the
forsaken
army

HEINRICH GERLACH

Translated from the German by
Richard Graves

CASSELL&CO

CASSELL MILITARY PAPERBACKS

Cassell & Co
Wellington House, 125 Strand
London WC2R 0BB

Copyright © 1957, 1979, 1983, 1986, 1989, 2000 by Nymphenburger in
der F. A. Herbig Verlagsbuchhandlung GmbH, Muenchen

English translation © George Weidenfeld & Nicholson Ltd
and Harper & Brothers 1958

First published in Germany as *Die verratene Armee* 1957
First published in English by Weidenfeld & Nicholson 1958
This Cassell Military Paperbacks edition 2002

The right of Heinrich Gerlach to be identified as the author of this
work has been asserted by him in accordance with the Copyright,
Designs and Patents Act 1988.

All rights reserved. No part of this book may be reproduced or
transmitted in any form or by any means electronic or manual including
photocopying recording or any information storage and retrieval
system without permission in writing from the Publisher.

British Library Cataloguing-in-Publication Data
A catalogue record for this book is available from the
British Library

ISBN 0-304-36278-6

Printed and bound in Great Britain by
Cox & Wyman Ltd., Reading, Berks.

CONTENTS

PUBLISHER'S NOTE

Because it tells a story of human folly, fortitude and suffering in terms of the personal fate of a number of characters, this book is correctly described as a novel. But in spite of this, it is a factual document, an authentic account of real happenings and an historical source of the first importance. It is an eye-witness account of one of the decisive battles in history. An account not only of the feelings of a single participant, but a complete cross-section of the hopes, the fears, the disillusionment of the men of the doomed Sixth Army and the complex pattern of a military disaster from the point of view of those involved in it.

Gerlach is neither a professional novelist nor a professional soldier. He was impelled to write because he survived a catastrophe so immense that he felt it was his duty to leave an account of it to posterity. He was born fifty years ago and became a schoolmaster. When Hitler came to power he joined the Nazi party to keep his job. The secure and uneventful life of a provincial schoolmaster seemed to be ahead of him.

Then came the war: Gerlach served in Poland, France, Yugoslavia and Russia. In 1942 he caught dysentery and had to go to hospital, but he rejoined his unit just before the Russians broke through and cut off the Sixth Army. On January 30th 1943—the tenth anniversary of Hitler's accession to power—Gerlach, severely wounded, was among the men marched into captivity from Stalingrad.

The callousness with which Hitler had sacrificed a quarter of a million of his men because he had publicly pledged himself that he would never abandon Stalingrad, the senselessness of all the suffering and death made Heinrich Gerlach resolve that, if he survived the years of captivity, he would tell the German people and the world what he had seen.

From the moment he entered his first prisoner of war camp, he began to ask his fellow prisoners how they had fared and so gathered an enormous amount of first-hand material on all aspects of the battle. He talked to men of all ranks, from the humblest private to the Commander-in-Chief himself, discussed what he had learnt with those best capable of evaluating the evidence and so acquired a complete picture of the many facets of the *débacle*.

It is from this vast collection of first-hand evidence that Gerlach constructed his novel. With great difficulty he preserved his growing manuscript from being detected by the guards. When it was completed he spent long nights in copying the book in tiny handwriting into an exercise book of only 20 pages. A fellow-prisoner tried to smuggle this miniature version of the book out of Russia, but the MVD found it and took it away. They also discovered and confiscated the original manuscript.

When Gerlach was finally released in 1950 he had lost his precious manuscript and he had reached such a pitch of nervous exhaustion that he was incapable of reconstructing it from memory. Only after he had undergone hypnotic treatment did parts of it begin to return to him. Gradually he regained his memory, but it took him five years to reconstruct the book.

THE FORSAKEN ARMY contains two kinds of characters. Important figures who are shown only in situations and episodes that are fully attested by the historical records and appear under their real names: men like Goering, General von Paulus, General von Seydlitz, General Manstein, General Hube or General Hoth and some of the members of their entourage. Other characters bear fictional names; these are composites. All the episodes and events described actually happened during the battle of Stalingrad, but the author has rearranged them.

Heinrich Gerlach insists that the book contains *nothing* which did not in fact happen. In a letter to us he says: 'I am of course able to provide the real parallels for every single scene or episode in the book and I could also name the people who vouch for their authenticity.'

The English version is shorter than the German original. Some passages of political discussion meant for a German audience which might still need to be convinced that Hitler caused the Stalingrad disaster have been omitted.

PART I

Thunder and Lightning

Chapter One

PROSPECTS OF HOME LEAVE

❦

'HELL, IT'S COLD!'

Lieutenant Breuer pulled the rug firmly round his knees and slid back deeper into his seat. Through the window he could see the landscape slipping past, the dirty brown plain, smooth as a potter's wheel, an endless monochrome. The little car moved briskly over the lonely road which the black frost of these November days had transformed overnight into a sort of asphalt. They were coming from the great depression between Volga and Don, where the staffs and supply services had their burrows, and they were making for the northern front of the salient.

'Just our luck to get a cold snap now—of all times.' The officer pulled at his cigar and stamped his feet on the metal floor. A few days back, during a spell of belated summer weather, it had been warm enough to wash, stripped to the waist, in the open.

Beside him sat the driver, muffled up to the ears in winter clothing so that all that could be seen of him was a red snub nose and a pair of crafty eyes. He took his hands off the steering wheel and let the car run on. He was a truck driver in civilian life and felt entitled to take liberties with this pigmy, which he had already driven 12,000 kilometres. He pulled off his mittens and rubbed his hands together.

'It's the rear-engine that makes the damn thing so cold,' he said. 'Give me the ordinary *Volkswagen* every time, with heating from the exhaust gases.'

Breuer laughed and said: 'Suppose you give yourself a shot of this kind of gas.' He pulled a cigar out of the depths of his overcoat, bit the end off, lit it and put it into the driver's mouth. 'Even you couldn't have guessed that we'd still be driving around here in winter,' he said.

The driver blew out great clouds of smoke, which remained stationary for an instant and then dispersed in trembling wisps and rags.

'Yes, and this is the second winter,' he said quietly.' God damn Stalingrad! It makes you wonder if the war will ever be over.'

'Don't talk such crap, Lakosch!' growled Breuer. 'We ought to be glad that we've got here at last. This is where the war will be won, one way or the other, whatever the cost.'

Lakosch glanced quickly at his passenger. Breuer was staring in front of him with a strained expression. He had a bad taste in his mouth. The operation known as the Russian Campaign was now in its second year. The grandiloquent phrases had a hollow ring now and the noble ideals they were fighting for were beginning to lose their glamour.

There was no time to think about anything except how to keep alive. Each man went on doing, out of habit, what he couldn't help doing, and called it his duty—just an animal reflex, thought Breuer. But even these gloomy thoughts couldn't stifle the joy which he had been feeling all the morning. His spirits rose as he listened to the drone of the engine and the rumble of the wheels which were carrying him away from that devil's hole behind him, Stalin's own city. Breuer felt ashamed of this primitive satisfaction and tried, with little success, to think about the events of the last months, during which he had vegetated in holes in the ground and under the ruins of houses in the borderland between life and death. And of his comrades, who had to remain there.

Lakosch braked sharply and stuck his nose out of the door.

'Crossroads,' he said, 'which way do we go?'

'I'll go and look,' said the officer. 'Meanwhile you might wipe the windscreen.'

Breuer got out of the car, slapped his arms across his chest a few times and waddled stiffly, like a penquin, across to a sign-post bearing a brightly-coloured shield covered with obscure military symbols and above it four weatherbeaten arms at right angles to one another. He managed to make out on the left arm the word *Vertyachi* inscribed in Russian characters, which showed that they had reached the main East-West road.

'We go left,' he said, 'thirty more kilometres.' Now they were going westward towards the Don. Behind them lay the Volga and Stalingrad.

Lakosch sniffed the air through his turned-up nose. He, too, felt happy and relieved. He had not known where they were going, and had supposed that they were doing one of their unpleasant daily drives to some part of the battle front. Now that he realized they were going in the other direction, he ventured to put a question which had been on his mind for some days.

'Is it true, sir, that we're going into winter-quarters?'

Of course he didn't expect a straight answer. A service secret: he knew all about that. Captain Siebel, the former Intelligence Officer, a professional soldier, would have snubbed him at once. But Breuer was a reservist, a schoolmaster or something like that, with less red tape about him and more humanity. Lakosch was right: Breuer took the bait.

'Well,' he said, 'there's been some talk about it. I think it's probably true. When we have done the job in the elbow of the Don, we move on to Millerovo. The advanced troops are already on the way. But, meantime, we have to stay where we are, d'you follow?'

'My God, yes,' said Lakosch with a sigh of relief; and then in soft and hesitating tones came a question which he knew he had no right to ask. 'Do you think there'll be a chance of leave?'

Leave . . . Lakosch was thinking of his mother and of Erna in Gleiwitz, who had not written for ages. It would be good to be able to go and put things in order. Breuer had snuggled deeper into his winter greatcoat and the same thoughts were crossing his mind. It would soon be two years since he had seen Irmgard and the two boys, shortly before the campaign in Jugoslavia. Jochen, the elder, had just gone to school for the first time and little Hans was still hanging on to his mother's skirts. The strange man in uniform had frightened him. 'A soldier,' he had said, and with those words had banished his father from the family circle into the distant grey-clad host of nameless men.

When all this was over, the first thing he had to do was to recapture the love of his children. But when would the end come, and where? Would it be here at Stalingrad? Very few people managed to get leave from Russia. Once he had hoped to do so. That was, yes, only a fortnight ago. He had come back from the field-hospital to his staff-billet, half recovered from an attack of dysentery, with a letter in his pocket from the PMO, recommending him for three weeks convalescent leave. But General Heinz had shaken his head. 'Leave . . . now? No, my dear boy. The Intelligence Section has gone to pieces. For the last six weeks they haven't given me a single report of the enemy's order of battle. As far as I'm concerned you can go and rest in your dug-out. Perhaps at Christmas . . .' His rest had consisted of daily visits to the field-hospitals and POW assembly stations and to battalion and brigade staffs, which were housed in dark cellars somewhere among the ruins. Sometimes he took Special Service Officer Fröhlich to interpret for him, but Lakosch was always with him driving his little car around the front and dodging the unexpected shells from distant guns and the salvos of the rocket-batteries they called the Stalin Organs. At night he slept restlessly in a damp dug-out on the hill above Gorodishche, which the Russian U2s, the 'sewing machines', used to plaster with bombs all night. Of course others had a worse deal, but that was no consolation. Now, perhaps, at last . . .

'There she is!'

'Who? What?' cried Breuer, coming out of his trance:

'There, in front—the Don.'

The car stopped for a moment. They could distinctly hear shots on the right and the noise of fighting. Not far away was the constantly threatened and sternly contested left flank of the Stalingrad front. And there behind was the Don, drawn like a steel-grey ribbon through the tawny plain. The car slipped past the dirty cottages of a village, rolled into a depression, jolted over a patch of log-surface and finally rumbled across the loose planks of the long pontoon-bridge.

Breuer couldn't help thinking of the day when he first crossed the river. Then it was high summer, far down in the south. The motorized division, advancing from Voronesh, had crossed in feverish haste and pushed on over the sultry steppe, past the weed-grown ruins of former settlements, dumb witnesses of the bloody battles of the Revolution, and then through neat, coloured villages with friendly inhabitants. They had expected to meet with desperate resistance, but, in fact, they had hardly come in contact with the enemy. The Russians had moved faster than they and had disappeared into the East. At that time Breuer had been commanding an infantry company.

Then one day they had seen the Don in front of them. There was sharp fighting at the crossing by the village of Zymlianskaya, a picturesque and peaceful place among its vineyards on the hillside. And then at last came a whole day of rest, with nothing to do! They tore off their clothes, crusted with sweat and dust, and waded in the river, like naked white frogs with brick-coloured hands and faces. The river flowed gently on, reflecting the dark-blue skies and the cream-coloured cloud-masses. Homely cottages were visible, half-screened by the silent wooded banks. The Cossacks called it the quiet Don. Even the dead Russian airman on the gleaming sand-bank lying beside his broken aircraft with a hand pointing to the sky couldn't disturb the peace of the scene.

A few days later all their hopes of seeing the mountains of the Caucasus and the palm groves of the Black Sea coast were shattered. The division was diverted to the north-east and it was then for the first time that they heard the name, never to be forgotten, of Stalingrad.

They marched on over the Kalmuck steppes with sand, as fine as dust, filtering into their pores and into the motors of the cars. Squadrons of Stukas pointed the way. A huge mushroom of smoke reached up to the sky, silver-grey and solid as a monument by day, a blood-red pillar of fire by night. That was Stalingrad. The troops fought their way into the burning, quaking town more easily than they had expected. Victory—the victory that would decide the war —seemed within their grasp. At home the papers were exulting and preparing to celebrate the victory, but in fact the real fighting was only now beginning—the fighting that was to stamp a city into the ground and eat up men as April sunshine melts the snow. Now it was a hand-to-hand struggle for every house, every cellar, every ruined wall.

Breuer shook himself and took a deep breath. Where had his memory taken him? All that lay behind him on the far side of the great river. But somewhere in his inner consciousness a thought kept nagging him—the thought of his new, as yet unknown assignment . . . He did not let it bother him too much or spoil the enjoyment with which he gazed at the wooded hillsides and smelt the scent of moss and pine needles. The Don lay behind him. He was not going to cross it for the third time. When the division, rested and reinforced, was ready to go into the line at the new year, the fate of Stalingrad would long ago have been decided.

Lieutenant Colonel Unold, the GSO1 of the division, stood bending over a map. Over his small head, with its scanty crop of hair, was drawn a tight sheath of bloodless skin which revealed the white bones of his skull. He was recording on the map with a charcoal pencil the details contained in a bundle of wireless messages. He worked quickly and surely and often made use of the ruler to draw lines separating the new positions of the different units. As he did so, Unold bit his lip. He didn't like the look of things.

The map, to scale 1:300,000, only showed a small section of the northern bend of the Don—the section between Kietshayer and Serafimovitch. The positions here were held by Roumanian divisions, which were already showing signs of uneasiness under the continual threat of a Russian attack. The German Armoured Corps, hastily assembled from bits and pieces and newly arrived units, had been put in to stiffen the morale of the Roumanians during these critical November days.

There was as yet no urgent cause for anxiety. A few new Russian divisions in the line and two or three fresh bridges over the Don— that was harmless. Rumours of greater enemy reinforcements were unverifiable and probably untrue. But the fact that here on the long north salient of the Stalingrad front, which jutted out like a huge nose towards the Volga, the great majority of the troops were Roumanians, an occupation force rather than a fighting force, with no heavy artillery—and the same situation south of Stalingrad— that was something to worry about. It was a dangerous way to dispose one's forces. Unold knew his Clausewitz: 'See that your wings are strong!' Since the battle of Cannae this had been the iron principle of all strategy. In the previous year there had been a similar situation at Kiev, with the roles reversed; the Russian wings had been enveloped and the resulting slaughter had been almost fatal to them. It was lucky, thought Unold, that we haven't got German troops against us instead of the weakened and exhausted Russians.

Captain Engelhard, the senior administrative officer, who was working at the next table, got up and silently laid a signal, just brought in by a messenger on the table in front of Unold. He liked doing things in the right way and didn't ask questions. Unold took a fleeting glance at the paper and then picked it up in his hand to read more carefully. 'Wireless announcement from the Army Group!' he said. 'Another lot of rubbish, I suppose.'

He read the message again reflectively and the shadows darkened on his face. 'Very well,' he murmured, 'let them come!' He took a red pencil and drew a tidy circle in the great forest region north of Kletskaya with a firmly marked 5 in the middle and below it the oblong sign representing a tank. Engelhard watched him from his table with ill-concealed interest.

'Do you really believe in this tank force, Colonel?' he asked.

Unold didn't answer. He put down the pencil and walked to the window, where for several minutes he seemed to be immersed in memories and secret thoughts. Then he returned to the table and rubbed out the tank and the figure 5 till no trace remained but a pale mark on the green of the forest.

'It's nonsense, Engelhard,' he said. 'The Russians aren't coming. They're finished.'

The town of Verchnaya Buzinovka consisted of several one and two storeyed stone houses, a modern hospital with a tiled roof and a wretched-looking wooden church which, according to the Russians, was no longer 'working'. One of the houses was ear-marked for the Intelligence Section.

Interpreter Fröhlich inspected the premises. What a stupid bitch! he thought. The fool still believes in Papa Stalin.

He was thinking out loud and as he spat the words out of his large mouth, his eyelids fluttered nervously over his deep set eyes.

He was speaking of the woman who rubbed her hands on her skirt in embarrassment as she followed him through the two rooms. She wanted to know if the Bolsheviks were coming back. She was clearly in a state of panic, because her husband was working for the local German administration. But she had said 'our people' when she asked if the Bolshies were likely to return.

'Where German soldiers have set their foot,' said Fröhlich in Russian, rolling his R's in his Baltic fashion, 'no Bolshevik comes any more—*ponemaish?*'

The woman kept silent and stroked the blond head of her little boy, who was hiding in her skirts. The family had moved into the stable and slept between the legs of the only horse that the war had left them.

'Tomorrow there must be a table here, and chairs, and the windows must be nice and clean, *ponemaish?* The place is a damned pigsty.'

Fröhlich thought that one could get most out of the Russians by abusing them. In reality he was very pleased with the wooden cottage. It lay on the road leading to Manoilin, thirty kilometres behind the front, and was fairly safe from air-bombardment. Moreover Lieutenant Dierk had installed his four-barrelled anti-aircraft gun behind the house, and the Russian airmen would treat him with respect. All this promised a quiet life. Fröhlich looked on while Sergeant Herbert and the long-legged Geibel dragged the cases full of office furniture into the room and, as he watched, he gnawed the nails of his bony fingers. He couldn't imagine what the idea was in settling down in this great elbow of the Don and was inclined to think that Buzinovka must be the first stage in the move towards winter quarters in Millerovo for which everyone was longing.

Private Geibel was carrying straw into the house. His round, childish face was beaming with happiness. He laid the straw against the back wall and spread blankets over it. At last there was a chance of peace and warmth in clean quarters with a watertight roof and a floor of dry wooden boards. His wants were few and he was happy.

In the next room Herbert was slicing potatoes and putting them into a pan by the light of the fire on the hearth. He was one of those

18

tender clerkly plants, which only thrive in the atmosphere of an office, and enjoyed doing household chores above all things. Later on Lakosch joined the other two, having parked his car in the court-yard.

'For God's sake, what's this? Fried potatoes?' His eyes bulged. 'It's two months, no three, since I had my last potato.' He fished out a crisp piece with his sharp fingers. With his freckles and his red hair reflecting the firelight, he looked like a little goblin.

'Take your paws out of the frying-pan, you filthy pig,' growled Herbert, 'and wash them before you touch my things.'

'Look at him!' cried Lakosch, smacking his lips. 'Soon as he gets out of the dug-out he starts acting like a lord. Frying-pan— that reminds me, do you know the one about the frying-pan? As the bishop said to the actress . . .'

'Oh, shut your trap!' said Herbert dispiritedly. Lakosch's funny stories were known and dreaded by everybody; which didn't in the least damp his ardour as a story-teller.

'Listen, Herbie, I know something you don't know,' said Lakosch, creeping behind Herbert's back towards the frying-pan.

'If you mean Millerovo, that's stale news.'

'Something much better! Something really great!'

'It can't really be much,' muttered Herbert, but his curiosity was aroused.

'If you promise to bake me a cake, I'll tell you. But I want a proper cake, a nice rich yellow one. I've still got a bit of baking powder and we'll get some flour out of Panje.'

'Don't be ridiculous. Take the potatoes in. No, you take the milk and I'll carry the potatoes.'

Breuer was still with the Colonel in the office making his report. When he came at last it was already dark. They all sat in candlelight round a wash-basin full of potatoes which they ate with dripping out of a tin, and drank hot milk. In the corner stood the Ikons illu-minated by a little oil lamp which had been kept alight ever since the days of the Czar. Stalin hadn't been able to put out these lamps, which now shone on Hitler's soldiers and seemed likely to go on burning as long as there were Russians on Russian soil.

When the basin was empty, Breuer started speaking. 'Your

colleague in the XI Corps sends you his best wishes, Herr Fröhlich. Those fellows know how to live, I must say. The whole of Ossinov-skoye is one great sanatorium, with a movie-theatre of course, concerts and a casino—just like peace time.'

'Why did we come here?' asked Herbert.

'The Roumanians asked for us. They found life here too dull and wanted our company.'

'Oh, heavens, let's hope it's not for the whole winter.'

'The Colonel reckons from a week to a fortnight. What he wants now is a revival of cultural activities—cases full of books, gramophone records and games are on the way. And he's deter-mined to get the Rembrandt film shown here—I can't think why. Anyhow he has promised me that administrative job as a reward, if I can get the film here.'

An administrative post in the intelligence branch had long been vacant.

'Why now,' said Fröhlich, 'when we don't need administering? In two weeks we'll be in Millerovo.'

Breuer smiled knowingly and said, 'Perhaps somewhere quite different.'

'Where?' said Herbert, looking at Lakosch.

'Yes,' said Breuer with a smirk, 'it looks like that. Do you know what the CO said to me in the mess? He said "You're only here for a few days as guest artists, because your division is going home to Germany."'

At these words there was a tense silence, and then everyone burst out talking.

'Home to Germany! Back to the Fatherland! Home to Mother! My God, am I going mad?' Fröhlich slapped his knee and showed his equine teeth saying, 'look, *Herr Oberleutnant*, that's just what I was saying. The first divisions are being withdrawn and in six months the war will be over.'

'I know, Herr Fröhlich, I know,' laughed Breuer. 'And then you'll build a branch factory on the Volga and supply your shops on the Kurfürstendamm with your own salmon and caviar.'

'Well, Herbert, what do you know?' asked Lakosch. 'D'you feel like baking me that cake now?'

Herbert nodded: there were tears in his eyes.

'Man, we must celebrate,' he whispered, 'we must celebrate.'

During the following days the weather changed. A fine drizzle plastered the trees and bushes with frozen pearls and covered the houses and roads with a blue skin of ice. Breuer went to visit the Roumanian staff at Kalmykov. Lakosch had a lot of trouble keeping the skidding car on the road and they took hours to cover the short distance.

A black-haired, slender captain in well-cut khaki readily showed Breuer the blue-prints of the enemy positions.

'Look at this, Lieutenant,' he said, 'these bridges are new. They were destroyed, but in the night they put them up again. And these divisions are new, too. This one here only arrived two days ago. And look at that wood. We don't know what's hidden in it. Some say a Russian cavalry corps. That may be right, and it may be wrong. If it's right, it's bad. What do they want cavalry for except to attack?'

'Well,' said Breuer, 'we're here now.' That sounded foolish and he went on in some embarrassment, 'that is to say, we soon will be. It's true that our division is only providing the tank regiment with about twenty tanks and the artillery. The grenadiers had to stay behind in Stalingrad. But the other Armoured Division, the 23rd, is a quite new formation, and of course your first Armoured Division is here too. I suppose they're going into action for the first time.'

'That'll be very nice, I don't think,' said the Roumanian. 'We have no tanks here and no heavy artillery and our men are tired. We were not meant to go to the front.'

As he spoke he looked at the two photographs on the wall showing Marshal Antonescu and the young King Michael covered with medals and gazing self-consciously at the camera.

'Do you know Bucharest, Herr Kamerad?'

'I was there for a few days before the war.'

'Bucharest is very beautiful. Beautiful women, beautiful cafés, beautiful warm sunshine . . . it seems very far away.'

As he spoke the Roumanian picked up a broad-bellied bottle and filled two long-stemmed liqueur glasses from it. 'You must be cold,

Lieutenant,' he said. 'Drink this; it is genuine *Chuica*. And if you smoke, here are some cigarettes—Turkish.'

'To the success of our partnership,' said Breuer, tipping up his glass. The strong plum-spirit did him good and drove the cold out of his limbs. 'Let us drink,' said the Roumanian, 'to the thought that you will soon be here with a lot of tanks and guns. We can't afford to wait very long for them. We were expecting a Russian attack on the 6th and the 7th—the anniversary of the Revolution, you know. But it didn't come.'

'I don't think it will, either.'

'Let's hope you're right, Lieutenant.'

On the way back they made a detour and visited the front. Breuer was trying to digest what he had just seen and heard. He did not think that the new divisions that had come to reinforce the Russian bridgehead at Kletskaya gave serious cause for anxiety. They consisted of old men over fifty or half-grown youths and were badly equipped. Some of them were armed with model 42 muskets with unrifled barrels. In fact the picture was the usual one, and it showed clearly how near the Russians were to the end of their resources. And this talk of a cavalry corps, magnified sometimes into an army of tanks, that was just fantasy—the product of overstrung nerves. Soldiers holding an endless front line without heavy armour or artillery could hardly be blamed for seeing ghosts.

Lakosch stopped the car. In front of him stood a lonely figure with a rifle under his arm. It was a sentry wearing a great fur coat reaching almost to the ground with a square of tent-cloth rigged above it. On the man's head was a conical lambskin cap and on the top of that, presumably to keep out the rain, a Roumanian steel helmet. The rain-drops ran off the edges of the helmet on to the tent-cloth and dripped on to the ground. The scarecrow ordered them to halt. They had reached the front line and could go no farther.

Breuer got out and walked a few paces forward. In front he saw the chain of hills growing smaller and smaller towards the north. Some fifty yards farther on he saw a pale stripe running across the brown plain. That was the line of Roumanian trenches. A few houses were visible in a hollow. That must be Kletskaya. And behind it a pale grey band—the Don again. The Don was always there, getting in the way, even when one had crossed it. But far behind there was a dark smudge, sensed rather than seen, a monotonous patch of deep grey, which must be the great forest region. Did it really conceal secret forces?

About this time the new Divisional Commander arrived at Buzinovka. He at once expressed the wish to meet informally the staff and officers commanding units. So a fairly numerous company was assembled one evening in the Church Hall, which the staff used as an officers' mess. Captain Fackelmann, the officer in charge of the Staff Headquarters, had by some miraculous means given the room an air of festivity. The damp wooden walls were draped with maps and hung with green pine-branches, and there were candles on the clean tablecloth. The room was full of officers who bombarded Engelhard with questions about the new CO. But Engelhard, who looked like a film star, was not forthcoming. It was not for him to talk, so he kept silent. Even the Adjutant, Captain Gedig, a little Berliner with merry eyes, restrained his tongue and contented himself with repeating the words 'wait and see, gentlemen, wait and see'.

Fackelmann, who was managing the entertainment, bounced around among the guests like a rubber ball, completing the arrangements as he wiped the sweat from his bald head.

Punctually at eight o'clock the orderlies flung the doors open to admit the General, a massive figure with a round, red face and two pale blue blobs swimming in the middle of it. He was accompanied by Unold, on this occasion wearing the black uniform of the Tank Corps. Dr Mueller, the white-haired PMO of the Division, followed with the bow-legged Panzer commander Major Kalweit, who looked like a Mongol. Unold, pale and reserved—he had been hoping to get the division himself—presented the officers one by one to the General. 'Captain Mühlmann, head of the Information Service . . .' 'Captain Eichert, leader of the Anti-Tank Section . . .' As they were presented the officers bowed and clicked their heels. The General favoured each officer with a handshake and a short glance, in which he tried, but failed, to put a gleam of fire. 'Captain

Siebel, our Messing Officer.' The captain pushed back his straw-coloured mop of hair and his right shoulder jerked convulsively, but the artificial limb as usual failed to function so he held out his left hand to the General.

'Where did you lose your arm?'

'At Volchov, sir.'

'How old are you?'

'Twenty-five, sir.'

'Is that so? A bit young for such a responsible job.'

'If I was old enough to risk my life, I must be old enough to cope with the potatoes, General.'

Everyone laughed and the company sat down, the General in the centre, flanked by senior officers and the others—a mixed assortment—lower down on both sides of the table. Fackelmann had prepared one of his famous surprises in the shape of liver-dumplings in golden-yellow sauce served with salted potatoes. And then, to the general astonishment, a couple of dozen bottles of Moselle suddenly appeared on the table.

'*Prost* Fackelmann! You old wizard,' called Major Kalweit from the other end of the table.

The Captain sprang to his feet, without thereby seeming to add to his height, and pressed his glass to his breast to acknowledge the toast of the Panzer leader. 'It's really delicious, my dear Fackelmann,' drawled Lieutenant Von Horn, Kalweit's assistant, flashing his eye through his monocle. 'And what a colour!'

'But, gentlemen, listen to me, I beg you,' called Fackelmann, waving his handkerchief. 'Perhaps you don't know that horse-liver is a great delicacy. The famous Brunswick liver-sausage always contains a certain amount of foal's liver.'

His hearers ventured to doubt him. Fackelmann's veracity was not always to be counted on in such matters as this. Captain Endrigkeit, the commandant of the Field-Police, a mustachioed East Prussian, reached for the third time for the potato dish.

'How do you like the taste, Zimmermann?' he asked the Paymaster sitting next to him. 'Next time you go to the Tschir you must bring back a few ponies with you and we'll make sausages of them.'

'I wish you'd shut up,' said Captain Siebel indignantly, pushing his yellow hair off his forehead. 'I won't hear a word against horses. If we've got to the stage of eating them, we shall soon be getting down to dogs.'

Someone sitting with the senior officers tapped on his glass for silence and the General rose to his feet. 'Gentlemen!' he began in an energetic voice that came incongruously from his plump-cheeked face. 'By the Führer's order I have come to take up this honourable command. I know what a distinction it is to be called to lead a division, which carries honour and glory blazoned on its colours. We have been through hard times and we have harder times in front of us, before we achieve the final victory which the Führer has promised us. We must be hard—hard towards ourselves and our people and mercilessly hard against the barbarous foe, who knows no mercy. To give the last ounce of our strength and to exact it from our men—that's what our country expects of us and that is our task as fighters for a new World Order. In this spirit I take over command of the division. To the health of our Führer and Supreme Commander.'

A painful silence followed. Breuer gave a long look at Wiese, the Information Officer, sitting opposite, who nodded slowly.

'*Donnerwetter!*' said Siebel quite audibly, 'it looks as if we're in for a glorious time.'

'Seen from the inside of a tank, the world looks somehow different,' observed Von Horn. 'I detect a strong smell of SS or Police.'

Fackelmann, who was once more on his feet and seeing to the distribution of cigars, bent over as he passed Endrigkeit and Fröhlich and, putting his hand before his mouth, said, with a snigger, 'to tell you the truth I'd rather have this chap's head roasted and served with a lemon in his mouth.'

These words gave Fröhlich such a shock that he nearly swallowed the match with which he was picking his teeth. However, Endrigkeit laughed so noisily that the people at the other end of the table stared at him indignantly. Even Captain Engelhard was pained. He disliked this lax attitude, which he blamed on the reservists, especially when it involved disrespect towards senior officers.

'I really must protest, gentlemen,' he said. 'The General has been a year in Russia and has commanded a tank division for five months.'

'Don't get worked up, Engelhard,' said Fackelmann soothingly. 'It's only a joke and besides . . . he will be good enough for France.'

France? His neighbours pricked up their ears. 'Yes, don't you know *anything*?' said the little Captain beaming with self-importance. 'Our division is going to France.' The Tanks Adjutant said, 'You must have read the news on the wall of some latrine.' 'No, sir, I have it from a good source—the very best. But keep it under your hats. The division is going to garrison the region round Havre, a stone's throw from Paris.'

This news was received with great excitement and Von Horn put in, 'Hasn't operational headquarters something to say to that?' Engelhard pretended not to have heard the question. Fröhlich slapped his left-hand neighbour on the knee to make him draw closer and said, 'Look, Padre, that's what I keep saying. The war here in the east is over. The Führer is withdrawing his troops to the west for the great attack on England.' 'Maybe you've got hold of the wrong end of the stick, my dear Fröhlich.' Padre Peters, the senior chaplain to the division had received the Iron Cross, 1st class, an unusual distinction for a chaplain: he went on, 'don't you think they may be throwing troops into the west because they're afraid of the Second Front?'

Fröhlich was silent, feeling, as usual, insulted when his optimism did not meet with a sympathetic response. Endrigkeit drew out his nickel-lidded pipe, which had a couple of tassels hanging round the mouthpiece, filled it carefully and lit it.

'Listen, Gedig,' he said quietly to the little Captain who was due to go to Berlin for a course during the next few days, 'don't forget to ask Unold to give us the address of the best brothel in Paris, otherwise you may not be able to find us in France.' 'He'll send a picture postcard first, Gedig,' laughed Siebel, 'showing Papa Endrigkeit with a bottle of bubbly in front of him, his corncob in his mouth and on his knee a nice little Parisian popsy. Very suitable for the family album and the edification of the grandchildren.'

At the upper end of the table the General was having a serious conversation with Colonel Lunitz, who commanded the Artillery Brigade, and the PMO of the division.

He was saying, 'Of course the division needs rest. I was talking to Zeitzler on the subject only a fortnight ago. He understands the situation perfectly and promised us time for thorough recuperation. We'd be in winter quarters already if it wasn't for this silly call for help from our allies. No one in authority takes them seriously, but of course we have to make a gesture to reassure them. After all we do need them, though they make you sick. They're not brave, not ready to sacrifice themselves and haven't a gleam of understanding of our world-wide mission and our aims—though they all want to profit by our victory. When the war is over let's hope the Führer will do some cleaning up among them.'

The gathering soon broke up, as the General wanted some time alone with his senior officers. 'I can't go to sleep yet,' said Engelhard to Breuer, as they were putting on their overcoats outside. 'Come and take a stroll with me in the open air to clear our heads.' Since he had had a bullet through one lung, which had caused his transfer to staff, he could not stand the atmosphere of smoky rooms. The two men walked along by the low cemetery wall towards the village. A fresh east wind had sprung up and dried the road. Light clouds were scurrying over the sky revealing and concealing the stars as they passed. In the distance a coarse voice was dragging out the refrain of Lily Marlene full of sentimental homesickness.

'If we really go to France,' began Breuer after a pause . . . but the Captain wouldn't take the bait.

He merely said quietly, 'If we only had all we needed here. Everything seems to be late. The Roumanian tanks are God knows where and the 23rd is only trickling in, to say nothing of our own deficiencies.'

'Do you really expect the Russians to attack?' Breuer was genuinely astonished. He had been thinking of France and Christmas leave.

'Army Group Intelligence has got hold of a detailed plan of attack by the Russians. It sounds absolutely crazy—a whole army of tanks, a corps of cavalry, several motorized infantry divisions with all the auxiliary services. Everything's ready behind the Russian front for the attack—they're obviously preparing something big.'

Breuer felt his hands trembling. None of this had been reported to his section.

'It's not possible,' he stammered. 'The Russians can never muster such forces.'

'That's exactly what the Army High Command said. They think it's all a brilliant hoax and that's why the story has only been circulated unofficially.'

'What do you think?' Engelhard was silent for some time. He disliked such conversations, but the night was dark and in the blackness he could forget his companion, so that when he began to speak, it was almost as if he were talking to himself.

'Up at GHQ they spend their time making calculations. They count up the divisions that have been annihilated and reckon that the Russian Army is dead. They get to believing themselves in the long run. But someone has calculated that the Russians have already put into the field forty divisions more than, according to the figures, they could have done. So the Russian's not only dead, he's doubly dead. For the last year we've been fighting an enemy who, on paper, is dead as a doornail. Yet every day it seems this dead enemy's getting stronger.'

In the western sky a red light blazed out and fell slowly to the ground. A cluster of brightly-coloured sparks flew up from the ground to meet it. After a while an explosion was heard in the distance.

'There, you see!' said Engelhard. 'A year ago the enemy couldn't do any night flying. That and the Stalin Organs and the automatic rifles and grenade throwers in every Russian infantry company are all achievements of this past year. We win battle after battle and all the time they are getting stronger. It's uncanny.'

'Yes, but now we're dug in on the Volga. We have them by the throat. Soon they won't be able to breathe.'

Breuer felt that he was getting strength from his own argument. But, the Captain showed no disposition to accept his companion's invitation to confide in him.

'Don't let's fool ourselves, Breuer,' he said. 'Nineteen forty-two hasn't brought us the success we had hoped for nor a victory that could be decisive. Timoshenko's retreat was a stroke of genius and it has succeeded. Although we've reached the Volga, we don't have the strength to crush the enemy.'

What's the matter with him, thought Breuer, and tried to read his companion's face in the darkness. What he had just heard was not at all like the silent, hard working, scrupulously correct Engelhard whom he knew. In a lighter tone he said, 'If we get any trouble here, do you think our General Heinz will be able to deal with the situation?' General Heinz was the former divisional commander who had recently been given a corps. While with the division he had been honoured and beloved.

'Our Heinz! Yes. What a pity he's not with us any longer. If the Russians attacked he'd go for them with our few tanks like a pack of hounds. But, you know, you have to have other qualities to command a corps. He's still very young. . . .'

Afterwards Breuer lay awake for a long time on his straw mattress. His thoughts kept turning in his head like mill-wheels. At last he went to sleep, having come to the conclusion that Engelhard must have had a particularly bad day. His fiancée lived in Essen and the morning radio had announced that the town had been heavily bombed.

Next morning Breuer was summoned to the General's office. With a roll of maps under his arm and a bundle of reports in his hand he felt rather uneasy as he made his way towards the wooden house on the other side of the street. Two orderlies, moving around on tiptoe, pointed at a door. Behind it sat the General at a table on which stood an open bottle of red wine and the latest number of the *Völkischer Beobachter*. When Breuer came in and stopped in front of the General, the latter looked up.

'You are?'

'The Intelligence Officer, General.'

'I know that. What I want to know is your name.'

'Franz Breuer, General, born in . . .'

'That doesn't interest me. You must discard these civilian manners. Your profession in civil life?'

'Schoolmaster, General.'

'I see—a chalk-pusher. I've never had much use for your profession. What have you been doing up to now about the daily reports?'

'I have reported daily to the Senior Administration Officer, General.'

'You have, have you?' fumed the General. 'In future you will report to *me* daily at ten-thirty. Is that clear? Now, show me the map of North Africa.'

Breuer thought he had misunderstood.

'A map of North Africa? We haven't one, sir.'

The General's face turned dark red. He pounded the table with his fist, making the wine bottle reel.

'What . . . no map of North Africa? You might be living on the moon! A masterpiece of strategy! We can all take a lesson from that.'

He waved the newspaper like a flag in front of Breuer's face. Huge headlines carried the news 'Successful retreat of Rommel through Libya. He went on, 'As from tomorrow you will appear every day with a map of the whole of North Africa, d'you understand?'

'Sir, where shall I . . .'

'Hell, what do I care where you get it from!' stormed the General, the veins on his temples turning purple. 'What are you here for? I must have a map of North Africa by tomorrow morning at ten-thirty.'

'Very good, sir.' Breuer had stiffened into a pillar of salt.

'With the latest moves marked.'

'Very good, sir.'

'Enemy positions in red, our positions in black. Black, sir, not blue.'

'Yes, sir.'

'Very well.' The swollen veins began to subside. 'What are you hanging about for? Have you something else to say?'

'No, sir.'

Breuer faced about with enough action to make the windows rattle and stamped his way out of the room. The orderlies grinned as they watched him go.

.   .   .   .   .

Everyone gets a break from time to time and Breuer, certainly, had the devil's own luck. In the first place he actually unearthed, from the collection of maps, an old one of North Africa, which found favour in the sight of the Divisional Commander, and secondly, as chance would have it, the Rembrandt film was running for eight days with the IXth Corps, who were obliging enough to lend it as well as the cinema-van for two consecutive days to Breuer's division.

When Breuer brought these tidings to Unold, the latter pounded his shoulder, laughing.

'That's a brilliant piece of work,' he said, 'and I'll keep my promise. You shall have your o3. Have you thought of anyone to take your place?'

'Yes, I thought of Lieutenant Wiese, sir.'

'The little Lieutenant from the Information Section? H'm. A nice lad, but very quiet, isn't he? Oh well, he'll fit in here all right as far as I'm concerned. Provided Mühlmann will let him go.'

At this point the staff began to be tremendously active. Anyone who knew how to use a paint brush was told off to paint posters under the supervision of the cartographers, while men who knew how to use hammer and nails took part in the campaign to transform the church into a cinema theatre, while the clerks typed out tickets of admission. Before long gaily-coloured posters announced in every corner of the village that the Buzinovka Film Theatre cordially invited everyone to come and see the première of the great German film *Rembrandt* on 19th November at 1700 hours. In the club, the officers and the soldiers' quarters no one talked about anything else. The whole division waited feverishly for the 19th.

'Rembrandt,' Lakosch explained to Geibel as they were washing cars together, 'was a man who lived in the middle ages and even then built submarines and aircraft and things like that. Yes; so they cut his head off because he knew too much. Don't stare, stupid. No one's going to cut your head off for that.'

Chapter Two

THE DON AWAKES

⌘

THE SKY WAS grey at dawn on 19th November. Private Geibel tossed and groaned on his bed of straw. He was having a nightmare. There was a ring—'Help,' he screamed, 'help'. He suddenly felt a sharp pain in his side and woke up.

'I'll help you, you brute!' cursed Lakosch, prodding his neighbour once more in the side with his elbow—'While you're having the willies, the telephone is ringing its head off.'

It rang again and Geibel noticed with surprise that he was holding the receiver in his hand.

'Intelligence speaking.'

'Hello, you drip. Administration Office speaking; Corporal Schmalfuss. Tell Lieutenant Breuer he has to come here at once, ready for the road, but without his car.'

'Lieutenant Breuer to Admin., ready for the road but no car,' repeated Geibel mechanically. And then he began to wonder. 'What, now, in the middle of the night?'

'Do what you're told and don't ask silly questions,' came the reply. 'In the first place it is seven-thirty, and secondly the Russians are attacking.'

Geibel jumped out of bed and rushed into the next room, suddenly wide-awake.

'Herr Oberleutnant,' he called: 'Herr Oberleutnant. They want you at once at the Administration Office, sir. The Russians are attacking.'

The message that had caused excitement and alarm when it reached the Corps Staff and Administration was that the Russians had been attacking since very early morning in the Roumanian sector. The message added that the position was unclear.

Colonel Unold was running around like a wounded tiger and snapping out orders and questions.

'Have Lunitz and Kalweit received orders to stand by?'

'Yes, sir,' said Captain Engelhard as he continued to write. 'The Artillery Regiment is already on its way with support to point 218.'

'Give me a line to Fieberg at once.'

'The line is still out of order.'

The Corps Staff was quartered about forty kilometres farther west. For the last hour telephonic communication had been interrupted.

'It's enough to make you sick!' stormed Unold. 'Situation still unclear!' he repeated scornfully. 'Like the stuff they put in the communiqués. What are we to do, I'd like to know? Let's ring up the Roumanians.'

'The Roumanians?' repeated Engelhard in astonishment. 'We have no line to the Roumanians.'

'It's enough to drive you mad,' said Unold. Then he threw the paper down and, running to the door, told Schmalfuss to order his car.

'Are you going out yourself, sir?' said Engelhard, surprised. This was the first time that Unold had left his office table to visit the front.

'I must know what's going on,' cried Unold. 'Or do you think the General will give us all the details.'

Engelhard didn't think so and said nothing.

At the door Unold ran into Breuer in full battle order with field-glasses, map-case and sub-machine gun. He said: 'You're to accompany the General. Keep your eyes open and see that nothing goes wrong. We'll be back by midday.' Then Unold dashed off in his car.

Breuer went across to the General's house, in front of which the grey Horch limousine was standing with its motor running. He was in a bad temper. After Gedig had gone, he thought he had the job of orderly officer to the General in his pocket. And what was going to happen about the film-show? It was damned bad luck that all this had to happen unexpectedly just on that particular day.

The General appeared in a fur-lined coat with a beaver collar, wearing a gold-braided peaked cap. In his mouth was a long Brazilian cigar. When Breuer reported he muttered something unintelligible and climbed groaning into the seat next to the driver without condescending to look at his companion. Breuer made himself comfortable in the back seat. The car started off with a bellow and rolled away through the village and along the high road to the north, overtaking lorries, anti-aircraft vehicles and tanks. Point 218 was the universal destination.

The first light of morning gradually ate its way through the thick cloud that overhung the Don valley. On the heights, where the Roumanians had their positions, visibility was better, though even there it was less than a hundred yards. Fur-capped men crawled out of dug-outs, trenches and shelters, relieved themselves and ran around unstiffening their limbs with comic gestures. When the light was good it was unsafe to show one's head in these positions, but that morning the troops felt safe on their brown plateau, surrounded by a grey void in which the hostile world seemed to have dissolved. Who would fight in such weather?

Here and there small groups met and chattered with excited gestures. They were not in a cheerful mood. The half-year, for which they had covenanted to supply troops for the campaign in Russia, was over and their divisions should have been relieved on the 15th. They had been waiting for this day for weeks and they were all feeling homesick—dreaming of the wild Carpathian forests, the dark-green fields of the Dobrudja or the sunlit café-tables in the streets of Bucharest. But the relieving forces had not turned up and the supplies had already been directed by some over-conscientious authority to a new position, and the division had now been on short rations for four days. It was no wonder that the men were cursing heartily at the unforeseen prospect of a hard Russian winter, at the wretched organization and above all at this infernal war which no one had wanted and which actually wasn't any of their business. . . .

Suddenly the air was full of an odd, sinister humming and hissing, like the buzzing of a thousand poisonous insects—a sound that broke violently through the lonely greyness of the misty sky. And before anyone could grasp the meaning of this uncanny noise, hell had broken loose. The earth crashed and split and fountains of soil

34

and fire shot up to heaven from bomb craters, showering red hot metal all round. The attack came so suddenly and so unexpectedly in this misty morning that even the front line soldiers lively instinct for self protection was of no use. Only a few had time to leap into cover, while the rest were thrown mangled and torn on the ground before they had time to realize what had happened.

For a few minutes the hail of bombs showered the narrow strip of earth on the top of the hill, and then moved a few hundred yards till it struck the gun emplacements before returning to its original target. Suddenly the racket ceased and all was still again, for the groans of the wounded and dying were scarcely audible after the din of the explosions. After the cloud of yellow smoke had rolled away the position revealed a mass of craters, which had swallowed up most of the casualties.

Here and there a head was sticking up out of the ploughed-up earth, its face a mask of horror and shock, as though it could not believe that the body to which it was attached was still alive. More men crawled out of cover. What had happened? How had it happened? By rights they should not have been there. They ought to have been nearly home by now. And this, horribly, was how it all had ended. They came swarming up out of machine-gun nests and bomb-shelters, all that could move; they streamed over the craters like frightened rabbits and vanished into the mist.

A few officers waved their arms, shouted themselves hoarse and fired their pistols into the air, but no one stopped for them. They were soon alone. And then they did what was not the most honourable thing but, in the circumstances, the most intelligent: they followed their men as quickly as they could.

The Russian tanks, carrying cargoes of infantry which clattered up the heights a little later, pushed deep into the enemy positions without finding anyone to oppose them.

At 1700 hours the film show was due to begin. A crowd of villagers collected in front of the Church, and Endrigkeit's Field Police had to work to keep order. The Captain himself sat in the Intelligence Section with Fröhlich, who did not want to start without Unold and Breuer. The latter had not yet returned. A fat pike was hanging from the ceiling and the coffee-pot on the hearth was half empty. They had been waiting for over an hour and had begun to reminisce. Starting with the good old times, they had reached the present and were now talking about the war.

'There have always been wars,' said Endrigkeit 'and there always will be. No one will ever put a stop to them. But as for this war with Russia, it was crazy to start it; I don't care what anyone says.'

'Do you really think so, Captain?' asked Fröhlich in irritation. 'I take a different view. After all we could hardly wait until the Red flood poured over us. Four weeks later the Russians would have attacked *us*.'

'H'm: to do that would have needed preparation. Did you notice anything like that? When we invaded them they were completely taken by surprise and hadn't a notion we were coming. I'm sure they weren't thinking about a war.'

Fröhlich laughed. He laughed very little and his laughter rang false. Then he said: 'Every child knows that the Reds are out to conquer the world. The Führer is fulfilling a historic mission in extirpating this cancer and one day the whole world will thank him.

German virtue, German worth
Will heal the ills of Mother Earth.

'And supposing the sick man doesn't want to be cured! What then, dear friend? The doctor only visits the patient who sends for him.'

Fröhlich raised his face and sniffed the air. 'We Balts have always been pioneers of culture,' he said with emphasis. 'It is we who first raised these pigs of Russians out of the mud.'

Endrigkeit broke off a bit of cake from one of the slices on a plate and put it slackly in his mouth.

'And to show how grateful they are, they finished up by throwing you out of your country,' said he with his mouth full. 'No, my dear fellow, it's not as simple as all that. And Adolf's conscience was certainly not clean. Otherwise he wouldn't have deceived us until the very last moment. Don't you remember when we came here how the people on the railways thought we were entraining for Asia Minor and India and told us that German Military Transport had been passing freely through the Ukraine for weeks? You don't suppose they had made that up; they got it from the top brass. I have a niece in Berlin who works in a big paper-mill. Do you know that in June '40 they got an order for 10,000 Red Flags with the Soviet Star? Getting ready for Stalin's friendship-visit to Berlin. The order came direct from the district propaganda people with the official stamp on it and the goods were paid for in advance.'

'Is that so?' said Fröhlich. 'No doubt it was necessary to take such measures in order to keep the secret from the Russians.'

'Oh, rubbish! The truth is they were afraid that the German people might not play, if they had time to think it over. I tell you the Russians didn't want war. Nor did we, but our rulers hadn't the courage to ask us what we thought.'

Fröhlich, bending his fingers till the joints cracked, said: 'The Führer decided on war, because he found it necessary. That's the decisive point—the only thing that matters—we've just got to be quiet and obey orders till we win the final victory.'

'Yes, yes, my dear Fröhlich,' laughed Endrigkeit. 'We are absolutely agreed on that. We have brewed the punch and now we must ladle it out. Let's hope it doesn't make us sick.'

He reached for the plate again and with dismay Corporal Herbert saw the last piece of cake disappear behind his moustache. He was glad he had taken the precaution of putting aside a piece for Breuer. But Lakosch would curse and swear when he came back.

As a matter of fact he didn't. When they both came in a little later, the red haired man crawled sulkily into his bunk without a word about either the cake or the film. No one paid any attention to him as Breuer was the centre of interest, but he too was out of spirits and disinclined to talk. However, they learned from him that since early morning the Russians had been attacking in several places after heavy artillery preparation, but that they had not used tanks. The first Roumanian Cavalry Division had stood up very well, but it was not yet known how things were on their left, where the heaviest assaults had taken place. Communications were interrupted in this area and it was impossible to get into touch with the German Tank Corps or with the Roumanian senior commands. During a reconnaissance towards the west they had come across tracks of a large force of tanks, which Breuer believed on account of their breadth to be Russian T34s.

'What had the General to say to all this?'

'He said "Balls". That's his favourite word. He's a smart fellow, I grant him that, but he simply doesn't believe what he sees. At one point we made out a group of tanks about twenty strong, driving south. He approached to within about 500 yards and told Lakosch to drive the Horch on to a hill top. "Be careful, General," I said, "Those are Russians." "Balls," he said. After a while he got the wind of a bullet that just missed the gold braid on his cap. But he stayed for quite a while, staring through his field-glasses, until he decided to turn round. It was high time, as we'd already had a few shots through the back of the car.'

Endrigkeit took his leave and went to move away the die-hards in front of the cinema and send them home. Then they went to bed quietly, but even the news that the Artillery regiment had taken a hedgehog position at point 218 did not allay the anxiety that everyone felt.

Late in the night a motor-cycle from the west buzzed into the village. A beam of light played hesitatingly over the street, searching among houses and fences till it struck a fur-coated sentry in front of the Administration Office. Then it went out.

'Halt, who goes there?' called the sentry, still blinded by the sudden glare.

'The staff,' gasped a voice in his face. 'I must see the staff.'

'Who is it?' cried the sentry. 'Give the password.' But before he could bring up his rifle he felt himself pushed aside and stumbled down the steps.

Engelhard was sitting reading the latest messages in which Colonel Lunitz reported that all was quiet at point 218. Thank God, he thought. Things seemed to be all right again. Then he heard heavy footsteps in the corridor but did not look up till the door of the room opened noisily.

'What is it?' he said, springing to his feet. 'What's the matter?'

A man was standing, in the doorway, bareheaded, without belt or weapons and wearing fatigue dress as though he had come in from the next room. But his clothes were torn and smeared with blood and clay, there was a grimy bandage on his head and he could hardly stand. He was supporting himself against the door posts so as not to fall down.

'Good God! Where do you come from?'

The man stared at Engelhard with glassy eyes. 'From over there —behind there——' he groaned. 'The Russians . . .'

'What's that you say?' said Colonel Unold, who had woken up and came in wearing his bath robe. 'The Russians? Where? Speak up and tell us.'

He was walking towards the man, but Engelhard got ahead of him, for he saw that the man was finished and might pass out at any moment. He picked him up carefully under the arms and let him slip into a chair. Then he put a bottle of brandy to his lips. The spirit had an immediate effect. The man became calmer and his expression more normal.

'Come now, who are you and where are you from?'

'Sergeant-Major Schlüter, sir, from the Veterinary Stables in Manoilin.'

'Have you come straight from there?'

'Yes, sir, on my motor-cycle.'

'And you say the Russians are in Manoilin?'

'Yes, Captain.'

'Impossible,' cried Unold. The word made the man shrink into himself, and his face took on the hunted expression it had worn when he came in. Engelhard glanced imploringly at the Colonel and said to the soldier.

'Now just tell us quite quietly what happened, one thing after another.'

The Sergeant-Major took a few deep breaths. 'We had already gone to bed. We'd been having a good time—everyone was pretty sound asleep. Suddenly the house seemed to be falling down. They'd dropped one into the middle of the room—I jumped up, I was the only one who could, and jumped out of the window. There was all hell going on outside. It was as bright as day, and half the village was on fire. Horses, peasants and everyone running round in circles—while their tanks drove through the mess, firing their guns. Our stables were on fire with all the horses inside—my God, how they screamed!

He was on the point of collapsing when Engelhard handed him the brandy bottle again.

'How long ago did all this happen?'

'An hour ago at most. I came straight over.'

'Tanks, you say. How many of them, about?'

The man shrugged his shoulders. 'Five, six . . . perhaps even twenty . . . it was hard to make out.'

'Infantry too?'

'I saw some sitting on the tanks.'

Engelhard got up and looked at the Colonel, who was gnawing his lower lip.

'Very well,' said Engelhard, 'now go and lie down on my bed and rest. We'll send for the doctor. You don't look too good.' When he had put the man to bed and tucked him up, he turned to find Unold looking at the map.

'In Manoilin,' he murmured. 'It's a catastrophe.'

'By night everything looks worse than it is,' said the Captain. 'But after all, if three or four tanks managed to break through, that's not a disaster.'

'What, thirty kilometres behind the front? That can't be only three or four. It's a hell of a mess,' said Unold as the gravity of the situation began to dawn on him. He picked up the foot-rule. 'Manoilin, man—why that's only fifteen kilometres away. Fifteen kilometres down a good road, with nothing in the way.' He dropped the foot-rule and looked at Engelhard, his face white as chalk. 'If they turn eastwards, Engelhard, they can get here in half an hour,' he said quietly . . .' Then he raised his voice, and shouted: 'The alarm . . . sound the alarm at once!'

The scream of the sirens woke Breuer. He had no idea what was happening, but he did not want to go for information to the Staff Office. At such moments it was better to keep out of Unold's way. So he went across to the Information Bureau, where he could always get the latest news. When he opened a door bearing the notice 'Head of News Service', he found Lieutenant Wiese before him.

'Hullo, Wiese,' he said. 'You here?'

The other got up from his chair and held out his hand.

'Are you surprised, Breuer? I have now been here two days as signals officer.'

'What! You're running the signals? Sorry, don't get me wrong. Of course I'm glad for your sake, but I had managed to get Unold to promise he'd move you to my office. Now that's a lost hope.'

'The best laid plans . . .' quoted Wiese with a smile. 'Anyhow we'll be able to see one another.'

Breuer had taken a chair and lit a cigarette. He said: 'All the same, it's a disappointment to me. We'd all have been glad to have you. Do you remember one evening in the gulley near Aksai, when it was raining in torrents, and you recited Rilke and Hofmannsthal the whole evening. That was fine—something to remember.'

Breuer looked at his companion, who was so much younger than himself but seemed much more mature and integrated.

'Tell me, Wiese,' he asked after a pause for reflection. 'You're not a professional soldier. What are you really? I mean, you must be a schoolmaster or a theologian or a librarian or something.'

Wiese laughed. 'You're on quite the wrong track. I'm nobody really. I work for the State Railways.'

'Really? That would have been my last guess. What on earth were you doing in that outfit?'

Wiese smiled again—a sad smile in which his eyes had no part. 'It's not a very interesting story,' he said.

Breuer was still puzzling over it when he went back to his quarters. He tried in vain to imagine Wiese punching tickets or issuing them to passengers. And then he suddenly remembered that he hadn't asked why the alarm was sounding.

The clerks, cooks and drivers, with the exception of three of four who were indispensable, had recently been organized into an Emergency Unit which could be called to arms if need arose. Captain Fackelmann, who was nominally in charge of the unit, knew all about the catering side of army life, but so little about the duties of an infantryman that he had gladly resigned this honourable post in favour of Sergeant-Major Harras. The latter was a keen young man with blond hair and bright eyes—in fact he would have made an ideal subject for the cover of a soldier's magazine. After being in

Class II of a secondary school he had joined the army firmly resolved to become an officer. He seemed to have all the qualities for commissioned rank and no one, himself least of all, understood exactly why he had failed twice at the examination of candidates for commissions. When the war came he cheered himself with the thought that distinguished service at the front might rectify the mistake and win him promotion. And then he was unexpectedly appointed to the staff of a division. No wonder Harras had undertaken responsibility for the Emergency Unit with enthusiasm. Here, if anywhere, fortune would offer him the chance of performing some improbably gallant feat of arms, which despite all obstacles would secure for him the coveted epaulets. In the firm expectation of such an event he was now wearing Russian leather top-boots, riding breeches made to measure and an officer's collar from which he had removed the silver edging. He also took a good deal of trouble when speaking to use the sharp, staccato tones, which he imagined to be the hall-mark of the 'officer-type', and his ear-splitting cry of 'Attention, everybody' had caused the troops to nickname him Ten Shun.

Today Harras felt that his great hour had come. He mustered his troop of some forty men on the road to Manoilin at the west end of the village and gave them their final instructions.

'Attention, everybody. This is the first time we go into action. The eyes of the whole staff are on us: you know your duty. One thing more—remember what you've learnt and let the enemy come on till you can see the whites of their eyes. I don't want any clot to go off half cocked. Wait till I give the order to fire—then let them have it. Pull yourself together, men—there are medals to be won.'

The soldiers in their greatcoats and caps with earflaps handled their rifles hesitatingly and looked doubtfully at their leader as he stood before them, tall and slim with a couple of hand-grenades in his belt, his sub-machine gun slung over his breast and a well-greased steel helmet on his head. His get-up was impressive but alarming. The unit marched in two files, one on each side of the street. It was cold and the ground was wet. Thick wet snowflakes were falling. Lakosch was in charge of one of the two machine-guns. He was one of the only men in the unit who knew anything about

42

them—Geibel on the other hand, who had been detailed as his number two, had never seen such an object before. After a short period of training he had come straight to the staff eight weeks before and since then had never left the clerk's room.

'Tell me,' he asked anxiously, 'what'll we do if they come in tanks? Is there anything at all we can do?'

'Of course there is, you dumb bastard,' said Lakosch, 'all you have to do is to jump up on top, pull open the shutter and throw a hand-grenade inside.'

'Is that so?' Geibel seemed enlightened by this advice, but after a while he felt new misgivings.

'But look here,' he said, 'we haven't got any hand-grenades.'

'Then you'll have to use something else. A brick or something. Or you could stick your side-arm into the tracks. Then the tank keeps on turning round until it runs out of gas.'

Feldwebel Harras, with a flashlight in his hand, strode once more down the line. When he reached Laskosch he stopped and inspected the machine-gun. Suddenly his expression stiffened. 'What's this, eh? Where's your side-arm?'

Lakosch, who had been bending down by the gun, pulled himself up to standing position. In his greatcoat, which was so much too big for him that he had to roll back the sleeves, and with the hood coming down to his nose, he looked like a garden-dwarf.

'My side-arm, Sarn-Major . . . my side-arm is in the car, ready for use.'

'In the car, you idiot! I'll have to break you of these driver's habits of yours. You're in the infantry now, understand? The back-bone of the Army. An infantryman without a side-arm is like a dog without teeth, good God!' He felt for his leather notebook which as usual was tucked between the buttons of his coat, and recorded the offence. 'You're sure to get three days,' he snorted and stamped away.

'Very good, Sarn-Major, three days sure,' repeated Lakosch, saluting stiffly before he slumped down beside his machine-gun.

'You see,' bleated Geibel, 'not even a side-arm, and if the tanks come . . .'

'Shut your trap,' said Lakosch, who was beginning to feel cold.

Hours passed and nothing happened. The snow fell thicker and thicker and the damp penetrated clothing and boots. Harras stood in the road staring into the darkness through his field-glasses, changing feet from time to time and cursing his boots. If only he had put on his old felt shufflers.

Suddenly he heard something. The wind had carried to his ears a sound which was out of keeping with the stillness of the night.

Harras strained his ears to hear. Yes, there was something like the murmur of voices and the tramp of feet. Or was it only the blood throbbing in his ears? No, now he could hear more clearly and could detect voices and the thud of boots and the clink of metal. There was no doubt about it. They were coming. Harras told himself to keep calm as he wondered how many they were? A battalion? A regiment? They were marching normally and were obviously not suspecting anything. Well, he was going to prepare a warm reception for them.

'Attention!' he whispered hoarsely.

The order was passed along the ranks.

'Ready!'

'Ready . . . ready.'

A tense excitement stirred the little group.

'Present!'

'Present . . . present . . . present.'

Twenty-one, twenty-two. Harras counted softly to calm his own nerves, and searched the darkness through his glasses. He wanted the enemy to come as near as possible, before he gave the order to fire.

Then suddenly putting down his field-glasses he roared 'Halt!' into the darkness, after which he made his unit stand at ease.

He had recognized the white lambskin caps of the Roumanians.

The disappointment was fearful, but Harras took it without wincing. He even acted as if he had been long expecting something of the sort. He held up the troop of dishevelled figures who came marching along the road, and subjected them to a severe catechism. He found they had come from the neighbouring section where everything was in confusion. They had been on the road for hours, but Russians . . . no, they hadn't seen any Russians.

44

The rest of the night passed quietly. Towards morning the unit, half frozen and wet through, was relieved by detachments from the local command.

The attractions of heroism now seemed more questionable. Even Sergeant-Major Harras had learnt something worth while, namely that high-boots were not the most suitable footwear for the front line.

The snow went on falling in thick flakes all the morning and since the early hours the Roumanians had been marching through the village. They came from the west. They came one by one, leaning on sticks or home-made shepherd's crooks, some of them barefoot or carrying their boots. They came in small groups trotting one behind the other like sheep, half asleep and propping each other up, too tired to shake off the heaps of snow that had collected on their caps and shoulders. Some of them were mounted, often riding two at a time on the back of some exhausted beast that could hardly go any farther, or on ambulance wagons which bent and creaked under their load of sick and wounded. Some of them were still carrying their weapons or pulling old-fashioned machine-guns on wheels, like toys, behind them. But most had abandoned these burdens. The roadway was strewn with rifles, boxes of ammunition, cartridge belts and steel-helmets, which the snow was gradually covering as if a pitying God were ashamed of the tragic sight. It was as if the ghosts of the broken Grande Armée had returned. They were marching eastwards, but they didn't seem to care where they were going—all they wanted was rest and sleep . . . sleep wherever they could find a resting-place.

The men of the Intelligence unit stood by the garden fence and gazed at the sight.

'You see,' explained Lakosch to Geibel. 'They're all fed up. Now they're going home.'

'Home?' said Geibel doubtfully.

'Of course, chum. They're through. You can see that. As far as they're concerned the war's over.'

A strange-looking rider came by at this moment. He was sitting on a car. His feet were bare and his uniform in rags, but he had an appearance of easy-going distinction emphasized by a helmet that had slipped over one ear. And the fellow actually had the heart to whistle and wink mischievously at the Germans as he passed. Lakosch picked up a frozen piece of sacking from the ground and threw it at the rider who caught it deftly and made a lordly gesture of thanks.

'My God! If that happened to us,' said Herbert, shaken.

'To us?' said Fröhlich heatedly. 'These are Roumanians? It *couldn't* happen to us. You must realize that.'

The Roumanians poured into Buzinovka like a swarm of locusts. They filled the streets and farmyards, the barns, stables and sheds and crowded into the houses like vermin. And wherever they found a little warmth they lay down and slept so deeply that no one could wake them up. Even in the corridors of the Intelligence Section they were lying beside and on top of one another and didn't move when anyone accidentally trod on them. Dirt and wounds and wet clothes all contributed to the disgusting smell. Breuer had given them the use of his room in the hope of getting some information about what had happened, but from the Roumanians he learned nothing.

Down below there was a panic at the crossroads. From the north came a bunch of five horses harnessed together and mounted by a single rider who was powerless to control them. One of the beasts ran into a post and fell, bringing down the others in a struggling mass—the shouts of men and the screaming of the beasts, as well as the sound of motor horns, created a pandemonium. The field-police, who were trying to regulate the traffic, lost their nerve and opened fire.

The wildest confusion reigned round the Town-Major's quarters. There was a board with a notice saying in German, French and Russian: 'Rations will only be given to parties under the command of an officer.' But you couldn't expect hungry soldiers to understand that. Besides there were no parties and no commanders any longer. Inside stood the Town-Major behind a table, which he hoped would protect him from the seething mob, waving his arms and crying *Nix Kuschait nix manger,* in that form of Esperanto which the war had created and which was understood by the soldiers of all nations. But nothing could be heard through the din except an ugly rasping sound. Suddenly an officer with a riding-crop fought his way through the mass of Roumanians. He was wearing a lambskin jacket and riding-boots, breeches and spurs on his bow legs. The sides of his breeches flapped like elephants' ears.

'Allow me,' he said in a Viennese accent. 'I'm Captain Popescu,' and he raised his riding-crop in salute. 'I require at once, please, stabling and forage for 500 horses of the first cavalry division. We have been riding for two days without stopping and haven't had a grain of corn.'

For a moment the Town-Major stood speechless. Then he summoned up his strength for a final effort and gasped: 'What are you talking about? Stabling and fodder for your filthy brutes? You'd better slaughter them and give them to your men to eat!'

The cavalry captain turned the colour of a boiled lobster. His thoroughbred riding horses were the pride of his life and this common fellow spoke of slaughtering them.

He shouted back: 'My horses have fighted. For whom have they fighted? For Hitlair, do you understand? And now must they die of cold and hunger? I shall go and complain to the staff and requisition all the oats, all the fodder and all the stabling they need—everything.'

He fought his way, raging, through the crowd.

'And the best of luck!' croaked the Town-Major after him. And then he had the same thought as Fröhlich. What are we doing mixed up with these filthy peasants?

In his office Unold was pacing up and down. The General was sitting by the map-table in his fur coat drumming with his stubby fingers on the table-leaf. Ten minutes before Colonel Lunitz had telephoned for the third time to say that the position at point 218 had become untenable.

Unold remained standing and said: 'No, this can't go on. Lunitz has run out of ammunition and is almost surrounded; he can't last another half hour. General, you *must* give him orders to retire.'

'And I tell you there's no question of retiring. Don't you know the Führer's order?'

47

Unold's face twitched. 'If you mean last winter's order, sir,' he rejoined, controlling his voice carefully, 'in which the Führer reserved to himself the right to withdraw any unit, even at battalion level . . .'

'Yes, that's just what I mean.'

'That order arose out of the special situation on the Moscow front. Now it's out of date. It's no longer binding.'

The General laughed sardonically. 'You think so? Maybe a court martial would have something to say about that. The Führer doesn't joke about that sort of thing. Anyhow I don't propose to risk my neck.'

Unold kept quiet, but the blood drained from his face.

He said: 'It's not a case of anyone saving his life. After all, to lose it is one of the risks of war. It's a question of saving our best artillery regiment and our precious 8.8 anti-aircraft guns, which we need here like our daily bread. It may be worth while sacrificing troops to gain a military objective, but this sacrifice does nobody any good. It's senseless!'

The General tried to flash his china-blue eyes as he answered: 'No sacrifice is senseless. The glorious, heroic end of the artillery regiment will be an inspiration to the whole division.'

Unold was a National-Socialist and proud of it. But he was also a self-respecting GSO. At this point his self-control left him and, trembling all over, he said: 'I can't go on like this. The division has to be commanded—otherwise let's shut up shop and make propaganda speeches instead.'

'That's enough!' snapped the General, springing to his feet. 'Pull yourself together, man! You don't know . . .'

'I know very well what I'm saying,' said Unold, his voice shaking. 'I've been running the division alone for long enough, and I know that I can run it. But I can't do it with an idiot for a chief.' As he said these words Unold suddenly felt a shock of fear. He realized immediately the significance of what had just happened. He looked dispiritedly at the General, who was gasping for breath like a fish on dry land. His red face was almost blue and the thick, dark veins stood out on his temples. He slowly shrank back into his chair and propped his head up with his hand. The skin of his face had suddenly became slack and yellow—'My nerves . . .' he said. 'It's too much for me. I need a thorough rest.' He got up again, felt for his cap without looking and moved with uncertain steps towards the door. With the handle in his hand, he said quietly without looking round:

'With regard to Lunitz, please do what you think right.'

Unold picked up the receiver with a shaking hand and sweat on his forehead.

The line was dead.

It was reported from Manoilin that two regiments of the enemy were attacking. Hastily collected fighting groups had indeed secured the roads leading westwards and Lieutenant Dierk, with his two four-barrelled flak-guns was in position there, but that was little enough to deal with an emergency. As the anti-tank section under Captain Eichert had still not turned up, the division, since the loss of its artillery, had no proper means of defence except four still service-able tanks, with which Major Kalweit was now on his way towards Manoilin.

At this point an idea came to Colonel Unold and he passed it on to the assembled staff-officers.

'We don't know,' he said, 'where to find enough men and ammunition, though the place is cluttered with Roumanians, lounging idly around. This has got to stop. We've got to get this mob functioning again.' As he looked round the circle his eyes fell on the rosy, smiling face of Captain Fackelmann and he said: 'That's a job for you, Fackelmann.'

The little Captain was thinking deeply about a culinary problem. On the night of the party at the mess the General had declared that the heads of beetles tasted strangely of nuts. He wondered where the old swine had acquired that piece of knowledge. If it was true, it suggested possibilities . . .

'Well, Fackelmann, you see what you can do.'

'Very good, Colonel,' stammered Fackelmann, still thinking of the cockchafers.

'Listen, then,' said Unold. 'Get hold of as many Roumanians as you can find in the village. Endrigkeit will help you. In two hours I expect you to have got together a couple of battalions ready to go into action.'

'Come along, old man,' said Endrigkeit at the door, dragging the wavering Captain out of the room.

They began the round-up by getting Endrigkeit's Field Police to picket the street and lay hands on any men found walking about. But the news spread like wildfire and in a few minutes there was no one to be seen except for the fifty or so they had been able to collar. Endrigkeit then announced that there was going to be an issue of food. The news created unexpected enthusiasm. The Roumanians began to chatter and gesticulate and to push each other around so as to get to the head of the queue. Some even volunteered to fetch other comrades, and soon the fighting force had reached 200. Fackelmann viewed this success with silence and suspicion. Endrigkeit beckoned to one of his men and said: 'Listen to me, Otto, you and Franz have got to see that this crowd gets fed at the Supply Stores—but properly, mind; they're very hungry. I'll expect you back here in forty minutes.'

In half an hour Otto and Franz were back. They were alone.

'Yes, sir,' said Otto, pushing his cap forward and scratching his head. 'Everything went well as far as the depot. There was bread and dripping and a bowl of thick pea soup for everyone. Yes, and then suddenly the bastards all disappeared. God knows where they all disappeared to.'

Endrigkeit looked at Fackelmann. 'Doesn't seem to have worked,' he said. 'I'll have to search the houses. Their officers must be somewhere.'

So they combed the houses. In the second house they found a room full of officers lying on the floor, or sitting with their heads on the table, sleeping.

Only one of them was awake. He looked daggers at the intruders, but Fackelmann walked up to him and explained what he wanted. The officer didn't move, but sat glowering at Fackelmann who repeated his request, sweating and stuttering in French. The Roumanian gave no sign of understanding, but after an endless pause, he suddenly said in German: 'Our Colonel is asleep in the next room. He has given orders that he's not to be woken up, but you can take a chance if you like.'

Fackelmann opened the door cautiously and looked into a sort of compartment. There he saw a giant lying on a camp bed. The man's swarthy face looked almost black against the white of his hair. He was lying on his back snoring. Fackelmann began to sweat more than ever. He beckoned to Endrigkeit to come to his help. Endrigkeit, who had no fear of barbarians, gripped the Colonel firmly by the shoulder and shook him violently. Inquisitive Roumanian faces looked in at the door. The Colonel knitted his bushy brows and grunted protestingly. Then he opened his eyes and sat up slowly. Thunder and lightning were in his glance and the Roumanians at the door vanished.

Fackelmann had taken off his cap and was wiping his glasses with his handkerchief like a man trying to polish a billiard ball. He introduced himself and began to formulate his requirements, but he did not get very far.

'Listen to me,' broke in the Colonel with a voice of thunder. 'I went to see your staff this morning. I asked for food for my soldiers. Your Colonel chased me away like a mangy dog—and now he has the nerve to send you to me.'

Fackelmann hastened to assure the Colonel that he had come on his own initiative. He said he had always had a high opinion of the Roumanians, he knew Bucharest and was a great admirer of Roumanian cooking which he praised enthusiastically. He seemed to have found a soft spot in the Colonel's armour; the giant's expression grew milder. And then Fackelmann had a bright idea. He told the Colonel that he had really come to speak in the first place about the question of supplies. It was clear that all freshly formed Roumanian units should be generously supplied with food. The Colonel, impressed by this decisive argument, explained that he would himself take the matter in hand and promised by the evening to provide 500 Roumanians for the defence of the village. He got to his feet, crammed his lamb-skin cap on to his head, picked up his knobbly stick and stumped out of the room. The sound of his voice had been heard in the next room and had caused a commotion among the officers. In a few moments they had all vanished. Soon afterwards Endrigkeit and Fackelmann saw them in the streets shouting and using their riding-crops on their men, and they came to the conclusion that their cause was in good hands.

Meanwhile Breuer hunted round from quarter to quarter. Unold had ordered him to collect rifle ammunition at all costs, but everywhere he met with shrugged shoulders and expressions of regret. It seemed there wasn't a single cartridge left in Buzinovka. Finally in a workshop on the northern edge of the village he came across three assault-guns which were being repaired. The three young officers in charge of the guns were sitting playing skat. They politely invited Breuer to join them, treated him to cognac and cigarettes and got him to tell them the latest news, which they found fresh and surprising. 'You want ammunition?' they asked. 'You can have as much as you like—will you take 2000 rounds or 3000?' One of the three officers went over with Breuer to the workshop and called the men together. 'Come on now. Bring out the MG ammunition.' Their faces expressed embarrassment. A Sergeant-Major said something like: 'There's very little here and we need it ourselves.'

'Nonsense—all the reserve boxes are full.'

Silence.

'Well, what's the matter? Open up the boxes.'

The Sergeant-Major very reluctantly opened the ammunition boxes of one of the machine-guns. They were full to the brim with cigarettes and chocolates. The others were the same.

'You must be drunk,' cried the Lieutenant, but there was a gleam of amusement in his eye. He shot a sidelong glance at Breuer and raised his voice: 'If such a thing occurs again I'll beat the hell out of you.'

The men saw the twinkle and answered: 'Certainly, sir,' in chorus, grinning all over their oily faces.

In the end they collected a few machine-gun belts and Breuer was able to supply Unold with about 400 rounds for the defence of Buzinovka.

He came back to find Kalweit's tanks just clanking into the village. A crowd of soldiers greeted them enthusiastically, shouting: 'What's the score, Major? Is Ivan coming? Did you scare the daylights out of him?' The Major stood in the turret of the leading tank, waving his cap and laughing. His camouflage tunic and shirt were open at the neck and his Knight's Cross was swinging on a hook.

'We had terrific luck,' he cried as he jumped down lightly from his tank—'we must have shot up a couple of battalions. No one's going to show his nose here before tomorrow morning.'

Towards evening two companies of Roumanians marched to the west boundary of the village in good order. Their Colonel accompanied them in person and inspected every single rifle barrel. Raising his powerful voice, he consigned to the flames any soldier who dared to leave his post without permission, and from the way he brandished his swagger-stick it looked as if he meant it.

Chapter Three

A DOOR IS CLOSED

THE DIVISIONAL STAFF was on the run.

Even the optimistic Fröhlich could hardly find any other description for the hurried abandonment of Buzinovka. But the Special Service Officer was not worrying. With an open mouth and eyes half closed, he was standing in the street, wool-gathering. As usual, when the situation was not in harmony with the confidence which he invariably felt, he had let himself drift into a semi-comatose condition. Winter had come overnight. The village houses beneath the tall pines had a fairy-tale look, their little windows spangled with crystals of ice. But no one could spare a glance for their beauty. Winter in Russia is a hostile season, and with it comes calamity.

A few steps away from Fröhlich stood Captain Endrigkeit looking along the grey line of cars. The collar of his sheepskin coat was turned up and he was shivering. Under his frosted moustache, his metal-lidded pipe was dangling as usual. But now even the Captain didn't notice that it had gone out.

Breuer was sitting in his car. His three men had seized the opportunity to warm themselves in one of the cottages and to poach themselves a few eggs. He himself had no wish to eat.

When, after a quiet night, the fire of field-guns and 'Stalin Organs' had suddenly burst upon Buzinovka, events had followed one another with such headlong speed that Breuer could only recall disjointed pictures of what had happened. The warriors on the staff of the stick-carrying Roumanian, skipping off like frightened rabbits after the first attacks; the Roumanians in the farm yard blown to pieces by mortar-bombs, which had torn away half the stables; the faces of the Russian family setting out in flight from

54

their own people, bundles in their hands and a weeping child on the father's arm. They said nothing, the man and his wife, as they fled from their ruined home, but on their faces was a look of satisfaction: look, they were thinking, they're coming after all—our own people: and then Unold, lying on his belly, covered with dust, entangled in the blown-out window frame. Breuer could not help laughing when he thought of the Colonel's look of incredulous surprise as he stared round the devastated room and remarked: 'Christ Almighty! Looks like it's time to move on.'

Then came the order instructing the divisional vehicles to clear out of Verchnaya Buzinovka as quickly as they could, separately, by whatever route they chose, and to assemble in a village lying two kilometres to the east on the far-side of a ridge of hills. This order sounded unpleasantly like the classic '*Sauve qui peut*'. Cars raced through the ruined village, through the smoke of burning houses, the crash of bursting shells and shouting, panicking troops. Breuer put his hand before his eyes and forced himself to breathe calmly. As an infantryman he had been in many a tight corner, but he had never witnessed a scene of such chaos, such helpless despair. To think that three days ago they had been talking about films and home leave!

Some twenty cars had mustered in the main street of the next village and others kept on driving in from every possible direction. Unold hurried along the grey column. His face was grey too—almost as grey as his shabby leather coat.

He called out: 'The General. Where's the General? Anyone seen the General?'

Since his collision with Unold on the previous day no one had set eyes on the General and until then Unold had not missed him. He stopped alongside of Breuer's car. His eyes were rimmed with red and his chin was covered with stubble. He said: 'Fackelmann's not here, Harras's not here and the Divisional Commander's God knows where! Got to do everything myself . . . Breuer, go back at once to Buzinovka and look for the General. Tell him that the new rallying point is in Verchnaya Golubaya and bring him there dead or alive.'

Driving out of the place Breuer passed Fackelmann standing

upright in his Volkswagen and waving his arms. As the cars passed one another he shouted: 'They almost got us. Boy oh boy! Look at this here,' and he pointed to the bullet holes in his radiator.

Breuer forked left up the hill over which the bitter wind was sweeping the snow in eddies. From the crest he could see, down in the valley, the clustered cottages of Buzinovka black with smoke and burning in many places. On the highest point of the ridge, where the wind was blowing most violently stood an 8.8 Flak Gun in position, with its long barrel turned towards the west. A few soldiers were standing around it.

'Hullo!' called Breuer to one of the men. 'Have you seen a car with the divisional standard on it? A big Horch?'

The man did not move, standing with his collar turned up and both hands in his pockets. His back was turned to Breuer and he was looking to the west. 'No,' he answered in very unsoldierly fashion over his shoulder. 'Can't say I have. We've got more important things to do.'

'Look over there, Lieutenant!' said Lakosch, pointing in the direction in which the soldier was gazing. Over the white shoulder of the hill on the other side of the valley, there was a thick brown stream that looked like syrup. Breuer walked up to the gun team and looked through his field-glasses. He saw that it was a body of Russian cavalry riding to attack the village. He could see their sabres gleaming.

'Give it them, man,' he cried, taking the soldier by the arm. 'Go on, blow them to hell!'

'Not yet,' said the soldier, shifting his cigarette with his tongue from one side of his mouth to the other. 'There aren't enough of them.' He spat out the cigarette-butt. 'They've tried to do it twice and each time we wiped them out. But they keep on coming. They're tough bastards.'

Breuer drove to fetch the General. Perhaps he was wounded, helpless . . . Lakosch turned off the engine and let the car coast down into the village, which they found almost deserted. A few stragglers were skirting the walls of the houses and a pair of unarmed Russians, escaped prisoners, were foraging around like jackals.

'There's the Horch!' called Lakosch, and sure enough there was the big limousine standing in front of them in the street. They recognized it at once by the black, white and red standard. Not far off, under the lee of a house, they could see the armoured car which accompanied the General on his rounds. The General himself was standing alone in the middle of the street wearing his gold-braided cap and smoking a cigar. He paid no attention to passing rifle bullets or the flak shells that boomed over his head. He was standing near a wooden case. The crew of the reconnaissance car were dragging a second case out of the burning depot.

'No,' he shouted. 'That's red wine again. Didn't I tell you, Cognac! In you go again, and this time fetch some cigars—Brazilians if possible, d'you hear? They're always good.'

Breuer stood unobserved behind him for quite a while and then he said: 'Excuse me, General.'

The General turned round. 'What are *you* doing here?'

'Colonel Unold has sent me to inform you, sir, that the divisional staff is . . .'

The General's eyes seemed to be popping out of their sockets.

'You can go to hell, sir,' he shouted. 'You and the staff with you.'

Breuer snapped out: 'Very good, General,' and hurried back to his own car. There was nothing more for him to do in the village. But where was Lakosch?

'Lakosch!' he called. 'Lakosch!'

Then he saw somebody crawling out of the ruins of the depot with blackened face and hands and singed hair. The figure waddled up, its greatcoat bulging like the skirt of a market-woman.

'Good heavens, it's Lakosch!'

'The chocolate's a bit singed,' said Lakosch, grinning. 'But these cigars'—he drew a box out of the depths of his coat—'are genuine Brazilians and the General says they're always good.'

In the Golubaya Valley, about 500 yards north of the village of that name, there was in the middle of a clearing in the pine-woods a group of small huts, which looked in the distance like a kaffir kraal. They were Finnish tents, circular dwellings made of weatherproof paste-board, the height of a man and with conical roofs. They were usually built about three feet deep into the ground and cushioned with straw to keep out the cold. But here the builders had been careless and the wind blew merrily through the joints, sweeping the frozen snow right inside.

In one of these tents the Intelligence section had established its office. This was a stroke of luck, because the village was crowded with units of the XIth Corps in whose territory the division now found itself. Communications with the Tank Corps were cut and the troops had retreated eastwards.

Soon after they had arrived Fröhlich had scraped together some straw and threw himself down in it, as he was, in greatcoat and boots. He was resolved as far as was possible to sleep through all incidents which did not suit him. Meanwhile Herbert and Geibel had been foraging for firewood, and had converted some boxes into makeshift office chairs. They had also fixed up lighting arrangements for the unit, consisting of a gasolene lamp of the kind used in coalmines. They did what they could to dry their stinking felt boots.

Breuer did not arrive till long after dark, as Unold had found different jobs for him to do all day. He expressed satisfaction in his surly way that his quarters were 500 yards away from the staff and that there was no telephone. At last there was a chance that he would be left in peace. Then he threw himself down in a corner and at once fell asleep. Lakosch covered him with all the coats and rugs he could find and then fetched in the cushions of his car, sat down on them and with a lordly gesture lit a Brazilian cigar.

'What have we got to eat?' he asked.

'Oh, bloody hell,' said Herbert, whose good manners had not stood up to the ordeal of flight, hunger and cold. 'The paymaster hasn't brought us our rations yet. God knows if he'll ever find us here.'

Lakosch grinned and pulled out of his overcoat a two pound box of meat-loaf and threw it across to Herbert, saying: 'All right, old man, then you can make us a dish of roast veal out of this.'

'Well, I'm blowed!' said Geibel. 'What have you been doing? Robbing a Jew?'

'It's a professional secret,' said Lakosch. 'If you'll shut up, you might get some.'

Herbert opened the tin with his bayonet and shook the contents into a cooking-pot, which he placed on the stove. Soon there mingled with the stench of dirty straw and felt boots a heavenly smell, which raised everyone's morale.

Geibel produced half a loaf of bread which he had been hoarding and set to work to cut a few slices from it. Suddenly he stopped and said: 'Christ, I'd almost forgotten. Ten Shun told me to tell you that you're on sentry duty from ten to twelve.'

'Who, me?' Lakosch let his spoon fall. 'Me of all people? He must be pissed. Fancy putting me on night duty after I've been running errands the whole day . . .'

'Probably it's instead of the three days—you remember—the business of your side-arm.'

'The rotten bastard! What time is it?'

No answer was necessary for at that moment the door flew open and a voice growled into the room. 'Where the hell's the relief? It's ten past ten already.'

Lakosch cursed as he got to his feet, pulled on his still damp felt boots and put on his greatcoat. He was still cursing when after fixing on his ear flaps he crammed his steel helmet on his head, picked up his rifle and stumbled out into the darkness.

The wind had subsided but it was very cold.

The moon was riding across the spangled sky and its light filtered through the white smoke that rose from the tents. Below on the road an occasional motor vehicle drove noisily by and from the staff HQ isolated calls and the buzz of conversation floated faintly across. Otherwise all was still. Lakosch trudged along the path which the previous sentries had trodden out between the tents, going round left handed and right handed by turns. And as he marched he gave himself up to thinking about home.

Life was hard, but it was something to have Erna, the little black devil! He started. Hadn't someone called out? The lights went up at HQ and a shot was fired. And then quite clearly he heard someone shouting the word 'Alarm!' In an instant Lakosch was wide awake. He ran from tent to tent and awoke the sleepers.

When in a few minutes the occupants of the Finnish tents had assembled in front of the Administrative Office, they found everyone bustling about in wild confusion. 'What's happened?' Don't know. Seems there are Russian tanks in the village.' Colonel Unold, his hair unbrushed and his leather coat slung over his shoulders, was running about like a dog that had lost its bone. Then Major Kalweit, who had been reconnoitering in one of his tanks, came back.

'Well, Kalweit, what's doing?'

'Not a thing—latrine gossip, that's all it is.'

'Oh, not again,' groaned Unold. 'It's too much. One more false alarm, and I'll go stark, staring, raving mad.'

The railway station at Tschir was the terminus of the long thin feeler which stretched out into enemy territory. The leave trains came through here—if the partisans didn't wreck them first—on their long way home. Every German soldier on the Volga and the Don dreamed of the station at Tschir. On 17th November Captain Gedig entrained here for his course for senior adjutants in Berlin. The staff supplies car had given him a lift to that station.

The heavy Büssing was now on its way back; with headlights full on it was humming along the frost-bound road towards the north.

Chief-Paymaster Zimmermann had buried himself in his fur coat. 'What's the date today?' he asked, yawning.

'The twentieth—or, well, it's the twenty-first now because it's twenty past midnight.'

'Damnation! We're two days later. They'll give us a bawling-out at HQ.'

'We're bringing them a lot to make up for being late,' laughed the driver. 'They won't grumble when they see what we've got.'

Zimmermann beamed. He had provisions for twenty-four days in the car—that was ten days more than he was entitled to—the change of position had enabled him to misrepresent his requirements in his favour, and he had no pangs of conscience when he brought it off. He wasn't such a mug as to miss a chance like that. Behind in the car he could hear the jolting of barrels and boxes. There was another sound, too—an excited scrabbling and cackling.

'Hear that?'

The driver nodded and smiled. 'Our Christmas dinner!' he said.

Zimmermann leaned back comfortably in his seat. It was something of a feat to have got hold of these geese in a remote collective farm, at a time when there wasn't a feather to be seen anywhere. Endrigkeit would have a fit when he saw this collection of poultry. The two days' delay had really been worth while.

He went to sleep and only woke up when the car stopped. A sentry in a steel helmet, fur coat and felt boots with his rifle under his arm had halted the car. He was standing in the light of the headlamps. Then he came stamping up and looked at the papers. When he saw the driving orders, he said, 'You're going to Buzinovka, are you? That's over by Kletskaya. You'd better drive through Kalatsch and follow the east bank of the Don as far as Vertyatchi. It's safer. There are supposed to be Russians on the other road. We've had a warning.'

'Oh, nonsense!' said Zimmermann. 'Do you want us to lose five hours? Come along, we'll go straight on.' And as he spoke he thought to himself, 'The old story again! When anything happens anywhere, the battalion doesn't get worried, but the regimental staff gets nervous. They start packing up at divisional HQ. At Corps HQ they burn the supply stores as a safety precaution.' He had long been a troop paymaster and had won the Iron Cross, second class. He took a poor view of staff in general. However, he made the driver dim the headlights.

A lonely moonlit winter scene slid by the windows. They missed the support of their own lights. The empty landscape seemed dead and unreal. Perhaps they would have done better to go by the other route.

They had been driving along without lights for an hour or two when they saw ahead of them lights at a distance from one another. Looked like a column of tracked vehicles on the march. Zimmermann thought with relief that the tanks wouldn't be travelling with headlights on if there was any danger. Then he thought, 'but why should our tanks be going southward?' He wondered if there was anything wrong. He let down the window and stuck his head out.

By this time they were alongside the first tank. The vehicle was painted white. It looked like a German 4, but he couldn't quite make it out. Soldiers in camouflage were sitting on it with the Commander standing in the turret.

The officer called out: 'Which is the way to Kalatsch?'

'Straight on and then to the left,' answered Zimmermann and then he called: 'Everything all right ahead?'

But by this time the tank was too far away for them to hear the answer. Soon the second tank, which was also carrying armed soldiers, rumbled up.

'How are things ahead?' cried Zimmermann.

One of the soldiers answered something and Zimmermann noticed his white teeth as he laughed. Idiot, he thought. Trying to tease in a place like this! The man had called 'gut, gut'.

When the third tank rolled by, Zimmermann called out again, but there was no answer. Dumb bastards, he thought. And then something flashed into his mind like a thunderbolt and pulled him back into the car.

'Step on it!' he cried ducking low in his seat. 'Step on the gas, man!'

He had noticed that one of the men was carrying a Russian carbine with a round magazine, and immediately he realized that something monstrous, something inconceivable was going on, and that far more was at stake than the arrival of provisions at HQ. Perhaps the fate of the army depended on his arriving alive to report what he had seen.

The frightened driver pressed the accelerator and the car leapt forward. The Büssing shot past the next tank, the last of the convoy, like a frightened deer.

Christ! thought Zimmermann and began to offer up thanks for having got away with it. He wiped the sweat from his forehead.

But then he heard the crackle of rifle fire and the whizz of bullets. Suddenly the driver beside him slumped over the steering wheel. He pulled open the door and jumped out, but as he was in the air he felt something hit his back. That was the last thing Zimmermann felt. His lifeless body fell heavily on to the road.

The driverless car staggered on for a moment and then fell side-long with a crash. Boxes and crates burst open and the geese, cackling and hissing, dispersed over the snowy steppe into the darkness.

The false alarm had excited everyone so much that it was impossible, for the time being, to think of sleep. In consequence a regular swarm of officers found themselves assembled in the wooden hut which one of the signal units of the XIth Corps had made over to Unold. Everyone was on fire to learn something new about the situation. The senior officers occupied the few chairs round the table, while the others stood around or sat on boxes. The low-ceilinged room was soon full of smoke. Major Kalweit sat almost buried in a kind of wicker chair with his arms hanging over the sides and his legs stretched out as far as the crush in the room allowed.

'What's really going on?' he asked. 'For the last two days we haven't heard a thing.'

'I'll tell you, damn it,' answered Unold crossly. 'The Russians have broken through between Kletskaya and Serfimovitch—which is not surprising, considering how thinly held the front is there.

'Have they got far?' asked somebody.

Unold's eyelids twitched nervously. He said: 'We mustn't take these break-throughs too seriously. The same thing happened several times last winter. After thirty kilometres or at most forty the Russians have to stop, and meanwhile the area is sealed off. They haven't got what it takes either in supply or leadership. They haven't even got wireless in their tanks.'

After that, everyone began to give their opinions. Fröhlich, jammed into a corner by the door near Padre Peters, slowly raised his eyelids and began to take interest. Suddenly the telephone rang.

'Corps speaking, Colonel,' said Engelhard, passing the receiver to Unold. Conversation ceased. Engelhard listened in on the extension and scribbled the message in shorthand. Then Unold repeated: 'The Golubaya Valley main front line as from now—not a step backwards—yes sir. That's capital, excellent. Soon, let's hope . . . all right, that's all!'

He put back the receiver, his eyes gleaming with satisfaction.

'Good news, gentlemen,' he said, 'the 24th and 16th Panzer Divisions are coming up to stop the hole. They're on the way now.'

In a moment the atmosphere changed and everyone began to talk at once. 'The 16th . . . yes, that's the one that pushed through on its own up to the Volga at Rynok in August . . .' 'Yes, and at Nicolaiev last year.' 'Quite right, they were behind the Russian lines for several days.' 'Ivan's scared stiff of them.' People also had good things to say about the achievements of the 24th, which had been constituted from the East Prussian Cavalry Division.

'Well, gentlemen,' summarized Unold, 'within two or three days it'll all be over. It even looks as if we're starting a pincer movement.'

Fröhlich nudged Peters in the ribs, saying: 'you'll see, Padre. We have them in a trap. I hope plenty of them have got through, so as to make the encirclement worth while.'

'Wouldn't this be the right moment for a toast?' proposed Kalweit. The applause that followed compelled Unold to have some of the cases opened. These were found to contain French white wine and cognac. The company drank out of cups and mugs as the bottles passed from hand to hand. A feverish gaiety soon prevailed. Kalweit had undone the collar of his tunic, his face was red and moist and he told East Prussian funny stories which were received with such resounding salvos of laughter that the sentinel outside halted in his round and listened, shaking his head. Unold drank only cognac and the bottle in front of him was soon half empty.

'I must say you've laid in a nice store of drinks,' said Kalweit. 'From what source did these blessings flow?'

'Our Divisional Commander organized all this. He got it himself from the supply stores in Buzinovka!' answered Unold somewhat thickly. 'It was his last bequest to us.'

'What do you mean? Where is he, anyhow?'

Unold was astonished. 'I thought everyone had been talking about it. He left today at noon.'

'Left? Funny time to pick isn't it?'

'Well, he *has* left and taken the Horch with him. He got me to give him a truck for his things. I just let him go.'

'But he can't go off as easily as that,' said Lieutenant Dierk, outraged. 'That would amount to . . .' He stopped, and his listeners remembered that a gunner had been shot for deserting the colours a few weeks before.

Engelhard thought himself obliged to intervene and said in a formal manner: 'The General has left for Vienna with special approval of the Army Command. An old cardiac disorder which has lately become worse made it necessary for him to take a cure.'

Silence. 'Well, here's to his health!' said Kalweit, and poured half a class of cognac down his throat.

Endrigkeit said, 'Let's hope he'll soon recover.'

Someone from behind said, 'That sort always recover.'

A voice said, 'If by any chance you're referring to me, you may be quite right.'

All heads were turned. No one had heard the door opening. Unold rose to his feet and stared at the speaker as though a ghost, 'Lunitz,' he whispered, and then he came to himself and cried. 'Lunitz! Man, is it really you?'

'Yes, indeed, it's me, and no deception!' said the Colonel dryly and came forward through the lane which the officers had opened for him.

'You didn't expect to see me again.'

'To tell you the truth, we didn't,' said Unold as he embraced the other. Then he noticed that Lunitz's neck was bandaged and that he was carrying his left arm in a sling under his camouflage jacket.

'Come on,' he said. 'Tell us about it. Who else have you got with you?'

'Six men. The others . . .' Colonel Lunitz made a significant gesture. 'We didn't give up easily, but when our last round was fired the Reds rode into us and cut us down. I and the other surviviors lay for two hours under a heap of corpses before we could get away.'

There was dead silence.

'Come and sit down,' said Unold, 'and have something to drink.'

The Colonel screwed up his eyes and looked around at the gathering: then he put up the hood of his coat and said, 'No thanks. I won't interrupt your party. Besides, I'm tired. Have a good time!'

And before anyone could stop him, he was outside. They talked about the incident for a while, but no one felt cheerful any longer.

The occupants of the Finnish tents returned to their quarters in small groups. The moon, round which thin wisps of cloud were hovering, bathed the valley in a flickering light. Breuer and Dierk tramped together through the frozen snow. Breuer was talking about the incidents of the day, but Dierk didn't seem to be listening. Anyhow, he didn't answer. Breuer was describing his vain efforts to find a pioneer unit, which was supposed to be somewhere in the area, when Dierk suddenly burst out, 'That swine! That rotten brute!'

Breuer looked at him, perplexed. His companion's sharp-featured face with its over-prominent chin looked in the fitful moonlight like a landscape battered by a storm.

'Don't take it to heart, Dierk,' he said. 'It's the best solution. The division isn't losing anything.'

'That's not what I mean,' burst out the other. 'A soldier gets stood up against the wall for the same offence, and a pig like that dares to quote the Führer. . . . How can such a creature call himself a National Socialist?'

Breuer began to understand.

Dierk was a professional Hitler Youth Leader. He was considered indispensable, but after tremendous efforts had managed to get himself sent to the front.

'There are good chaps and bad ones everywhere,' said Breuer soothingly. But Dierk replied, 'Not with us. With us there shouldn't be any black sheep. And war, when all's said and done, is the final test. We can only be a credit to the Führer if we conduct ourselves properly, whatever happens. There can be no arguments about that. But one man of this sort can tear down what it's taken years to build up.'

Breuer could find nothing to say. He was ashamed. He too was a Party-member, one of the multitude who had joined in 1933, attracted by the dynamic force of the movement and by all the hopes it had aroused. Practical considerations and professional and economic interests had helped him to make his decision. At that time he and his wife were expecting their first child. He had been offered a teaching job, but the school authorities made it conditional on his joining the Party. It had not been difficult for him, but he was never quite free of misgivings and within his own four walls had tried to preserve a world of his own, independent of the pressing new ideas. He could never have shared Dierk's uncompromising devotion and almost religious enthusiasm, and in fact was not really very interested in the ideology of the movement.

They arrived at the tents without saying another word. As they parted Breuer gave his companion a powerful handshake. It was lucky, he thought with pleasure, that there were such youngsters about. They would make everything alright in the end.

Next morning Lieutenant Wiese was summoned to Unold's office and didn't feel very happy about it. Probably something had gone wrong with the communications. It often did, and at such moments the Colonel could be very awkward. Wiese was too thin-skinned to enjoy a bawling-out from the Colonel. He was therefore much surprised when Unold shook hands with him and said in a kindly voice: 'I'm really sorry, Wiese, to have to call on you for extra duty, but the new CO of the division needs someone to take him round and I have no one else available. I can't send just anyone along with him, can I?'

Wiese thought to himself that the old boy knew very well that he had no right to utilize the Signals Officer in this manner, but decided to heap coals of fire on his head. He said, 'I'm very glad to be able to do you a service, Colonel!' At which Unold gave him a bitter-sweet smile.

Wiese was told to go to an office where he found a strange officer. He introduced himself as the officer turned towards him. He looked very clean and *soigné*, and Wiese had the feeling that after four weeks in filthy trenches, he would look just as spotless.

'I'm your new Divisional Commander!' said the officer, extending a slender hand with a big, gold seal-ring. Wiese looked into a refined, clean-shaven face and bright friendly eyes. The newcomer's hair was parted with extreme accuracy. Don't I know this face? he wondered. The CO said, 'I hear you are going to show me round. I'm very glad to have you. Wait here a moment.'

The Colonel went out to see to his kit while Wiese looked round the room, in which there seemed to be the faintest possible trace of perfume.

On the table were some flasks, a few books, a travelling toilet-set and a pile of pure white handkerchiefs. Among these objects stood a photo in a silver frame, showing a young man in air-force uniform. Wiese at once realized why the Colonel's face had seemed so familiar to him.

'Why, that's Ferdy,' he cried.

The Colonel, came back. 'You know my son Ferdinand?'

'Ferdy von Hermann? But of course I do.' In his pleasure Wiese had forgotten his formal military manners. 'Why, we were school-friends. He was in the class above mine, but we were in the same Youth Group and went around a lot together. How is he?'

The Colonel smiled as he looked at the photo and said, 'Well, as you see he's in the air force. Wireless Officer in a transport squadron. His great sorrow is that he's not a fighter pilot. Still, it's good for him to know that we can't always have what we want, and that every job needs to be done conscientiously.'

'In the old days he used to be crazy about the army,' said Wiese.

'I hope you are, too.'

The young officer stood to attention and pushed his chin forward, making a comic little dimple over his collar. Then he said stiffly, 'I do my best, sir.'

Colonel von Hermann sized him up with an understanding glance and said, 'Don't torment yourself. Luckily we don't only need soldiers in this world.'

Wiese discovered with pleasure that he lisped slightly—just like Ferdy. A lisping Colonel was quite a novelty, he thought. He helped the CO into his driving-coat which bore no badges of rank, and they went outside to find the two reconnaissance cars and the arm-oured personnel coach waiting for them. The Colonel had chosen the latter for his rounds. He had to go to Buzinovka which they had left on the previous morning, but which was still being held against Russian attacks.

The road was empty. The two reconnaissance cars darted on ahead like puppies, rushing up the hills and stopping on the summits to see that all was safe. They had to keep look-out for Russian patrols and cavalry scouts.

They met a few stragglers, slightly wounded men, and the Colonel stopped his car and asked them about their units and where they had come from and about the situation in Buzinovka. The men were reluctant to speak at first, but when the Colonel explained that he was the new Divisional Commander, they said, 'Everything's going fine, sir. The Russians haven't a hope of taking the place.' The Colonel nodded and said nothing.

In the waste country on both sides of the road they saw an occasional wrecked tank, motionless and thickly coated with snow. The CO said, 'Those fellows were shot up by my Artillery Brigade in the fighting last summer, when we occupied the bend of the Don. Things were pretty hot here then. Who'd have thought we'd be fighting here again, facing the other way?'

Meanwhile Unold was running up and down in his office swinging a foot-rule in his hand and saying, 'It's really disgraceful to appoint a young Colonel over my head! I've been trying to get the job for ages, and God knows I've proved I can run the division on my own.' His face showed a trace of hangover from the night before and the top buttons of his battledress were undone. He went on talking to himself. 'Of course it's all Zeitzler's doing. He had it in for me because I didn't help his nephew when he was in trouble. But I won't do the dirty work here much longer.'

Captain Engelhard was the silent witness of this soliloquy. He knew his Chief's lack of self-control and burning ambition, but he could make allowances, for he knew his history. Unold had grown up in St. Petersburg and had lost his parents in the revolution. As a boy of seventeen he had found his own way to Germany. Without money or influence, he had enlisted in the ranks, obtained a commission and fought his way to the General Staff through brains and sheer hard work. Engelhard couldn't help respecting and admiring him in spite of everything.

The three cars reached Buzinovka unscathed. The village looked very different from the previous day. Now, there was a feeling of order and security. The few men to be seen on the streets had work to do. Even the occasional rattle of rifle-fire and the thud of mortar shells seemed to be part of the picture. A detachment of engineers was at work on the still smoking ruins of the Supply Stores. The crews of the reconnaissance cars, thinking of the loot that had been picked up the day before, got into conversation with the salvage party.

'Made a thorough job of it, didn't they?' said the NCO in command of the working party, bitterly. 'Everything burnt or dragged away. And us sitting here with nothing to eat, while some chap who's employed to prolong the war burns the camp down just because he's scared silly. A fellow like that ought to be hanged. But of course, he'll get a medal instead.'

In the middle of the main street stood a Sergeant-Major holding a rubber hose in his hand leading to a barrel at the side of the road, against which a board was leaning with the notice: 'Stop here! Tank up!'

'Have you got plenty of gas?' called the Sergeant-Major.

'Yes, thanks.'

Well, fill up all the same and fill your reserve tins. No one can pass without filling up.'

While the three vehicles were at a halt, the CO got into conversation with the Sergeant-Major who said: 'These are Colonel Steigmann's orders, sir. We've a big stock of gasolene here and it'd be too bad to burn it or leave it to Ivan.'

'You're quite right. Where's your CO?'

'Straight ahead of you, Herr Oberst. On the northern side of the village. You'll see notices everywhere.'

The staff was quartered in a blockhouse at the foot of a hill up which the line ran. Bullets were whistling and shells crashing all around. The meeting room was full of officers called to a conference to discuss the situation.

When Hermann and Wiese came in, heads were turned. An officer as tall and broad as a wardrobe, who had been bending over a map, stood up straight. It was Colonel Steigmann, leader of the battle group which since yesterday had been attached to the division. Colonel von Hermann introduced himself and asked for details of the situation. The other man's broad face lit up as he replied, 'The Russians will never get through here, Colonel. They attacked three times today with cavalry and infantry and three times we sent them home with bloody noses. We can hold the place, no doubt of that.'

The other officers noisily confirmed his statement. Their morale seemed excellent.

Then Colonel von Hermann said slowly, 'I'm sorry that my first duty in my new assignment is such a disagreeable one. You and your group must retire to the East, or to the Golubaya Valley. We're evacuating Buzinovka.'

'Giving up Buzinovka?'

'Yes, by tomorrow morning at seven o'clock you must be in occupation of your new sector. Here are the maps.'

There was a painful silence. Every face was stiff with anguish.

'Oh, God!' said the Colonel, passing his hand over his eyes. Then he straightened up and said, 'Very good, sir! After a while he shook his head and groaned: 'How am I going to tell this to my men?'

During the drive back the Colonel's car passed an airfield in which long lines of fighters, perhaps forty or fifty of them, were drawn up in good order, looking as if they were ready to take off. But in fact there was something wrong with every one of these machines. One of them had a wing missing, another had lost its propeller, a third had a damaged undercarriage. Some of them were quite black. And there was not a soul to be seen except for a solitary sentry, standing on guard in the road.

'They couldn't take off because of the fog,' he explained. 'A few tried to and they crashed over there. We had to destroy the others.'

'And the men?'

'On ahead, in the trenches.'

Wiese looked at the scene of destruction and then at his Chief. What must he be thinking? His son, Ferdy, was an airman, but the Colonel's face was unmoved.

On the morning of November 23rd, Breuer went to get his orders at Divisional Intelligence. At the door he met Captain Engelhard, who seemed to have aged ten years overnight.

'I'm glad you've come,' he said in a toneless voice. 'I was just going to send for you. We've got to retire—behind the Don.'

'Behind the Don?' Breuer didn't understand. But he had a feeling that some terrible doom was approaching.

He said, 'But I thought we were behind the Don already.'

'I mean we must retire to the east, man. Don't you understand? We've got to go back to the Volga. We're surrounded.'

'Surrounded? Who by? How? What do you mean?'

'I see you haven't heard . . . Listen. Down in the south at Beketovka there was the same bloody business as here. The Roumanians again. Yesterday the two enemy columns which had broken through joined up at Kalatch and we're surrounded. The whole Sixth Army, more than twenty divisions! Now do you get it?'

Surrounded! Breuer felt a lump rise in his throat and stick there. Surrounded! A whole army . . . it couldn't be true. It must be a bad dream, a nightmare. But we're winning, we mean to win . . . Surrounded! The word beat like a hammer in his brain. Surrounded . . . surrounded . . . going home to Germany . . . perhaps for Christmas . . . surrounded.

Captain Fackelmann came by. He too looked appalled. 'Have you heard?' he asked. Breuer nodded. A mist veiled his eyes—'Terrible, isn't it? Did you hear they were using captured German tanks . . . what about that?'

By midday they had moved to a point about three kilometres to the east. On the map it was marked '*Dairy Produce*', but there was no sign of a farm, only a few dug-outs in a hollow, hidden under bushes. Very comfortable dug-outs too, lined with wood and equipped with stylish looking rustic furniture, iron bedsteads and brick fire-places. The OC's dug-out even had a bath-tub and a shower. An infantry staff had installed all these fittings with a view to spending a quiet, comfortable winter there. They had already left in a desperate hurry, leaving plates and cooking-pots unwashed and a fire burning in one of the grates.

Unold chased Breuer back to Golubaya, where Russian tanks were said to have broken into the village. On the road leading down to the place there was a moving mass—baggage trains of motor-cars and peasants' carts—and marching between them small bodies of troops, Roumanians singly or in clumps, among tanks and self-propelled guns. A slow-moving welter of weary men and vehicles. It was clearly impossible to get through this stream of traffic, so Lakosch had to clear off the road and find his way through the fields. The road ran down in a curve to the village and to right and left on the heights two-centimetre flak batteries were in position. The men serving them in their white camouflage stood motionless on the look-out, the only still points in the general turmoil. The village itself was full of motors and men and noise and shouting.

When Breuer got back, it was already dark. Over the screen of shrubs surrounding the square he could see flames. As he came closer he witnessed a fantastic scene—something like an enormous funeral pyre crackling and vomiting flames, round which moved a swarm of smoke-blackened, howling, dancing devils, who dragged up boxes and packing-cases, packs and parcels, tore them open and ransacked them and then, shouting and laughing, threw the lot into the fire. Boots, blankets, bits of uniforms, bundles of letters and documents, all went the same way. Unold was hovering around pale as a ghost, with bulging eyes and restless hands.

'Everything into the fire,' he croaked. 'Everything must go, except arms, ammunition and food. We've got to make do with bare necessities.'

Sergeant-Major Harras carried out these orders ruthlessly. He crept under the vehicles and climbed on to them and found in the most unlikely places things which had suddenly become super-fluous. Breuer stared helplessly at this orgy of destruction. Then he was himself carried away by the stream. *Surrounded*—the thought beat like a hammer—*surrounded*.

Lakosch wanted to get by with a wooden box. 'Hey, where are you going?' said Breuer. Lakosch walked close up to him and whispered: 'We've got room for it in our car, sir. We can put it behind the back seat.'

'Nonsense, man; throw it away.'

Breuer dragged his own box to the pyre. It contained a tunic, some washing, boots and a few books, newspapers, letters and photos: he hurled them all one after another into the fire and with each piece something of his past was burned to ashes. Breuer stared into the flames, not realizing how his face glowed nor that the soles of his boots were burning. Near his feet a few photos were crinkling in the heat. *Surrounded!* he thought. It's all over. The life-line to the outside world is cut. He bent down and picked up a photo and stuck it in his pocket, and he also rescued a bundle of letters from his wife which had not yet been burnt.

Lakosch popped up again out of the darkness. This time he was dragging an iron-bound box behind him to the bonfire. He opened it with his side-arm and pulled the contents out—green silk shirts, pyjamas . . . Harras pounced on him like a hawk.

'What are you up to now? Keep your hands off!'

'Oh, it's the Sergeant-Major?' said Lakosch feigning surprise. 'Wouldn't you perhaps like Sarn-Major . . .'

'I wouldn't like anything. But it's my box and I'll attend to it myself.'

'You mustn't get your fingers dirty, Sarn-Major,' said Lakosch with a shamelessly friendly air. A civilian suit flew into the fire, then the well-known top-boots, and some pairs of shoes. And then, under them, appeared an officer's sword made of light metal which burnt in the flames like a magnesium wire. Harras watched the holocaust like a steam kettle under pressure, his hands opening and closing from emotion. Suddenly he turned away and disappeared. In the distance they could hear him roaring.

The bunker with its carved wooden furniture and curtains on the windows looked cosy by the electric light, which was still working, but it was over-crowded because the Intelligence section had to share it with the Maps—though only for a few hours. The men squatted about the rooms, eating or dozing, waiting for the next move. Herbert was roasting slices of cheese on the fire. Fröhlich was crouching in a corner, asleep. He had once more switched himself off. Breuer produced a bottle, which he had saved from the burning, containing Cointreau, from the last consignment sent to the officers' mess. He had meant to take it on leave with him. Leave! Would there ever be leave again?

Then someone pushed through the door. It was the clerk from the Registry. His eyes wandered over the company till they reached Breuer.

'Lieutenant,' he stammered, 'we've still got the files of Operational Orders—could you . . . could you possibly take them in your car?'

'What!' laughed Breuer. 'You want me to take your files, when we've just burned all our own stuff?'

'But they're top-secret and confidential.'

'Burn the damned things. We shan't want Operational Orders any longer.'

And then he suddenly felt sorry for the helpless man. So he poured out a full glass of Cointreau and handed it to him. He drank it like a sleep-walker and passed his hand over his forehead as though recovering from some great effort and murmured: 'All the same they're confidential documents.' Then he slipped out without saluting the company.

Soon afterwards Breuer was called to Divisional Intelligence, where he found Unold standing beside Colonel von Hermann before a map.

'Just look here, Breuer,' said Unold. 'You see this road leading to the Don . . . we don't know either if it's practicable for traffic or if it's still clear of the enemy. You must find that out at once. Endrigkeit will go with you—make quite sure, because a lot depends on it—indeed everything.'

The night was clear and cold. Lakosch had already started the motor and now helped Breuer into his overcoat. Endrigkeit was studying the map by moonlight. Then Corporal Herbert, came up panting, with a look of horror on his face.

'Lieutenant! Lieutenant!'

'Yes? Good Lord, what is it now?'

'Sir, he's lying there in the office.'

'Who the hell are you talking about? Speak up, who?'

'The clerk from the Registry . . . in the office. He's just shot himself.'

Chapter Four

RETREAT ... TO THE EAST

❧❧❧

IN THE LIGHT of the full moon the snow had a greenish tint, the colour of verdigris. It was bitterly cold. Captain Endrigkeit, who was sitting in the back of the car, had mislaid his pipe and was chewing a cigar without enjoyment. Breuer was in front with Lakosch. He kept his eyes on the road and never said a word.

Surrounded! As they drove, they passed Russian farm-carts heaped high with boxes and barrels, or with hay, and drawn by rough-coated cobs. The wagons creaked and grated as they jolted along the edge of the turnpike. Occasionally the car overhauled a truck. To right and left a reddish glow was visible, where the bonfires of destruction were still burning, lamps of victory for the enemy. . . .

Surrounded! Surrounded!

A crowd of men were trotting along the road like a herd of sheep, Russian prisoners of war on their way to the east. Two guards, recognizable only by their weapons, marched wearily behind them. They and their captives both wore the same stoical, hopeless expressions.

'Isn't today the 24th?' asked Breuer in the midst of the silence.

'Yes, Lieutenant,' replied Lakosch. 'It has been for about the last half-hour.'

'Aha!'

Lakosch cast a glance of surprise at his companion. He could not guess why the Lieutenant said 'Aha' with such grim satisfaction. And he would have been still more astonished, had he been able to read Breuer's thoughts.

The 24th, thought Breuer. Of course, the 24th. Today the Don should have been crossed. A great column of men would have to be got over the river at daybreak and the approaches to the river would certainly be blocked by the multitude of soldiers. They would make an easy target for enemy aircraft, who were probably already alert. There would be panic and a massacre. That would be the end—the crowning catastrophe. It was fitting that it should happen on the 24th.

The 24th had a particular significance for Breuer. When he was a schoolboy in the Upper Third at the High School in his little East Prussian town, he was in Doctor Strackwitz's class for German and gymnastics. The master was a man of middle age with a long, narrow face which was made even larger by his centre-parting, and uglier by a pair of rimless spectacles. He always wore knicker-bockers and a green tweed coat which sometimes had the Stahlhelm badges pinned to it. Strackwitz was a favourite with the boys in spite of his strict discipline—or perhaps because of it. During drill in the courtyard he often made the boys sing as they marched.

When they heard the sound of marching songs the other masters, elderly and unprogressive, would shake their heads and close the windows in disapproval. But down below the youngsters sang twice as loud in jubilant protest against a dreary and reactionary world. And Doctor Strackwitz smiled triumphantly.

Red-letter days occurred when Doctor Strackwitz, who among friends was inclined to drink a little too much, came staggering to school. Then all discipline vanished. The master sat at his desk reading the newspaper and let the boys do what they liked, only murmuring from time to time: 'You'll have to watch your step in a minute.' Sometimes he used to give his class romantic accounts of his experiences in the last war, which filled his own eyes with tears and he usually culminated in the hope that he would one day see all of them serving in his machine-gun group.

Years went by and Breuer became a university student. One night he had a frightful dream. In the middle of his last year at school he saw himself walking into a dark hall with huge Gothic windows. There stood Doctor Strackwitz with his usual centre-parting, facing his class, wearing puttees and glasses. He said in a cold, firm voice: 'The decisive hour has come. You are all to march with me against the enemy and, so that you shall be under no

77

illusion, I am going to tell each one of you the date of his death.' He took out his notebook and adjusted his glasses. 'Abel . . . Arras . . .' a date followed after every name. Breuer felt the cold creeping up his limbs. He wanted to cry 'Stop' but found himself unable to open his mouth . . . Strackwitz went on: 'von Batocki . . . Behrend . . . Breuer!' and gave him a piercing look—'On the 24th.' Breuer screamed and woke up, bathed in sweat.

Since that time he had had a complex about the 24th. Every month, as the ill-omened date drew near, he became restless, kept to himself and preferred not to leave the house. On the other days of the month he was so certain of his immunity that he failed to take the most elementary precautions, and had had several narrow escapes.

The road suddenly narrowed and curved down into a gully. At a river crossing they found a long line of vehicles waiting. Breuer produced the black-white-and-red divisional pennant. He always kept it hidden in his sleeve, having no real right to use it, but it had often served him well. Here again it enabled him to pass quickly up the column and over the bridge. After that they had to climb up a slope and when they arrived at the top they could see a village in flames. A parachute flare was swinging overhead and bombs were falling on the houses. Breuer halted the car. To the right of the road a vehicle was burning. Little blue flames were darting all over it. Near it lay the driver on his back—a dried-up, shrunken mummy. His hands reached up to the sky, with crooked fingers, as if in prayer or to ward off calamity, and his white teeth shone in the middle of his blackened face. Russian POWs stood around the burning car. They had put down their tin boxes on the hot metal and were laughing and chattering, happy to have found some warmth. One of them had his foot on the body of the dead driver. Breuer and Endrigkeit studied the map by the light of a torch. At the village in front of them the road forked. The motor-road, which led to the right, seemed better for traffic but it made a suspiciously wide sweep towards the south. Who could tell if it was free of the enemy? Misgivings on this point caused them to choose the other road, which was considerably shorter.

At first they made good progress, but after a few hundred yards they lost the track in the snow among trees and high bushes. The car reeled and jolted and kept slipping into treacherous holes.

'No good,' said Breuer. 'Turn round!'

Lakosch was starting to turn the car, when he felt the Captain's hand on his shoulder.

'Wait a moment, lad!' he said. 'Isn't that a man ahead of us?'

Was it possible in this lonely spot? The three gazed intently to the front and in fact it looked as if there was a man standing some fifty yards ahead of them. He didn't move, so they thought it might be an effect of the moonlight. 'That's funny,' muttered Breuer. But Endrigkeit had already got out of the car. 'I'll go and see,' he growled, 'perhaps he can put us on the road.'

Breuer thought it unnecessary. He was dead tired and wanted to turn round. He yawned as he watched Endrigkeit's bear-like figure growing smaller and mistier in the moonlight.

'Look out!' came a cry and from the bushes there was a volley of rifle-bullets, which passed screaming over the car.

'Out.'

Breuer hunted for his sub-machine-gun, but couldn't find it. He felt paralysed and remembered the 24th . . .

But Lakosch was quicker. He tore his hand grenade from his belt, aimed it as he ran and flung it in the direction of the shots. A bush disintegrated in a flash and something white disappeared like a ghost into the night.

Just at the point where the road appeared again a groaning, human ball was rolling. Lakosch bounded up and, seeing the back of a close-shaven head, he whipped out his bayonet. Hesitating an instant, he plunged it into the body. The steel crunched against bone and then slid off, ripping the soft flesh. Lakosch felt as though the cold blade was running along his own spine. He dragged out the weapon and when he saw the dark red stain of blood, he went to the side of the road and vomited.

Breuer had emptied his magazine into the bushes and combed the area. In the undergrowth he found a pair of snow-shoes and he noticed that ski-tracks led away to the south.

Meanwhile the Captain had come out of cover. He had been badly shaken up. 'Hell's bells!' he snorted, feeling his limbs. 'What a rotten bastard!' They searched the corpse, which was that of a powerfully built man with a broad, pockmarked face. Under his camouflage shirt he was wearing a Russian wadded jacket. He carried no papers.

'A scouting patrol,' said Breuer, 'probably three or four men. They wanted to pick up a prisoner or some documents. If they'd caught us between the trees . . .' They covered the body with snow and turned back to try the other road, which turned out to be free of enemy troops and suitable for traffic. The road to the east was clear.

Endrigkeit had not yet got over the shock of his experience. On the way back he growled: 'Listen, young Lakosch, I'm not in the mood for chatter, but if I can do you a favour any time, you've only to ask.'

And Breuer said: 'Lakosch my boy, I'll get you an Iron Cross for this, if it's the last thing I do.'

Between the Volga and the Don, not too far from the town of Stalingrad there was a great airfield near a village called Gumrak. Its flanks were lined with the dug-outs of former Russian flak gunners. The Commander-in-Chief's headquarter staff had just installed itself here. Hitherto, they had remained outside the periphery of the encircled forces, but that afternoon they had received orders from the Führer's headquarters and had flown into the ring. In these bunkers lay, about 100 yards away, the HQ of the GOC of the 51st Corps to whose command the divisions on the Volga front and in Stalingrad itself belonged.

On that night Colonel Clausius, the Chief of Staff to the Corps, was sitting working by the light of a lamp. In front of him lay the army's instructions, received by wireless, for breaking the Russian cordon—everything was prepared. Only the Führer's final approval was to come. The General had gone across to Army HQ to find out about it. He had already been two hours away.

The Colonel was drafting the final orders. If it came to breaking out of the town and pushing through to the west, there would be a lot of action here. The operation had already started. The 16th Tank Division and the 3rd Motorized Infantry Division had already evacuated the north-east corner of the town. During the afternoon they had destroyed their superfluous kit and tools, including all clothing, except what each man was actually wearing. There was a ring of bonfires, still burning.

The orderly came in to fix up the two camp beds for the night and to examine the mousetrap, which had been rigged up out of a cartridge box.

'Well, Müller, caught any more?' asked the Colonel over his shoulder.

'Of course I have, sir. That's the twenty-eighth I've taken in four days.'

'If you were the Supreme Commander and the Russians the mice, the war would soon be over!'

The orderly scratched himself behind the ear and said, 'Ach, Herr Oberst, the creatures are almost as bad as the Russians. Yesterday I found them having a go at the General's boots.'

But the Colonel wasn't listening. He was making diagrams and calculations and thinking how devilish difficult the evacuation of troops from built-up positions was going to be. The two divisions in the north-east, which had to retire to a shorter line, were kicking up hell about it. But it was going to be more difficult for the others. They should have carried out the plans which provided for the withdrawal of the Stalingrad front to the Donetz with the coming of autumn.

There was a sound of footsteps on the stairs and the door opened to admit a fur-clad, snow-sprinkled figure. It was Artillery General von Seydlitz, the GOC of the 51st Corps.

'Stop it, Clausius,' he cried, 'don't go on with that.'

'The orders are ready to be signed, General! Has it come through?'

'Yes, it's come through,' the General laughed bitterly as he peeled off his outer garments. He came of a long line of cavalry officers and was himself a passionate horseman. You could have guessed that from his upright, youthful figure, though his hair was nearly white, and his sharply-cut features, at present red with anger, had the breeding of a racehorse.

'The Commander-in-Chief has made further representations to the Führer,' he announced.

'And what was the answer?' asked the Colonel, rising to his feet.

'A blank refusal. We must wait to be relieved from the outside. Here's the new Army Order. All divisions still in positions west of the Don are to be withdrawn to the east bank, and both armies under the command of Paulus are to adopt a hedgehog formation.'

'Does that mean there's to be no break-out? But that's . . . that's a . . .' the Colonel looked at the General. Words failed him. With an effort he regained his self-control.

'If that's so,' he went on, 'I give up.'

'It's madness, perfect idiocy. Imagine putting two armies in a position like that. It probably only needs one push to break through the ring. There's never been anything like it in history.'

'And what does the C-in-C say?'

'Paulus? Well, you know him. He shrugs his shoulders. He's a smart enough fighter in the field, but he has no idea of boxing with his own bosses. Besides, he had a bad time with them over our taking back the two divisions. We can't expect any help from Paulus.'

There was silence. The General walked up and down. He halted before the plank-faced wall and stared with unseeing eyes at a newspaper, doing duty for wall-paper, on which was printed in large capitals 'PREPARING FOR FINAL VICTORY IN THE EAST'.

'We ought not to take it lying down,' said the Colonel. 'We really oughtn't, General.'

'Of course not. But what can I do? I've talked myself hoarse, I assure you.'

He began to pace around like a lion in a cage. Colonel Clausius drummed with his pencil on the table and said: 'We must approach them in writing . . . we must send Paulus a written memo.'

The General stopped.

'A memo? Not a bad idea! It should be a written protest based on an accurate judgment of the situation and drawing all the logical conclusions. Maybe that would stiffen his back. He's not obliged to take a stand. He can simply forward it without comment . . . Come on, let's get it on paper.'

Colonel Clausius picked up a writing-pad and pencil. He smiled to himself. The General had taken the bait and now he wouldn't let go. What was it he always said? 'Throw your heart over the fence, and horse and rider will follow.' Now he'd have to rein in the galloping horse and ride him at a steadier pace. But the great thing was that they were going to ride! Perhaps they would succeed after all.

The General dictated and the Colonel wrote it down.

'To the Commander-in-Chief of the Sixth Army.

Conscious of the gravity of the hour I feel myself obliged with reference to the most recent Army Order . . .'

The terse, hastily drafted sentences described the situation. The Sixth Army and almost the whole of the Fourth Armoured Force, twenty-two divisions in all, were packed tightly in a poverty-stricken steppe area, offering no natural means of defence. There was no material for building positions, no fuel for heating and the Russian winter was at their door . . . The Volga divisions depleted and bled white . . . No reinforcements . . . No flak protection . . . and the Russian cordon growing stronger every day.

The General went on dictating. He had been thinking over the problem all day long. He was familiar with such situations. Demjansk for instance. In the previous spring he had organized the break-out of an encircled force which, thanks to supplies dropped by parachute, had managed to hold out during four long Russian winter months. The operation had been carefully planned and, in spite of considerable casualties, had been a success. But in that case the force involved had been six divisions, not twenty-two. It wasn't possible to supply twenty-two divisions by air. The General's corps required in munitions, liquid fuel and food alone something like 1000 tons per day if it was to be able to fight defensive battles. And it was clear that the Russians would attack. They wouldn't miss a chance like that.

'The probable action of the enemy,' dictated the General, 'is easy to predict. He will make every effort to achieve a quick victory. He may be expected to pursue his attacks against the encircled divisions with undiminished violence . . .'

The General paced up and down as if reading the text from the smoky walls of the bunker. Demjansk! The Führer had ordered him to give a lecture on the operation. 'One of my toughest officers,'

Hitler had commended him later. It was not child's play, the break-through from Demjansk. It had needed months of preparation and weeks of fighting. The Sixth Army couldn't afford to wait that long. By then it would have perished of starvation.

'The conclusion we must inevitably draw is that the army in its present hedgehog formation can only avoid annihilation if it is effectively relieved from the outside within a few days and the enemy is forced to discontinue his attacks. At present we have no cause to expect anything of the kind.'

The General passed his hand over his eyes. Demjansk came off, he thought, and as a result the people at the top have lost their sense of proportion. If Demjansk hadn't been a success, we shouldn't have been in this mess today. It was a tormenting thought that he was partly responsible for the threatening catastrophe . . . The army must get out, at once and without delay. There must be no catastrophe at Stalingrad.

Only a few hours ago he had personally submitted all these views to the Commander and his bustling Chief of Staff. They had listened to him and haggled about words. 'Can we say that? Isn't that too strong?' And then they had sent off their anaemic wireless message. It had failed, of course . . . Now he must get his views past the General Staff to the Führer himself who would listen, perhaps, to the words of one of 'my toughest officers'. Perhaps . . .

He went on dictating in a clear voice in the way he would have spoken, simply and without prevarication. Colonel Clausius, calm and discriminating, helped to formulate, clarify and round off the phrases.

'The order to maintain the hedgehog formation till help arrives is unrealistic. It cannot be carried out and must lead inevitably to the destruction of the army. If we are to avoid this, we must be given other orders.'

Only one other order would save the situation. An order to break through to the west at once with all available forces. They must realize that.

'The army,' dictated the General, 'must while uncovering the North and Volga fronts, set free shock-forces with which to stage a break-out at the point where resistance is weakest. At the same time

Stalingrad must be evacuated. Every hour of hesitation means a loss of fighting men and munitions. With every hour of hesitation the enemy is growing stronger.'

Every hour! Every minute was precious. The army must keep its hold on the Don and maintain its bridge-heads. Alternatively the break-out could be made in the direction of Kotelnikovo . . .

The General went on dictating. He had now begun to repeat himself and the hands of the alarm clock pointed to 2 a.m. The Colonel, too, felt his energy ebbing and was writing almost mechanically.

'That's all. You'll go over that carefully, won't you?' said the General. 'And after you've polished it, make a fair copy. We can send it off early this morning as a top-secret signal. They can't very well throw it into the waste-paper basket, can they?'

Colonel Clausius pulled himself together. He went back to the beginning and read the draft aloud. Its many pages were less a dispatch than a dissertation. The Colonel read and the General listened with his eyes closed, nodding approval when Clausius extemporized a new sentence or proposed a change in wording.

The alternatives emerged very clearly: either the army defended itself in hedgehog formation until all its ammunition was exhausted and it was defenceless, or shock-troops arrived immediately to blow a gap in the surrounding ring.

Then came the final passage, in which mention was made of the claims of conscience and the duty of the Government towards the people and the country.

Last came the statement, clear and unembellished, that in case of necessity—if the lunatic order to form a 'hedgehog' was not revoked at once—the Commanders in the field must be free to arrange the break-out themselves.

The Colonel jibbed and re-read what he had written. Had the General really dictated it? He felt vaguely as if he himself had made the suggestion . . .

'Freedom of action!' he repeated and shook his head. 'That won't do, General. We can't leave it like that. Freedom to act against the Führer's orders?'

The General looked at him uncomprehendingly.

'I mean to say, if the Führer reads this himself . . . You know he's not going to stand for that.'

'The Führer?' asked the General quietly. 'Ah, yes. Of course. But what can we do? We have no choice.'

In a feeble endeavour to postpone a decision Clausius said, 'We might make a broader basis for our recommendations. Supposing we consult the other Commanders . . .'

'Nonsense, Clausius,' said the General, dismissing the suggestion with a wave of the hand, 'that would mean starting all over again and getting all the others to agree. No, this must stay as it is. God in Heaven! It *must* make things happen.'

The Colonel put down his writing-pad and looked at his chief with wide-open eyes. He knew that it was useless to say another word. But he didn't want to leave unexpressed the thought that had been weighing down the atmosphere of the room.

'But this is mutiny, General. It might cost you your life!'

General von Seydlitz hesitated for a while. He bit his lips and stared tensely at the top of the table. Then he said calmly, 'You may be right, Clausius. But there's more than that at stake—not my reputation or my life, nor yours or Paulus's, but the lives of 300,000 German soldiers.'

Endless columns streamed through the night—units of the XIth Corps marching to the east. Steigmann's detachment brought up the rear with a clinking of cook-pots and a clashing of arms, while their boots scraped and skidded over the icy road. 'Like Moscow a year ago,' they were saying. 'Yes, just the same bloody shambles!' 'Ah, Moscow! Yes, but then we were marching to the west. At least we knew where we were going.' The uncertainty that filled the men's minds was the heaviest burden they had to bear during this forced night march. They had got out of the way of marching and their feet were sore. They breathed heavily under the weight of their weapons, but they gripped them all the more firmly for now it was the arms which were carrying the men—their only stay and hope.

Colonel Steigmann drove in his jeep along the column, encouraging his exhausted men. By the side of the road a truck had stuck fast. The crew stood around it, staring apathetically. 'Come on!' a very young officer was shouting. 'Get cracking, you bastards, damn you!' They seemed not to hear him. But the Colonel heard and said to himself, that's not the way to get things done on a night like this. He got out of his jeep.

'Now, men, what's the matter? Won't she move? Let's give her a shove.' He started pushing the back of the truck. Two or three men sprang forward and the rest of the crew joined in. The wheel whizzed and spun round and the truck took the road again.

Baggage-wagons with balloon tyres rolled by, drawn by snorting, steaming horses with white clusters of icicles hanging from their harness. A cyclist platoon was hauling its machines through the snow, the wheels looking like discs of ice. Behind, the man-handled guns rumbled along, the steel of their heavy wheels cutting ruts in the roadway. Each piece was dragged by a dozen men harnessed by long ropes to the gun. 'Hoy . . . yup! Hoy . . . yup!' they shouted as they pulled. Sergeant-Major Strack was in charge of the operation. Recognizing Colonel Steigmann he went up and reported to him.

'How are things going, Strack?'

'All right so far, Colonel. We've brought everything with us. But these guns . . . we could do with a few tractors . . .'

'Yes, I know, Strack, I know.'

The Sergeant-Major said, half to himself: 'I only wish I knew what the object of all this was.'

'Better not ask, Strack,' rejoined the Colonel kindly. 'I'm not allowed to ask either.'

The Colonel set off once more, passing horse-drawn wagons, the trucks and the long column of marching men. A three-ton truck with a broken axle was standing across the road. A lot of men had crowded around and some had climbed into the truck to forage. The Colonel noticed bottles passing from hand to hand. 'Put that liquor away!' he shouted. 'Put it away at once!' He knew that alcohol taken in large quantities on such a cold night could be fatal. The men obeyed him and the bottles were collected and loaded on to another vehicle.

A little farther on a young soldier, full of drink and oblivious of the fact that he was freezing to death, came staggering across just in front of the Colonel's radiator. His ears and nose were already quite white. The Colonel put him in his jeep and wrapped him in blankets, and he fell asleep at once.

A torch flashed a message in the darkness.

Shouts of 'Halt! Right face! Are you bastards deaf?' Someone jumped on the Colonel's footboard. It was Lieutenant Behrend, wearing, instead of a fur cap, a thick bandage round his head. Two days before he was to have been flown off to a sanatorium at home, but he had refused to go. Now the road was cut off and his company had to be home and hospital for him. He recognized Colonel Steigmann and explained.

'This is a hellish piece of road, Colonel!'

And so it was. The road graded down steeply and was coated with ice. Every vehicle had to be roped before going down. One of the guns broke loose and crashed down the slope, running over two men. The first fatal casualties of the night.

Below glinted the grey surface of a small ice-bound river. And there were the tractors at last! But one of them had broken through the light wooden bridge and hung suspended and helpless among the beams and planks. The other had tried to cross over the ice but had broken through and now was sunk up to the top of its wheels in the water. Sergeant-Major Strack came hurrying up.

'I'm damned if I know what to do, Colonel.'

'Scuttle them!'

What! Destroy the tractors, after getting them this far? There were tears in the Sergeant-Major's eyes, but when he looked at the Colonel's stony face he dared not say another word.

A village came into sight: or rather, the smoking, smouldering ruins of a village. Was that their destination? No, not yet. Not by a long shot. But they had a short pause for rest, and men and beasts sank down on the outskirts of the village, caught between burning heat and ice cold: huddling against one another's bodies they fell asleep. But after a few minutes they were on the road again.

Morning was already visible in the east and with the new day fresh confidence was born. Discipline was stricter and the men marched more quietly and with surer-footed steps. A message came from the rear-guard saying, 'We have successfully fought off enemy attacks and have knocked out two T34s.' 'There, you see, they haven't got us yet!' 'Not by a long shot!'

Colonel Steigmann drove once more along the column. Now that the first night of retreat was over, he looked old and tired. 'One day,' he thought, 'we shall know what all this was for.'

There was a steady grey-brown stream of men winding down from the wooded heights beyond the Don, hurrying over the broad pontoon-bridge at Peskovatka, marching noisily through the miserable village full of astonished ragged women, dirty children and stragglers before disappearing at last into the numerous depressions of the treeless, houseless, uninhabited steppe that lay between the Don and the Volga. To the north the grumbling of artillery sounded like a heavy thunderstorm. The northern crossing at Vertyatchi had for several hours been subjected to heavy gunfire, but for some peculiar reason the Russians had shown no interest in the bridge at Peskovatka. From time to time an aircraft, flying at a great height, dropped a few bombs at random on the plain. Meanwhile a whole army corps had crossed the Don without incident and in perfect order.

Colonel von Hermann drove out with Unold to visit the staff of the VIIIth Corps, which was quartered in Peskovatka. New instructions awaited the division there. It was already known that the western units of the VIth Army were to retire to a line of defence west of Stalingrad, which Hitler himself had selected.

The bunkers of the staff had been cleverly built into the face of a high cliff and provided perfect cover against bombing. The staff quarters were equivalent to a ten-room house with every modern comfort.

While the Colonel and Unold were conferring inside with the GOC, Breuer was sitting behind a white-painted door in the anteroom, turning over the pages of illustrated papers. '*A German Girl in Kiev*' was the headline on one page, and underneath was a story about the exciting life of a young typist in the Ukrainian city. There she was striding along the main street looking very self-conscious in a dark suit while a *native*—as the paper expressed it—walked behind carrying her bag. And there she was again sunning herself in a bathing suit on the bank of the Dnieper, a blonde and smiling figure. Breuer looked at the pictures sourly. So that's what we're fighting for, he thought.

Officers, smooth and shiny, hurried busily about with papers and dossiers, staring at the unshaven, grimy guest sitting in their basket-chair, his boots leaving marks on their clean carpet.

The conference behind the white door was over. The old Corps Commander with the square, leonine head rose from the sofa and shook hands with his visitors.

'You must know General Heinz,' he said as they were taking leave. 'Didn't you belong to his corps?'

'Yes, sir,' replied Unold, 'our division was in support of the Tank Corps until quite recently.'

'Well, in that case you'll be interested to hear that he has broken through to the west with the two other divisions. Almost without casualties.'

'General Heinz is our old divisional CO,' said Unold, with pride.

'Ye-es,' said the General, nodding his head thoughtfully and screwing up his green eyes. 'He and his Chief of Staff have been relieved of their Commands and both of them are to be tried by court martial.' His eyes were wide and flashing. At first they hardly understood him.

'What? For God's sake, why?'

'Because of their successful break-through to the west. Because they hadn't anticipated the brilliant idea of bottling up a whole army, or taken the appropriate measures to carry it out. That's why!'

'It doesn't seem possible,' stammered Unold, overwhelmed by the news. Colonel von Hermann turned very pale but said nothing. The General looked at him with what seemed a mocking gleam in his eye.

'Well, Hermann,' he said at last, 'You're a Divisional Commander, too, and it won't be long before you're a General . . . You have my most heartfelt good wishes in advance!'

The cars of the staff had driven up into the open country north of the village, not far from the river. Nothing was left behind. Major Kalweit had even been able to bring all his tanks with him, but they were still on the other bank of the Don together with those of the 16th Tank Division, in position to defend the bridge-head.

PART II

Between Night and Morning

Chapter Five

'MANSTEIN IS COMING'

～⌘～

AT THE BEGINNING of December a keen east wind was blowing across the Volga and raging into the mortally wounded city. It screeched among the jagged ruins, angrily rattled metal sheets and roof-ends, howled through the yawning window-spaces and round the corners of the deserted streets and, free at last, stormed out into the open steppe. White curtains of snow swept along with it, filling the hollows with deep drifts and contemptuously powdering the lonely men, who cowered under awnings in their shallow fox-holes.

The echoes of General von Seydlitz's protest died away in an ominous silence. His dangerously hot-tempered memorandum had been forwarded by the army with a disparaging marginal note to Army Group Headquarters. There, it had been received in a gingerly manner and quickly buried in a heap of forgotten dossiers. Hitler was never informed that one of his Generals was on the verge of mutiny. In fact, by a stroke of irony, it was not long after this that the Führer, as a mark of his confidence in this General, added the divisions of the Northern salient to his command. Von Seydlitz accepted the honour without comment.

However, the VIth Army had retired in three stages to the line drawn diagonally through the steppe between the Volga and Don by a chalk pencil on a map in the Führer's HQ. The limits of the Stalingrad Cauldron were now definitively set.

To the west of the airfield at Pitomnik, almost exactly in the centre of the Cauldron, the village of Dubininski was marked on the Russian maps. In fact, it consisted of two or three half-ruined houses, the remnants of an agricultural settlement which had proved a failure in the barren plain. But a few hundred yards to one side where the steppe sloped gradually upwards to the north, a regular town had sprung up during these winter days. Hundreds of cars were parked there, sheltered from observation by mounds of snow or by their own white camouflage. The crews of these vehicles were housed in tents or holes in the ground, some of which had originally been dug by the Russians. Strangely enough the Russian U 2s—'sewing machines' as they were called—which flew over the Cauldron all night dropping small-calibre bombs, left this enormous assemblage of cars almost unmolested. Possibly they took the place for a bogus car-park or a car-cemetery, although smoke by day and fires by night should have betrayed the presence of occupants. The three ruined houses standing by the side of the village street unfortunately didn't enjoy the same advantages. Above the door of one of them was a board with a notice painted in white letters saying 'Staff HQ.' Captain Fackelmann had recently taken up residence here.

Sergeant-Major Harrass came out of the house and looked up at the sky. He was in a hurry to get away because the place got very unhealthy after dark. On the previous evening a bomb had fallen close by the wall of the house and the explosion had blown out the last of the windows. The occupants of the house now had to work by candlelight day and night.

Harras trotted nimbly in his felt shoes towards his quarters. He was wearing a close-fitting sheepskin coat with the skirts standing out from his knees, like a ballerina's tutu. His peaked fur cap was completely in keeping and a soldier meeting him in this costume had addressed him as Captain.

On the left the road led round to the dug-outs, losing itself in a network of footpaths. Harras stumbled over something and kicking angrily at the obstacle detached a piece of brownish cloth. Looking closer he found that the object lying under the snow in the middle of the road was a human corpse—Russian or Roumanian, to judge by the cloth. The man had probably been killed while the ground was still soft. The heavy vehicles had rolled him flat and pressed him into the earth. Imagine leaving such a thing lying about! Harras's sense of order was scandalized. It was bad enough to have decomposing horses lying all over the place, without this. Shaking his head, he went on his way.

Dusk was already beginning to set in, although it was only three o'clock in the afternoon. Over the airfield at Pitomnik the first parachute flares were flaming and the far-away boom of shells could be heard. Harras threaded his way between vehicles, dug-outs and snow banks and cursed as he went. He had lost his way and was furious at the thought that there were no signposts to guide him through this maze. The posts had long since been looted for firewood. At last he came on a familiar-looking wireless mast. The Command car next to it was the Divisional Intelligence bus and to the right of it was the field-kitchen truck and behind, at the very edge of the warren of bunkers, a small car alongside a white mound. That could only be the Intelligence Volkswagen. Thank goodness!

Suddenly he fixed his eyes on a white object showing clearly not far from the Volkswagen, which he recognized as a bare human backside. He pounced on it like a hawk.

'Are you mad?' he cried.

The backside covered itself and a figure rose to its feet and turned to face him. It was Lakosch.

'Don't you know that troops are forbidden to defecate within fifty yards of the billets?'

Lakosch held up his trousers with one hand and with the other felt for the place where the seam of a soldier's trousers ought to be. He said, 'Yes, I know, Sarn-Major, but it's too cold for that. I don't want to freeze to death.'

Harras inhaled audibly and his chest rose under his sheepskin coat. 'Look here, man,' he said, adopting a fatherly love. 'Can't you see how beastly it'll be when the spring comes and the place is full of your stinking messes?'

Lakosch rolled his eyes like a scolded spaniel. 'Quite right, Sergeant-Major,' he said, 'but the soil will be well manured, and that'll suit the potatoes a treat, if we're still here to plant them.'

Harras's mouth tightened and he hurried away in search of the staff bunker. Lakosch fastened his belt with a grin and then, taking one of the aluminium seats out of the staff car he disappeared with it into a hole in the ground.

The word 'bunker' had by now lost most of its meaning. Six square yards of damp soil, four bare clay walls, down which the water trickled, seven inches of earth and planks for a ceiling and, close under it, a narrow slit of a window—such was the bunker in which for the past ten days the Intelligence staff had been housed. At first they had to share this hole with the Map section and the Signals and at night the thirteen men lay on the ground as tightly packed as sardines in a tin—but gradually the others had left and only Lieutenant Wiese and the Intelligence people remained.

When Lakosch with his aluminium seat stumbled down the slippery steps, he was greeted with an emphatic 'Sh'. Breuer was sitting at the table, which at night had to serve as a bed for him and Wiese, holding the telephone receiver to his ear.

'VIIIth Corps—yes.' Graf Willms, the Chief Intelligence Officer, was going through the daily summary. This he did as circumstantially as a three-year-old telling a story. 'Er, movements of Russian tanks are reported to—er—to the south . . .' Breuer was automatically drawing little circles on his writing-pad. 'And on the front held by the XIth Corps, er, there are apparently, er, altogether only four Russian tanks, er, as far as we can, er, ascertain.'

Lakosch had made himself comfortable in the seat borrowed from his car. Beside him sat Senta his bull-dog bitch. He had taken her off a flak-officer in Peskovatka, who had been on the point of dispatching her to a better world, because she seemed to be expecting a litter. Since then she had not left his side. Lakosch stroked the tawny head which she had pillowed on his knees, while she looked up at him with a questioning but resigned expression in her dark eyes. 'Yes, yes, old girl,' he said. 'I know you're hungry.' Who wasn't hungry? But not everyone showed it in such a gentle and modest fashion. Lakosch thought he must try once more in the kitchen.

Herbert was crouching in front of the stove and heaping fresh wood on the crackling fire.

'Still stoking the fire, you idiot?' said Fröhlich. 'This blast-furnace is visible for miles. Can't you hear the bombers up there, looking for a target?'

'And you moan because it's cold,' replied Herbert. 'It doesn't matter what I do—you moan.'

'Shut up!' called Breuer.

'What? Er, did you say something?' said the Intelligence Officer on the telephone.

'No, no, please go on.'

'So, er, yes . . . no, what was I saying? Oh yes, so, er, we have now ascertained that there are no tanks in front of the IVth Corps . . .'

'Good God!' said Breuer. 'What's Ivan up to now?' Withdrawing all his tanks?'

'What? Oh, you mean, why is he withdrawing them? Yes, er, well I don't know either. And, oh yes, I was going to say that the usual nuisance fire has been directed on Marinovka again today.'

Breuer sighed and rang off. Now all that remained for him to do was to record these futile messages in intelligible form and pass them on to the subordinate units. In the old days there had been some life in the intelligence. Pilots' reports and air-photos had to be evaluated, visits by car to the front had to be made and prisoners interrogated as well as circular messages from other fronts—then it had been possible to keep in touch with the war as a whole, as well as getting an insight into the riddles of the enemy's plans. All these advantages had made his transfer to the staff worth while. Things were different now. Breuer gazed like a prisoner round the narrow room till his eyes came to rest on a photo of Irmgard and the two boys on a Baltic beach. He had received no letters for a long time and he hadn't yet got over the shock of the encirclement. He stared angrily at the quotation stuck in capital letters on the wall near his postcard. Since Fröhlich, full of enthusiasm, had pasted it up, it had caused Breuer continual irritation, but he couldn't keep his eyes off it. It was an oleograph from a soldiers' periodical and the quotation was from Ulrich von Hutten:

I do not dream of what is past and gone,
I shall break through, with not a backward look.

Colonel von Hermann was shaving when Unold came in with a

paper in his hand. 'We're being ordered into the line,' he said. 'The whole division.'

The CO put down his safety-razor and said, 'Really, Unold? At last.'

Up till that moment Colonel von Hermann had been feeling angry and frustrated. After the Cauldron had been stabilized the division had lost Steigmann's group while the two Grenadier Regiments were stuck far away on the Volga front and had to be written off. What remained of his division consisted of the anti-tank force, which had long ago lost its guns and could only be used as infantry, the Artillery Regiment, seriously weakened by the loss of its flak-detachment at Buzinovka, the Tank Regiment, whose tank effectives varied, according to the capacity of the repair shops, between five and eight units, the Signals, and a few supply services which had been unlucky enough to have come inside the cordon. All of these lay in the Dubininski area, in the middle of the Cauldron, far away from the fighting line and out of range of the Russian guns.

Dependent as it was for its supplies on the XIVth Tank Corps, the division received its fighting orders direct from the Army Staff. 'Why call me a Tank Commander?' said the CO grimly. 'Captain of the Fire Brigade would be a better title.' There was trouble enough on the 150 kilometre front, even though the Russians for the most part refrained from attacking. But when there was an assault, fractions of the division were sent out to deal with it—either the anti-tank section under Eichert of Kalweit with his tanks or one or two batteries of artillery. These troops were sent as necessity arose to reinforce any threatened division. Meanwhile the Colonel sat with his staff inactive in Dubininski while the reports of his division's losses in men and machines came in. The CO was far from satisfied. It was bad enough that the army, on the Führer's orders was confined to one area and had to wait to be relieved from outside. Even so, it would have been preferable to remain in the front line with direct responsibility for defence and the opportunity to show your teeth to the enemy, rather than be condemned to squat here like an old woman by the fire, while the whole division went to pieces.

'At last, Unold!' said the Colonel. 'Just show me on the map what is happening.'

He took the paper in his hand and went with it to the map. Once more the trouble was in the north-west corner, the stormy corner of the Cauldron, where the Vienna division was holding the line. It was clear that the Russians knew that and hoped to find a weak spot there. According to their official theory, the Austrians had been forced into the war as unwilling allies of the Germans.

'What! Have they got through as far as the Rossoshka valley this time? That's bad. It looks like quite a job of work for us.'

To all appearances he was delighted that things looked so bad. His own private views were quite otherwise, but he preferred not to express them.

Colonel von Hermann studied his instructions carefully. The Tank Division with every available vehicle was to seal off the salient in co-operation with the 44th Infantry Division and to drive the encroaching enemy back to their original front line. When this operation had been successfully carried out the reserve division would be once more withdrawn and the front line occupied by troops from the 44th Division.

'Well, what shall we do? I think we'd better send Eichert out now, as it seems to be urgent. Tomorrow at daybreak we'll counter-attack with the rest of the division.'

Unold and Engelhard started at once, to work out the orders for the counter-attack and that evening the Anti-Tank Section rolled off on its trucks towards the north-west corner of the encircled area.

There was a heavy snowfall in the night and in the grey light of dawn a thick mist overhung the earth like a wet sack. The grass and the car-tracks and the dead horses were all buried under the mushy snow. The steppe lay still and lifeless, a forlorn expanse of earth in the great grey nothingness. Breuer might have continued to sleep quietly in his bunker instead of driving with the troops into the unknown and at one point he thought of going back. Unold had left him free to accompany the expedition or not, as he thought fit. 'The people on the spot will provide us with all the intelligence we need,' he had said. But Breuer was glad of the chance to get out of the dug-out, perhaps to interrogate a few prisoners, to draw maps, in fact to justify his existence.

Padre Peters had also asked to be allowed to go with the others. Now he was sitting in the back seat, and his presence had an uncomfortably inhibiting effect on his companions' language. As there was no trace or track to follow—for Kalweit's tanks had not yet started —Breuer had made Lakosch drive north-west by the compass across country. Under its soft covering of snow the ground was very treacherous. The car jolted laboriously over hidden obstacles and in and out of holes and, coming unexpectedly to the edge of a steep hollow, had to turn aside. Before long it came to another and all the time the mist made it impossible to see a yard in front of one's face. Even the impatient Fröhlich refrained from expressing his thoughts aloud for fear of upsetting the Padre. Not that the Padre would have been shocked. It was simply that he carried about with him an indefinable air of sincerity which impressed everyone who met him. This was an intangible quality; it had nothing to do with his appearance. Peters looked like any one of his comrades. He wore a yellowish sheepskin coat over his greasy tunic, and on his head a grey ski cap with furry ear-flaps crowning his stolid countryman's face. This harmony, this interior relaxation had often caused Breuer to wonder and once, as he was thinking about the Iron Cross on Peter's breast he had had the courage to say to him in a quiet moment: 'A priest in uniform—don't you find that a contradiction in terms?' Peters had answered, 'We're not communists, Breuer. We don't think we can create a paradise on earth. But does that mean we should renounce the privilege of helping men in loneliness and need? We have to be the guardians of that image of mankind which Christ bequeathed to us. We are neither for nor against the war—we stand apart.'

Visibility improved and it was now possible to see a chain of grey monsters, like mammoths, moving to the left—Kalweit's tanks. They must be on the highway. The car could move faster now and they reached the village of Baburkin at the same time as the tanks. The mist had almost cleared away and the sun wandered through the misty sky like a pallid disc of paper. Between the wooden houses the snow had thawed into brownish slush and an uneasy activity filled the village. Soldiers with suspicious, unshaven faces scuttled about like rats frightened out of their corners. The streets were lined with furniture, beds, chests and barrels, and vehicles of all sorts piled high with baggage interfered with the traffic. To the right, between the houses, a long drawn-out shallow depression could be seen. It was the valley of the Rossoshka river. Far below there was a line of bunkers with doors and windows open towards the west. Round them all was bustle and movement. In the distance small figures scurried about like people in front of a burning house, before the firemen arrive. Small cars raced up and down the slopes and men with stretchers hurried to and fro. The place was clearly a hospital. The white surface of the surrounding snow was dotted with black spots like a leopard skin and yellow tufts of smoke kept rising from the snow and revealing, when the wind blew them away, fresh black blobs.

'Please stop, Breuer,' said Padre Peters. 'This is where I get out.' As he walked down into the valley his figure grew smaller and smaller. The plumes of smoke hid him now and then, and soon he was just a dot among many others.

Sergeant-Major Harras did not take part in the first large-scale operation of his old division. Before it began he had been posted to the Motorized Division at Karpovka in the southern sector.

His introduction to his new duties was unpromising.

'I suppose you're the newcomer from the divisional staff,' said the CO with an oblique look down his beaky nose, when Harras presented himself. 'Very well. Go and take off your crinoline and put on a proper camouflage dress, so that at least you look like a soldier.'

Harras had to pack his mess-jacket, his smart-waisted overcoat and his lamb-skin cap in his box and get himself supplied with the most unremarkable uniform he could find.

At the end of the autumn fighting the division had been pulled out of the Stalingrad front for recuperation. Destined for a planned attack on Beketovka, a few miles south of Stalingrad, it had been kept in reserve until the Russians had encircled the German forces.

It was the only unit in the army still up to full strength in men and weapons. The divisional positions, inherited to some extent from the Russians, followed the Karpovka valley and a half-finished railway embankment. It was an admirable line of defence—there was no prospect of a Russian attack succeeding here.

When Harras examined the quarters of the Company to which he had been assigned he could not get over his astonishment. In the roomy bunkers there were wooden bunks, iron bedsteads, tables, chairs and cupboards and even proper windows and doors. He couldn't help thinking of the filthy hole in Dubininski in which he had been housed.

'It's good enough for a brothel,' he growled with a mixture of envy and relief.

The Lance-Corporal, who was going round with him, grinned broadly. 'We shipped all this by rail from Stalingrad, Sarn-Major. We could build a whole town here and we've enough firewood to last us through two winters. What do you think of that, Sarn-Major?'

Harras took a very poor view of this casual form of address. The next thing would be for these fellows to clap him on the shoulder. He determined by the use of good, old fashioned methods to bring order into the pigsty. 'Put your heels together, can't you?' he snapped. 'Don't you know who you're talking to?' The soldiers gaped at him in silence. From then on, however, they looked on him as an enemy and lost no opportunity of making him look a fool in front of the officers. Harras changed his tactics and tried the effect of a clumsy familiarity, which antagonized them even more.

He got on much better with the OC of his company, a Captain in his thirties. He was about the same height as Harras and had a very long body and strikingly short legs, on which he wore a pair of ancient cord breeches of indeterminate colour. The leather-covered seat of these riding breeches, not even partially concealed by a serge monkey-jacket, was stretched across a rump that would have done credit to a carthorse and which earned him on all sides the nickname of 'the Bum'. The Bum, more from the lack of anything better to do than from inclination, had studied law for three terms during which he had become an officer in a student's club. From this period he had retained short hair with a knife-blade parting and a couple of reddish scars. With the hasty expansion of the Wehrmacht in 1932 he had taken advantage of the favourable conditions granted to lawyers and had joined the army as a regular. The Bum was known as a go-getter. During the heavy autumn fighting for the tractor factory of Stalingrad, he had won the Knight's Cross. It was surprising that he was still a Captain and Company Commander, but it was due to his addiction to alcohol. Certain uncharitable persons said that since the beginning of the war the Bum had not been sober for a single day. That was probably an exaggeration but, nevertheless, his weakness had attracted the attention of his superiors, and he had now given up all hope of getting a Major's epaulets and was proud, after his fashion, to describe himself, inaccurately, as the oldest Captain in the German Army. The Bum asked a great deal of his men, but they were prepared to admit he never lost his nerve and was always in the forefront of the fighting. They liked, too, his incorruptible honesty and his unpretentious, friendly way of talking which Harras tried in vain to copy.

At Harras's first meeting the Bum asked him:

'Do you play skat?'

'Yes, Herr Hauptmann.'

'All the conventions?'

'Yes, sir.'

'Very good. We shall see.'

Since then there was a game of skat almost every evening in the main bunker. The assistant MO and the battalion paymaster took it in turns to make a third. If by chance both were free, they played a four-handed game. Harras regarded these games of skat as an essential part of his duties. He did not enjoy cards, did not play well, and the Bum was no easy partner. For him skat was a science and every false card a sacrilege, but Harras endured his reproaches with clenched teeth and made up for his mistakes by laughing heartily at the stories the Bum told, between the hands, of his adventures in France. His reward was the Sauterne and Cognac of which there seemed to be inexhaustible supplies.

In many respects things were better in his new billet than Harras had dared to hope. There were almost always potatoes and very often fresh meat and bread baked by the company. After months of short rations, Harras was again able to satisfy his appetite.

'It's remarkable,' he said one evening as he was eating goulash with the Bum, 'it's remarkable how different horsemeat tastes here.'

'Horsemeat!' The three card players looked at one another and then burst into delirious laughter. 'Horsemeat! 'Don't make me laugh!'

Harras did not understand what there was to laugh at. When he tried to explain that since the first days of the encirclement the divisional staff had only eaten horseflesh the Bum said: 'No more silly jokes, please.' The paymaster's only explanation of this miracle of catering was to say, 'If you go hungry, it's your own fault.'

Harras simply couldn't understand it. 'Aren't you supposed to return the surplus supplies?' he asked. He remembered an army order recently issued with the object of securing a fair distribution of supplies.

'Return the surplus?' cried the paymaster, red in the face. 'So that others can eat themselves sick while we starve? Not on your life. God helps those who help themselves it says in the Bible?'

The staff of the Austrian division was housed in bunkers built like swallows' nests along the upper edge of the steep face of a hollow, and only accessible over a complicated system of wooden paths and bridges. These bunkers had been constructed on the assumption that the front would face to the east and now they offered their vulnerable and unprotected side to any attacker from the west. The Russian tanks that had broken the line had already done some damage to the system without, however, driving the staff out of their holes. When Colonel von Hermann and Unold arrived, the CO of the division came to meet them with outstretched hands.

'I'm very glad, gentlemen,' he said, 'to be able to greet you with good news. Your excellent anti-tank section started to counter-attack last night, and they've already reached the old front line. The enemy tanks have all been driven back or shot up . . . apart from three or four which are still causing us a bit of trouble.' He made a gesture expressing regret, which at the same time was one of farewell, while the GSO1 sitting at the map table, smiled with an air of polite dismissiveness.

'This is er, very agreeable news,' murmured Colonel von Hermann, making an effort to hide his disappointment. 'Well, Unold, it seems there's nothing for us to do here.'

Meanwhile Breuer and Fröhlich were reporting to the Intelligence Officer, while Lakosch had gone on a visit of inquiry to the field kitchen. The Intelligence Officer, a morose looking Captain wearing ribbons from the first World War, was consuming a couple of meat dumplings on an aluminium plate and didn't allow himself to be deflected from this agreeable occupation by the presence of visitors.

'We weren't expecting guests,' he said, as he chewed his dumplings. 'We've only just enough to go round and horseflesh is getting scarce.'

'Are you eating the horses?' said Breuer in surprise. 'What will you do later. . . .'

'We'll go on Shanks's pony. Better on foot and alive than in a carriage and dead, don't you agree? If your cars were eatable you would eat them too. You know, when our people have run out of food, we can call it a day.'

Then he told how, when the division was shifted to the line, it was supposed to find new quarters ready. Battalions of POWs had been allegedly working on the job. But they had found nothing ready for them—nothing but snowcovered, frozen ground as hard as iron. It was too hard for them to dig themselves in and anyhow they had no time, so now the men were lying in holes in the snow, such as children build for themselves for fun, covered with tenting and a few rags, day in, day out, without relief. 'Excuse me,' he concluded, 'I must have a bit of shut-eye! I didn't get a wink of sleep last night.'

The Captain withdrew into a cabin at the back of the bunker and further instruction was supplied by the O3, a fellow as tall as a tree, in a grey pullover. His bullet-head was covered with tousled black hair and his jawbone looked as though it had been carved out of hardwood. He spread out the map showing the enemy positions and, pointing with his finger, said, 'Now, those are the divisions facing us. All old men over fifty or boys . . .'

'No morale and rotten supply services,' interrupted Breuer. 'A musket to every third man with an unrifled barrel, isn't that so?'

'Yes, how did you know that?' said the astonished O3.

Breuer laughed. 'Tell me one thing,' he said, 'how did an enemy like that manage to break through your lines?' The O3 thoughtfully pulled the hairs that protruded from his nostrils. He didn't know the answer.

Colonel von Hermann could very well have gone back, but he felt unable to tear himself away. It seemed to him that he was waiting for something. Then it occurred to him that he might as well take back Eichert and his people with him, so he asked the GOC of the Vienna division to give an order for their release. However, the General didn't seem anxious to do this. He murmured something about 'premature' and 'not as easy as all that'.

The Colonel found this strange, but said very politely: 'If you're worried about the Russian tanks breaking through again of course our tanks will remain at your disposal.'

At that moment the telephone rang. The General grabbed the instrument and said curtly, 'Eichert? . . . what's happened now?'

Colonel von Hermann had heard the name and picked up the other receiver without noticing the irritated look on the General's face and listened in. He heard Eichert say: 'Very heavy bombardment from guns of every calibre. Up to now casualties amount to around twenty per cent. I must ask the General to authorize an immediate withdrawal. We have already fulfilled our mission and it isn't our job to hold this position.'

'Yes, yes, yes,' said the General rather crossly, 'but don't get nervous, man. These things take a little time.' He replaced the instrument and said quietly, without looking at the Colonel, 'I've always said this damned hummock was untenable. Whether it's occupied by the Russians or by us, it only take ten minutes gunfire to leave it as bald as a skull.'

Colonel von Hermann opened his eyes wide and understood everything. He said as quietly as possible: 'As I'm instructed to collaborate with you, may I ask if you have made representations on the subject to Army Headquarters?'

The General laughed curtly and said, '"Made representations" is good. Every day I badger the corps and the army about it. But they won't give up this height. The line of defence which has been laid down by the Führer himself may not be altered without his personal approval. What do we do next?'

A tide of rage welled up inside the Colonel against this wretched mound, on which his men were being killed. 'Well,' he said coldly, 'that is for you to decide. It doesn't concern my division. We've carried out our orders and put back the front line to where it was before. I ask you once more, General, to instruct my detachment to withdraw forthwith.'

The General flushed but, before he could answer, the door flew open and a voice said, 'We can't carry on like this, General.'

It was Captain Eichert, still holding his sub-machine-gun in his hand, and breathing heavily. A bloodstained rag hung down from under his fur cap. The General rose to his feet. He was not used to such outbursts from his Viennese officers. But Eichert was no longer looking at him: he had suddenly seen his own CO and gasped at him, 'Colonel, the position is absolutely impossible. Nobody could hold it. For an hour we've been up there as exposed as if we were on a plate, plastered by every gun on the Russian front . . . then they attacked and now they're sitting up there.'

'Casualties?'

'Can't estimate them yet, sir, but I'm afraid . . .'

Colonel von Hermann took up the telephone.

'Army Staff-Command HQ I want to speak personally to the Chief of Staff. Yes—urgent. Put me through at once.'

After a few moments the connection came through. The Colonel put the receiver to his ear and there was the Chief of the Army Staff, Marshal Paulus's right-hand man. It was an open secret that he was the real leader of the army. There was the clear vibrant voice and the Colonel thought he could feel the compelling, slightly mocking steel-blue eyes focused upon him. In a moment, feeling small and embarrassed, he had forgotten what he had to say. Meanwhile, Major Kalweit had come into the room. He whispered to Unold an account of his experiences in the line. He had driven the last Russian tanks back over the main line of defence and had knocked out one of them while another had been lost through damage to its tracks. He rubbed his hands together and beamed. The Colonel was listening to the Chief of Staff, saying, 'Yes, yes, sir,' from time to time and unconsciously accompanying the words with a clicking of his heels. This time the General was listening in through the extra receiver, and now and then he cast a significant glance at the Colonel, who finally put back the instrument with a deep sigh. Then he turned to Kalweit and said to him in constrained tones, 'Ah, it's a good job you're here. New orders for you. Tonight you're to take your tanks up the hill and hold the position till dawn, when the infantry will relieve you.'

The Major's expression changed—incredulous amazement was printed on it. 'What!' he said quickly. Then the blood rushed to his face and he raised his voice and cried, 'What! by night! We aren't cats. We can't see in the dark! And they want us to hold the position, so that when daylight comes the enemy will be able to pick us off like flies. Tanks aren't toys for children.' He swallowed a few times and the muscles of his face twitched. Then, without saluting, he rushed out of the room and banged the door behind him. The General collapsed into an arm-chair with his arms hanging down. He stared with an expression of dismay at Colonel Unold, who looked as if his last ten-mark note had been stolen from his pocket.

The tanks stormed the hill at night, and morning found the Russians in possession again after they had knocked out two German vehicles with anti-tank rifles. Twice more Eichert's force was sent to the attack and twice they occupied the height only to evacuate it in the morning. In the process they lost over thirty per cent of their effectives killed and wounded. Then at last, after the General had assured Army HQ that he would keep the enemy off the hill by gunfire, he was allowed to draw the front line of defence along the foot of the hummock.

That was the last time that the line was substantially reinforced by the reserve division.

Sergeant-Major Harras gradually grew accustomed to life at the front. He already knew the difference between the impact of a shell and the report of a gun and no longer trembled under the mocking eyes of the Bum when the batteries on the railway embankment began their nuisance bombardment. He learnt from the noise they made to know the direction and probable point of impact of projectiles, became familiar with the whiplash crack of anti-tank shells and was able to distinguish them from the clear unexpected bangs of the mortars, and the dull stutter of the Russian Maxims from the busy rattle of the German MGs. He had soon learnt that exaggerated cleanliness was not considered a virtue here. They used to say, 'nothing suits a soldier like a dirty face', and Harras acted accordingly. He grew a beard and followed its progress daily in his shaving glass. A shell from a mortar, bursting near by, caused an insignificant graze on his head, which qualified him for a wound medal. This he secretly exchanged for an old one, which had become shiny with age and looked like gold in the distance. Of course when the Russian night-bombers swept along the German positions and dropped sticks of bombs into the river valley, or when artillery bombardments caused the frozen ground to shake and the earth to trickle down between the beams in the bunker, fear overwhelmed him like a great black spider. But he concealed it and that was the great thing.

Harras had passed his probation successfully and nothing more seemed to stand in the way of his promotion. Unold had promised to ask for his return to the staff after his promotion to commissioned rank. But could one trust Unold? In any case Unold, who had recently called on this division in company with his own CO, had greeted him in a very friendly manner. 'Hope to have you back with us soon' was what he had said.

But there was another thing that filled Harras with anxiety. A lot of rumours had recently got about concerning relief operations from the south. It was said that there were plans for a simultaneous break-out towards the relief column. Harras wondered if the mysterious visit of von Hermann had any connection with that. The Bum kept his mouth shut and seemed to have no information. But if such a plan existed, there could be no doubt that this division, already stationed in the south-western corner of the Cauldron, would be one of the first to be thrown into the battle. After his arduous and successful attempts to improve his position, the prospect of dying a hero's death in battle held no attraction for Harras. He sometimes asked himself whether it wouldn't be a good idea to revive some old physical weakness, so that he could get a bit of temporary leave. Or better still, he could try to get a further promotion which would entail being posted away from the front line before the real trouble started. Sergeant-Major Harras looked around eagerly for an opportunity to distinguish himself in a manner that would neither escape notice nor entail undue risks.

In the bunkers and field-hospitals, in the latrines and at the issue of rations—in every place where the soldiers collected, the news was bandied about.

'Have you heard? Manstein is coming.'

'Is he? Manstein? At last.'

'Didn't he take the Crimea?'

'Yes, of course, and Sevastopol too ... with sixty-five centimetre mortar!'

'Well, I expect he'll fix them. It's high time someone put a stop to all this nonsense.'

An order from Hitler had recalled Manstein with his staff from Vitebsk and placed him at the head of the newly-formed Don Army Group with the lapidary order 'to liberate Stalingrad'. Though none of the soldiers in the Cauldron knew him by sight, his reputation was such that every heart beat faster when his name was spoken.

There was one man whose name was never mentioned although he had to bear the burden and responsibility of the relieving operations. That was General Hoth, the Commander of the 4th Tank Army. Only the officers and a few soldiers of the encircled tank divisions remembered a short, springy man, who used to bob up in the most unlikely places and clear the air like a thunderstorm. They called him 'The Goblin'. He knew how to get things done. In the summer of 1942 he had crossed the 200 kilometres of Kalmuck steppe, a red, sandy desert, in a few days, taking Remontnaya, Kotelnikovo, Aksay, Shutor I and II in his stride, and had burst into Stalingrad from the west. Now the bitter winter had set in, the steppe was frozen hard and deep in snow and his best divisions had been bled white in Stalingrad while those that had survived the murderous autumn fighting were encircled with the remnants of the Sixth Army. He was to march on Stalingrad again, supported by other divisions of which only one was properly rested and refitted. It looked as if he would now have to pay the debt from which fate had granted him a temporary respite in the autumn. Fighting and, especially, attacking had long been thought an impossibility in winter. In the beginning of the Russian campaign the German General Staff had dreamed of a sort of winter-sleep—a hibernation —on both sides. It was only the disaster on the Moscow sector and the heavy defensive fighting that followed in the winter of '41–'42 that had dispelled this dream. They had to think again. This was the first great offensive operation undertaken by the German armies in the middle of the Russian winter. It had been appropriately named 'Operation Winterblitz' and the depleted divisions went ahead yard by yard through snow and cold and in spite of the Russians.

But on the southern front of the Cauldron the troops stood to their posts and strained their ears to hear sounds from the snowy waste in front of them. The Russian front seemed to have gone dead, but on still days some listeners thought they could hear a distant rustling, carried by the wind, a faint humming sound, which might have been their own hearts beating—'Do you hear? They're coming!' But on clear, frosty nights, when the sky was sprinkled with stars, sometimes above the far-off horizon, single points of light would appear like tiny glow-worms. 'They're coming, my God! They're coming!'

In the Intelligence Section bunker in Dubininski the daily announcement from Corps Intelligence was awaited in tense excitement. 'What's the news, Herr Rittmeister?' was the opening question. By now Graf Willms had become much less phlegmatic. 'Yes, Breuer, er, something doing today. They have been unloading tanks on the Tchir, fresh from Africa—still painted brown—yes, they're going ahead . . . progress, er, yes, quite good progress. And behind the tanks, innumerable columns.'

They were all worked up. Even Herbert's ill-humour had disappeared. 'At Christmas, Lieutenant, you must all come and visit me in Dessau. We'll serve you a feast . . .' and he went on to sketch out a most elaborate menu. Meanwhile Fröhlich couldn't be induced to stop looking at the map and Geibel gladly received instructions from him. 'Come and look at this, man, we've just patched up this bit of line and when the next big push comes from the west we shall have five or six Russian armies in the bag. Isn't that so, Breuer? At least five or six. That will be something.' He clapped Geibel on the shoulder so hard that he almost brought him to his knees.

'It'll be the greatest encircling movement in the world's history.' He gazed at the verse pinned up on the wall and clenched his fingers till the joints cracked. 'Yes, yes . . . We're going to break through all right,' he said with a laugh . . . 'A great man, that von Hutten.'

The operational staff of the VIth Army followed the course of the relieving operations with the closest attention. It had been decided, without paying too much attention to orders from the Führer's HQ, to break out of the cordon and advance to meet the relieving force. A spearhead was to be forged out of all available tanks and motorized vehicles and the man selected to command it was Colonel von Hermann. This order acted on the Colonel like a blood transfusion and he blossomed into boundless activity. Every day, accompanied by Major Kalweit and Breuer and occasionally by Unold, he visited staffs and workshops and inspected the sectors of the south-west front. Meanwhile Unold and Engelhard sat day and night studying maps and plans, working at orders and drawing up dispositions. The break-out was to be made from the Karpovka-Marinovka area and was to be launched as soon as the relief force was near enough.

But opinions were divided over what was 'near enough'. The Army Staff wanted the spearhead of the IVth Tank Corps to advance to a distance of thirty kilometres from the German line before launching the break-out, so that the two forces could connect between daybreak and nightfall. Colonel von Hermann considered this estimate over-cautious. 'The sooner the better' was his idea, and he even summoned up the courage to oppose the Chief of Staff on this point. 'Any action that we take on this side will make things easier for Hoth. And if we can't get through in one day, we'll have to make a hedgehog. It won't be the first time.' But the army said, 'thirty kilometres'. The risk would be too great otherwise.

The staff in the Cauldron worked feverishly. All tanks and guns fit to go into the line—there were about fifty of them—were pulled out, mobile battle-units were put together and sent to the areas where the coup was being prepared. Vehicles were requisitioned and parked in empty columns waiting to be used to bring up supplies. The army had asked for 700 trucks, but the divisions managed to produce double that number to meet the emergency. They knew what at stake. Units of the Field-Police were ordered to watch all the exits. No one was allowed to leave the Cauldron without the written authorization of the Army Staff. And so the Field-Police began to guess what the fighting command had known for so long, namely that the only object of Hoth's operation was to provide a funnel through which new strength—munitions, fuel and supplies as well as replacements in men and material—could be pumped into the encircled army. The withdrawal of the exhausted troops from Stalingrad and the surrender of the city was not contemplated in spite of all that had happened. 'Where we stand we stay' the Führer had said.

The senior staff officers knew that, but the soldiers in the Cauldron did not. They were preparing for a great trek southwards. Even the sleepy bunker-city of Dubininski stretched itself and began to swarm like an ant-heap in spring. Motors were thawed out and machinery greased. The snow-covered giants awoke from their sleep rattling and groaning and shook off their crests of snow. Geibel was learning to drive a car. He lay for hours, black and oily under the motor with Lakosch, listening with awe to the curt explanations which the little man deigned to give him. At other times, like a curious cat, he haunted the omnibuses and the trucks carrying field kitchens and his only preoccupation was whether they were in good enough shape to stand the long journey to the south. Lakosch, too, moved about a good deal and watched the preparations. Senta never left his side and he could be heard saying, 'Look, Senta, this here is a Büssing with three sets of wheels, and that over there is a thirty hundredweight Ford, captured from the enemy, isn't that right, old girl?' Lakosch had the impression that his dog understood more than Geibel. And sometimes, as he strolled along, he would hum the refrain of a song, which he had found in a book about the Peasants' War and had adapted to the present situation.

> Manstein is coming, he's on his way,
> Manstein's already here, hooray.'

Chapter Six

HUNGER AND MORALE

THE DAYS GREW shorter and dimmer, the nights longer and more painful. The days were full of noise, full of a droning sound like a thousand telegraph wires that swelled and sank and seemed to come from near and far. The air force was flying in provisions for the encircled VIth Army.

This was the result of a conference that had taken place weeks before, when the news of the encirclement of the Stalingrad divisions had arrived and the question of what to do next became urgent. This happened at a place where gold braid, oak-leaves, epaulets and orders were still being worn and the war was represented by figures and diagrams. The HQ staff of the air force and the QMG's staff were conferring together—Reichsmarschall Göring in white uniform with his two generals, Milch and Jeschonnek, and the Quartermaster General of the Army with his experts and advisers, and finally—and nothing could have emphasized the importance of the conference more strikingly than this —He was there: He, the One, the All Powerful in whose hand lay the fate of them all. It was not so much the fate of an encircled army but the vindication of a sentence that had been spoken not long before. 'We have decided to take possession of Stalingrad, and nothing will ever persuade us to leave the place.' Now something had happened to challenge these words and to cast a doubt on the infallibility of the man who had spoken them.

The orderly officers who had been hurrying hither and thither with documents and whispering messages into the ears of their chiefs had disappeared and closed the doors behind them—the movement of chairs and the hum of conversation had been silenced.

General Jodl gave a summary picture of the position at Stalingrad in the light of the latest reports.

General Wagner, the QMG of the Army, was leaning back in his chair, doodling on his writing-pad and listening with half an ear to the different speakers. The news from the Stalingrad front, although it represented only a part of his preoccupations, had really shocked him, but he couldn't help having a slight feeling of satisfaction, for he had seen it coming.

There was his memorandum submitted by the DQMG of the southern army-group as far back as September, when everything was going well and the capture of Stalingrad was daily expected. In this memorandum it was shown in clear and unadorned language supported by sober figures that it would be quite impossible to keep the troops in the long projecting salient, which ran up to Stalingrad, adequately supplied. There was only a single line of railway running through Morosovskaya to the Tschir and even this had not yet been completely adapted to the German gauge. Two armies depended on this for their supplies. Everything had to be pushed along this wretched little line—supplies, munitions, spare-parts, tools, petrol and even horse-fodder—for half a million soldiers, and in addition it had to serve for the transport of the wounded and men going on leave. The troops could not live on the country, the steppe was too barren, and then the railway only ran as far as Tschir. There everything had to be loaded on to trucks of which the number was quite inadequate, especially as they had to carry water from long distances. The report concluded in clear and courageous fashion that the Stalingrad front should be withdrawn to the Donetz, which could be done without risk to the Armies of the Caucasus because the Russians in the steppe-region had to contend with the same difficulties as the Germans and wouldn't be able to conduct an offensive in winter. 'Otherwise' the DQMG had written (and General Wagner remembered the exact words) 'when winter comes, the forces between the Volga and the Don will find themselves in a catastrophic position.'

He had been quite right. The catastrophe had occurred. Other officers had reached the same conclusions in good time. One of these was General von Schwedler, CO of the IVth Army Corps.

He had expressed his views to Hitler's face, and Hitler had sent him into the wilderness to join the others who had had the courage to tell him the truth. The army had not been withdrawn to the Donetz, and the Luftwaffe had undertaken to supply the Stalingrad armies by air.

Now they were in a fine mess. Somehow or other they would have to make up for what they had neglected to do in September. Thank God the damage was still reparable, though the job would be difficult, but it was better to face the facts now than never.

General Wagner twisted his pencil in his fingers as he listened to the speeches. What was the point of going on when it was clear that it was quite impossible to supply the VIth Army from the air. Now the Führer would have to fight a rearguard action. Nobody was anxious to admit his own mistakes and Hitler needed a scapegoat. A good thing that he seemed to be looking for one in the ranks of the air force.

At this moment General von Richthofen, the Commander-in-Chief of Air Fleet No 4 was speaking.

'Since August we've borne the chief burden of carrying supplies to Stalingrad and the Caucasus,' he said in abrupt and temperamental tones. 'As the nine transport groups of JU 52s, of which we disposed, were not adequate to our needs we had to use our own means of transport.' His eyes met those of General Wagner, who said to himself that was what you wanted—'We had formed truck columns from our own air force rolling stock.'

'By dint of a reckless expenditure of men and materials we carried on until the two railway lines had again become usable. But recent events have created an entirely new situation, which has got to be recognized. To keep an army of 300,000 men supplied by air is a task unique in history. It is far beyond the capacity of an airfleet. That would require special measures. I should say that from five to eight hundred machines would have to be made available for transport alone. Then a complete smoothly-working ground organization would have to be set up. It would be necessary to establish at least four efficient airfields for day and night service. Only if all these conditions were fulfilled would it be possible to keep the VIth Army supplied, and even so it would scarcely be possible to carry the necessary 300 tons daily.' Six hundred tons, thought General Wagner; that was the calculated minimum. But he said nothing. What was the good? A sandwich without cheese was as bad as a sandwich without ham. And it seemed to come to the same thing if they couldn't fly in either 600 or 300 tons.

'The 4th Air Fleet,' Richthofen continued, 'will not be able to contribute much from its own resources. First of all it will be necessary to free the 8th Flying Corps from all combat-duties.' He took a piece of paper in his hand, which his QMG had passed to him, and went on: 'the number of our usuable planes after deducting losses which . . .'

'Yes, yes, yes, we know all that,' interrupted Göring—(Wagner thought 'how damnably the fellow treats his generals. Like an NCO with recruits.')

'Morzik, please!'

Morzik was Chief of Transport to the Luftwaffe or something like that. He looked like a book-keeper as he peered through his glasses at his thick bundle of papers and talked about figures. The figures showing the strength and distribution of the different Air Transport Forces in Norway, with Rommel in Africa, in the Crimea and the losses over the Mediterranean . . . There was no additional transport available for Stalingrad without risking serious repercussions on other fronts . . . Even if something were done, the fresh planes made available would not nearly suffice.

The Reichsmarschall had been drumming nervously with his fat, beringed fingers on the table.

'Milch,' he snorted.

The Field-Marshal shot up like an india-rubber ball. 'He makes them stand up like school children' thought General Wagner and smiled. This chap Milch always amused him. As he stood there waving his little, soft hands, with his rosy sucking-pig's face beaded with sweat, he had a superbly unmilitary appearance more like a company director. But he had a string of military and civil titles which would have done honour to a prince in the Middle Ages.

It was of Milch that Göring was said to have remarked: 'I am the one to decide who is of Aryan descent.' Well, anyhow, the man was a specialist in planning, calculation and organization. It was he who had built up the Luftwaffe in a few years, he needed no documents and no papers, he had all the statistics in his head. He selected the most essential figures employed by Morzik, added a few details and then concluded:

'Let me summarize. To supply the VIth Army with 300 tons daily—always supposing that this amount is sufficient to ensure a minimum subsistence, which is certainly open to question—will, if we reckon on normal wear and tear and losses due to enemy action, require from 450 to 500 JU 52s. Counting the fighters we shall need for the protection of the supply planes, we must raise this figure to 700. We haven't got these machines, so at the present moment it is impossible to supply the VIth Army by air.'

Well, there it was. General Wagner laid his pencil down and looked at the man at the other end of the table, who, unusually enough, had remained silent so far—the man for whose benefit the whole session had been arranged, and to whom the final word belonged.

Deep silence, broken at last by a dull, throaty voice speaking as if from the bottom of an abyss: 'It *has* to be possible. The impossible does not exist for us.'

Hitler's words pierced General Wagner like a bullet and shook him out of his apathy. Was there to be no withdrawal? Could Stalingrad hold out in the conditions they all knew? There was no sense or understanding in the decision. It was madness——

Hitler's cornflower-blue gorgon's eyes swept round the line of faces. In his expression lay a question that had to be answered, and few of them dared to look him in the face. They lowered their eyes or looked away.

'What do you say, Jeschonnek?'

General Jeschonnek, the Chief of Staff to the Luftwaffe, had the face of an ascetic, with ice-cold eyes and a slit for a mouth. His tight-lipped mouth seemed hardly to move as he answered.

'In the circumstances described to us today I must refuse all responsibility for transporting supplies to the VIth Army.'

General Wagner waited in embarrassment for what would come next. He was familiar with Hitler's uncontrolled rages when things did not go as he wished. But nothing of the sort happened—only the question: 'Is that all my generals have to say to me?'

Yes, that was all! Whether secretly and evasively or in clear and unmistakable tones the generals had said their 'No'. God be praised, thought Wagner, and dared to hope again.

Then Göring sprang to his feet. There he stood tall and gross— a mountain of flesh. Around his neck hung the gold-rimmed Grand Cross of a great order.

'My Führer,' he cried, and the rolls of fat on his face turned a dark red. 'You are right, as always. Nothing is impossible for us! We shall build giant planes, glorious Messerschmitts. By the light of the moon we shall fly in immense convoys to Stalingrad. Milch —that is your task. My Führer, I will guarantee the provisioning of the VIth Army.'

The occupants of the Intelligence bunker spent the days before Christmas waiting. On the Sundays in Advent they lit a candle, sipped black coffee, crunched their toasted bread and thought of home. Graf Willms rang up less often now and, when they wanted him, he was often not to be got. He had become more reserved in his communiqués. Of course we were making progress, but things were difficult in winter and they must be patient. 'We certainly shan't be here next Sunday,' he would say, or 'Of course we shall be gone by Christmas.'

Breuer played the harmonica. At the end of his last leave his eldest boy, Jochen, had pressed his own instrument into his hand, at the railway station crying: 'Take it with you, dad, and play to the soldiers in Russia.' Now he was glad to have it, for it helped him to pass the dreary hours. He sat in one of the seats from the car playing a Chopin Étude. But no matter what tune he started, he always came in the end to the song which goes

Tout est fini,
La terre se meurt,
La nature entière subit l'hiver,
Tout est fini—

Lakosch sat and stroked Senta's smooth, silky coat, muttering endearments to her. She had grown noticeably fatter lately and it looked as though she was going to have her puppies. He never let her out of his sight. There were too many Roumanians and hungry Russian POWs loafing around, and the dogs and cats which had formerly haunted the bunker-town had disappeared.

From outside came a fiendish noise of firing and bombing and Wiese got up and went silently out into the open air. Breuer played a few chords on his harmonica, but he was no longer in the mood. He got up, too, and pushed his way through the narrow entrance into the open. The cold gripped him like a wild beast. The sky was black and starless. A red rocket went up over Pitomnik and came down in single stars which soon went out. Then for a short while a searchlight swept in a circle through the night. A multiple droning filled the air, like uncanny voices behind the scenes, coming through the lonely blackness. Breuer recognized Wiese in the gleam of the searchlight. He was staring motionless into the night. He went up to him and said: 'They're firing again.'

Silence . . . and then he heard Wiese say very quietly: 'I can't go on any longer!' He spoke in a whisper but it was like a cry of pain. Brcuer started. 'Wiese—you?' Wiese, always calm, always equable. It seemed that even he was overwrought. 'Look, man,' he said, 'you mustn't give way, you of all people.'

'I can't stand it any longer. The air of this country is full of death. It is killing me.'

'Now listen to me, Wiese,' said Breuer taking him by the arm and shaking him. 'Why do you think Fackelmann comes up here every other day? Why does old Endrigkeit come along to smoke his pipe in our bunker—and Dierk and the others? I'll tell you. It's because they want to draw strength from us, because our little den is an island of peace in the middle of this pandemonium. And it's you who make it so. You, who help everyone, all of us. Don't you realize that?'

'Island of peace!' said Wiese bitterly. 'Don't you see that everyone's going to pieces—me just the same as the rest. Here we are, 1,500 miles away from our homes, cut off from everyone we love. We are all going rotten in this awful place. I can't stand any more of it.'

'But think; only a few more days, man,' said Breuer almost crossly. 'In a week we'll be out of here.'

'Do you really think so?' said Wiese sadly.

'And if we do really get away, we shall no longer be the same. We shan't take home with us the best of ourselves. That lies buried here under the snow.' Then, feeling that he was not understood, he went on. 'But, of course, you're right. We are still alive and still can and must go on fighting.'

They heard foot steps shuffling through the snow. It was Geibel, who had been to draw rations. The two men followed him into the bunker where he was greeted with enthusiasm.

Geibel hadn't much to lay on the table. Two packets of rusks, a small tin of bully beef, sugar and a weighed-out portion of coffee—'Only three cigarettes per man!' 'What! Oh, hell! Cigarettes too! —is that the lot?' Geibel produced a few little packets of sweets and then six brand-new toothbrushes wrapped in cellophane, and three large rolls of toilet paper. 'One for every two men,' he said.

There was also a packet of newspapers, dating from October and announcing that the battle for Stalingrad would soon be over, but there were no letters from home.

In the Bum's bunker they were playing skat. It had been an unusually quiet day. The Russians seemed to be busy with the relieving force, which was coming nearer and nearer. On clear nights there were lights on the horizon and the grumble of distant fighting was getting louder. 'Something's going on outside, Herr Hauptmann,' said the sentry, looking in through the door. 'Would you come and have a look, sir?'

'All right: I'm coming.' The Bum got up and tightened his belt. 'Don't look at the cards, doctor,' he said. 'We'll finish the hand when I come back.'

The sentry had shut the door and moved away. What could be happening? Something to do with Manstein? No, the weather was too thick for that. It wouldn't be possible to recognize anything so far away. The Bum draped his fur coat over his shoulders and went out with Harras following.

The night air was damp and heavy, full of the monotonous

din of the transport planes, which nobody noticed any longer. The two men stood on the embankment and stared into the darkness. They could see nothing, absolutely nothing.

'All nonsense,' said the Bum. 'Quiet and gloomy as the Prophet's arse!' He turned to go, thinking of the hand he had left on the card table. Suddenly he felt a hand seize his arm.

'There, Herr Hauptmann!'

And over there, where the Russian line was supposed to be, a bright fireball went up and, after turning over once or twice, dissolved into single red stars, which slowly fell and went out.

'What is it, I wonder?'

'That's one of the things they're always sending up over Pitomnik, Herr Hauptmann.'

'Is that so? I wonder what it means?'

Out of the droning which sounded like the rumble of a powerhouse, they could hear an isolated buzzing sound growing deeper and stronger all the time.

'I know,' said the Bum. 'They're trying to tempt our aircraft down.'

The flares went up again and the drone of motors became louder and louder. There was no doubt that an aircraft was gradually coming down.

'Damnation! What do we do now?' said the Bum, hopping nervously from one foot to the other.

'Shoot,' said Harras.

'D'you think anyone up there would hear you?'

'Send up warning lights.'

'You'll have to hurry up for that. Besides do you know how to signal to the air-boys?'

The plane came down very low over the embankment. It had put on its landing lights and between them the black stem of the aircraft looked like the body of a bird. A searchlight blazed up far away and threw a brilliant cone of white light on the surface of the snow. The machine shot into the beam, touched down and rolled swaying and rocking out of the light. It was a JU 52 and it came to a halt a few hundred yards from the embankment, between the lines. A few men clambered out and looked round them dazzled, while from the darkness at the side a group of Russians advanced towards them. On the left a machine-gun started barking.

'Don't shoot,' shouted the Bum. 'You'll hit our own people.'

Then the searchlight went out and the darkness was blacker than before.

A few moments later the Russian guns opened fire, and the two men had to hurry back to their bunker.

Göring had done what he could, but not what he had promised. No transport gliders or Giants flew to Stalingrad but from time to time, to make up for their absence, a plane swooped down through the ceiling of cloud and after circling over the Cauldron a few times to the deep and comforting sound of its four powerful engines came down on the airfield of Pitomnik. The soldiers told themselves wonderful stories of the masses of stores that such a monster would be bringing in. There were two or three machines of the Focke-Wulf Condor type, which had been put on this run from the south of France and an occasional JU 90 or JU 290, but they were few and far between and on the uneven, snow-covered surface of the airfield they soon knocked themselves to pieces and only added to the number of mournful wrecks stranded there.

In addition the airfields of Tatsinskaya and Morosovskaya, both of which were situated more than 200 kilometres away from Stalingrad, were used by the good old corrugated iron machines, the JU 52s. Twenty years ago they had first flown round the world and they were still in service. Each of them could carry two tons of cargo. In addition there were fighters from the VIIIth Flying Corps, the Heinkel 111s and some other types capable of carrying a ton and a half of supplies in their bomb racks. All these machines flew by day and night through mist and clouds and snowstorms. They flew when the ice was an inch thick on fuselage, wings and propellers, threatening them continually with disaster. What was almost worse they flew on glass-clear sunny days, when there wasn't a cloud in the sky and visibility was unlimited. On such days the old, defenceless JUs had a modest fighter escort, but were an easy prey for enemy flak and fighters. Many of these machines flew three or four trips a day and their pilots swallowed pep-pills and answered questions with a dull and empty look and moved their hands mechanically on the joy-stick as they dreamt of sleep. On an average ten machines a day were lost: shot down, crashed or badly landed.

The people on the airfield and at Army HQ conscientiously recorded the daily tonnage of supplies arriving from the west—93 tons, 114, 52·4, 216·2, 84—gasolene, weapons, spare parts, munitions and food stuffs. Only once had deliveries totalled nearly 300 tons, which the army had promised to supply as an average, though the forces in the Cauldron needed at least 500 tons. The QMC's department figured and figured but didn't make allowances for death. They reckoned that with careful rationing, supplies would last till the 28th December. That would be the end unless a miracle happened. If Hoth didn't come. . . . Why didn't he come? The rations graph was falling—200 grams of bread—150—100. Since 15th December each man had been getting 100 grams of bread per day. Any unit was lucky that still had a reserve saved up from before the date of the famous army order about rationing. But it was hell for those who had no more to eat than a litre of fatless soup with a handful of semolina or oats, a single teaspoon of bully beef and the 100 grams of bread. The divisional staff in Dubininski had no more. The paymaster was missing and with him supplies for three and a half weeks.

A hundred grams of bread amounts to a moderate-sized slice. What can you do with that? You can eat it in various ways. You can swallow it in a few seconds or you can live on it for a whole day. In the Intelligence bunker each man had sharpened his knife to the keenness of a razorblade. With it he divided the slice into slices. Fröhlich was the expert at that and was sometimes able to cut a slice horizontally into five. He regarded this as a sign that nothing was impossible and derived courage and strength from the thought.

'How on earth do you manage to do that, sir?' asked Geibel. 'I couldn't do that even with a slice of Dutch cheese.' He kept on dreaming that he was at home in his grocery store stuffing himself with chocolate and ham and cheese, while his wife clung crying to the skirt of his battledress. The sub-slices of bread were roasted in the oven till they were dark brown and hard as stone. Then they powdered them, mixed them with saccharine and chewed them for hours together. Hot, sweet coffee deadened the pangs of hunger. Herbert had laid in a large supply of saccharine. Once he had wanted to exchange it for eggs and milk but where in the world could such things be found?

On the steppe to the west of the bunker-city some horses had recently been seen grazing. There were about twenty of them. Small and shaggy, they wandered feebly about, cropping the prairie grass which protruded here and there through the snow. Some unit that used horses must have sent them out to graze in these mournful pastures. Lakosch thoughtfully contemplated this new phenomenon from afar. A soldier with a gun and a few Russian 'helpers' were guarding the animals.

One day Lakosch paid a friendly visit to the kitchens and shortly afterwards he might have been seen lounging aimlessly over the steppe. As if by chance, he approached the sentry, who was sitting, muffled in a long sheepskin coat, on the ramp of an old flak position, with his rifle over his knees.

'Morning,' said Lakosch and sat down with a grunt beside the man, who mumbled something unintelligible, without taking his eyes off the horses. 'A bit warmer today, isn't it?' tried Lakosch, but the sentry didn't answer. He evidently attached no value to visits. Lakosch took a metal case out of his pocket and opened it with an air of boredom. It was tightly packed with cigarettes. The cooks had all contributed to the collection. Lakosch tilted out a cigarette with his finger and felt with his left hand in his coat for matches, while he offered the box to the sentry. The soldier looked sideways at the cigarettes and then at Lakosch, who didn't seem to be paying any attention to him, and at last pulled off a glove and fumbled in the case with trembling fingers.

'You been laying in a stock?' he asked. It seemed a miracle that anyone should offer him a cigarette.

'What d'you mean?' Asked Lakosch innocently. 'You mean these few I have here?'

'Well,' said the soldier, holding Lakosch's hand tightly as he took a light from him, 'with three cigarettes a day . . .'

'Three?' said Lakosch in an astonished voice. 'Why, we get ten.'

'Well I never—how bloody unfair!'

'What d'you mean, unfair?' said Lakosch slyly. 'Why, we laid in a whole stock of groceries from July on—schnapps and cigarettes and biscuits and rusks and jams—no, chum, we aren't starving yet.' He blew a few rings into the air. 'In the evening each of us gets a tin of tuna-fish.' As he told the tale he almost began to believe it and his mouth watered at the thought.

'Tuna, my God!' The sentry was so excited that the butt of his cigarette fell out of his hand. Lakosch handed him the case again.

'Look here,' began the soldier, sweat breaking out in beads on his forehead. 'Couldn't you manage to slip me a tin of tuna? Oh, not as a present. If you need a fountain pen or . . . or . . . or . . .' He rose to his feet, holding his rifle between his knees and felt in his trouser pocket.

'Here, look at this: genuine stag's-horn, with eight blades and a tin-opener. Here's something that would suit you.' He produced a monstrous pocket-knife, opened the blades and held it under Lakosch's nose. And all the time he didn't notice a lorry which had stopped at the side of the road. It was only when the Russian 'volunteer' workers began to shout and wave their arms, that he turned round.

With a curse he threw up his rifle, but it was too late. One of the horses had already got a wire noose round its neck. The car drove on pulling the struggling beast after it. And suddenly horse and car had disappeared. The sentry shot off his magazine into the flurry of snow, but they were already out of range.

Lakosch, too, had risen to his feet and was viewing the scene with interest. 'Well I'm blowed,' he said, shaking his head. 'What do they want a skeleton like that for?'

'Why, to eat, of course!' cried the sentry. 'Hell's teeth, that's the third. The old man will kick up hell.'

'What! Eat horseflesh?' said Lakosch 'You wouldn't catch me doing that. Well, we'll talk about the tuna-fish some other time. S'long!'

He went away with rapid steps. The sentry eyed him suspiciously. It dawned on him that he would never see that tin of tunafish.

For supper there was goulash in the mess and a special covered dish was brought for Lakosch, to share with Senta.

Soon afterwards Lakosch had a further opportunity to improve the menu in the mess. One day he was detailed to assist the working party which from time to time was sent to collect precious firewood from the ruins of Stalingrad. Lakosch wasn't looking forward to the job. He went off, cursing, having given Geibel precise instructions to look after Senta. 'If anything happens to her,' he said, 'I'll break every bone in your body.'

In the ruins of the wooden house on the western edge of the city they had loaded the lorry with planks and charred beams. But as they were driving out over the heaps of debris they had a breakdown and had to improvise a spare part. It wouldn't be possible to get back before noon the next day. Lakosch roamed through the ruins. He found the town quieter than in the autumn and was astonished at the busy activities of numerous vehicles and fatigue parties. The city was being taken to pieces.

And then a piece of good luck befell him in the heart of the city. A voice called to him across the street from the basement entrance of a house.

'Hey, what are you doing here?' The NCO who stood there was a butcher's assistant from Gleiwitz whom Lakosch had known in the Party organization. Now he was a platoon-leader in a unit which had been sitting by the Volga since the autumn. The two men went into the dug-out and celebrated their meeting with a drink. The NCO said that things weren't too bad on the Volga. The Russians were quieter just now and as for food, they were fairly well off thanks to a Russian boat that lay half submerged in the river. 'Full of flour up to the gunwale, old man, not far away from here—three or four hundred yards. It's really in the next sector, but since the characters next door are too cowardly to go and forage it's up to us. Tonight we're going there again.' After a few more glasses the platoon-leader said: 'You must come with us, Karl. That's obvious, I'll fix it up.'

That night Lakosch, by this time a little drunk, with his friend and two other men, climbed over the lumps of ice that had piled up into miniature icebergs. Afterwards he remembered vaguely rooting round in a good-sized tug half-covered with ice and running into mortar and machine-gun fire on the way back. One of the party stopped one on the return journey and they had to carry him the last few hundred yards, which had a sobering effect on Lakosch.

Next morning, pale and exhausted, he rejoined his unit carrying a canister full of syrup and a twenty-eight pound sack of flour. During the drive back he slept with his head on the meal sack and with the canister under his arm.

When, at last, he reached his bunker, Senta wasn't there. Geibel was almost weeping. He said he had walked with her once through the camp and she had kept close to him all the time, he was sure of that. Then, suddenly, she wasn't there. Lakosch gave him a terrible look and then, weary as he was, rushed out. He climbed into every bunker, searched every car over a wide area and examined the snow for prints, but found no trace of Senta.

Meanwhile the Junker lay, grey and lifeless between the lines. No one knew what was hidden inside her. Bread, perhaps, or gasolene or munitions. Two tons of precious cargo, doomed to fall into the hands of the enemy? But they hadn't got it yet and it seemed that the Russians hadn't done much about it either. By day they couldn't approach the machine and it would be no easy job to unload two tons of cargo in the dark. But something had to be done quickly. That was the view of the Regimental Commander, who had said: 'Plaster the cases with machine-gun bullets. If there's gas inside, it'll burn.' They had tried this, following the flight of the tracer bullets through field-glasses. It was clear that there was no gasolene there. The regiment asked the division for authorization to destroy the JU by gunfire. The division allowed them three free shots, the third of which looked like a bull's-eye, and the machine must have been riddled with shell-splinters. But she still lay there, huge and grey, a source of annoyance to everybody.

'What do you think about blowing the damned thing up?' said the Battalion Commander to the Bum. The latter nodded. It might be possible, with luck, to reach the machine under cover of night. 'But,' he said, 'we shall have to ask for volunteers. We can't order men to do the job. It isn't really worth while.' Sergeant-Major Harras, who was present at this conversation, said: 'I'd like to have a try, sir.' He had considered the matter with the speed of lightning. This was his chance, perhaps his only chance.

'You?' Harras had improved as a skat player but the Bum had no great opinion of him as an infantry soldier. He looked at the Sergeant-Major for a while in silence and, at last, shrugged his shoulders and said: 'All right, if you really want to—but you can't do it alone.'

Corporal Hempel, who understood something about explosives, also volunteered and, unexpectedly, Seliger, known as 'the Sausage'. They had clearly assumed that wherever Harras was, the danger would not be great. As no one else showed any ambition to take part in the adventure, the Bum gave his assent.

The following night they set out. The job was evidently going to be much more difficult than Harras had foreseen. The three men had put on white camouflage and had chalked their faces and boots. As soon as they got past the embankment they had to crawl. Harras was in the middle and the two others were to right and left of him at an interval of about ten yards. Two or three hundred yards is an insignificant distance on foot. But to a man lying on his belly things look different and if one has to cover the distance crawling, it seems like a mile. Keeping well down on the ground, Harras crept forward. He found his sub-machine-gun a hindrance and the steppe-grass blades, as sharp as knives and as hard as glass cut his face and hands. Moreover he was haunted by the fear that the charge in his pocket would explode and blow him into the sky. After a few minutes in spite of the intense cold he felt the sweat running down his forehead and flowing, mixed with chalk, into his eyes.

He could hear nothing of his two companions. 'Pst, pst,' he whispered. 'Here, Sarn-Major,' came the answers, from which he judged that Hempel was level with him and Seliger a little way behind.

The Russians seemed very uneasy. They continually sent up flares, by the yellow light of which Harras had to steer his course.

He saw the JU in front of him and felt that she wasn't getting any nearer.

He would now have gladly renounced all hope of promotion and distinction, if he could only be sure of getting back safe. But in desperation he crawled on. Drops, which might be blood or sweat, fell from his face. Another flare went up and Harras stretched his body up to look. Was he never going to get up to that damned aircraft? However, he was glad to see that he was already nearly half-way.

Then an MG started firing and another and a third . . . and quickly two or three fire-balls shot up. Damnation, they've spotted us, he thought. What next? Harras pressed himself so flat against the ground that he squeezed the wind out of his body. And then there were sharp crashes—mortar-shells in front and behind—to left and right.

When, after ten minutes, the firing died down, the night was filled with a piercing, protracted scream, sounding like nothing human. It was heard inside the bunkers and roused the sleepers from their wooden cots. And it went on and on—by morning it sounded like a long-drawn whistling interrupted by pauses for breath and in the afternoon it was a sort of groan. Towards evening it became a thin, piercing whine. During the night a search party crawled out towards the sound. The Russians refrained from shooting.

They found Corporal Hempel. He was dead by the time they brought him in. They had only been able to make a perfunctory search for the other two, who were never found.

Lieutenant Dierk had just got his two four-barrelled flak guns in position on the north-western edge of the bunker-town. At night the Russian fighters came down so low over his shelter and discharged their stuttering MGs at such short range that he became furious. These machines calmly dropped their parachute flares and let slip their bombs without being molested, though Dierk could often have brought them down with a single shot. But this he couldn't do, for he only had permission to shoot in the event of an attack on the divisional staff.

By day, it is true, the Russians hardly showed themselves in the air. They had some respect for the last five fighters in Pitomnik, some of which were almost always in the air covering the transport planes. But whenever all five were grounded at the same time, you could be dead sure that the Russian bombers would be up within a couple of minutes. They flew four or five in a line with a few of their short-tailed fighters swooping around them along the Rossoshka Valley or the positions in the north and sometimes had the nerve to come over the airfield. Their course was marked by grey mushrooms of smoke on the ground below them. Sometimes a black cloud rose skyward when a petrol dump had been hit. Dierk, who, to his chagrin, was only a spectator on these occasions, was astonished at the stop-watch regularity with which these raids were carried out, for by the time the Messerschmitts were in the air the Russians were far away behind their own lines.

Only once did they come over prematurely, while two Messerschmitts were still in the air. The Russians had not seen them and were flying straight for the airfield, when the silver-grey Me 109s dropped on them like hawks with their guns spouting fire. The bombers began to fidget. They staggered and dodged and peered right and left for ways of escape, breaking formation as they flew. But the Russian fighters accepted the challenge—they hadn't any choice, and soon the sky was full of humming, fire-spouting machines.

Down below the soldiers were craning their necks as excited as a football crowd.

'At him, man, at him! Oh well, what d'you expect if you won't get a move on! Now's your chance! Got him! There he goes, right into the cloud.'

The Russians had disappeared. Only two fighters remained in sight, swooping wildly round one another. Then one of them broke away and flew straight for the Russian lines with an ever-thickening trail of smoke oozing from its body. The Messerschmitt made one more attack, from below this time, spitting fire at its antagonist. A small black figure detached itself from the tail-end of the Russian machine. It fell faster and faster till suddenly something white spread itself out above it.

From the north-east a strongish wind was blowing. It drove the white ball along towards the bunker-town. Down below, the excitement was intense. Men crawled out of all the holes and stared up at the sky—including the Intelligence people, of course. The silver parachute glittered against the blue background of heaven. It grew bigger and bigger. It swept quickly on towards Dierk's gun position. By now it was easy to make out the arms and legs of the man who dangled helplessly at the end of the cord. Something fell from him to the ground. 'Look! Is that a bomb he's dropping?' 'A bomb? Don't be silly. He's dropping ballast.' Then there were four or five reports coming from the man in the air. 'Hell, he's got a gun!' A few cautious people threw themselves down in the snow, while others threw up their rifles. 'Don't shoot!' cried Dierk. Nevertheless a few shots were fired.

At last the parachute came down almost to earth. The man touched ground, sinking up to his knees in the snow, and then bobbed up again and was drifted a short distance by the wind. Then the parachute bulged out over his head like an enormous blister and suddenly collapsed.

The soldiers ran up from all sides through the deep snow calling to one another: 'Look out, he may start shooting again.' But there was no movement under the heap of silk.

Meanwhile Captain Endrigkeit plodded up with his pipe between his teeth. 'Leave it alone!' he said to the soldiers, who had begun to dismember the parachute. 'Papa Endrigkeit will attend to that.'

Dierk, together with Wiese and Breuer, who had just arrived on the scene, pulled the parachute to one side. They found the Russian cowering below in the snow. He still grasped his carbine. Endrigkeit took it away from him and looked at the magazine, which was empty. Meantime Breuer attended to the Russian, who didn't seem to be hurt as he helped the others to extricate him from the tangle of cords and to put him on his feet. As he stood there in his padded flying-suit he seemed somewhat weak in the knees, but was clearly unhurt.

Dierk walked round him, examining him from head to foot, and finally pulled his cap off. Stubborn flaxen hair stood up straight from a broad, white forehead. The rest of his face was brown and smeared with oil. He breathed deeply, looked at nobody and seemed to be waiting for something unavoidable to happen. Dierk handed him a cigarette. The Russian looked with a questioning expression at the donor and then took it with a trembling hand. He drew the smoke deeply into his lungs and breathed it out through nose and mouth simultaneously. It seemed to calm him.

The men crowded round, making remarks. 'A leather flying-suit, look! Smart-looking bastard! Probably some sort of a commissar.' 'He doesn't look too good.' 'Nor would you, if you were in his shoes, you clot.' 'He's in a bloody mess, and we're in a bloody mess—there's nothing to choose.'

'So, young fellow, come along with us now,' said Endrigkeit, taking the Russian by the arm. 'This is your pigeon, Intelligence; you haven't had one of these for a long time.' They walked off with the Russian between them to the Intelligence bunker and the crowd dispersed.

The Russian sat leaning forward on a stool, with his hands folded between his knees. His broad face had a coarse look, but his mouth and eyes looked intelligent. He seemed to be gazing through the walls of the bunker into an unknown distance, as if he were hardly aware of the officers sitting round him and sizing him up.

Interpreter Fröhlich took up a writing-pad, licked the pencil and prepared to catechize the prisoner. Come on, mister, tell us your surname—"*Nu dawaj, gospodin, kak wasche familia.*'

The Russian said nothing. He didn't seem to have heard the question. Fröhlich cleared his throat in embarrassment. He was afraid the others might suspect his knowledge of Russian.

'You're an airman, aren't you? What's your unit?—"*Wylot-chik, da? Kakoi polk?*"'

No reply. The Russian stared without interest in front of him.

'Why don't you speak, don't you understand?—"*Nu shto, patshemu nie gawaritye? Nie panimaitye?*"'

The Russian might have been deaf and dumb. Fröhlich had never met a case like this. 'He doesn't answer,' he said. The others had already noticed this.

All through this, Dierk had been fidgeting on his seat. At length, he couldn't keep quiet any longer.

'Give him a damned good thrashing if he won't open his trap!'

'I beg your pardon, Lieutenant Dierk!' said Breuer sharply. 'Have I got to remind you that you're an officer?' Dierk bit his lip and turned red. Breuer went on. 'Besides, as a prisoner of war the man has the right to refuse to answer. What d'you want me to do about it?'

'I wouldn't like to guess what *his* people would do to *us*,' growled Dierk, staring crossly in front of him.

Breuer told Fröhlich to stop the interrogation. He said: 'Let Corps HQ sort him out, if they like. We couldn't care less where their airfields are and what they've got to eat on the other side— Incidentally, Geibel, have we got anything left to eat?'

Geibel put on a dismal expression. The question touched his professional honour. He replied: 'We have . . . that is to say we just have the Herr Oberleutnant's usual ration.'

'No more? H'm—I was thinking we could all . . . Well, go across to the cook-house and see if you can scrounge a bit of supper for this chap. If you can't, you'd better give him mine.'

Suddenly the Russian spoke for the first time. His voice was slow and heavy.

'Please shoot me,' he said.

They all looked at him in astonishment.

'What do you say?' asked Breuer. He thought he had misheard.

Captain Endrigkeit slapped his thigh and said: 'This really is too much.'

'Shoot me,' said the Russian once more. 'Make an end!' This request, spoken in slow but correct German sounded earnest and impressive. The others gazed at the man with open mouths.

At last Breuer said: 'If that's all you're worrying about, let me tell you that we don't shoot prisoners here. We're not murderers.' Then he remembered the order about Commissars, but he thought: that's a long time ago and it was hardly ever carried out. He certainly remembered one case and then dismissed it from his memory.

The Russian looked at him meditatively as if there was something else worrying him. He looked round at Fröhlich and Wiese and finally his eyes came to rest on Dierk, who seemed to be about the same age as he was.

'No,' he said slowly. 'Not murderers perhaps. You do not shoot me. You give me food and cigarettes. Not murderers. You are—Germans.' The others did not interrupt him. The Russian's eyes ranged over their faces as if he were trying to fathom the inexplicable mysteries of a foreign land. He looked at Wiese and said: 'I have loved Germany. I have studied Heine and Goethe and Lessing and Hegel. And you have read them too . . . And then you come into our land in peacetime and destroy our cities, kill the Soviet people and hang them on—how do you say that in German?—yes, on gallows. Why?' He said all this quite quietly without a trace of excitement.

Dierk lost patience. He couldn't understand why they made such a fuss of this sullen fellow. 'Don't talk such rubbish, man,' he cried. 'You don't understand, because you're too stupid.'

'Yes, it is so. I do not understand,' said the Russian, 'but I have learned to hate Germany. The Germans are criminals.'

'That's enough,' said Breuer. 'You'd better have something to eat; it might put you in a better frame of mind. As time goes on you'll learn to think better of the Germans. Tomorrow you'll be taken to a camp, and when the war's over you can go back to your own home.'

But the Russian shook his head and it almost seemed as though he were smiling. Then he said: 'I shall not live and you will not live. Tomorrow I shall be dead and you the day after. Stalingrad—that is the beginning—Hitler *kaputt*, Berlin *kaputt*, Germany *kaputt*—that is the end.' He said it in a quiet, almost indifferent voice, as if what he said was self-evident. Then he devoted himself with interest to the plate of soup which Geibel brought him.

Old Endrigkeit had been so astonished by the pilot's conversation that he had let his pipe go out. He shook his head, saying: 'Ever heard anything like that?' It was beyond his comprehension that anyone should say such things, and this Russian apparently believed them. Amazing!

When Captain Endrigkeit returned next day, he seemed very much upset. He groaned as he sat down in his chair and pulled violently at his pipe.

'He's dead,' he said.

'What, not the pilot?'

Endrigkeit nodded and shrugged his shoulders, saying: 'What can you do, when a fellow is determined to do himself in?' On the way to Corps HQ, the car had had a break-down and the prisoner had run away, while they were attending to it. 'He didn't have a chance, of course. My fellows ran after him a long way and shouted at him not to be an idiot. Then they fired a few shots to frighten him, but that didn't work. He wouldn't stop. Well finally, Otto . . . well, the very first shot got him in the heart. Yes . . .' Endrigkeit's pipe puffed like a railway engine; then he drew out the carbine that he had taken off the Russian and turned it over in his hands. 'You know, Breuer, he was asking for it. He wanted to be killed.'

Since the successful horse-hunt Lakosch had been on the best of terms with the cook-house orderlies. This had its advantages. Occasionally there was something to spare for him, if only half-a-litre of soup. So it was no great surprise when one day he received a mysterious invitation to 'a small party'.

When, after the evening distribution of food, he came over to the kitchens, he was received with a shout of greeting. The whole complement of cooks was present with Corporal Klaucke, the fat chef, in the chair, looking like a Pasha. By an incomprehensible dispensation of providence this slim, long-legged journeyman-tailor from Berlin, had been attracted to the cooking-pots and he had never regretted it. In the course of time by the absorption of countless remnants of soup and food he had acquired an impressive belly of which he was very proud, though it hardly matched his lanky, calf-less legs and unhealthy grey complexion.

'Prost Karl!' said Lemke, the mess orderly, who had managed to scrounge a bottle of cognac out of Unold's stock, a good portion of which they had already drunk. 'Have you heard? Ten-Shun has gone west.' 'And Seliger, too,' said someone.

'Has he? Oh . . .' Lakosch had not heard about it and assumed that this party was a sort of wake. 'Well, then here's to them!' he said. He was sorry to hear about Seliger, the 'sausage', who had usually been able to find an extra morsel for him and Senta, but as for Harras he would have given ten like him to get back Senta.

The bottle went round once more and then Lemke produced another.

Someone said: 'You'd better take care, young fellow. If the Colonel finds out, there'll be a stink. He counts the bottles every evening.'

'Nothing to be afraid of,' laughed Lemke. 'Some of his bottles are already filled with cold tea.'

'But if he tumbles to it . . .'

'If he does, we'll just blame it on the late Seliger of blessed memory.'

'I'd watch out if I were you. The Colonel's quite capable of sending you to join our late friend.'

'No more drinking,' ordered the Chef. 'We're going to eat now.'

They started with pea-soup which was very much above the average issue. When the soup was finished each person was served with a lidded aluminium plate and a delicious smell filled the air. At the word of command the lids were removed and the others, who had been let into the secret, fixed their eyes on Lakosch. The little man stared as if bewitched at his plate, in which lay two dumplings as big as his fist and two splendid slices of roast meat in brown onion sauce.

'That's a surprise for you,' said the fat cook. 'Good grief!' said Lakosch, so moved that his eyes filled with tears. 'Have you caught another horse?' He looked round and saw all the others beaming at him. Lakosch cut a piece from his slice and tasted it. 'Marvellous,' he said. 'This tastes like—like veal cutlets.' The meat was light in colour and very tender. 'You aren't going to tell me that this is horseflesh?'

'Don't ask questions. Go on eating,' said the Corporal. Lakosch needed no further invitation. He filled his mouth so full, he could hardly swallow. The others ate likewise and kept looking at Lakosch with sly grins on their faces.

'Eat, man. Don't hold back!' said the Chef, replete and good tempered. 'There's a second helping for you if you want it.'

A full belly can transform a man. Lakosch felt the warmth flowing from his stomach into his limbs. He forgot his worries and everything seemed light and easy once more. He hardly had room for the second helping.

Over the brandy they all told funny stories but suddenly the laugh on Lakosch's freckled face froze into a grimace. He had just caught sight of something in a corner of the bunker. Under a heap of dirty linen, something had caught his eye.

Lakosch's face grew sharp and grey. Even the others were silenced by his appearance. Tension grew till it became unbearable.

'He's noticed something,' whispered the cook. 'Watch out for fireworks.'

Then Lakosch rose slowly from his chair and moved like a sleep-walker towards the heap. For a while he stood before it as if he had to remember something. Then with lightning speed he put his hand down and plucked something out of the heap—a tawny skin, as soft as velvet.

Much later when Lakosch came to his bunker the officers were asleep, all except Geibel. When the latter saw his face, he got a frightful shock, but he did not dare to question him. For the whole of the next day he looked fearfully at Lakosch, but the little man didn't seem to notice him. He didn't say a word.

The talk about Manstein had died down.

It is true that the die-hards continued to scan the horizon to the south and west by night and thought they were seeing signs and portents. Nevertheless the vehicles that had been got ready for a sortie in force kept gradually returning to their units. The slogan, 'Stick it, Manstein is coming to cut you out!' had lost much of its attraction. The fact was that something had happened to change the situation—something that people had heard about and some seen with their own eyes.

In the middle of December, probably to counter the German relieving action, a second Russian offensive had been launched in the bend of the Don west of the point where they had made their first break-through. The Italians, whose positions were here, were overrun at the first attack and the attackers penetrated deep into the elbow of the Don and cut the vital railway line to the Tchir at various points. Millerovo was surrounded on two sides and the important supply station of Morosovskaya, which for days was the scene of hand-to-hand fighting, was lost to the Germans. The Russian tanks pushed on as far as Tatsinskaya and swept the German transport-planes off the airfield. The Russian advance was aimed at Rostov, on the Sea of Azov. It was expected to be a death-blow for the Armies of the Caucasus which were also cut off, and to give the *coup de grâce* to the southern army group.

Meanwhile Hoth's fighting force had covered most of the intended distance. On 19th December the spearhead of its tanks had reached a small river some fifty kilometres south-west of the Cauldron and had established a bridge-head there. It was during these days that it had been possible to see the flares with the naked eye and hear the continuous thunder of cannon. Wireless messages saying 'Stick it, we're coming' and 'See you soon' kept arriving. That was the moment at which Colonel von Hermann kept appealing to the Army Staff and saying 'Now is the time, now we must attack.' The army continued to reply 'Thirty kilometres. We haven't enough fuel for a longer sortie. If Hoth has covered a hundred kilometres, he will manage to cover twenty more. It's only a matter of hours.'

But at that point General Hoth received an order from his army group to move his three tank divisions with all speed into the great elbow of the Don. With their cannons still hot from combat, the tanks raced back and arrived just in time to prevent the worst from happening. During these days no one talked of Stalingrad, which seemed far away. Hoth's remaining forces were subjected to a heavy attack by Russian tanks which penetrated deep into their flanks. The Russian armies had easily been able to spare them. In order to save what still could be saved, he had to return, but in a few days he had been thrown back behind the line from which he had started.

The staff of the VIth Army had learned very little about these successive disasters. It merely received from army group the laconic message 'Relieving action postponed,' together with a few vague expressions of sympathy. The VIth Army staff drew their own conclusions but did not guess the full extent of the catastrophe. They didn't yet know that the army group now had other worries apart from the fate of the VIth Army in Stalingrad.

When Colonel von Hermann came back from HQ with the latest information he looked years older.

'Yes, Unold,' he said wearily. 'Our dream is at an end, but the men mustn't get to know any of this.' He took the silver-framed photo in his hand and looked at it, wondering in what part of the sky his boy might now be flying. He had had no news of him for months. Would he ever see him again?

Continuing their conversation, Unold said: 'That's only right. It isn't good for a soldier to know too much, it undermines morale.'

'Do you think so?' The Colonel put the photo back on the table. 'My principle has always been confidence for confidence, and it has been proved true in the worst situations. Nothing damages the morale of soldiers more than lies, and even to say nothing is a form of lying. But what's the use of talking? For your information let me tell you that I have applied for a transfer to an infantry division.'

Unold's weary face betrayed a fleeting smile as he said: 'Well, sir, in that case I can reveal to you that I've put in for a transfer too. I'd be grateful if my application could be forwarded with yours.'

He took a sheet of paper from his table and handed it to his CO, who glanced at it and then looked up with a surprised expression.

'What's this, Unold?' he said. 'You're applying for a transfer to the SS? What's the idea? You know that there aren't any SS troops in the Cauldron.'

The last drop of blood seemed to drain away from Unold's face. Had he misunderstood the Colonel? He bit his lips and his eyes wandered along the wall. The silence was painful.

Then the Colonel said: 'I would advise you, Herr Oberstleutnant, not to send in this application. It might give rise to certain misunderstandings.'

Unold hastily took back the paper, turned about in silence and left the bunker. Luckily for him he did not see the look with which his Chief followed him.

As a consequence of the strict army order about the dissemination of news, even the Intelligence section was not informed of the reason of Hoth's non-appearance. It was no longer possible to get Graf Willms on the telephone. The orderly officer would reply that the Graf was over-burdened with work and that he himself, unfortunately, possessed no information. However, Fröhlich now began to bring in quantities of information. German tanks had been seen on the roads running along the ridges flanking the Don. At Kalatch three SS Divisions were standing ready to move off . . . His hearers shrugged their shoulders and were quite pleased when an order came from Colonel Unold to the personnel of the staff instructing them to build a new bunker. Emaciated and hungry, they nevertheless found this heavy work with picks and ice-breakers, if not a pleasure, a means of changing the current of their thoughts.

The soldiers in the Cauldron learned nothing of what was happening around them and for a long time they all believed in Manstein, then they began to believe in him with the pathetic faith with which children cling to a fairy tale, hoping that it may conceivably turn out to be true. Manstein had become as legendary as the Prince whose kiss was to free the Sleeping Beauty from her thorny prison.

Chapter Seven

BLACK CHRISTMAS

CHRISTMAS CAME.

Dressing stations, field and emergency hospitals could hardly contain the masses of wounded men together with those who were sick with starvation and frostbite, and in the graveyards of Yeshovka and Pestshanka, Gorodishtche and Gumrak, where the victims of the bloody autumn battles slept, the forests of wooden crosses grew ever larger.

Lakosch had his own cross to bear. Senta's death had upset him profoundly, as his companions guessed.

They didn't know the full story and the men in the kitchen said nothing about it. But they were struck by the change which had come over Lakosch since his bereavement. He spoke seldom, and then surlily or sarcastically and intimidated his companions. There was a strange, tense expression on his face as if he was continually listening to some inner voice. Lakosch had become a brooder. Alone and aimless, he wandered through the ice-bound bunker-city, or lay at night on the damp earth of his dug-out listening to Fröhlich's regular snores and the ebb and flow of sound from cruising aeroplanes. He felt the dark weight of this incomprehensible land pressing, like lead, on his chest.

Long ago his father had told him wonderful stories of Russia. He had talked of the Workers' Paradise, of the Liberation of the Proletariat and of a plan to rebuild the world. Lakosch hadn't paid much attention to the slogans which his father had borrowed from the Red Flag or the pamphlets he had studied. But in June '41 he had crossed the Bug at Sokal and had felt a certain curiosity about the fabulous country he had heard so much about.

At first everything looked the same and a forbidden thought had bubbled up in Lakosch's mind. Perhaps Stalin's aims were the same as Hitler's. His object might be to bring socialism to his country, to promote the brotherhood of nations and the well-being of his workers? If this was so the war was nothing but a ghastly misunderstanding, a piece of devilry contrived by the plutocrats of the west. Rosenberg, the Baltic Slav, must have talked Hitler into hating the Russians as much as he did. If it were only possible to get Hitler and Stalin to sit down together it might bring this beastly war to an end.

Lakosch had suddenly become desperately sick of the war—and not only because of Stalingrad and the encirclement of the army to which he belonged. He was familiar with the face of war, but the death of Senta had struck him to the heart.

Geibel watched the change that was coming over Lakosch uneasily and one day said to him: 'What's the matter? Are you hungry?' He broke his slice of toast in two and gave half of it to Lakosch who didn't look at the toast but gazed long and searchingly at Geibel. Then he said: 'You're lucky, man. I wish I was as dumb as you are.'

Lakosch now had to bear an Iron Cross as well. The news that he was to receive the decoration on 23rd December at noon from the hands of Colonel Unold had surprised him and helped to dispel his depression. He started early in the morning to brush his shabby, stained battle-dress, and, whistling a dreary tune, polished his boots with a mixture of soot and sugar, till they shone with a glossy brilliance.

Lakosch felt nervous about the imposing military ceremony of which he was to be the central figure. It was on tiptoe that he climbed the steps leading to Unold's bunker and halted before the wooden door. He heard voices inside, the Colonel's and that of Captain Engelhard. He had already raised his hand to knock, when something stopped him. 'Saving the world from bolshevism!' The words came ringing through the door. 'You really mustn't believe those fairy tales, Engelhard. This war is a business matter. Industry and commerce didn't finance the Party for nothing. They want to see a return on their money.'

Lakosch's heart was beating fiercely and he missed Engelhrad's hesitating reply. Unold's next words, however, were perfectly audible.

'Don't you understand, Engelhard? You disappoint me. The great confidence trick began in '34-'35 with rearmament. A few years later came the subjugation of central and western Europe and then the conquest of Russia. In Dniepropetrovsk, Kirovograd and Stalino you'll find the Reichswerke Hermann Göring, the United Steel Works, Klöckner & Co. and all the other big concerns. Of course the little man will have to be rewarded too. After the war thousands of peasant farmers will be installed here as smallholders. The dumbest German will be able to get a job as an overseer and the Russians will play the role of helots. But it's the big business, Engelhard, that really counts.'

This time Lakosch heard Engelhard's answer. He spoke of the German people's struggle for existence and of the deadly menace to the German way of life from the expansionism of the east and the west. He said that Hitler hadn't wanted the war and had offered to renounce his legitimate claims in order to avoid it.

'That's what people say,' interrupted the Colonel, 'and quite right too. You've got to disguise the smell of commercialism somehow. Every little shopkeeper knows that. But people like you and me, Engelhard, must face up to the truth.'

Unold's voice cut like a surgeon's knife. He could visualize the Colonel's yellow face, which always reminded him of a death's head. And now his voice was so harsh that the boards of the door seemed to vibrate to its resonance.

'Listen, Engelhard,' said Unold. 'Operation Barbarossa, the plan of campaign directed against the Soviets, has been in preparation for years. The order for it was given by Hitler as long ago as July '40 immediately after the French campaign, when we were supposed to be on the best of terms with Russia. At that time I was working in the Army High Command, and I myself worked on the details—so did Paulus. The whole thing was cleverly camouflaged behind operation Sea Lion, the projected landing in England, which wasn't seriously contemplated at the time. It's confidential now but when the war is over we'll be able to talk about it, for we shall be in the right. The conqueror always is. If things go wrong, we shall all be hanged together.'

In the silence that followed Lakosch could hear the sentry's footsteps, but the sounds seemed dim and far away. Lakosch felt numb.

Now Engelhard was speaking again, louder than before and excitedly. He spoke of the building of a new and better order in Germany and in Europe, of a union of peoples and of social justice, of the new faith of the German people and of the progress they had made in recent years. And from it all he inferred that Hitler was moved in all he did by a single principle—the welfare of his people —and he felt that Hitler wouldn't risk the destruction of all he had built up unless driven to it by the direst necessity. Lakosch had believed all this once but it moved him no longer.

When Unold spoke again the cynicism had gone from his voice.
'Christmas makes you sentimental, Engelhard. Don't talk to me about socialism. Do you seriously believe that Hitler's a socialist? Do you think he cares a damn if this man has enough potatoes or that man is paid extra for working overtime? The people need an idol made in their own image. They'd be horrified if they could see the reality behind this façade, the real Hitler. But we've got to see the truth. It'll give us strength to follow the right course. Hitler serves no cause and no persons; he carries within himself the purpose of his existence. He isn't a man in the accepted sense of the word but a solitary Titan, beyond good and evil, beyond love and hate. Hitler is the pure incarnation of the Will to Power. Two or three times I've seen this aspect of him at quite private conferences at which there was no public to tempt him to act. It was a fascinating experience. Don't look at me like that, Engelhard. Get it into your head that Hitler is capable of smashing the world to pieces.'

When he got back to his bunker Lakosch couldn't remember what the Colonel had said to him when he pinned the medal to his chest and he hardly heard the congratulations of his companions. He left seeing the face of his dead father and hearing the old man say: 'Hitler means war.' Lakosch began to understand. He took off his decoration and kept it in the pocket of his tunic. When Breuer reminded him that the cross ought to be worn for a whole day after the award, he murmured something unintelligible, but didn't put it back. Nobody else noticed its absence.

Towards noon on Christmas day Captain Fackelmann, who had taken charge of the staff commissariat again, paid a visit to the bunker.

'I'm very sorry, boys, but I can't do anything much for you today—only half a packet of rusks and three more cigarettes each. That's absolutely all. I haven't a thing, believe me.'

They believed him. He would have done anything to get them a Christmas dinner of six courses, but he himself was obviously undernourished. His chubby freshness had disappeared, and the skin hung loose and sallow on his cheeks.

'A touch of jaundice,' he murmured if anybody commented, or: 'I've lost so much weight that if anyone asks me later if I've come from Stalingrad, I shall be able to answer "partly".'

The men laughed nervously, then someone came in with a message. 'Lieutenant Colonel Unold says you're allowed to use our emergency rations for Christmas.'

They looked uneasily at one another. Their emergency rations had long ago been used up.

When it grew dark Breuer lit the lamp and the candles. There had been no letters, no visible greeting had come from home. But the men took out the little presents they had secretly prepared for their comrades. Fröhlich had drawn a number of sketches of the bunker with the caption 'In memory of Christmas in the Cauldron 1942'. Herbert produced some handkerchiefs which he had cut out of an old shirt and hemmed himself. Wiese had copied poems out of his collection in italic writing. Breuer handed Geibel two cigars and it then appeared that the latter had had the same idea. He looked embarrassed as he offered Breuer four black cheroots painfully extracted from his last remaining ten.

Meanwhile Lakosch had slipped out, unnoticed. When he came back he threw a linen bag and a round cardboard box on the table.

'There,' he said abruptly. 'Luckily I haven't been greedy.'

'My God,' cried Breuer. 'Look what he's got . . .'

149

He had brought a bag of biscuits and a box of chocolate. The biscuits were badly crumbled and mixed with mouse droppings and the chocolate was a bit mouldy, but that didn't worry the men in the bunker.

There was a sound of heavy breathing outside and the door flew open. Corporal Lemke walked in carrying a heap of aluminium plates in one hand and a steaming cook-pot in the other.

'Compliments of the season from Captain Fackelmann,' he announced, red in the face, 'they've picked up another horse.'

As he wiped the sweat from his forehead he enjoyed the men's astonishment. Then he fished two great meat balls from the pot and put them on the plates with a helping of white cabbage for everyone. Now they had a proper Christmas dinner. Fröhlich, as he munched his food, spoke with real gratitude of the Captain who had brought about this miracle.

After the meal was over, Breuer brought out his harmonica, played a few random chords and then started a Christmas car:

O thou happy, O thou blessed,
Grace-abounding Christmas-tide.

One after another they all joined in. Wiese in a firm, clear voice; Geibel, rather uncertaintly; Herbert's light tenor and Fröhlich's droning bass which was not at all in tune. Finally even Lakosch joined the singing.

In a world forlorn Our Lord was born.

Strange hoarse music poured from throats, which had not sung for so long, but the familiar line made even this bare room homely.

A storm howled over the steppes, driving flurries of powdered snow before it. The moon, pale and distant, seemed to hurry restlessly through the ragged clouds. No stars were shining as Padre Peters felt boots broke through the crackling surface of the snow. He trudged onwards, leaving tracks like an elephant's behind him, that the blizzard soon filled up again. He was on his way to the copse near Karpovka. On his left there was a momentary gleam of light. Peters walked towards it and saw that it was the back of an ambulance, the bonnet of which had pushed into an opening in the wall. A medical orderly came towards him carrying a pail.

'Good evening, Padre,' he said. 'We're busy as usual here. A happy Christmas to you!'

Peters climbed in through the back door. The hard bright light intensified by the cream-coloured walls dazzled him. At the operating-table two assistants were busy with an unconscious man. The Doctor was standing by the wash-basin drying his hands on a towel. His rubber apron was sprinkled with blood.

'Good evening, Doctor!'

'Ah, it's the Padre! We've had nearly a hundred new cases today, some of them very serious. We really don't know where to turn.'

'Why today?'

'Oh, it's been going on for some time. They can't fly out more than twenty cases a day and there are usually a hundred fresh casualties. Well, you'll see them in the hospital.' As he spoke he poured some hot coffee out of a pot and took a few quick drags at a cigarette.

'Do you want the fractured skull now?' asked the assistant.

'No, we'll begin with the amputations.' Peters could not see much point in talking about Christmas there, so he said good-bye and went out.

In the middle of the copse stood an enormous tent. Properly speaking the canvas walls should have been sunk in the ground but when it was put up the soil was already too hard. It was as much as they could do to get the poles and the tent-pegs into the frozen earth. Inside the patients were lying side by side on a thin layer of straw. Those near the walls were powdered white, for the wind blew the snow in where the canvas did not touch to the ground. Two lanterns, fixed to one of the tent poles, did little to dispel the darkness. In the middle stood an iron stove, which only warmed those lying round it. A cardboard cut-out of a Christmas tree was fixed to another tent pole and on it a few candles were burning.

When the Padre came in, a murmur went round the tent.

'There's the Padre! Perhaps he has news.' 'He won't leave us in ignorance on Christmas Day.' 'Evening, Padre, what news?' 'They must be within twenty kilometres by now.'

Peters had come to console them but, the consolation they asked for was not in his power to give.

'We must trust in God,' he said simply. 'He alone knows what we need.'

Stepping over the wounded men he tried, with the stuff he had brought with him, to create a semblance of Christmas. He opened a gramophone and put on a record of the Dresden Choir singing Christmas Carols. Outside could be heard the drone of the transport planes, flying in spite of the blizzard as well as the stuttering tack-tack of a Russian 'sewing-machine'. From the distance came the rumble of detonations. The various sounds in the tent were stilled, except for intermittent groaning from one corner.

Rejoice, rejoice, O Christians.

Then Padre Peters took his slender bible and moved to where the candles were burning. He read: 'And they wrapped him in swaddling clothes and laid him in a manger, for there was no room at the inn.'

Tears ran quietly down the faces of the men. They were the shepherds in the field to whom in their misery long vanished truths offered a new revelation.

When the Padre put on a new record the tent was filled with organ music which seemed to add to its height and breadth. It was the Toccata and Fugue in D-minor, by J. S. Bach. Peters had used his loudest needle in order to drown the din of engines which was getting stronger and stronger. A plane was circling over the Balka and its rhythmic thudding broke into the organ-tones. The tent was suddenly filled with fear and even the candles seemed to be burning down. Then something came hurtling down, and the ground vibrated like a metal plate. Then came another bomb, nearer this time. The tent rocked like a ship in a stormy sea, pitching and rolling.

The roar of the aircraft made some of the wounded men try to sit up and the groaning in the corner stopped. Padre Peters prayed, his head in his folded hands. 'Help us, Lord God. Let it not fall on us here—not now.' A deafening crash seemed to grasp the tent in an iron fist and shook it to its farthest corners; like a swarm of hornets a shower of shrapnel came humming through the canvas.

The lights went out and no one spoke. The organ was still playing, but no one heard it.

When someone struck a match the Padre lit the candles. Thank God, no one had been hit. A breath of new life blew through the room. In the distance the noise of the aircraft died away and the tones of the organ rang out victorious.

The Padre walked through the rows of wounded men. He got them to talk to him and listened quietly and attentively. The men were grateful to him and only here and there where a wounded man could not or would not unburden himself did the Padre dispense a few words of consolation. He spoke of the one way of escape that lay open to them, the way to Heaven.

One of the men he spoke to was an NCO, whose feet had both been amputated the day before. He had been an SA leader since 1929. 'If I get home, Padre, my attitude to the Church will be different. But did I have to come to Stalingrad to find this out?'

Outside on the steep face of a slope was a row of bunkers. Here they put the dangerous head-wounds and abdominal cases, as well as those who would be dead in an hour or two. The cold was intense in the bunkers as firewood was short and the living had more right to warmth than the dying.

A boy of nineteen who had come straight from school to Stalingrad had been shot through the belly. His face was deeply shadowed and his eyes shone with unnatural light.

'It's fine, Padre,' he said with a smile. 'That I don't have to shoot any more.' The Padre laid his right hand on the boy's folded hands and prayed with him. In the middle of his prayer, his young face grew waxen and his noise pointed. 'For thine is the Kingdom,' intoned the Padre as he folded his arms round the prostrate body.

The next room Peters went into was quite dark and he sensed that it was the mortuary. He was just shutting the door when someone said 'hallo' to him.

The Padre lit a match and saw a row of corpses, laid out tidily like cigarettes in a case, and someone moving in the corner.

'Padre,' said the voice, 'please give me a cigarette.'

A young man was squatting in the corner with one leg drawn up and the other, thickly bandaged, stretched out in front of him. There was a blanket over his shoulders.

'What are you doing here?'

The lad's face twisted into a tearful grimace.

'They've shut me up in here,' he said, 'But I've done nothing. Oh Mother . . . Mo-o-other.'

The Padre sat down by him and lit the stump of a candle.

'Listen, my boy,' he said earnestly. 'Today is Christmas. Think of that and then of your mother. You mustn't tell lies. You shot yourself in the foot, didn't you?'

The wounded boy clung to Peters and buried his head in his overcoat, weeping uncontrollably.

'They're going to shoot me,' he said. 'I know they're going to shoot me.'

The Padre was silent and he knew that they would shoot him.

At last he said softly: 'We must trust in God. That all He does is good.'

Later Padre Peters stumped off with his sledge to the front line trenches. By day it was impossible to get to them as the field was swept by Russian MGs, but at night it was safe enough. After walking for 600 yards he reached a trench and a bunker.

A sour steaming atmosphere struck him in the face. The men were lying on the ground, their faces black with smoke. Here too they had tried to make a Christmas tree. The outline of a fir tree had been cut from a piece of tent-cloth and stuck on the wall of the dug-out. A few wooden sticks had been driven through it into the clay and lighted candles were fixed to them.

Someone was playing a concertina and the men, coughing and snuffling, were trying to sing to its music. Peters had to lie down, too: there was no room to stand or to sit. He said a few words to the men and then taking Selma Lagerlöfs 'Legends of Christ' read them the story of the Holy Night. The men listened in silence.

Outside the trench again, he stood beside the sentry. The storm had abated and the front was quiet. On the left a flare went up and then a machine-gun barked once like a dog disturbed in its sleep. The Padre shivered.

'It's horrible out here,' he said. 'When are you relieved?'

'In two hours.' The sentry looked steadily across to the other side as he added, 'I volunteered for this watch.' After a while he said: 'I can't listen to Christmas carols any longer. For me God died at Stalingrad.'

'You're right,' he said. 'God has died at Stalingrad thousands of times. He has died with each one of our dead comrades . . . and here at Stalingrad He will rise again.'

After lunch on Boxing Day Breuer and Wiese were sitting alone in their bunker. Fröhlich had gone over to Captain Siebel's office which lay about a mile away in a wood. He particularly wanted to see a Russian Lieutenant-Colonel who was said to be at HQ. Herbert and Geibel were gossiping to friends in the map section, and Lakosch had gone off without a word. The unusual quiet was restful and Wiese was reading by the light of a wax candle, while Breuer was trying to write a letter home. Try as he would, he could think of nothing to say. He was alarmed to find that the gap between here and there had widened and deepened.

'That was a nice speech you made on Christmas Eve,' said Wiese, out of the blue, as he put his book down. 'How did you come to join the Nazi Party?'

Breuer gave him a puzzled look. The question itself and the way Wiese had phrased it seemed unusual. He noticed that Wiese was looking at him quizzically.

'What do you mean?' he said slowly. 'I don't understand.'

'Surely no one who really believes in Christmas can be a Nazi.'

Breuer put down his writing-block and sat up in his chair. He smelt danger and felt unprepared to meet it.

'Why not?' he answered casually. 'I don't see why the two things can't go together.'

'Yes, Breuer, you do. I'm sure of that. Other people may fool themselves—but not you.'

'National socialism is a political movement,' he said. 'Rosenberg's views are not a religious doctrine.'

'They don't make you recite a creed, perhaps, but they do require you to think and behave in particular ways. Haven't they ever supervised the use you make of your spare time? Or checked up on the place where you hang your picture of the Führer, or on the newspapers you read? Haven't they ever forced you to talk about things you don't believe in?'

'No they haven't, Wiese,' said Breuer with a thin, deprecating smile. 'In my home you won't find a picture of the Führer. I read the *Deutsche Allgemeine Zeitung,* pay my contributions to the NS Teachers League and the NS Public Welfare Fund and once a week do my turn of SA Service in a signalling section. Otherwise I'm my own master and I won't have anyone saying . . .'

'You've bought your own security,' interrupted Wiese, looking at the beams in the ceiling. 'You're lucky you're not a Jew or a Freemason or a Social Democrat. With your uniform, your "Heil Hitler" and the money you pay the Party you've earned a semblance of freedom in your own house. But don't deceive yourself, Breuer. The poison seeps through the cracks in the door and you can't buy yourself out. There's only one alternative, if you don't want to lose your own soul.'

Breuer looked at Wiese and their eyes met. Good heavens, he thought, What's this fellow saying?

'You exaggerate everything, Wiese,' he said in a strained voice. 'This either-or of yours doesn't exist. Life is full of compromises. I still read Thomas Mann, and in my book-case you'll find Heine as well as *Mein Kampf.* He tried to smile.

Wiese was not mollified by these explanations and said: 'You're a fellow-traveller—there are millions of them. They're the worst of the lot. It's they who give an air of respectability to the Nazi movement—even to the pogroms and the concentration camps. Stahremberg was quite right when he said that National Socialism was the German form of Bolshevism. The two systems are as alike as apples from the same tree. This war is a struggle for supremacy between two misbegotten brothers.'

'Do be quiet, Wiese,' said Breuer, who felt an indeterminate rage rising within him. 'This is pure enemy propaganda. Your picture is absolutely distorted. Things aren't like that in Germany. These atrocities, for instance—have you ever seen anything of that sort with your own eyes? I haven't.'

'There are none so blind as those who will not see.' Wiese turned over the pages of his book and took out an envelope. 'Here's a letter from my cousin who's a nun in the Convent of St Hildegarde in Eibingen—perhaps I should say, she was. The nuns were turned out of the convent by SS men at two hours' notice. They found themselves in the street with what they could carry and the convent became a school for the NS party . . . go on, read it.'

Breuer declined the invitation. 'You've got to know all the circumstances,' he said sulkily. 'And after all, what a way to look at things! You notice all the small defects, the black spots. Why don't you look at the great achievements of the régime, at what is being created? Work for everybody, social peace, progress and plenty and a unified German State—they're worth living for. Of course there are black spots here and there. You can't go through a great national upheaval without having a few bad elements coming to the top. But you must admit that things have changed a lot since '33. If only the war hadn't come . . . Do you think that the Führer doesn't notice what is wrong? You'll see, after the war he'll have a final clean up and victory will bring fulfilment to the Party and to Germany.'

Wiese looked intently at Breuer and then said bitterly: 'Hitler, of course, the Good, the Noble and the Pure—he only wants the best. It's not his fault, naturally, when things turn out for the worst. He's just been misled by his advisers. That's what you believe, is it?' Wiese's eyes blazed with passion. 'This man,' he went on, 'who has his closest friends slaughtered, who concludes treaties in order to break them; who invades other countries in peacetime and means to wipe them out as soon as he is strong enough to do so! Look again at the face that grins down from every wall. Can't you recognize the devil's smile behind the façade?'

Breuer was petrified by this blasphemy. His idol was being torn to pieces and shamed! Carried away by rage, he shouted: 'Stop! Say what you like about anyone else, but leave the Führer alone. He stands above your filthy lies.'

Wiese nodded like a doctor who sees his diagnosis confirmed.

'All right, Breuer,' he said, 'blow off steam, if you want to, it sometimes helps. At the bottom of your heart you know that I'm

157

right. The greatness you've been talking about has led you to the Cauldron of Stalingrad! We're not in Germany any more—we're at the end of the road. So we may as well face the truth. If we can't face it now we never shall.'

Stalingrad! thought Breuer. It's true I'm in Stalingrad. For a moment he had forgotten it, but now his arguments seemed to loose their force. The frozen air of the steppes had withered them.

Breuer breathed deeply.

'You say terrible things,' he said painfully. 'But you're right. Something has broken . . . I haven't thought it out yet, though I've often wondered if the way we're going was right. I've been tortured by the thought that because it wasn't we can't win this war.'

'We shan't win it,' said Wiese, 'and we ought not to win it.'

Breuer looked at him as if he thought him crazy.

'We ought not to win it! Wiese, for God's sake . . .' Wiese repeated his words firmly. 'We ought not to win this war, Breuer. I know that defeat—after all that has happened—will be terrible. But less terrible than what would happen if we won. I can only pray that our people will save their souls in the ordeal of their defeat. I can see no other way out for them.'

Silence fell and Wiese's words hovered in the room like great grey birds. Breuer seemed to feel their wings beating in his ears. After a while he found his tongue:

'What you're saying, Wiese, is horrible. I think we ought to stop this conversation, but I want you to tell me one more thing. If these are your views, and I believe you are sincere, how can you bear to wear German uniform?'

There was an odd change in Wiese's expression. He winced and he brought out his words with difficulty.

'Yes, Breuer, yes. You are right. Since my eyes have been opened, I ought no longer to be wearing uniform. But . . .' and the shadow of a helpless smile played round his mouth. 'But how many of us are consistent in everything we do? I've embarked on this course and I must go through to the end . . . I can only thank God that in His Grace He hasn't made me to shoot anyone. I swear to you, Breuer, that, whatever happens, I shall never raise a gun against a man.'

He leant forward and took Breuer's hand. 'We're terribly alone, Breuer,' he said. 'I wouldn't like to think that anything had happened to spoil our friendship. You won't hold it against me, will you?'

Breuer shook his head and got up and put some logs on the dying fire.

Gradually the others came back, last of all was Fröhlich who was cheerful and bursting with news.

'Siebel's mess is a damn sight better than ours,' he said. 'They've still got a stock of sweets, and French brandy. You ought to go over there, Lieutenant. Colonel Unold and Captain Engelhard were there and this Russian, Gontsharov, is an interesting chap. He gave Siebel an illuminated text with Christmas wishes in German, saying "German courage and German organization are a guarantee of victory". He's a Russian and one of our prisoners . . .' He looked at Wiese, as he spoke, and added: 'Doesn't say much for his loyalty, does it?'

Late in the evening Lance-Corporal Krause brought the post over from the divisional office. 'They've sent a comic paper too,' he said, 'It's got a few funny things in it.' The paper was called 'News for communication to the Troops' and it was sent to the Intelligence section for distribution to all units. It was one of the only things that the section still had to do.

Breuer glanced at the news-sheet and read parts of it aloud. '"A sanitary unit has fought and defeated three Russian tanks which broke through the line—a proof of the superiority of German morale" . . . "A regiment of Bashkirs has just come into the Russian front line. Ninety per cent are illiterate and their organization is defective . . ." We know that record by heart. Let's put on something else. Here's something interesting:

'"In the sector of Army Corps IV two German stragglers, who had spent four days unrecognized behind the Russian lines have returned. They were able to supply valuable information regarding the composition, strength and weapons of the enemy force in front of us. It appears from their report that discontent owing to ill treatment and lack of food is growing in the ranks of the enemy and no one any longer anticipates the defeat of the encircled German forces. The two soldiers, a sergeant-major and a lance-corporal have been decorated by the General."

'How could they have found out all that?' said Herbert sceptically.

'You're always doubting something,' said Fröhlich venomously. 'I don't suppose *you* would have found out much.'

'I suppose *you* would have,' retorted Herbert.

'Shut up,' said Breuer. 'Here's something else.'

' "The number of Russian deserters is growing. Two who came across in the Sector of the 376th infantry division yesterday said that their unit had had no hot food for four days. They preferred to be surrounded with the Germans rather than to starve with their own people." '

'Do they get extra rations over here?' asked Geibel. Everyone laughed except Fröhlich, who sat grumbling in his corner.

'Joking apart,' said Breuer, 'you mustn't let this rag out of here. If the Corps want to make fools of themselves, they can do so without our help.'

'But you can't do that, Herr Oberleutnant!' protested Fröhlich.

'Very well—you can hang it in the latrines. That's the best way of spreading news.'

Chapter Eight

THE STREET OF BONES

ON 31ST DECEMBER Colonel von Hermann and Unold made their way to Corps HQ. A curt army order, giving no explanations, had summoned them to an important conference.

The Colonel seemed as calm as usual. From the distribution list it seemed that, apart from him, only the GOCs of the five corps were to attend the meeting. He wondered why he, the only Divisional Commander, had been sent for. There must be a special reason. There had been rumours lately of a new plan for breaking the ring. But such a plan would be more difficult to carry out now than it would have been two weeks ago when Hoth was still facing the Mishkova Sector. Far more difficult. The distance from the Cauldron to the nearest German troops outside was now far greater and the physical condition of the troops had declined alarmingly—besides stocks of fuel and munitions were running out. Since airborne supplies did not get through, something had to be done. The troops simply had to get out soon or wait until the last man had died of hunger. It was rumoured that the army were considering the reduction of the bread ration to fifty grams a day.

Outside the wind was blowing the snow over the steppe and a dead horse lay sprawled by the roadside. Its bones stuck through its skin and its skull had been split and emptied.

'Today there must be a decision,' said the Colonel to Unold.

The latter meant to keep his thoughts to himself.

'Hube is back, I believe,' he said. Hube was the GOC of the Tank Force. Shortly before Christmas he had flown to the Führer's HQ to receive the Knight's Cross from Hitler's own hand. Later he had had a few days' leave for his daughter's wedding. The one-armed General was known for his reckless courage. He had been told to describe the situation in the Cauldron in the plainest and baldest terms to the Führer. He had flown off, full of indignation, and it seemed as though his fighting spirit must ensure the success of his mission. Everyone expected his return to herald some decisive action.

Most of the other officers had already assembled in the great bunker at VIIIth Corps HQ when Unold and his Colonel arrived. Only two of the Corps Commanders were present, the others had sent their Chiefs of Staff. That was a relief to von Hermann, who had dreaded the thought of having only his superiors to deal with. Nearly all these officers were known to him.

'Aha, there's the wizard of the tanks. Now we'll have a chance of getting things going, Clausius!'

'Have you heard what Hube has brought back from the Führer's HQ? You'll be surprised.'

Most of them were standing by the map on the wall and Colonel Clausius was holding forth.

'Why shouldn't that be possible?' he was saying. 'Of course it's possible. In the east we must fight a delaying action and in the west we must box our way out with every tank and motor vehicle we can throw in.'

'And so we shall advance, with our back's to the wall, slowly towards the homeland—ha, ha, ha!'

'No, Clausius, much as I admire your good intentions, it just can't be done.'

'Well, what other plans have you gentlemen got for breaking the ring?'

Colonel Clausius was excited. He had worked on his plan for the break-through all through the night. 'We have no alternative,' he said. 'To judge by what General Hube has to say . . .'

'What's that?' asked Hermann.

'He didn't get a chance to explain things properly. Hitler told him we ought to make a fortress—an *alcázar* he called it—and entrench ourselves in the ruins of Stalingrad, as there was no hope of relieving us before the spring.'

Hermann put his hand to his head. Could the Führer really have said that? Good heavens, his troops weren't in Spain, but in the middle of a snowy desert—300,000 of them. If that was his last word ...

'Gentlemen, the Commander-in-Chief.'

There was silence, and then a stooping figure came through the low doorway. It was Paulus, the Commander-in-Chief of the encircled divisions. Hitler's New Year's Message had proclaimed his promotion to full General, but no one in the Cauldron had yet heard the news. Paulus was slim and unusually tall, overtopping most of the others by a head.

'Good morning, Gentlemen,' he said.

They sat down. The C-in-C kept his hands folded in front of him on the table. He said in a quiet but vibrant voice:

'Gentlemen, you're all familiar with our situation, which is so grave that we're forced to come to decisions of the greatest moment. That is why I have asked you to come here today. We must decide once and for all what's to be done.'

Hermann who was sitting opposite him sighed with relief. The proposal to create an *alcázar* seemed to have turned the scales. He looked gratefully at the narrow, spiritual face and well-shaped forehead, the breadth of which was accentuated by the General's brushed-back hair. He looked like an intellectual and would have been handsome but for the twitches and tremors that ran over his face. The Colonel could sympathize with a man on whom destiny had laid so heavy a burden.

'After thorough and earnest consideration,' said Paulus, 'we have . . . that is the Army Staff has . . .' he hesitated and glanced across at his Chief of Staff who was smiling at his pencil. 'I think it would be better if you explained things to the meeting.'

The Chief of Staff bowed shortly and, while Paulus covered his face with his hands, he gazed round the table with a beaming smile which attracted all eyes to him.

'The Führer's message for the New Year is known to you.' His clear voice rang fresh and untroubled through the room. 'The Führer's words have clarified our situation and encourage us all to look to the future with confidence.'

Hermann knew nothing of the Führer's message. He couldn't

understand. Meanwhile Unold was moving uneasily on his chair. The clear, tranquil voice irritated him more and more.

'But this firm confidence,' he went on, 'doesn't free us from the obligation to do everything in our power to improve the situation. Only a fraction of our man-power is at the front; behind the lines are thousands of car-drivers, transport people and so on lounging about uselessly and purposelessly. We must comb out.'

Hermann felt the ground giving way under his feet. He leant back in his chair and closed his eyes. It's all over, he thought. This is the end. Overcome with weariness, he ceased to listen.

'Yes, a thorough comb-out, Gentlemen. I know that you don't like the idea.'

'Comb out!' said an old General banging his fist on the table. 'We *have* combed out. Every man fit to carry a rifle in my force is at the front.'

The Chief of Staff, beaming at the fierce green eyes of the old Tiger, said calmly, 'Well, as long as you find it possible to build such magnificent bunkers . . .'

'Nonsense!' said the Tiger. 'I protest.' But the Chief's shaft had been well aimed. A whole company of Pioneers had been working for weeks on a single bunker.

'Please, gentlemen,' said the Commander looking up with a pained expression. 'The situation is too serious for us to quarrel.'

The Chief of Staff continued as though nothing had been said.

'Here in the Cauldron we still have about 240,000 men. 40,000 of them are in the line while 200,000 sit around in the bunkers with nothing to do: drivers, signallers, gunners without guns, supply trains without supplies. These 200,000 men could furnish at least twenty new battalions. We need these battalions, if we are to hold out until April.'

Two hundred thousand men, thought Unold, but you have to reckon among them all the staff-personnel, the supply and sanitary services, the workshop people and the tens of thousands of wounded. This was thoroughly phoney arithmetic! It would be wonderful to be so persuasive, he thought enviously.

Colonel Clausius was representing General von Seydlitz and he deeply regretted that the General was not there. 'Is it clear to the army staff,' he said 'that this measure means mucking up the whole army? We shall lose our mobility for ever and with it the last possibility of breaking through the ring.'

Paulus seemed uncertain. He had been troubled by the same misgivings, but his Chief of Staff waved the objection away.

'We shall be relieved in the spring. The Führer assured us of that. We must hold on until then and contain the maximum number of Russian troops and prevent them from preparing a spring offensive. We are holding down five Russian armies, gentlemen.'

But Clausius would not own defeat.

'If the Russians were to withdraw their troops and leave us to be destroyed by hunger and cold, there wouldn't be anything we could do about it.'

But whatever he said was useless.

The Chief of Staff went on. 'A staff is being created to organize the new units, armed with far-reaching administrative powers. In that connection I have thought . . . ahem . . . of you, Colonel von Hermann, and your staff.'

Hermann started and sweat beaded his forehead. When this man spoke to him, he felt small and helpless. He was on the point of saying 'Very well, sir,' but recovered himself in time to register his objections.

'Allow me, General,' he said, 'to express certain misgivings. These motor-drivers and gun-team men have no experience of an infantryman's job.'

'We'll train them. We have time. We needn't expect any attack by the Russians before the end of January.'

'We have no qualified officers and NCOs.'

'I've arranged to have a number of experienced NCOs flown in.'

'Then there's the question of equipment, for instance field-kitchens.'

'Difficulties exist to be overcome, Colonel.'

Colonel von Hermann almost believed him for a moment. In the presence of this man all difficulties seemed to melt away.

'That's why I have selected you,' went on the Chief of Staff, looking at Hermann with shining eyes. 'You wanted a more responsible job than your present one, didn't you?'

Hermann suddenly remembered his application for a transfer. 'Yes, General,' he stammered, 'but. . . .'

'Very well, then. Now, you're in charge of the Supplementary Forces of the VIth Army. You have full authority over all the service departments in the Cauldron. I hope that you will devote all your energies and all your personality to this job—and that you will be successful.'

A short discussion followed about a name for the new units. They had to think of something attractive and suitable for boosting morale.

Unold suggested 'Fortress-Battalions', and was furious with himself when he found his pulse quickening under the grateful eye of the Chief of Staff. The others muttered.

'Whoever started this idiotic talk about a fortress?' growled the Tiger. 'A heap of ruins surrounded by holes in the snow is not a fortress!'

In spite of this they approved the name and Colonel von Hermann received orders to organize four new units within the following ten days—the Fortress-Battalions I to IV.

The post arrived with letters from home. It was as surprising, as contrary to all expectation, as the arrival of a man believed to be dead. There was something for almost everybody.

When Breuer opened his letter, postmarked October, a little envelope fell out of it. It contained a sheet of paper over which a childish hand had written in pencil:

'Dear Daddy! I like going to school. Our teacher is called Krakel. I have never been beaten. I send you a picture to give you pleasure in Russia. I painted it for you myself with my love. Mummy always says that you are coming soon. Hans is still too small, but I am already very afraid. Kisses from your Jochen.'

Inside the letter was a piece of drawing paper folded over several times. On it, drawn with coloured pencils Breuer was able to make out a few circular trees, some crooked cottages with red roofs and an enormous church with curiously barred windows. Behind a mass of billowing cloud the sun was pointing its rays like yellow fingers. To the right in a corner, strange to behold, was a second, larger and much yellower sun.

Lakosch got a letter too. When he recognized the handwriting he turned pale, hid the letter in the pocket of his tunic and slipped out. He walked some way into the steppe before he took out the envelope and tore it open. It contained a sheet of paper ruled in squares on which a letter in scratchy handwriting with the lines very close together was written:

'Dear Karl, I want to write to you again. The Kunzes say that you are surrounded at Stalingrad and that everyone will be killed. Now perhaps you see where Hitler has brought us and your father was right. It is your mother who is writing this and its all one to me if they read it. I am an old woman and so many people are dying. Konetzko's eldest has been four weeks at home. Both his legs are off. Yesterday there was again an air raid, but I don't go into the cellar. What's the good? They have taken away your grey suit. You know the one with the stripes as they are collecting textiles. Erna sends her love. Just now she is going with a Feldwebel in the Anti-Aircraft. Perhaps dear Karl you will still come home and let me see you once more. That is what your mother wishes.'

Lakosch did not notice the east wind blowing through his clothes and turning his limbs to ice. He stared with burning eyes at the sheet of paper which trembled in his hands.

Geibel had actually received a parcel. It was impregnated with benzine and so crumpled that it looked as if it had been used as a football. The contents consisted of a Bologna sausage, some gingerbread, sweets and a cake which had crumbled to pieces.

Geibel insisted that everything should be shared out equally and, in spite of the benzine, it tasted wonderful on New Year's eve.

About ten o'clock that night a tremendous noise drove the men out of their bunkers. Outside they saw an extraordinary sight. Above their heads the sky was pitch-black, but all the way round the horizon there was a brilliant garland of fire. Guns of every kind were being fired and the reddish blaze of the individual shots was merged into a single wave of flame. Red, yellow and green flares streamed into the sky in regular fountains and among them tracer bullets flew, sparkling like champagne bubbles. The earth shook beneath the ceaseless impact of explosions.

Breuer stood by Wiese in front of the bunker and watched this wonderful firework display.

'You see the boundaries of our country,' he said quietly. Never before had he seen the ring which enclosed 300,000 German soldiers so clearly—or realized how impossible it was to break through it.

'They're celebrating the New Year,' said Wiese. 'They've got something to celebrate all right.' And then, *à propos* of nothing, he asked: 'Do you remember the names of the two Consuls, responsible for the defeat of Cannae, who left 75,000 Roman soldiers dead on the battlefield?' Before Breuer could grasp the point of the question, Wiese answered it himself. 'The one who brought about the defeat was Varro, an insolent, incompetent clod. He escaped. But the other, who couldn't prevent it, was a cultivated man, an aesthete—and his name was Aemilius Paulus.'

In the morning hours of New Year's Day the men of the divisional staff in Dubininski were called together.

One after another, crawling out of the dug-outs, came the clerks from Intelligence, the drivers, the cooks and orderlies, the men from the registration office, the maps section, and the signals and Field Police. With bent heads they tramped round in front of the Intelligence bunker, slapping themselves with their arms to keep warm and turning their backs to the piercing east wind. The officers were there too—Captain Endrigkeit with his Roumanian sheepskin cap and his snow-powdered beard looked like a Canadian trapper; Fackelmann, yellow and ill, with Wiese, Dierk, Fröhlich and Breuer. They presented a variegated and fantastic medley of strange clothing and headgear, and looked like members of a polar expedition rather than soldiers.

Last of all came Captain Engelhard, stiff and slim in his close-fitting greatcoat. He wore a grey balaclava helmet of thick wool with a visor which covered the bridge of his nose and made him look like a crusader. He formed the men into line and dressed them.

As Colonel von Hermann arrived, Engelhard gave the command. Attention! Eyes . . . right!

A shock went through the men. It sounded like an echo from the past.

The Colonel said: 'Gentlemen, I beg leave to report.' The officers put their hands to their caps in salute. They looked in wonder at the Divisional Commander, who wore neither greatcoat, gloves nor headgear. He had come out, just as he was, from his desk. His face was as smooth as enamel and his thin, carefully parted hair glistened: but there was something disturbing about his exposure to the winter cold, it seemed like a silent but bitter revolt against the pressure of circumstances.

The CO did not tell the men to stand at ease and he himself stood straight and stiff.

'Men,' he said. The wind was blowing hard and snatching the words from his lips. Only some of his words reached the men.

'On the Volga, alone . . . in forsaken outposts . . .' The Colonel's face took on a bluish tinge with white spots on his cheekbones . . . 'but behind us in the west is our home . . . and mothers and wives and children.'

Breuer's hand was still at the salute. He had an irresistible desire to scratch his nose which had now gone numb, but he looked at the Colonel, whose eyes were running with tears of cold, and controlled himself. '. . . to break our way out of here, that's what we hope for . . . but if not, then we shall know that our sacrifice will not have been in vain . . . the front behind us. If that holds, that will be our doing . . . conscious of all this we look to the future with resolution and confidence . . . beloved German fatherland— hurrah!'

The cheer was weakly taken up by the men, caught by the wind, carried off into the snow and lost.

'Dismiss!'

The men dispersed and disappeared into their bunkers. Breuer rubbed his ears and nose with snow.

'The Colonel wasn't particularly hopeful,' he said to Wiese, who was walking near him. 'All the same, we *are* containing five Russian armies.'

'Do you really think so?' rejoined Wiese. 'The Russians have known for a long time that we can't move. They can withdraw whatever forces they want and complete their other operations at their leisure. We can't run away.'

Breuer looked at his companion with horror.

'Good Lord, man,' he groaned. 'You're really the limit. One has to believe something, or life won't be worth living.'

In the bunkers the men were brooding over the Colonel's words. What was it he had said? 'In forsaken outposts? Sacrifice not in vain?' What was the good of that? They shook their heads and listened to the forebodings of the first grey day of the year 1943. The transport planes were flying in spite of the blizzard.

Later the Führer's New Year Message arrived and everyone breathed a sigh of relief. There was no change. It was clear that they meant to come and relieve them. One couldn't sacrifice 300,000 men. The CO must have had some sort of a bee in his bonnet.

Hitler had broadcast——

'YOU CAN RELY ON ME WITH ROCKLIKE CONFIDENCE.'

Colonel von Hermann was not the man to neglect a duty because he found it distasteful. He had been given an order and his own wishes, misgivings and anxieties lost all importance. He set to work with an energy worthy of a better cause, and after a few days he had to admit that the Chief of the Staff was right in many of his conclusions. He found artillery units, who had no more ammunition, signals detachments without instruments, and an observation section without anything to observe. There was a regiment of grenadiers who had long run out of grenades and ammunition. The Flak Division, too, could spare some of their men to join the infantry. Then there were the Roumanians, who wandered about the Cauldron like vagabonds, and numerous stragglers of unspecified origin. There was no lack of men; the difficulty was to convert this untrained, neglected and half-starved rabble into decent front-line troops.

That came later. His first task was to build up the four battalions he had been instructed to have ready to go into the line in ten days. For this Hermann had to get hold of the remnants of his own division. He had an almost complete detachment of Signals, sixty per cent of whom were redundant, the remainder of the Artillery Regiment and the former Anti-Tank Section. During the battles of the autumn and the retreat, they had lost guns and vehicles. Later in the numerous rescue attacks which they had made as Eichert's Fighting Group, they had been further decimated, with the result that they were down to about a third of their original strength. However they were experienced men with trustworthy NCOs and if the remaining seventy per cent were drawn from the Gunners and the Signals, it would be possible after a few days' training to turn them into the first front line battalion of the new force.

Day and night Colonel Hermann worked out plans with Engelhard, had conferences with the leaders of units and drafted orders. Unold helped him with unexpected enthusiasm. He blossomed into a one-man commission of inquiry and had many show-downs with Colonel Lunitz and Captain Mühlmann, the OC Signals. He was like an auctioneer trying to see how quickly he could get rid of his own division.

All this activity was carried on more or less in public and its different aspects produced keen discussion. One day Breuer was talking things over with Wiese. 'Don't be in too much of a hurry,' said the latter. 'Better wait for things to happen.' But Breuer did not want to wait. He had served as an infantryman for the greater part of the war and thought it his duty to volunteer, before receiving an order to go where he certainly belonged. The small amount of Intelligence work that remained could be dealt with by Fröhlich. When he put his case to Unold, he was surprised by the answer he received.

'No, no, Breuer,' said the Colonel, 'Our staff has got to be preserved. An intact and hardworking Divisional Staff is invaluable, Breuer, and we mustn't squander it. I respect your good intentions, but I must ask you to put them out of your mind.'

Breuer went back to his bunker shaking his head. In the early days some staff belonging to disbanded divisions had been flown out of the Cauldron. Was Unold thinking of them? He dismissed the thought as absurd.

Four days later the first Fortress-Battalion marched off to the front line under the command of Captain Eichert.

Lieutenant Bonte, the battalion-adjutant, was furious. He thought the battalion was being disgracefully treated. Housed in half-ruined stables, where the snow swept through the holes in the walls, they had no wood, no stoves, no blankets, while in the neighbouring bunkers nitwits from the paymaster's office were throwing their weight about and puffing out their chests.

Bonte had served in the infantry in Poland, France, Greece and Russia and the fact that he was still alive in spite of the numerous bullets that had passed through him was due partly to his small and wiry frame and his tenacious and wide-awake character and partly to the fact that Providence, as he gratefully recognized, had performed several miracles on his behalf.

He had himself crawled through all the neighbouring dug-outs where, needless to say, he met an ungracious reception and had told the occupants where they got off. He said that a battalion which in a few days would be standing in the filthy trenches had the right to be treated decently as far as possible. He went on to ask them if they were familiar with the new combing out orders and to suggest that their own days in these comfortable quarters were numbered. He threatened to report the situation to the authorities and his hearers turned pale. Suddenly thirty blankets appeared and a truck to fetch fire-wood. The 150 grams of bread, which was the ration for men in the trenches, he meant to arrange even if Captain Eichert had to go to Corps HQ and demand it.

One day on his rounds he found two soldiers standing in front of him. They were wearing dirty camouflage clothing and were unshaven and shivering with cold.

One of them said: 'Lieutenant—have you . . . that is, can we have something to eat?'

'To eat? Where do you belong?'

He said this more roughly than he meant, but the area was full of odd people . . .

'We . . . we came here with the battalion's baggage and our Captain's things. We were told to wait here till we were fetched. We've been waiting now for three days . . .'

'Yes,' said his companion eagerly, 'for three days,' his eyes filled with tears. 'Without anything to eat.'

The Lieutenant nodded, no longer angry. Anyone who got separated was lost.

'I'll see what I can do for you,' he said, and wrote a few words on a piece of paper. 'Where has your unit got to?'

The men looked at one another and one answered in a soft, hesitatant voice: 'Kazatchi Hill.'

The Lieutenant went on. What's the matter with that damned hill, he wondered. He had already heard the name a few times and it was always whispered with a shy look over the shoulder, as though the speaker was talking of the Devil. He climbed into his bunker grumbling. He still had to see the Army Post Office and he was short of a field-kitchen. . . .

'There you are at last,' said Eichert. 'I've been looking for you for half an hour. We've been ordered into the line.'

'Already? They must be in a hell of a hurry,' said Bonte perplexed. 'I thought the battalion was getting a week for training. When do we start?'

'The trucks are coming to fetch us in half an hour.'

'Hell's bells! I must get cracking.' He visualized the things that had to be done and then asked casually: 'Where are they sending us?'

The Captain scratched his head—'Don't mention it to the men, but we're going to Kazatchi Hill,' he said.

The convoy of heavy Büssings ground its way slowly through the snow towards the west. The men sat closely packed together under the awnings, their rifles between their knees, sleeping or dozing. When the wheels slipped unexpectedly into a pothole, there was a clatter of rifles or kitchen utensils, heads knocked together and a few sleepy oaths were heard. Disjointed thoughts flickered through drowsy minds.

Going to the front line!

The experience held no novelty for the old hands who had survived many visits to the trenches when an attack had to be repelled. They knew what a snow-hole was and what it meant to crouch all day long in one without being able to raise their heads till they seemed to have become part of the frozen ground. But there was always an end to those experiences, a return to the refuge of a bunker and the comforting proximity of other units. Would there be any relief this time?

The new boys, those from the artillery and the signals, knew nothing of this. They had had some experience of artillery-fire and Stalin Organs and bombs and low-flying air raids and had milled around with partisans and tanks. But they had no experience to compare with what lay ahead of them nor had they the imagination to visualize it. What would it be like? Would they be fighting without interruption or would there be pauses and reliefs? Were these dug-outs and trenches? What sort of food would they get? And the business of relieving themselves—that couldn't be very easy in a rifle-pit.

The officers, distributed in different vehicles, sat in front by the drivers. Captain Eichert was in the leading truck. Through a portion of the wind-screen was kept clear of ice, he looked out into the greyness of a cloudy day and was grateful to the clouds. He wondered how the driver could find his way in this wilderness. He couldn't have attempted it.

Then he caught sight of something which made him screw up his eyes and lean further forward. By the side of the road, the leg of a horse was sticking out of the snow. And another, and another. On the left a pyramid of bones had been erected, and a little farther on a horse's skull had been stuck on top of a pole. Farther on he saw a man with his head and shoulders buried and his legs sticking through the snow like a pair of candles. A light coating of snow covered the yellow soles of his bare feet.

The driver had noticed Eichert fidgeting and said, 'The street of bones. We had to mark it somehow, because it's always disappearing under the snow. If we put up wooden sign-posts they grab them for firewood. They even collect the bones of the horses.'

Captain Eichert had been in the army for thirteen years and had become extremely tough, but the Street of Bones gave him the creeps.

The cars moved off swiftly because the area was under fire. The men stood in groups on the street, nervously fingering their weapons and listening to the wheeee . . . ow of mortar shells and the crash of detonations. A few threw themselves to the ground at each explosion. They were the new troops and could be recognized by their uniforms. They wore square-shouldered greatcoats and ear-flaps . . . Many of them had no felt boots and some of them were shaking with cold in the thin summer uniforms in which they had been sent to the war in 1941.

Lieutenant Dierk, who commanded the second company, walked up and down and did what he could to calm them. He had already had a lot of trouble with the new men and had come to regard himself as a kind of nursemaid, so helpless had they shown themselves. He hoped they wouldn't have to go straight into the worst of the fighting. Luckily he had his old gunners with him, Sergeant-Majors Menke and Hommen and the stout-hearted Corporal Häring from the second Flak battery—well-tried men who understood trench fighting.

Meanwhile Eichert and Bonte were reporting to Colonel Steigmann in the regimental command post. Eichert was tall—as a recruit he had often been put at the end of the line—but the Colonel was half a head taller.

'I'm glad you're here,' he said. 'You must man your positions at once. The fellows we put in three days ago are all in . . . They've had heavy casualties and must be relieved.' He showed Eichert a map. 'Here's your sector. It's a dangerous corner, especially the right hand side where we join on to the next-door division. You know that the Russians always pick on points like that. What have you brought with you?'

'Two hundred and forty-three men and four officers, Colonel, with eight machine-guns and two four-barrelled Flak guns.'

'That's fine,' said the Colonel with a nod. Eichert noticed the gesture with misgiving.

He said: 'The unit has only just been created. Seventy per cent have been combed out from other services and have had no infantry training.'

The Colonel's face clouded over. 'Too bad,' he said. 'When we heard the words "Fortress-Battalion" we thought they were going to send us men with anti-tank guns and flame-throwers and so on. I'd rather have half a dozen old toughs than a few hundred greenhorns, who merely provide targets for the enemy.'

'We were promised at least eight days training,' said the Captain.

'Well, I suppose the division knows what it's doing . . . We'll see how they turn out. These maps are very important. Look—these crosses here are two wrecked tanks, our chief landmarks. Here are the names of flowers—violet, rose and lily—they're the gunnery observation posts. Those green points with the names of colours—red, mauve and black—represent a further network of infantry-observers. They're linked by telephone and I've got them all connected up to me here, including the artillery. If the slightest trouble starts, it's reported from two or three points and within three minutes the Russians get the whole of our artillery shot at their heads.'

Eichert looked at the map dubiously. It reminded him of diagrams of complicated electrical apparatus and he felt like a stable-boy ordered to drive a train. The Colonel smiled at him and said: 'It looks funny, but without it the Russians would have thrown us out of our positions long ago. I count on you to keep the system working. I'll give you some guides to take you to your positions, but you'll have to wait till it's dark. Remember that Kazatchi Hill is a dangerous corner.'

Eichert felt a lump in his throat. He folded up the maps with unsteady hands. Then he said in a strained voice: 'Colonel, we're supposed to be an independent unit. We belong to no one and there's nobody to look after us. We're strangers everywhere. Do we get any rations here?'

The Colonel looked at Eichert without speaking, his eyes bright. Then he took Eichert's hand, pressed it and said. 'I promise you I'll call up Corps HQ today. But for the moment you have to go to your positions, there's nothing else to do.'

●　　　●　　　●　　　●　　　●

When Padre Peters opened the door of the mud-hut, he was greeted by stifling fumes, a mixture of ether, lysol and pus, as well as the stench of soaked clothes, felt boots and foot-bandages. The low-ceilinged room was crammed with men sitting on benches or squatting on the ground, plucking at their bandages, fingering their damaged limbs or just staring glassily at the wall. A medical orderly was busy with bottles and cotton-wool and a doctor was moving about among the patients. He was the only person who spoke and he shouted rather than talked. He did not notice the Padre.

'Come on, some iodine here! Off you go. Oh nonsense. Now unroll that filthy bandage, man; hurry, please.'

A small, insignificant-looking soldier, his face all eyes, was sitting holding out to the doctor a hand to which a dirty dressing still clung. The doctor unwound it.

'Can't you do it for yourself?' he said. He unwound the bandage roughly, and as the wrapping came off a blue-black gelatinous mass revealed itself. The doctor held in his hand the clean-stripped skeleton of five fingers. He looked at it for some seconds and then stormed.

'Another of these damned frostbite cases. But don't think you can deceive me. I know you and I know exactly how you do it. Shall I tell you what I call it? Self-mutilation—that's what it is.' The man stared at his fleshless fingers and then looked at the doctor helplessly with his mouth hanging open. The doctor pulled himself together, and said more quietly:

'All right, man, don't stare at it like that. Go into the room next door, they'll nip off the bones and in a week you'll be able to shoot again. Off you go. Next!'

So it went on. There were feet, blue and half gangrened, hands, noses, ears and faces terribly swollen and discoloured or covered with blackish boils—malnutrition oedemas and frostbites of the second and third degree. The doctor made the orderly powder them and apply ointment and a green liquid and then bind them up.

'Fit for duty, fit for duty! The next!'

At last there was quiet. The orderly tidied up his things and the last patient slunk out. Only Padre Peters remained and the doctor noticed him for the first time. He showed no sign of pleasure as he grumbled to himself and fingered a cigarette. His lighter would not work and with a curse he threw it on the table and felt with unsteady fingers for matches.

'What's come over you, Doctor?' said Peters, perplexed. 'I hardly recognize you.'

The doctor had at last lit his cigarette. He greedily inhaled a few times.

'Spare me your sermon, Padre,' he said bitterly, 'I know what you want to say—word for word.'

Peters sat down on one of the benches and thought how the man had changed. His hunted air, his angry look, his tobacco-stained fingers. He shook his head.

'I hardly recognize you.'

The doctor threw himself on the plank-bed and gazed at the ceiling.

'D'you know,' he said quietly, 'I hardly recognize myself . . .'

Neither spoke for a moment. The clatter of instruments could be heard from the next room. A glass fell to the ground and broke and the noise brought the doctor to his feet. With a disgusted expression he threw his cigarette stub to the ground and started pacing up and down like a caged tiger. 'Listen, sky-pilot,' he burst out, 'I used to want to be a doctor—not just a medicine man, no, a doctor, a doctor! I wanted to help, to heal, to bring light, sunshine and health—I wanted to see sanatoria made only of glass—I would have liked to invent new methods for curing TB and cancer—to be able to say "We are conquering death". Ha!'

He struck his forehead with his open hand, turned around suddenly and stared at Peters.

'What's the good of trying to conquer death—if this is to be the destiny of man?' He came close up to the Padre—'Do you know,' he whispered, 'what I ought to do? I ought to send all these men straight home, keep them in bed for four weeks, heal them, feed them, coddle them—and then send them to convalesce for three months at the seaside or in the mountains . . . Then, perhaps, they might recover.' He shouted—'But I can't be a doctor. I'm no longer allowed to be a doctor.'

Standing with his back to the door he went on: 'Would you like to know what the SMO told us the other day? He said that the number of casualties was disgraceful and anyhow we were officers first, second and all the time. It was our business to look after the interests of the Command. Do you understand? The interests of the Military Command—the sick, helpless, suffering soldier was of no interest. Only the man who could be made fit to fight and to carry arms was worth while. A tank that had been shot up must be repaired and geared and oiled; if it doesn't get that treatment, it doesn't function. But apparently a damaged man needs no repairs. He's treated like dirt and pushed back into the line. He goes on till he falls and becomes, as it were, scrap-iron. Well, what does that make us doctors? Repair men for fighters, according to the SMO's theory.'

'You've still got a mission, Padre. You have to help the troops into the next world and the way there has become damned easy. We've got to help them to get back to their holes in the ground. But look out, Padre Peters, they'll be coming to you soon and ordering you to dig up the dead and bring them back to life again!'

Peters sat in silence. Yes, he thought to himself; 'To bring the dead to life,' that's it. He wanted to restore to life all the dead hearts he saw around him. He included the young doctor who seemed alive but who, in reality, had lost his life at the siege of Stalingrad.

That night the column plodded slowly down the footpath towards its front-line position. The men stumbled in the darkness, which seemed full of lurking dangers. Cooking-pots clattered and there was a click of rifles while the panting breath and the whispers of the men could be heard along the moving chain. Outlines of wrecked tanks, deep in snow, the tail-end of an aircraft and other unidentifiable shapes showed up suddenly in the darkness. The front was getting near and the air was full of strange, uncanny noises. A flare went up and its limelight glittered evilly over their heads, painting black shadows on the snow. A machine-gun started shooting and the men bunched together, it sounded so close. The path led down to a hollow where it forked. Number 2 Company moved to the right, while the others kept straight on. Suddenly there was an orange flash in front and another and another. The detonations of three shells merged into a single shattering crash. Mortars were at work. The men waited for another volley and then hurried at the double across the danger zone. A toboggan was lying upside down in the snow and near it was a groaning man. They put him quickly on the toboggan and dragged him along with them. Behind them they heard the crash of shells once more. And then they came to a bunker, the battalion's front line HQ. An officer was standing outside. He only noticed the toboggan.

'You too, Jahnke,' he said mournfully, 'an experienced old bugger like you!' He took hold of the wounded man and carried him into the bunker with the help of Eichert and Bonte.

'Where did it get you, old man?' They laid him on the wooden bunk. He was wounded in the thigh and the bone seemed to be damaged.

'I've got another here,' said the Lieutenant, looking at the two officers like a beggar. He was distraught and now, for the first time, seemed really to notice the new-comers.

The bunker was so low that they could not stand up straight in it. It contained a few boxes, two wooden bunks and a wicker table on which a Hindenburg lamp was burning. Garments and weapons hung on the walls. Distant music could be heard coming from an army radio, interrupted from time to time by a metallic, staccato voice.

Eichert seated himself on one of the boxes and fingered a hand grenade he found lying on the floor.

'What are you fussing about?' he asked. 'We're the relief.'

The word 'relief' roused the officer from his trance. 'Relief, yes, yes that's right. Scherner, come along. The relief is here.' Immediately he went into feverish activity. From the second bunk there rose a grey, hollow-eyed figure. 'Come on,' said the Lieutenant, 'first the boxes and then that thing there.' As he spoke he pulled out the cord of the radio. 'Everything on to the sledges—we'll tie Jahnke on the top.' He suddenly stopped talking and seemed to be brooding over something. Then he said absentmindedly: 'You've got to watch it here. Meyer got his yesterday at . . .' and then he stumbled round the bunker as if he was looking for something. 'Where is it . . . I thought it was there . . .'

He went with Eichert to show him the positions. There were fox-holes that only came up to a man's middle and three bunkers to get warm in.

'All full again,' said the Lieutenant, 'full of people—like three days ago.'

Then he took his leave in great haste as though he could not get away fast enough.

Eichert arranged the bunkers with Bonte and the man who had accompanied the party and tested the telephone connections. Everything was in order and the battalion occupied the positions without a hitch. He fixed up a time-table with the Adjutant. They agreed to watch in turn for the first night. . . .

Sergeant-Major Menke said: 'If Ivan comes, he'll be surprised when he gets a bellyful of shot!'

Lieutenant Dierk went over his section once more. The first of the four-barrelled flak guns was well positioned and camouflaged and had a wide field of fire. There was even a bunker in the neighbourhood. The men were in high spirits. Even so Dierk could hardly believe his eyes when he saw that three men had made a fire in the hollow and were talking loudly and carelessly.

'Are you drunk?' he said. 'The Russians'll blast you out of this before you can make a sound.'

The men looked at him incredulously—they were new to the front line.

A voice said: 'It's so cold here, Lieutenant!' Dierk found a man cowering in a hole without felt boots and with only a thin greatcoat. He was quivering like an aspen, and Dierk felt he ought to bring him a few rags and perhaps a blanket or at least a square of canvas. The man wouldn't let him go. He kept on asking questions.

'It's true, isn't it Lieutenant?' he asked through chattering teeth, 'that the Führer won't leave us here? He'll take us out again, won't he?'

The Lieutenant was silent. He remembered the *alcázar* and thought of the General with the message who wasn't able to speak when he came into the Presence. Frederick the Great's generals had thrown their daggers on the ground in front of the King. How was it that the generals of today won battles and wore decorations, if they were so cowardly? Dierk was astonished that such thoughts should come to his mind. The Führer can't know anything about the situation here, he thought. To the half-frozen soldier he said: 'Certainly, man. What d'you think? Of course the Führer will take us out of here.'

As he crept along on his round he felt a lump in his throat and wanted to cry like a baby.

Eichert lay on his wooden bunk and slept on his back. The lantern threw his profile sharply against the mud wall: his short, thick nose, and domed forehead. He snored noisily.

'Captain, Captain!' Bonte was shaking and tugging at him but could not wake him up. At last Eichert sat up, saying: 'No—yes—what's the matter?'

'Dierk's on the line. There's trouble in his sector.' In a trice Eichert was up and had his ear to the receiver. He heard the rattle of machine-guns and Dierk's voice sounded very far away and very faint.

'The Russians are in . . . on the right where the second flak gun is . . . No, we can't get to them. It's a complete surprise without any artillery preparation.'

'Damnation, what a mess! Are the enemy following up?'

'Don't think so. It's fairly quiet for the moment.'

'Try and seal up on the right. I'm coming at once.' Then he rang up Colonel Steigmann.

'Hell and damnation,' said the Colonel. 'What a bloody awful business.' But he was not as agitated as Eichert had expected. Apparently such things happened fairly often. He said: 'Go and fix things up so that it will be all right by morning. Perhaps I can send you some men: and you'll get a barrage.'

Good heavens! thought Eichert—a counter-attack with these half-trained men.

Eichert called out every one of the old hands who still remained. He would be leading the counter-attack in person.

But it didn't come to that. Things happened differently. During the night the Russians, after violent artillery preparation, attacked with tanks and infantry at the place where the line had been breached and smashed in the whole length of line occupied by the battalion, as well as part of the neighbouring sector. It needed the combined efforts of the two divisions to seal off the salient created by this attack in depth, but the old line was never completely restored.

Meanwhile Fortress-Battalion Number 1 had ceased to exist.

Chapter Nine

IS THERE A WAY OUT?

CLEAR FROSTY DAYS began to follow the long spell of grey weather. The mornings were wonderful: with the first light of dawn a violet carpet of fleecy clouds became visible in the east while high in the heavens the last deep-blue shades of night faded slowly. Then the sun rose over the snow-fields, blood-red and gigantic.

The sun climbed higher and higher up the steep, metallic floor of heaven and made millions of tiny ice-crystals glitter in the transparent air like a crust of diamonds. The world looked like a great ice-grotto, majestic but hostile to all that lived. Midwinter, with its cruel beauty, had arrived.

In staff headquarters and in the fox-holes a faith in miracles blossomed and flourished. It was known that the arrivals of transport planes were diminishing daily, but everyone said: 'in three days' time a huge quantity of supplies will be arriving!' It was common knowledge that the Russians were reinforcing along the whole Cauldron Front but reports to that effect were ignored. A rumour that a new relief force was being assembled on the Tschir with fresh divisions from France spread like wildfire. Pilots claimed that they had to fly from Novo-Cherkask or Voroshilovgrad and that Salsk was to be evacuated immediately, but no one believed them—300,000 soldiers could not be sacrificed; it was an absurd idea! The Führer must be preparing a coup, so wonderful and so unique that the world would tremble when it was delivered. People didn't believe their senses any more; they believed a sentence as full of certainty as a prophecy in the Bible: 'You can rely on me with rock-like confidence.'

One of the few men who did not succumb to this dream-world was

Lakosch. He had nothing more to dream of. He saw now that the road which he had followed so far was a false one but he could no longer go back. He saw himself caught like a mouse in a trap. This was the end, without sense or consolation, like a criminal's end upon the electric chair.

He had another trial to bear: his little car had at last ceased to function. Lakosch had taken it over in the spring of '41 in the Volkswagen Works and from then on it had been *his* car. The idea of giving it up had never occurred to him. He had lovingly run it in on the autobahns of Central Germany and had driven it via Sokal into Russia. He had driven it through the dust of the country roads and the cloudbursts of the noon-day thunderstorms, through the wheat-fields and sunflowers of the Ukraine right down to the Black Sea. In the autumn he had driven it through deep mud to Kursk and Orel and then into the icy winter south of Moscow. He had driven it back through the Russian wastes to Voronesh, through the Cossack villages in the elbow of the Don and the yellow sand of the Kalmuck steppe, past caves and tents and camels, to the Volga and at last to Stalingrad. In twenty months of intensive driving Lakosch had learned to love his car; he understood the song of its motor, anticipated all its needs, and had greased and cleaned and fed it. He had taken it to pieces and made spare parts for it, kept it warm with blankets and a small wood fire and even murmured words of encouragement to it as though it was a faithful horse. When BMWs or Horches got hopelessly stuck in the mud; were worn down by the sand or lay helpless by the side of the road, his little car had never stalled. He had driven it over every obstacle until they came to the dug-out at Dubininski. There the little Volkswagen had to stand out all night in the snow, without shelter against the blizzards or the crackling frost. It had waited, patient and uncomplaining, like the others, but it had become more and more difficult to start on the rare occasions when he still had to drive it. One day the clutch would not work any longer; the lining had finally worn away.

His head sunk between his shoulders and his hands deep in the pockets of his greatcoat, Lakosch stumped back through the gorge. The snow crunched under his feet, and red-brown shell-holes pitted the road. Behind him he heard the thud of hammers and the clatter of machines. They told him it would take three weeks to repair but who could tell what would happen in three weeks? Lakosch had said good-bye to his car, feeling sure that he would never see it again.

It was dinner-time and the men stood in a long queue with their pots and pans. Round the field-kitchen the ground had been trodden into brownish slush on which the frost outside was always encroaching from the edges.

Lakosch was wondering how he could manage to get a plateful of soup when somebody called:

'Hey, Karl!'

Lakosch looked up casually. Karl is a common name and he did not expect to find acquaintances in the southern sector. In the doorway of a bunker stood a man with two cooking-pots in his hand, calling and waving. He was trying to attract Lakosch's attention. The latter turned to the left and walked across and the nearer he came, the wider he opened his eyes. The man there was . . .

'I'll eat my gas-mask!' he cried. 'I thought you were dead.'

He found himself facing Lance-Corporal Seliger, the 'Sausage', the mess orderly who had vanished and been reported dead. But here he was grinning all over his face.

'Dead! Hell! Did you really think that?'

This man with his baby face, was really Seliger. The ribbon of the Iron Cross, second-class, shining brightly in his button-hole was new. He had two saucepans full of snow in his hands.

'You old bastard,' he said. 'What are you doing here? Come right in and warm yourself. The old man's out.'

They went together into the bunker which was large and cheerful like a cottage room. There was even a table-cloth and curtains in the windows.

Seliger helped Lakosch out of his heavy overcoat.

'Sit down and tell me what the staff's doing?' He pulled out a box of cigars and put a bottle and a couple of mugs on the table. Lakosch couldn't get over his surprise.

'No, you tell me about yourself,' he growled. 'I thought that you and Ten Shun had gone off and got yourselves killed.' He couldn't take his eyes off Seliger's ribbon.

Seliger poured out a full glass. 'I suppose you've stopped reading,' he said. 'There was a lot about it in the bulletin.'

'About what?' asked Lakosch crustily. Seliger was throwing his weight about and giving himself airs which he did not appreciate.

'Why, man, the bits about the Sergeant-Major and the Lance-Corporal; how they got behind the Russian front.'

Then Lakosch remembered. It had been in the news shortly before Christmas that the men had made jokes about it.

'D'you mean to say that was you?'

'Certainly it was. Cheers!'

They clinked their mugs, which made a tinny sound, and drank powerful rye spirit, tasting slightly of benzine.

'I'm here with Captain Kollasius as his batman—supposed to be convalescing after my fright. The Captain does something about spare-parts for the army. He doesn't get back before the evening, so . . .'

He took a cigar from the box, bit off the end and spat it on to the floor. Lakosch did the same. He felt extremely hungry, but it wasn't the moment to think of food. They'd all thought the report was a hoax and he was very much looking forward to hearing the real story.

'Come on then, tell me about it. It must be quite a story.'

'You're right—it was.' Seliger took a pull from his mug, put the saucepan on the stove and shoved in some more wood, and then he began. He explained about the JU that had gone astray, lured by Russian signals, and the plan to blow it up. He and his companions had been surprised by Russian fire while sheltering in a bomb crater. and had seen that they were cut off from behind by a Russian patrol. Then there had been nothing for it but to go on, through the Russian lines. Seliger told his story cleverly; it was evident that he was making the best of it—and not for the first time. They had found an empty bunker far behind the front and had crept into it. The two occupants had gone out to fetch food. When they returned Seliger and his companion, maddened by hunger had killed them and taken their uniforms.

He went on to tell of adventurous experiences with Russian stragglers, of the atmosphere on the other side and of their many dangers and daring deeds until at last one foggy night they had risked the return journey to their own lines. In the intervals he addressed himself to the bottle and gradually his speech grew heavy. He didn't notice that Lakosch had become silent and that his face had clouded over. Finally he began to speak of the numerous occasions on which they had received special privileges since their return.

'Shut up!' interrupted Lakosch curtly. Such a story was just possible of course, but he knew Seliger for a hopeless coward.

'I don't believe it,' he said.

'Whatever d'you mean?' asked Seliger stupidly.

'About you and Ten Shun, of all people!'

'Now, perm—permit me to say,' said Seliger, opening his glassy eyes.

Lakosch recognized his mistake. There was something wrong with the story. The bit about the JU and the party who volunteered to blow it up was official; so was the fact that the volunteers had been absent for days and then suddenly turned up again. Everything else was probably a pure invention. What could really have happened?

He had to get it out of Seliger.

'I didn't mean you,' he said, diplomatically. 'I was thinking of Ten Shun, old man. He would never have had the nerve . . . After all, I know him as well as you do.'

Sliger's head nodded up and down. He made convulsive efforts to regain control of himself.

'Ten Shun,' he growled. 'That creeper.'

'Yes, yes,' put in Lakosch. 'That's just what I mean.'

Seliger raised his forefinger and wagged it under Lakosch's nose.

'I'll tell you something, Karl. You've always been my friend. That fellow is a lousy great bastard. Do you think he talks to me today? Before it was Seliger here, Seliger there all the time. But now that he's a Lieutenant with an Iron Cross, first-class, he doesn't want to know me.'

'Disgusting,' confirmed Lakosch eagerly. He saw that he had found Seliger's weak spot.

'A swindle, that's what I call it,' said Seliger, sweeping his hand over the table and upsetting one of the mugs. 'Pay attention, Karl, to what I'm telling you. The dirty dog is going to fly home, while he leaves me to rot here. In six days I've got to go back to the unit—then what'll I do with this piece of tin?' He brought his hand down with a bang on the Iron Cross. 'But he can't do this to me, Karl. If I have to stay, that bastard will stay too.'

The water on the oven was boiling over, but neither of the men noticed it. Seliger grabbed Lakosch's mug and drained it. Then he leant far over the table and grasped the other man's hands.

'You—hic—you were always my friend Karl—you remember how . . .'

'Of course I remember. But now . . .'

'You're my friend, Karl, my only, only friend. You must—hic—avenge me, when I'm dead.'

Seliger emitted simultaneously a sob and a belch.

'Promise me that, Karl.'

'Yes, of course I will—but why?'

'You've got to get this bastard out for me. You'll know—hic—everything. That is my tesh—teshtament—the teshtament of a dead man. When the green grass covers me, Karl, promise me that.'

The notion of his death overwhelmed him. He clutched at the bottle with trembling hands and began to sing.

'*Upon my gra-ave shall crimson ro-oses bloom.*' Lakosch stood up and took the bottle out of his hand.

'Your testament. Let's hear it.' Seliger heard no more. He sang and tears rolled down his face. '*Rohoses red as blood and . . .*' Lakosch caught hold of him and shook him. 'Your testament, I'll break your bones, if you won't tell me.'

'My testament,' trolled Seliger. His head fell forward and the spittle flowed from his mouth. He fell heavily over the table. Lakosch hit him and shouted curses into his ear, but there was nothing to be done. The hero had departed, taking his testament with him.

Lakosch stood up thoughtfully. If he had only taken the bottle away in time. The whole story stank of trickery and he was determined to get the truth somehow. He did not mean to let go of Seliger, who lay there snoring like a walrus.

He put on his overcoat, muffled up his head and looked round the bunker for something to eat.

He found a crust of bread and the remains of some meat-loaf in a tin and took them away with him as well as four of the cigars. When the Captain came and saw the mess, Seliger would get it anyway. He didn't think the four cigars would greatly matter.

Lieutenant Breuer had been busy for a long time.

During the battles of the autumn a vehicle belonging to the anti-tank brigade had been captured in an evening ambush. In it there had been orders and instructions marked 'Secret' and 'Distribution to Military Personnel Only.' When the loss was reported Captain Eichert received an angry questionnaire from the army which he took to Breuer saying: 'You might fill up this rubbish for me, Breuer. I was never much good at pen-pushing.'

In the meantime the anti-tank brigade had ceased to exist and the Russians had captured masses of orders identical with those lost with this vehicle. This had not prevented the third questionnaire from arriving.

(1) Why had the brigade continued to carry instructions dating from the time of the campaign in France which, according to instruction XY No 6, should have been destroyed not later than 1.8.41?

(2) Was the driver of the vehicle entitled to carry secret documents and had he taken the necessary oath to perform such duties faithfully?

(3) Had he been properly instructed about the handling of secret and top-secret documents according to the regulations, i.e. had he furnished evidence in writing of his familiarity with the regulations?

(4a) If not, because of what special emergency had the conveyance of the said instructions been entrusted to him?

(4b) If the answer to question 3 was in the affirmative, why had he not, when he recognized the danger, obeyed the instructions and employed the hand-grenades provided for the purpose to blow up the vehicle, irrespective of the possibility of destroying it by fire?

Breuer read out this document to Wiese, who laughed more heartily than he had done for days. They concocted a reply together. It ran:

'A searching examination of the driver in respect of points 1 to 4*b* of your questionnaire unfortunately led to no conclusive result, since the man in question had died in the meantime. The cause of death, as certified by the medical officer, was an apoplectic stroke which carried him off as he was reading your third questionnaire.'

Just as Breuer finished copying out this reply, someone pulled open the door of the bunker and called 'Lieutenant! Quick! Something's happening.'

He recognized Geibel's childishly excited tones.

'What's up?' called Breuer, but Geibel had already gone. He put on his greatcoat and hurried out, arriving just in time to see a JU 52 coming from the west diving steeply towards the ground. A grey fighter was just behind spitting tracer bullets into her. The JU ducked still deeper and in doing so brushed the ground, breaking off the undercarriage; then, reeling and staggering, her grey body slid over the ground for a bit in a flurry of snow. The fighter shot away, but returned and swept once more in a scornful dive over its victim after which it vanished like an arrow into the blue.

Soldiers rushed from all sides towards the wrecked machine. Lakosch ran up panting with Herbert and Geibel. As he ran, a thought came to him and he called to Geibel: 'Go back, Tiny, go and fetch all the pots and pans and a square of canvas as well.' Geibel obediently trotted back. A JU was a gift from the Gods. She might contain chocolate, or dripping or bread—tons and tons of bread. The stuff they dreamt about at night in the bunkers. Of course, she might be carrying munitions or fuel oil, but no one dreamt of them.

Breuer was one of the first to reach the spot and walk round the machine. It had left a deep track skidding through the snow and was leaning slightly to one side. The left wing was broken off and one of the engines had made a hole in the body of the plane when it struck the ground. Blue flames were stealing out of the fracture like will-o-the wisps.

Meanwhile a crowd of men had gathered. They pulled open the side door out of which a stream of cardboard boxes flowed. Some of these burst open and a yellow powder poured out of them into the snow. The soldiers tasted it and one of them cried 'pea-flour', and they all began to carry it off in their caps and their pockets. Then some of the men climbed into the plane and started throwing out parcels which were immediately carried away.

The burning engine roared and crackled. The blue flames licked greedily around them and, turning yellow, shot up hissing into the air. The snow below started to melt and form dirty puddles and from the stern of the machine smoke began to issue.

Suddenly there was a cry.

'There are still people inside.'

Of course—the crew. No one had thought of them, but now they could be seen. Faces showed through the windows of the pilot's cabin, past which the smoke was streaming in clouds. Now they could hear the sound of hammering and shouting—sounds muffled as though they were coming from a cellar. The door leading to the cockpit from the inside of the machine must have been blocked in the crash and the crew were imprisoned. 'A hatchet!' called someone, 'get a hatchet!' A few men ran back to the bunker-town.

Now the fuselage was on fire too, and, in the hope of getting at the flour quicker, someone tore off the hatch at the stern of the aircraft. The rear-gunner rolled out. He had been wounded in the head and was unconscious but apparently still alive. They laid him on a cloak and carried him off.

In the forepart of the plane the heat grew greater and kept the curious crowd at a distance. Suddenly, with an explosion which shook the ground, a great flame shot into the air. The fuel tank had burst. The motor glowed red hot and now the material of the wings caught fire. Purring and hissing the bluish-white flames devoured the woodwork. All the time the distorted faces remained glued to the window.

'God!' groaned Breuer. 'We must do something. We can't stand by and see two men burnt to death. The hull of the plane must be broken up.' But he had nothing to do it with—not even a side-arm. Lakosch was carrying his bayonet, thanks to Harras and an additional spell of guard-duty. He sprang on to one of the wings and rushed into the smoke followed by another man. They broke the glass panes, but to no purpose, for the openings were too small for a man to get through and the fresh air only prolonged the agony of the imprisoned men. Their piercing cries could be heard through the roar and crackle of the flames.

'He . . e . . lp—— He . . e . . lp—oooh !'

A few paces away the soldiers were busy gathering up the flour. Shouting and fighting they pulled off their coats and tunics and scooped up meal and snow and dirt together and carried it away in cook-pots and boxes and caps.

There was a detonation and cries of 'look out'. The mob dispersed as the ammunition went up. Cartridge cases buzzed through the air and one of the scavenging soldiers caught fire. He rushed screaming from the blaze and rolled himself in the snow like a dog.

At last the tools arrived—hammers, iron bars and jacks—but by now the cabin was wrapped in flame and it was impossible to approach it. Through the smoke the pain-distorted faces were still visible leaning out of the broken windows. The bystanders could see the whites of their swollen eyes and their agonized faces. Their cries were terrible to hear; shrill at first, then sinking to a deep croaking and flickering up again to more piercing and rending screams.

Breuer groaned and felt his stomach heave, but he couldn't tear his gaze away. Wiese stood by him—a figure of stone. He wanted to run away too, but he could not move. He was aware of nothing around him, only of these faces surrounded by flames—no longer human faces. He was waiting for a miracle, but no miracle took place.

In a sort of trance Wiese felt for his holster, took out his pistol, loaded it, pushed forward the safety catch and raised the weapon to the height of his eyes. Six times he fired the pistol and the faces disappeared from the window; only the crackling of the fire was heard as the flames consumed the plane.

Breuer watched and breathed a sigh of relief. He too would have shot, if he had had a weapon handy . . . Then he suddenly realized that it was Wiese who had fired. Wiese, who had sworn never to raise a weapon against a man, come what might. He looked at his friend, who stood there with his face as white as chalk and his eyes

G

unseeing. The pistol had fallen to the ground. Breuer laid his arm on his shoulder and led him away. Wiese moved like an old man and the crowd of soldiers made way in silence for the two officers.

Behind them the mob still battled for flour, their faces black and their eyes red from the smoke. The ground near the plane was black and so was the pea-flour and sparks were glowing in the midst of it. But they scrabbled and scratched, and, panting, carried away what they could.

The JU burned out completely. For yards all round the earth was blackened and the wreck glowed and smouldered for hours.

Colonel von Hermann appeared later.

They had recovered the bodies of the two airmen——or what remained of them. The Colonel took off his overcoat and spread it over the bodies.

That evening there was pea-soup in the Intelligence bunker——a full saucepan for each man. It was so thick that a spoon would stand up in it and the slight taste of burning put no one off. Geibel even found it exciting. And Lance-Corporal Herbert, who had taken a lot of trouble preparing it, was indignant because Lieutenant Wiese wouldn't eat any.

When Lakosch went back to see Seliger, he was greeted gruffly. Seliger seemed determined not to let him into the bunker and his face mirrored his unpleasant memories.

Lakosch, however, was determined and had no intention of allowing Seliger to slam the door in his face.

'I've come about your testament, chum. What is it you want me to do?'

Seliger looked blank and said he couldn't remember anything about it.

When Laskoch pressed him, he only said: 'Stuff it!' and turned to go into the bunker. 'All right,' said Lakosch. 'You've already told me enough. I'll report you.'

'Told you what?' said Seliger, casting around, 'I haven't told you anything at all.'

'Quite enough,' said Lakosch on the off-chance, 'to get you and Ten Shun hanged.'

Seliger stared at him in horror. Then he took Lakosch by the arm and drew him into the bunker. This time there was no rye and no cigars, but to make up for that Lakosch was able to get the whole story out of the frightened Seliger.

The two men had been surprised in their bomb crater by a Russian patrol. Harras, who had been hit on the head by a lump of earth during the firing and half-stunned, was quickly brought to life by kicks and blows from rifle butts and they had been taken back at the double behind the Russian lines. There they were first relieved of their watches, wallets, pocket-knives and rings and then made to pass a ghastly night in a hen-house in the expectation of being shot through the back of the neck in the morning. Sure enough soon after it was light they were blindfolded and the Russians fired a few shots past their ears, but in the end they were put into a truck and driven at breakneck speed to some staff office. There they got friendly treatment, food—'white bread, I tell you, and butter and a bit of bacon as big as your fist and tea with sugar and . . .'

'Yes, yes, go on,' urged Lakosch, not interested in the Russian menu.

Then came the questioning. 'Do you know, Karl, they knew more about us than we do ourselves. They knew everything. The name of the Company Commander and the Sergeant-Major and how strong we are and all about the 100 grams of bread . . .'

Then two Germans had suddenly turned up.

'Germans?'

'Yes, chum, Commie deserters or something.'

It appeared that these men had told them that the Russians proposed to polish off the Cauldron in a few days, that the German defence would be smashed to pieces and that it was all Hitler's fault. They asked them to agree that Hitler had brought bad luck to Germany. Harras had kicked him under the table and they had both nodded and said yes—they did. 'Then one of them, a fellow with a criminal-looking face, asked if we wouldn't like to return to the Cauldron and advise our friends to break away from Hitler, who was ruining everything, and put a stop to this senseless resistance. The Red Army would guarantee their safety—you know, the same stuff we get in the leaflets.' At that point Harras kicked him again and they had looked at one another and pretended to think it over. Finally they had said that they would be glad to.

One evening they had been blindfolded and led back to the front, where they had been given back their watches and rings and money. In the night they had sent them back to their own lines with a packet of leaflets and newspapers and a hand-written letter to the regimental CO.

Lakosch couldn't keep quiet any longer, 'What did you do with the leaflets?' he cried.

'Sh,' said Seliger in terror, and hurriedly told the end of the story. They had sheltered in a bomb-crater and buried all the stuff in the snow and invented a story to tell when they got back. 'He gassed about promotion and medals and said they would certainly fly us out to submit a report to the Führer's HQ. It made me quite giddy to hear him, Karl. Well, you know what happened after that.'

Lakosch's hand moved backwards and forwards along the table. He was clearly in a state of tremendous excitement.

'Germans, did you say these blokes were? Real Germans?'

'That's right, the one with the criminal face and the little one. He said he was a writer from Hamburg and that we must know him from the leaflets. Later a tall chap came in, with a squashed ear, and said he was a Captain and had been a prisoner since '41 and that all the talk they feed us about the Russians shooting their prisoners was absolute bunk.'

Lakosch bit his lower lip and said: 'Listen to me. It's a bit thick not having reported all this. Just imagine what would happen, if Paulus knew.'

Seliger sprang to his feet and raised his hands imploringly. 'For God's sake, keep your trap shut, man,' he cried. 'They'd put us all against a wall. You swore you'd hold your tongue.'

'Yes, yes,' said Lakosch quietly. His thoughts were far away. With a curt 'so long' he started to walk home accompanied by the protests and supplications of the jittering Seliger, who walked with him as far as the gorge. If Paulus knew . . . a plan was forming in his head.

Next morning when the occupants of the Intelligence bunker awoke, they found that Lakosch was missing. They supposed that he had gone off on one of his lonely walks, but when he didn't return in the afternoon, they began to be anxious. They found that none of his things were there and a suspicion arose, so dreadful that no one dared to voice it. Geibel ran around the bunker-town searching and asking, but nobody had seen Lakosch. In the evening Breuer decided to report his absence to Unold.

The Colonel burst out in a rage:

'Deserted of course—that's as clear as daylight. And from our staff! I never cared for that red-haired Slav, blast his guts! But, of course, you didn't notice anything, you innocent, silly sheep! Don't report this case to anyone higher up for God's sake! It'd ruin our good reputation.'

The incident knocked the stuffing out of Breuer. Now he thought how quiet and disturbed the little man had been for a long time past, and he reproached himself bitterly for not having done something about it. I should have noticed it and spoken to him, he thought. My God, how little we know of one another.

Lakosch's disappearance disturbed all his companions. Everyone thought about it, but no one dared to talk of it. His name was never mentioned.

Colonel von Hermann was sitting alone in the Staff bunker. He had a cheap title and fewer worries, and that pleased him. After three Fortress-Battalions had been formed out of the remnants of the Tank Division, the army had handed over the duty of finishing the job to the CO of the mortar regiment, whose unit was next for incorporation in the new force. Unold and Engelhard were on their way to see about the transfer.

There was a knock. It was Corporal Schmalfuss, a clerk in Divisional Intelligence.

'Excuse me . . . Is Colonel Unold not there?'

'No. What have you got there? Is it anything important?'

'Not particularly, sir—it's about the property of the two dead officers from the Junker. I wanted to know what we should do with their things, as there are no papers left.'

He put a few blackened but undamaged coins, a half-melted silver pencil and a yellow lump, that must have been a ring, on the table. The stone round which the gold ring had melted was intact. It was red and smoothly polished. On it was a crest——

'Colonel!'

Corporal Schmalfuss took a step towards von Hermann. He looked frightened to death.

'Thank you,' said the Colonel in an unrecognizable voice. 'Leave me alone, please.'

When Unold returned later and wanted to speak to his chief, he was shocked at the change in his appearance. He didn't dare to ask for an explanation when he looked into Colonel von Hermann's eyes. He forced himself to act as though he had noticed nothing, but wondered all the more. Had the evil genius of the Cauldron gripped this self-confident steadfast man—this model soldier? He couldn't help feeling a kind of malicious satisfaction and drank a cognac on the strength of it.

He had failed to notice that the photo in the silver frame, which had been on the Colonel's table, was no longer in its place.

The car was ploughing its way painfully through the snow. In the back, warmly wrapped up in overcoats and rugs sat Breuer and Captain Gedig.

Gedig had arrived the night before at the Pitomnik airfield. His plane was late—much later than was expected. Gedig had chafed at the delay. He did not realize that no one had missed him. He had come by the mail train from Germany and had run into the middle of the catastrophe between the Donetz and the Don. Arriving at Tatsinskaya he found that the train went no farther. However the place was one of the airbases for the transport fleet and was only 250 kilometres from Stalingrad. He was met with sardonic laughter when he showed his ticket. 'Stalingrad? Why do you want to go to Stalingrad? Stay here, there's trouble enough here.' It was no longer possible to fly from Tatsinskaya into the Cauldron. Two days before the transport fleet had had to clear out at the last moment, when the T34s bombarded the runways. They would not allow Gedig to leave and put him in charge of an emergency unit consisting of leave-men and stragglers. When his unit had ceased to exist and the situation was stabilized, he at last managed to get away. A supply column took him as far as Morozovskaya. But again, he was too late. On 2nd January, Bomber Squadron 55, which carried supplies for Stalingrad, had transferred to Novocherkask, as the airfield at Morozovskaya could only be used for short-range flying. After working his way to Novocherkask on the Don, he managed to find a corner in a Heinkel 111 and covered the 350 kilometres to Pitomnik, cooped up among barrels and packing-cases.

At last he had arrived.

He did not tell any of his friends about his experiences during the past two weeks. What was the good? He had seen with his own eyes that the army had nothing to expect from outside, but almost as soon as he had got down from his plane he realized that here they still believed the opposite. Gedig was touched by this unshakable confidence and began to look on Stalingrad as a battle of heroes. He had not seen the Roumanians streaming in flight through Buzinovka or the funeral-pyre of the retreat. He knew nothing of the fox-holes in the west nor the slaughter at Kazatchi Hill; nothing of the 100 grams of bread. His box was full of Christmas cakes and biscuits and chocolate. Even the memory of the house-to-house fighting in the autumn and the companies reduced to a dozen men had faded. He still believed he saw an army of twenty-two divisions in a fortress; twenty-two unconquerable divisions entrenched behind ramparts of concrete and steel. He did not realize how much the seven weeks in Germany had changed him, and that he was looking at Stalingrad through the eyes of those at home. Whereas, while in Germany, it had been his duty to put people on their guard against cheap optimism, he believed that it was now his duty to strengthen the confidence of his companions here.

He told no stories of his experiences on his way to the front; instead he talked of Berlin.

'Yes: I had a wonderful time there. Not much to show that a war was going on except the black-out and occasional air-raid warnings. Theatres, cafés, bars and cinemas packed. People have to do something with their money. Everything was just as it used to be. Morale? Well, of course news filtered through from the front and the relatives of the dead felt bad about it, but otherwise everything was normal . . .' Breuer listened to him quietly. It sounded like a tale from the 1001 Nights and Gedig seemed like a being from another planet.

Colonel von Hermann sat in the front seat by the driver, staring fixedly at the snowy road. His face looked waxen. He was thinking of the new job which was bringing him to the southern sector at Zybenko, and was forcing himself to think of that alone and nothing else. The job was a strange one.

The car stuck in a drift and they had to get out and push. It was bitterly cold on this January day and the men's breath went up like smoke in the keen air. Some Roumanians dressed in rags were shovelling the snow away, their shaggy faces ash-pale. They helped to push the car, but they were so weak they could hardly hold their spades. The Colonel gave them a few cigarettes.

By the time they reached their destination it was dark. A triangular pennant pointed the way to a narrow defile, with a row of dug-outs from the entrances of which a faint light issued. The staff of the Infantry Division lived here.

The General's bunker was lit by two electric lamps. At a table covered with maps sat a Lieutenant-Colonel. He had a young, fresh face, and was eagerly making notes with a charcoal pencil while, with his left hand, he held a telephone receiver to his ear. The General was pacing up and down the room wearing a shabby battle-dress, open at the top, his skinny neck protected by the rolled-collar of a woollen pullover. With his whitish hair and the long grey stubble on his face he looked like the skipper of a trawler.

Colonel von Hermann introduced himself and the gloomy eyes of the General lit up.

'Thank God you're here! Thank God!' said the General, shaking both his hands. 'What are you bringing with you?'

Hermann looked up in astonishment. Doesn't this man know what brings me here, he thought?

'I'm bringing these two officers of mine,' he said.

'What do you mean? That's impossible. They told me . . . Where are your tanks?'

'Tanks?' A flicker of a smile passed across the Colonel's face. 'We have had no tanks for a long time, General.'

The General's hand went to his neck as though his collar was too tight for him.

'What shall I do, then?'

His hand fell and his quivering lips murmured again, 'What shall I do?' He walked quickly to the map-table.

'Come and look. Yesterday the Russians broke through at these two places and we sealed off one of them by scratching up all the men we could lay hands on. I have thrown the Signals people into the second breach. The regiment on the left has just reported that the Russians have got through, one battalion strong, and are marching to the north. Marching, d'you understand? Marching! There's nothing to stop them, nothing. I can't spare a single man.'

The telephone rang without interruption with a series of disheartening messages. The lively Colonel, with the rosy face, dropped the receiver for a moment with a look of discouragement: then his pencil began to move across the writing-pad again. The telephone rang again: 'What, Colonel? You can't do it? It *must* be done. It *must* be possible to withdraw two more sections from the battalion . . . Post a man every thirty yards and keep the rising ground raked with MG fire. No, I can't send you anyone. You've *got* to do it like that. The General? Yes, these *are* the General's orders. That's all.'

'You're an experienced Tank Commander,' said the General to von Hermann. 'You understand situations like this. Tell me honestly, do you see any way out?'

Von Hermann shrugged his shoulders and said nothing. The task the army had assigned to him seemed absolutely meaningless. He was to take over the command of the regiment on the right of one division together with the regiment on the left of the adjoining division—a new sort of divisional command. The army staff seemed to think that by creating a new command they could save a desperate situation. It was lunacy! Soldiers were needed not commanding officers. Rested, fighting-fit men! He thought of the three Fortress-Battalions, which he had created, but they had long ago been put into the line and he had heard no more of them.

The General broke the oppressive silence:

'The Corps promised me 200 more men. One might do something with them . . . We've been waiting for them since noon.'

There was another silence. The feeling of helplessness weighed heavily on the Colonels and the General continued to stride up and down.

Breuer and Gedig sat on a bench by the wall. Gedig laid his hand on Breuer's arm and his eyes wandered to the General, the Colonel at the map-table and from him to von Hermann and back to the General. He hadn't grasped the situation.

The door creaked on its hinges, the curtain was pulled aside and two officers pushed into the bunker. One of them wore white camouflage and looked like an old man, walked bent over and seemed hardly able to place one foot in front of the other. With an effort he raised his hand to salute and announced in a muffled voice:

'Captain Ulrich with 200 men for duty . . .' The General rushed up to him. 'At last! We've been waiting for you. You must immediately . . . but you don't look well. Is anything the matter with you?'

'Just got up, sir. Been in hospital for six weeks—rheumatism in the joints.'

'Good Lord, what are you doing here? I need soldiers, not cripples.'

'Soldiers,' the officer said swallowing, 'All my men have come from hospital either wounded or sick—and only a quarter of them have winter clothing.'

The General stared helplessly at Hermann and the Colonel for a few seconds, then he turned on the Captain with a stream of angry words.

'The situation is deadly serious. I can't help you, man. We shall probably all die like dogs here . . . Now look. This ridge is your section. You've got to hold it at all costs—hold it to the last man. Tell the men that the fate of the whole VIth Army depends on them.'

The Captain didn't move but looked at the General in silence. Then slowly and with a visible effort he said:

'General, we have had nothing to eat since early morning. Could we . . .'

'But of course, naturally. Here, Supplies Officer, issue these 200 men with marching rations. Quickly, there's no time to lose.'

The Supplies Officer, who had come into the room with the Captain, breathed audibly.

'It's impossible, General.'

'What? It *must* be possible. That's what you're there for.'

'I *have* nothing, General. We get 150 grams of bread each. I receive it daily and issue it daily. I have no more. Really I haven't, if it was two or three men I might manage—but not 200!'

The General seemed to crumble up. He made a helpless gesture and said quickly:

'Well, then you'll have to go as you are.' He walked up to the speechless Captain and seized his hands as the tears ran down his face.

'It's frightful,' he whispered, 'I know it. But I can't help you.'

There was dead silence in the bunker, while the Captain slowly turned and went out.

'My God,' murmured Gedig. 'My God!' At last he understood what he had come back to.

After some delay the army, at the instance of Corps HQ, cancelled the idiotic order creating Colonel von Hermann's new command. The General said good-bye, casually, to his visitors and stood for a while by his Chief of Staff looking at the map.

Colonel von Hermann and the other two climbed into their car. As they drove slowly off they saw, through the misty safety glass, the ghostly company of the 200 marching past them—a row of faces, looking less like men than like death masks. The drive back was very quiet. An icy wind was blowing. It came through the sides of the car and ate its way through rugs and overcoats but the officers hardly noticed it. What they had seen had chilled them to the heart. Gedig talked no more of Berlin and his experiences between the Donetz and the Don seemed like a childish adventure. Only one thing now possessed his mind—the death march of the 200. He could not forget the sight of them dragging themselves past the car in their summer coats and field-caps with their ears and hands tied up with bits of cloth. Some of them were walking with sticks and there were some with their limbs still in plaster. Never, to his dying day, would he forget that afternoon. Obsessed by this terrible pectacle, he imagined a series of others that passed before his eyes like a film. He saw the 200 staggering through the night, knee-deep in snow, hungry and shivering with cold. The rifles knocked against their backs unheeded and their ten cartridges clinked together in their pockets. Here and there a man fell with a cry, pulled himself up and stumbled on for a few paces before he collapsed again and lay still for ever. A procession of dead men was marching out to save the VIth Army.

Gedig imagined the hand of the limping Captain pointing vaguely to the front. There was the height, the post they had to occupy. The expressionless, infinitely weary faces of the men stared into the dark, lit only by the muzzle-fire of Russian guns. There were no trenches, no dug-outs. The plain seemed to stretch out for ever with clouds of powdered snow sweeping across it. This was the road of no return, the street that led to death.

The marchers separated and spread out over the steppe. One after another they let themselves sink to the ground to be gradually covered by snow, while the tracer bullets from Russian machine-guns whistled over them. Not an order was heard, not a question, not a sound. Such deathly silence can only be kept by those who no longer hope.

Gedig groaned and rubbed his forehead. He knew the meaning of war. He had seen children and old people die in air raids and exhausted prisoners shot in the streets. Still there was something which made the sick and helpless sacred to friend and foe alike, and those who broke this law forfeited the respect of all men. The symbol of the Red Cross ought still to be respected.

Total war could not put an end to conscience and reduced the individual to a cypher. Those 200 men could not save the VIth Army. It could no longer be saved by anyone, and there could be nothing worth saving where such things were done. It was all over. . . .

'It's a crime.' The officers sitting behind drew together. Had someone spoken or was it the wind rattling the door? There it was again, ringing loud and clear in the night.

'It's a crime,' said Colonel von Hermann again. He was not speaking to the officers behind him nor to the driver who stared at him and almost let go of the steering-wheel. He was speaking to himself.

He added: 'None of us is free from guilt, but there's no way out.'

No way out, thought Breuer in despair. Is there really no way out?

During these days not much happened to relieve the monotony for Geibel and Herbert—Herbert's face grew more transparent and Geibel's head became more and more like a leaking balloon. Since the disappearance of Lakosch they had both fallen into a state of apathy. When Breuer returned from his night-drive with the CO, he found everyone awake and in a state of considerable excitement. Wild rumours concerning the Colonel's trip had been going round.

'Is it true, Captain, that air staff has been transferred to the south front and that a fresh break-through has been planned?'

'Take it easy, men!' said Breuer repressing. 'We're staying here for the moment. It's all nonsense.' 'But the interpreter has been telling us,' said Geibel rather sulkily, 'that over there . . .' Fröhlich was embarrassed and said: 'There were two wounded men from Karpovskaya who said that a parachute-division had landed near Kalatsh. They said they could hear the fighting from the hospital.' 'Yes, and at Divisional HQ they are saying that the Colonel is certainly going to lead the Tank Division.'

Breuer was not even annoyed. He thought of the 200 wounded men who had been pulled out of hospital as the last reinforcement to save the army from defeat. . . .

He turned over the pages of the information bulletin which Herbert fetched daily from Corps HQ, without much interest. The IVth Corps reported a break-through in depth by the Russian forces at Zybenko. Counter-measures had been taken . . . He knew all about that. Then he noticed an item which read: 'In front of the 376th Infantry Division the enemy has massed 120 rocket throwers.' Breuer's eyes dwelt on the figure. He handed the paper to Herbert saying:

'There seems to be a misprint here. Please correct it. It should be twelve.'

'No, no, sir,' Herbert replied emphatically, 'that's quite right. I thought it looked funny, so I asked them again. And there's another place in which eighty are reported.'

Breuer had turned pale. One hundred and twenty Stalin Organs! Each one of them, mounted on a truck and served by 6 men, had the fire-power of a light artillery brigade with 12 guns, more than 80 vehicles, 510 horses and at least 600 officers and men. With 120 of these machines concentrated on an area of a few square yards not a mouse would be left alive. The last act of the tragedy seemed to have begun at Zybenko.

'You can rely on me with rock-like confidence,' Hitler had said.

Towards noon on the next day a man came panting down the steps leading into the bunker. It was Corporal Klaucke, the flabby-looking chef.

'Hullo, Wilhelm? Come to offer yourself as a nice bit of roast pork?'

'No, no,' said the cook—'I haven't come about the food. Too early for that. It's about this thing here.'

Carefully rubbing his hands on his once white apron he fished out a folded paper from his trouser-pocket.

'We've been talking ourselves silly about it, and at last I said: "Give it to me and I'll go across to Intelligence with it—they'll know what it's about."'

Breuer took the thing from the cook's hand. It was a blue, torn piece of paper, printed on both sides in blurred and still damp letters.

He read: '*To the Commander-in-Chief of the Sixth German Army General Paulus.*'

'Where did you get that?' he said. The cook wiped his nose with the back of his hand.

'We were standing by the soup-bowl,' he said, 'making the mid-day brew, and as there wasn't enough powder, I thought it would be better to make less, so that it shouldn't be too thin. Half a litre per head would do I thought, but this fellow Emil who's always spouting about justice and so on, he says "You can't do this to us, William. Each of us has a right to a litre and you can't reduce that." "O.K. Emil," I said. "Your full share lies right out-side the door. Get out and bring in an armful of snow." So Emil throws a tarpaulin full of snow into the pot and I keep stirring and stirring and the soup gets thinner and thinner and the single horse's leg in it just tosses up and down. Then suddenly I find this thing sticking to the spoon.'

As the cook talked Breuer glanced at the paper shaking his head. At last he said, 'Now listen to me. This is absolutely crazy.'

He began to read out:

'To the Commander-in-Chief of the VIth German Army or his representative and to all the officers and men belonging to the German forces besieged before Stalingrad.'

The men crowded together and tried to read the words over his shoulder.

'Look at that,' said Geibel gaping. 'It's addressed to us, too.'

Only Wiese paid no attention to what was going on. He remained sitting in the corner with his book.

'The German VIth Army with detachments from the IVth Tank Army and other units sent to reinforce the above have been completely surrounded since November 23rd, 1942.'

'That's right,' said the fat cook, 'nobody can deny that.'

'The troops of the Red Army have encircled these German Army Groups with an unbreakable ring. All hopes of saving your troops by means of an offensive by the German Armies from the south and south-west have failed to materialize. The German forces hurrying to relieve you were beaten by the Red Army and are now retreating on Rostov.'

'Sounds a bit exaggerated,' said Herbert. He had no idea where Rostov was, but supposed it was somewhere far to the rear. He remembered that there had been fighting there in August.

'That's all boloney,' said Fröhlich indignantly. 'It's quite evident that now that the parachute troops are upon them . . .'

'What's the matter?' said Breuer crossly. 'Either I'm going to read or you're going to chatter. Can't have both.'

He continued:

'The German Transport Air-Fleet, which was bringing you

starvation rations in food, munitions and liquid fuel has been obliged, owing to the successful and rapid progress of the Red Army, to change their air-fields several times, each time increasing the distance they have to fly to reach the besieged troops. Moreover the Transport Air-Fleet is suffering enormous losses in planes and personnel and the help they can give the besieged troops is illusory.'

'What does illusory mean?' whispered Geibel to Herbert. The latter shrugged his shoulders. He didn't know either.

'The situation of your encircled troops is grave. They are suffering from hunger, sickness and cold. The grim Russian winter has hardly begun. Keen frosts, cold winds and snowstorms await your soldiers who are not even provided with proper winter clothing and are living in very insanitary conditions.

'You, as Commander-in-Chief, and all the officers of the encircled troops understand perfectly well that you have no possible means of breaking through the cordon at your disposal. Your position is hopeless and it would be futile to prolong your resistance.'

Fröhlich was shifting from one foot to the other and at last he could contain himself no longer.

'Throw the bloody rag away, Captain,' he cried. 'It's just filthy lying propaganda.'

'No, no, not yet,' protested the cook. 'The most important part comes later—please read on.'

'Seeing that the situation in which you now find yourselves has no future for you, we propose the following conditions of surrender, in order to avoid needless bloodshed.

1. All the German troops in the encircled area, with you and your staff at their head, to cease fighting.

2. All persons belonging to the German Army together with their weapons, fighting equipment and all army property to be surrendered undamaged to our authorities.'

'What a hope!' growled Fröhlich.

'We guarantee to all officers and men, who cease to resist, life and security and their return to Germany at the end of the war or to any country to which prisoners-of-war may wish to proceed.'

They knew all this, having read it *ad nauseam*. It was the stereotyped formula of the Russian leaflets. They had often laughed at it and made jokes about it. But, as things were now, it suddenly looked different somehow; more worthy of credence.

'All members of the German Army who surrender will be allowed to retain their uniforms, badges of rank and decoration, as well as their personal property and valuables. The Senior Officers will be also allowed to keep their swords.'

Fröhlich laughed. 'You can see by that what a complete hoax the whole thing is, "Their swords," indeed. They *must* know that no one here wears a sword.'

'Shut up,' said Herbert angrily.

'All officers, NCOs and men who surrender will at once be issued with normal rations.

'Medical treatment will be given to all wounded, sick and frostbitten persons.'

'Well?' asked the cook, 'What do they mean by normal rations, when they themselves have nothing to eat?'

'One moment, gentlemen,' said Breuer. 'I've nearly got to the end. Afterwards you can pull the damn thing to pieces as much as you like.'

He went on reading:

'We shall await your answer on January 9th, 1943 at 10.00 hours, Moscow time. Your reply must be in writing and entrusted to a representative nominated by you personally, who is to proceed by a personnel car bearing a white flag along the road as far as the siding at Konny, near the station of Kotlubany. Your representative will be received by Russian plenipotentiaries in sector 13 0.5 Km south-east of siding 564 on January 9th 1943 at 10.00 hours.

'Should you refuse our terms of surrender, we must warn you that the troops of the Red Army and the Red Air-Fleet will be

obliged to wipe out the encircled German forces, for whose annihilation you will bear the responsibility.

Signed:

The Representative of the Central
Command of the Red Army,

General of Artillery Voronov.

The Commander-in-Chief of the Troops of the Don Front.

Lieutenant-General Rokossowski.'

'If one only knew whether the Russians made any arrangements
at all for POWs,' said Geibel. He added that no letters from
prisoners-of-war had ever come out of the Soviet Union and no
news of them, except for a few leaflets which might have been faked
and the photos put in by the Russians. The pictures showed men
with close-cropped hair, but German soldiers no longer wore their
hair short. Lately a leaflet had been dropped showing a bald-headed
fighter pilot. He was said to be a great-grandson of Bismarck and
wrote that the old man had also been opposed to war with Russia.
The pilot wore the Knight's Cross and was said to have three enemy
planes to his credit. Even Geibel knew that pilots didn't get the
Knight's Cross for shooting down three planes. What would
Lakosch have said? But, of course, Lakosch had gone. . . .

'If only it was the English,' reflected Herbert. 'But the Russians . . .'

'They'll throw us all into the Volga, man,' said Fröhlich bitterly,
'and then you'll be able to ask the fish if the Russians make proper
arrangements for POWs.'

'What, several hundred thousand men?' put in Herbert. 'And
Generals as well? They couldn't do that.'

'You'd be surprised at what they can do,' said Fröhlich with a
laugh.

The fat cook wiped the sweat from his face. 'What they say
about the position here—isn't so silly,' he said. 'They're quite
right about us being hungry and freezing.'

He himself had not yet reached this stage, but he did not want to.
If the Russians took everything over in good order and guaranteed
normal rationing, then they would also take over his field-kitchen

and he would somehow be able to get through his period of captivity.

'And what do *you* think of this thing, Captain?' he asked.

Breuer gazed at the paper again. The Colonel had said: 'There is no way out'. But this looked like a way.

'I think . . .' he began slowly, forgetting the fact that, as an Intelligence Officer, he had no right to allow discussion of an enemy leaflet. 'I think we've come to the end of our tether. The Russians might kill us, let us starve or send us to rot in Siberia, but there is a chance that they wouldn't. But to go on fighting here spells certain disaster for all of us, including the wounded and sick men.' He thought of the column of cripples limping through the wintry night. 'No one can take the responsibility for that.'

The cook nodded eagerly.

'That's just what I was saying to the others.'

'That's nonsense,' shouted Fröhlich. 'When Riga was freed from the Bolsheviks we found a cellar full of German corpses cut to ribbons. Capitulation!' he snorted, 'there's no question of such a thing. The German soldier never capitulates. Never in the whole of German History.'

'You're wrong, Fröhlich,' said Breuer. 'Even Blücher surrendered at Radkan, when he had no more bread or ammunition. A perfectly honourable act!'

'I keep thinking,' said Geibel, 'about the Senior Officers, I don't mean the Colonel, but those higher still. They've got a lot on their minds and they've no time to bother about what the little man is thinking and feeling.'

'Stop bellyaching, Geibel,' said Breuer impatiently. 'General Paulus knows very well what everyone is thinking and he worries more about us than you imagine. That's why I believe that if he thinks there is any chance of the Russian proposals being genuine and honourable, he will accept them.'

For some time Wiese had been looking up from his book, now he said:

'No, Breuer, he won't accept them.'

'Quite right, Lieutenant,' cried Fröhlich.

'He won't even answer such filth as this. It's laughable . . .' He pulled the paper out of Breuer's hand. 'Look at this. What do they say . . . "We shall await your answer on January 9th, 1943 at 10.00 hours Moscow time——" I ask you. If anything had happened, we should have heard about it by now.'

'What? Show me!' Breuer looked for the passage feverishly. 'Yes, he's right. January 9th. Today's the 9th and it's nearly 14.00 hours.' Taking the leaflet in his hand, he hurried out of the bunker.

Breuer ran across to the staff bunker and pulled open the door. Unold and Engelhard were both out, but he saw Colonel van Hermann in the next room. Breuer stopped in the doorway. In the middle of the bunker stood an open box, clothes were laid out on the plank bed, on the table was a row of bottles and tubes and by them an immaculate heap of white handkerchiefs. The Colonel, tidy and well-groomed as ever, was busy packing. He looked up for a moment and Breuer saw that his eyes were glassy and lifeless.

'Is that you, Breuer? Then I can say good-bye to you now.'

'Colonel,' stammered Breuer, 'are—are you going away?'

'Yes, I'm going to a division in Stalingrad. Tell Wiese to be here in half an hour ready for the road. He's coming as my orderly officer. His CO has been informed.'

Breuer stood in silence. The Colonel going, Wiese going . . . The Divisional Staff with its little circle of friends was being broken up.

'What have you got there?' asked the Colonel looking at the paper which Breuer was holding in his hand. 'Oh that . . . please destroy it. The army doesn't want the troops to know about it.'

He took a sheet of paper from his pocket.

'This concerns your section,' he said. 'You'd better take it with you.'

Breuer looked at the paper and read:

'Gen: Cmd XIV P K. Sect: Intelligence.

For the Information of the Troops.

Yesterday enemy envoys under a flag of truce came to our lines bearing a sealed communication, allegedly a summons to surrender, addressed to the Commander-in-Chief of the VIth Army. The document was rejected unopened, and the officers who brought it sent back to their lines.

'Now that the enemy has recognized that he cannot defeat our armies in the Cauldron by force of arms, he is endeavouring by means of clever propaganda to undermine our resistance. He will not succeed. The VIth Army will hold Stalingrad, until it is relieved.

'In future enemy negotiators approaching our lines should be driven away by rifle-fire.'

PART III
The Painful Truth

Chapter Ten

SO FAR ALREADY

‸

BREUER WOKE WITH a start and found himself sitting up. Cold sweat was beading his forehead and his heart was in his throat. What was it? He had been dreaming . . . but it wasn't only that.

He got up and listened. The dark bunker was full of the even breathing of the sleepers and through the window he could see the first faint blue-grey light of morning. He heard a slight, hardly perceptible vibration and oscillation, which made the tiny flame of the oil-lamp flicker.

Breuer turned the wick up.

'Wake up, Fröhlich,' he said.

Fröhlich's face appeared from under the table, blinking lazily at the lamplight.

'Ye-es. What's up?'

'Listen . . .'

Fröhlich listened with his mouth open. He heard a continuous murmuring and rumbling like rollers beating on the shore a long way off.

They tumbled into their clothes, put on their greatcoats and stepped carefully over the sleepers on their way to the door. As they raised the flap, a rush of cold air struck them and simultaneously they heard an angry growling and knocking like the sound of an approaching thunderstorm. In the east the light of dawn was high, but on the western horizon, over which the last shadows of the night were still hanging, they saw a sight which rooted them to the ground. It looked as if the earth had split open, down to its fiery central core. A solid wall of fire was flaring and glowing, pierced by white flashes, its red tongues of flame licking into the darkness above.

The two men stood and stared. Their ears were blocked by the unceasing drumming and droning and the earth shook beneath their feet.

Breuer grabbed Fröhlich's arm.

'They're coming,' he said hoarsely . . . 'it's the big attack . . . that's what's happening.'

A field hospital not far from the Rossoshka Valley—one of many—was housed in some old, half-ruined stables with walls and rafters blackened by the smoke from the petrol barrels which served as stoves. It was meant to accommodate 200 men but at the moment it held about 600. No one kept count of the exact number and fresh patients arrived continually. They lay on stretchers or tarpaulins in the snow before the entrance waiting to take the places of those who died and were dragged out every morning to the low ground behind the stables. Many were frozen to death or died of their wounds as they waited outside.

Padre Peters had been living here for days. His visit to Fortress-Battalion Number 1 had led him here and his work in this place of torment left him no time to himself. In the half-darkness of the room into which the frugal daylight filtered through cracks in the wall and a few holes that had been breached just below the roof, the Padre felt his way through a curtain of stinking exhalations. He guided himself carefully over bodies which strewed the ground in twisted poses, towards the groans and sobs, issuing from dark corners. Those men needed his ministrations.

He worked incessantly helping the dressers and comforting the wounded, and he hardly knew day from night. Now and then he was able to snatch a few hours sleep in the corner of a dug-out.

Waking or sleeping he saw them sitting, the 600. They were pressed close together, leaning against one another or propped against the walls of the loose-boxes, some fitted in between the legs of the men behind them. Even the mortally wounded and dangerously ill had to sit. There was no room to lie flat. He looked into eyes bright with fever or dull with resignation, listened to stammering words, whispers, and piercing cries. And there was the silence, which hung like poison-gas over the dark corners. He saw disfigured bodies creeping on all fours through the narrow gangways or supporting themselves painfully on sticks till they reached the operating table. There they pleaded for a shot, from a gun or a syringe, they no longer cared which.

He saw assistants and male-nurses moving like ghostly machines through the room, sometimes collapsing from sheer exhaustion. He saw brutal orderlies dragging patients in and out like logs. And one day when he happened to be in the hollow he saw two bearers tip their burden into the snow. He saw the grey body fall in among the others; the face was stiff but the eyes were moving and the fingers of one hand were opening and closing, as though they were picking flowers in a field. The bearers watched stupidly for a moment and then looked at one another. After a long time one growled: 'Come on: we'd better take him back.' And so they lifted up the body again and stumbled back with it to the stables.

And he couldn't get his mind off a particular surgeon, whom he had seen working in one of the boxes by the light of a lantern. He was wearing a cap and had a cigarette between his lips and from his rubber apron the blood kept flowing till it formed a black puddle which never dried up. Day and night he stood there at his task, keeping himself going with black coffee and pep-pills. He classified each wound according to its curability. 'Shot through the belly? No, can't do it. Not now—perhaps later.' Later meant never. A belly wound he counted as equal to three amputations or a dozen frostbites. All very businesslike.

Padre Peters witnessed these scenes day in, day out. Unheeding and half asleep he often stumbled over injured limbs without hearing the groan or the muttered curse. He looked at hands stretched out in entreaty and into disfigured faces and saw nothing. Without his knowledge or will the chambers of his heart had closed up like the bulkheads of a leaking ship, leaving him only able to recognize need and suffering in the measure that his shattered spirit could assimilate them. Imperceptibly he had become just like the doctor, ready to contribute his services only for certain practical purposes. In the beginning he had always accompanied the bearers outside and said a short prayer as they threw the body into the snow. He no longer did this. The dead men outside were at peace. Every word he addressed to the dead was lost to the living inside.

The motorized division was occupying its new sector. The idea of withdrawing the most efficient fighting force in the army from its safe and well-constructed positions in the south and transferring them to the western sector was perfectly understandable. The men wondered why the staff had taken so long to decide on this solution. The dangerous piece of the line between the 'nose' at Marinovka and the Kazatchi Hills had been occupied by a single infantry division since the Russians had closed the ring. This division had been severely mauled during the retreat and only consisted of fragments of its original strength. The Russians had announced in their leaflets that the division had been destroyed and it was a miracle that the remnants were still there and still fighting.

The advance parties from the south were greeted with enthusiasm, though people smiled at their self-satisfied action. At night they crawled about the trenches and shook their heads at the knee-deep rifle-pits. In the miserable dug-outs they screwed up their noses: 'Not very high-class accommodation. We'll have to do a bit of trench building.' 'What with?' grinned the others. 'Don't you worry: we're bringing what we want.' Sure enough columns of vehicles arrived full of railway-sleepers which were piled up behind the line. The force they were relieving did not worry; they were as happy at the thought of taking over a quiet sector in the south as if Karpovka were the Promised Land.

Few of them could see beyond the narrow framework of their own division, but those few were beset by many misgivings. One of these was Colonel Steigmann. He was not to be corrupted by figures, equipment or big words—he knew from bitter experience how little these things counted. The fighting on the western front of the Cauldron was a peculiar form of warfare not to be measured by normal standards. Most of the men he had brought over the Don with him had been frozen to death in the rifle-pits, had died of exhaustion or had been killed during the continuous Russian attacks. The few who had survived were capable of something far above the average level of performance, they were more valuable than units with twice their manpower. This part of the front had held out for so long because of these men, who had grown to look like shadows from the kingdom of the dead. Would the troops from the south be able to do as well? They looked suspiciously healthy and smelt of cleanliness and hot stoves. Steigmann wondered, what would happen to his plan of fire—a masterpiece of military art which he had improved from day to day and without which it was impossible to hold the sector. The officers from the southern front looked at his multi-coloured maps with feigned interest and thanked him politely for making them available. The expressions on their faces barely concealed their feeling that the whole thing was a sort of game. Anyhow theirs was a motorized division as well as being the best in the Cauldron and for them the last humiliation was to be given advice by flat-footed infantrymen.

But the self-satisfied assurance of the motorized soldiers faded quickly. The toll of casualties through frostbite and dysentery rose to alarming heights and many of the rifle-pits could no longer be manned. The construction of proper dug-outs could not be undertaken in spite of all the wood they had brought with them. Both the Russians and the state of the ground, which was as hard as cement, precluded that.

The most miserable man in the division was the newly-commissioned Lieutenant Harras. Everything had gone wrong for him. He had become an officer and Battalion Adjutant, and above his wound badge he sported the Iron Cross, 1st Class. The men no longer looked askance at him, but there was no further talk of his being flown out. To add to his misfortunes he had been transferred to this devilish piece of the line, where there wasn't a safe corner to be found. He would gladly have risked an attempt at breaking out, but the possibility seemed to have vanished for ever. His spirits had reached rock-bottom.

There had been a series of days full of incident before the Bum, who now commanded the battalion, found an opportunity to collect the skat-playing fraternity once more in his bunker. It was 9th January and the troops were enjoying their first peaceful hours since their arrival. A few bottles had been broached and the players were immersed in their game, though Harras and the Assistant MO had trouble hiding their uncontrollable yawns behind their hands. The Bum paid no attention to the fact that they were dog-tired—he was losing money and had no intention of ending the game.

'Just imagine,' he was saying as he played the knave of Clubs. 'The bitch sat down on the General's lap. Just sat on his lap and said "Oh là là, you fat little man"—she said "*Dickerchen*" in German—God, you should have seen the old man's face.'

Harras laughed shortly. He had already heard about all the Bum's disreputable experiences in Paris, and he knew when to laugh without having to listen. He shuffled the cards listlessly and glanced at his watch. Good Lord, it was getting on to morning. These long hours were enough to kill a mule. The doctor stared vacantly at his hand, murmured 'pass' and closed his eyes . . .

Rurr—wu hummm—Wu hu hu—wummm. Suddenly everything lost its outline. The bunker, which passed for a safe shelter in the frozen ground with a roof a yard thick made of oak, earth and ice suddenly seemed like a tinfoil toy in a giant's hand. The Bum sat as though nailed to his box. He still held his cards in his hand and his face looked like a paper mask. The shock had brought Harras and the Doctor to their feet and thrown them against the wall. Harras felt for something to hold on to. His fatigue had been blown away and it flashed through his mind that they were being bombed from the air. He waited feverishly to be delivered from the murderous din, but it did not stop: the crashes continued louder and louder, sounding like a titanic roll of drums.

Harras saw that the table they had been using was bounding around the room, then the light went out. Something seized him and hurled him into a corner. The ground heaved and sank under his feet and the atmosphere pressed on his body like a hundred tons of water. His ears felt as though they were full of boiling lead. He covered them with his hands so as not to hear, but the fearful crashes could not be shut out: they pierced through skin and bone to the very marrow, to the innermost filament of the brain.

Harras pressed himself to the quaking ground. He wanted to creep into the earth. His eyes started out of his head. He felt himself shouting but didn't know why. He was, in fact, pouring out his soul with these cries of his which were drowned in the uproar of the unchained inferno. Earth fell on him and then a body, heavy as a sandbag. A warm stream flowed over his hand . . .

He didn't know how long he had been lying there. Was it minutes or hours? When he came to, the echoes of the uproar were still resounding in his breast and limbs: his ears felt as if their drums had been pierced by red-hot needles and his intestines seemed to be tucked up in a tight knot. But around him things were different now. The ghastly din had ceased and the silence that followed it was as painful as the suction of a vacuum pump.

He groaned as he worked himself free from the mass of earth that had fallen on him and the heavy body. He looked at it and saw it was the Doctor, stone dead. With dust-filled eyes he blinked around and tried to get his bearings. Then he saw that one corner of the bunker had fallen in and the grey light of dawn was filtering through a hole. Before him was the black outline of a figure. It was the Bum standing with his legs apart, his steel helmet on his bowed head. He looked as though he were carrying the entire weight of the roof on his shoulders. Harras felt his aching limbs with stiff fingers. Then he suddenly noticed that he was very cold. He tried to say something but his voice failed him.

Then someone shouted through the doorway.

'Out! They're coming.'

Harras dragged himself to his feet. Without thinking he crammed his cap on his head, pulled a fur coat out of the debris and grabbed automatically at his sub-machine-gun which was still hanging from a hook.

He trod on a body, yielding as india-rubber, and stumbled feebly up the steps. He crouched as he looked over the top of the flap that curtained the entrance and his teeth chattered.

A few steps in front of him the Bum was standing, his gun in his hand, as motionless as a statue. He was looking towards the front. Harras gazed past him at the foreground which sloped gently to the west. He couldn't believe his eyes. The white carpet of snow on which the sun had been shining yesterday was replaced by a monochrome surface of brown clay, pitted like a lunar landscape, a field of craters, beyond summer and winter. Over this brown field some white objects were pushing their way. White points were crawling forward and white tanks moved slowly like tortoises turning their heads now this way and now that, and spewing out red flames through grey tufts of smoke as they crept on their way. Looking at them Harras forgot his fears and what had just happened and stared incredulously at this unreal picture.

Then there was a blinding flash beside him and a shell-blast threw him to the ground. But where the Captain had been standing, there was now only half a man—a pair of legs up to the belt and then the legs slowly, very slowly tipped over.

Harras sprang up with an animal cry. He bolted like a hunted beast over holes and craters, ruins and weapons and soft bodies. Another shell whizzed past his head and the blast blew him over. He got up and dashed on seeing and hearing nothing more, his brain emptied of thought—but on his eyes was stamped a picture—two legs up to the waist, falling slowly over; then standing there again and once more toppling over . . .

He rolled down a slope. Strong arms picked him up at the bottom. In the safe keeping of those strong hands Harras lost consciousness.

The inhabitants of Bunker-town had gradually grown used to the faint grumbling of the battle coming from the north-west, like the nagging pain of some internal lesion. It was only when the west wind made it more audible and more menacing that they listened uneasily. Now the rumble and drone of the distant fighting continued without pause along the wide expanse of the western horizon and the noise crept nearer and nearer like a thousand-footed monster. The sky, too, had become dangerously lively and was often full of bombers and fighters of a new type. The four Messerschmitts wrestled bitterly and in vain with a crowd of grey fighters. But on the high road, on which even a single car had been a rarity, a long column now wormed its way to the east.

Bunker-town had been awakened with a painful start from its winter sleep and was seething with restless movement. Time, which, during the weeks of waiting had passed with leaden-footed slowness, was now hurrying on like a fever-driven pulse. No one knew anything for certain and people lived on rumours which seeped up from the street into the bunkers. The Russians were through, the front broken, gun-positions, field-hospitals, baggage-depots had all been over run and the staffs were in flight.

The terrified eyes of stragglers and fugitives saw in their own experiences a universal calamity and their exaggerated fears gave rise to a measureless crop of alarming rumours. It was only from Fröhlich that hopeful news could be heard.

Between Kalatch and Karpovka the 'Grossdeutschland Division' had already taken up its position and this Russian attack was only a last desperate attempt to force a decision, before they themselves were encircled. It was only necessary to stick it for a few days more and then everything would be all right.

Breuer rang up the Tank Corps staff. After a lot of trouble he got an answer from the Orderly Officer of their Intelligence Section.

'Sorry, Breuer, no time to talk. We are in the middle of moving. Willms? He's gone, flown out with dispatches. Is the situation bad? I wouldn't say that. It has been necessary to withdraw to the Rossoshka Valley—be seeing you!'

About midday Breuer received a curt order to come across to Divisional HQ. He thought there would be a conference about the situation and took his map-board with him. Unold no longer lodged in the little dug-out which, to his discomfort, he had to share with Colonel von Hermann. Since the day before he had transferred to a new bunker with a separate bedroom, tiled stove and a ceiling made of tree-trunks.

When Breuer entered the room he found Unold, Engelhard, Captain Endrigkeit and two of his military policemen. Then he stepped backwards and found himself leaning against the door-post in astonishment. He looked helplessly at a little figure in a torn greatcoat standing between the two policemen, his grey face bristling with red stubble. Unold, who was standing behind his work-table, was looking at him with thin-lipped scorn.

'Well, Breuer,' he said out of the corner of his mouth. 'Here is the fruit of your slackness. Deserted, of course. What else did you think? Dishonoured the German Army. At least he admitted that.'

Breuer couldn't take his eyes off the man who stood there small and shrunken as though he was hanging in his outsize greatcoat on a hook in the wind. How changed he was! For days he could not have eaten or slept.

'Lakosch,' he said hesitatingly. 'You actually deserted?'

Lakosch looked at him shyly and said, 'Yes,' in a quiet voice.

'You mean you wanted to leave us all in the lurch, just to save your own life?'

Lakosch looked at Breuer with wide eyes; his upper lip trembled, but he did not answer.

Breuer looked helplessly round the circle.

'Maybe it wasn't deliberate desertion,' he urged, pleading for the man. 'It was probably a nervous breakdown. We're all suffering from nervous strain. I know the man well.'

Unold looked at Breuer contemptuously.

'Is that what you think?' he said and stifled a smile between his lips. 'Nervous breakdowns of this sort are dangerous, my dear sir.'

The court-martial was convened for the same afternoon. Unold as acting Divisional Commander presided, Captain Engelhard sat as assessor, and Corporal Kuhlmann, Colonel Unold's batman, represented the non-commissioned ranks. The act of desertion was clearly established and confirmed by a confession. The accused was sentenced to death by shooting. The whole thing was over in five minutes.

At the end Unold sent for Captain Endrigkeit. He said: 'The execution will be carried out by the Field-Police. Please see that there is no publicity. It had better take place tomorrow morning at dawn perhaps at the old flak positions. You know what to do. Report to me at ten o'clock tomorrow that this order has been carried out.'

The old Captain shook his head and said very decidedly. 'I can't do it.'

Unold said rather helplessly: 'What did you say? I don't understand . . . You can't do it? What does that mean?' No one had ever given him such an answer to a direct command.

The Captain moved his lips a few times, then repeated quietly—'I can't do it.'

A quiver ran over Unold's face and for a moment he closed his eyes. Of course, he thought. The fellow's a reservist, an old fossil left over from the last war. These fellows put on uniforms, but they never become soldiers again. He curbed his anger.

'Endrigkeit,' he said, 'I have really got more important things to attend to. Be so good as to refrain from making a scene here. I have no one else. After all you're not a schoolboy, due for your first communion. You must have had fatigues like this before.'

The Captain passed his tongue over his lips. Yes, indeed. This wasn't the first time. He had had to shoot the Commissar at Lubny and the three civilians suspected of being partisans and the two stragglers condemned for looting. But Lakosch!

'I can't do it,' he said once more.

The Colonel lost the last remains of his self-control. The sweat came out on his forehead and he stormed: 'Don't drive me mad, man! I order you as your superior officer to perform this duty. You know, I should hope, the consequences of refusing to obey an order. About turn, march!'

The old Captain turned on his heel like a recruit and stumped stiffly out of the bunker.

The snowclad plain lay dull and drab under the ashen sky. The air was full of humming and howling. Fighter-planes swooped, like birds of prey, on to the airfield at Pitomnik with red flashes spouting from their wings. In the west a low-flying line of bombers planted black smoke-columns in the earth. In the distance, not so distant now, the front was droning and growling.

Captain Endrigkeit was not aware of all these things. He looked unseeing at the smooth path of beaten snow which his feet followed mechanically. From time to time he emitted a groan. He was alone with his thoughts and in revolt against fate for giving him such a devilish duty. The men he had executed in the past, had been partisans or looters—Germans and Russians—and he carried out the orders for their execution without moral misgivings. But this fellow Lakosch . . . there were limits.

'God blast him!' muttered the Captain to himself and immediately knew that he was wrong. He felt he could see into the heart of things, like an X-ray, and could no longer be satisfied with surface appearances. The ground which had supported him for over fifty years had begun to rock beneath his feet. The old unshakable world had melted and was running like quicksilver through his hands. Was Stalingrad to blame?

He stood still for a while and snorted and then suddenly made up his mind. He walked hastily back to Bunker-town. A low-flying aircraft streaked over the plain, screaming and belching out a random spray of machine-gun bullets, which sang as they dived into the ground and kicked up tufts of snow and earth. The Captain went on his way undisturbed. He would not have minded if a bullet had hit him.

In front of the former Divisional HQ bunker, in which the condemned man was awaiting his last hour, he found a Sergeant-Major in a steel helmet with a police badge on his chest. Heinrich Kruschkat was the son of an innkeeper from Krautupönen near Gumbinnen. He, too, was depressed and thinking of the next morning. Endrigkeit replied to his greeting with a grunt and, lifting the flap, entered the bunker.

The room was bare and cold and the evening light filtered faintly through the dirty window-panes. In a corner at the back Lakosch was sitting huddled on a bench. When Endrigkeit came in he raised his head and for a moment showed the whites of his eyes in terror. The Captain drew up a stool, sank down heavily and began to fill his pipe. When, at last, he had it between his teeth and was blowing out the first clouds of smoke, he leaned against the wall and gazed at Lakosch in silence.

Lakosch was still wearing his absurdly large greatcoat with skirts that swept the ground and sleeves that covered his hands. On his head was a crumpled service-cap with the flap turned down to cover his ears. A grey layer of dirt coated his sunken face but over his cheekbones, where the dirt had flaked off, were two bright hectic patches. Round the tight line of his mouth were a few white wrinkles. The stamp of infinite sadness, which had begun to appear on the faces of all the Stalingrad soldiers, had here crystallized into a timeless death mask. With a gesture Endrigkeit invited Lakosch to sit down. He felt a spring of pity rising within him and prepared to fight it down.

'How could you do it?' he exclaimed, 'Run away and leave the others sitting here in the dirt.' He gave a groan of disgust and said: 'But of course it didn't occur to you that some poor devil would have to shoot you.'

At these words a curious change came over Lakosch. His face came to life and the sullen fixed look with which he had received the Captain's words disappeared. He was ready to be bawled out, beaten-up and put to death, but he was not prepared for a word of human kindness. The attitude, which bitterness and frustration had forced on him, vanished and he suddenly felt small and helpless, and remembered himself as a little boy in his first pair of trousers with his father looking at him as he cut up the latest Trade Union news-sheet and sailed it down the gutter in the street.

He stammered: 'I . . . I . . . thought of that, but . . .'

'But what?'

'But I thought perhaps I might be able to save the army.'

'What!' burst out the Captain, half-rising from his stool in surprise. 'What did you want to do? That's the limit!'

Lakosch nodded eagerly like a schoolboy who wants to explain a bad report—'Yes, Herr Hauptmann, really. You know there are Germans over there, real Germans . . .'

And then it all came out. Everything that he had carried about with him in his desperate loneliness, that had tormented him by day and night, poured out like a long dammed-up stream. Gleiwitz, his wretched childhood between bare walls, his father who had died in a Concentration Camp and who had always said 'Hitler means war.' How he had refused to believe it and had thought that Hitler would bring in real socialism and set the workers free. Then the story of the Jews and Senta and his little car and his poor bewildered mother and her last letter. What he had heard before Christmas outside Colonel Unold's door, and the meeting with Seliger. Now he knew that there were really Germans on the other side who hoped to save the men of the VIth Army from a senseless death . . . It all came out in a confused flood, but the Captain understood. At first he had sat there, shaking his head. Then he had lit a candle so as to be able to see the other man better and now he was leaning his head on his hand and listening.

'Then I thought that General Paulus, if he knew all that, would perhaps . . . perhaps act quite differently . . . and that if they sent me across like Seliger and I could explain all that to the Commander, everyone might still be saved, perhaps, and everything would turn out all right in the end . . .'

It was quite quiet in the bunker. The candlelight threw Endrigkeit's bearded profile on the wall. He sat there with a man's destiny spread out before him like a landscape, clear and transparent and free of all secrets.

Suddenly the Captain was overwhelmed by a flood of unreasoning rage. He sprang to his feet and Lakosch crumpled up before the unrecognizable expression on his face——

'Get out!' he roared so loudly that the candle flickered and the window rattled. 'Get out, you scoundrel, you rotten bastard!'

Lakosch looked at the Captain with dispirited eyes. He did not understand.

'Get out, do you hear me!' shouted the Captain. 'You miserable idiot! Get out!'

Then Lakosch began to understand. A small, incredulous smile stole into his face. He took a hesitating step towards the Captain, but the latter was trembling all over and looked so terrifying, that Lakosch had to summon up all his courage to duck under Endrigkeit's outstretched arm and rush out of the door, up the steps and past the abashed Heinrich Kruschkat into the darkness.

Endrigkeit stood for a while longer, listening to the echoes of his own angry shouting.

Gradually he calmed down and sat panting on the stool, while he wiped the sweat off his forehead. He slowly became conscious of what had happened. He had done something monstrous. He had helped a deserter, condemned to die a shameful death, to escape. The more clearly he realized the nature of his action, the more light-hearted and unconcerned he became. He felt as if a burden had been lifted from him—a burden that had been weighing on him for a long time. He had set Lakosch, the deserter in the dock to be judged by his conscience and his conscience had acquitted him. He was not afraid. If they shot him, it wouldn't matter? The death sentence had already been pronounced on everyone in the Cauldron, even on those who presumed to call themselves judges. But he had given some meaning, some point to his death.

Swarms of wounded men and stragglers overflowed the hospital. Sheltering from the wind behind the stable walls they squatted in clusters, cowered round wretched fires and pushed their way into the field-kitchens. With eyes still full of fear, they told of the break-through on the western front. They got food to eat, had their bandages attended to when possible, and were pushed off farther to the rear.

But inside the hospital, men sat and listened to the hum of voices and the unwonted noises and the roar of battle which gradually came closer. The hospital orderlies pretended that it was nothing, but their wavering eyes proclaimed them liars.

Then the first defence troops appeared, dug fox-holes and laid their machine-guns in position behind ramparts of snow. Peters watched them and so did the doctors and public health officers. The days—no the hours—of the hospital were numbered.

The SMO of the hospital was on the telephone.

'We've got to clear out, sir,' he said to the PMO.

'Yes, yes—Get moving. As far as possible towards the east, pre-ferably to Gumrak, where you'll find everything ready for you.'

'But what about vehicles, Colonel?'

'Vehicles? My dear chap, where do you expect me to get them from?'

'For God's sake, sir—The Corps can't leave us in the lurch. We've got nothing here.'

'Well, you must forage for yourselves. Look for a column of empty supply trucks.'

'Can't you let us have ten trucks, Colonel?' called the Doctor, 'or five . . . or three?'

But the Colonel had hung up.

In the afternoon an officer appeared wearing a white camouflage suit, a steel-helmet, and field-glasses. He examined the terrain and contemplated the swarming crowd with disapproval as he sniffed round the walls of the stable.

231

'You've got to get out of here,' he shouted to the SMO who was standing some way off. 'The front line is coming here.' The Doctor's eyes were wide with astonishment and his face. He understood what that would mean.

'When?' he asked in a toneless voice.

'Tomorrow,' said the other. He hesitated a moment, but found that he had nothing more to say. He shrugged his shoulders and walked away.

The Doctor jumped into his little beetle of a car and drove off at speed into the night.

As far as Marinovka he was driving downhill and then he climbed up to Baburkin and Bolshaya Rossoshka visiting staffs and supply depots and artillery units. All those he spoke to either refused to listen to him or, after the first few words, made a gesture of regretful refusal. They had more than enough on their hands already.

A U2 came swooping down over the highway and dropped its bombs. A flame darted from the car in front of them and the Doctor and his driver dragged two men from the burning car. Both were badly wounded—two more to add to the hundreds in the hospital. That was all that the Doctor brought back from his nocturnal drive.

Nevertheless some transport was forthcoming. Next morning four heavy Büssings were standing before the entrance, throbbing and steaming. They belonged to a column that was running empty after carrying munitions to the front. The hospital bearers, shaken out of their indifference, hurriedly set to work to move the sick. They stacked the pale-faced patients on top of one another, fifty to each car, covering the heaps with blankets and tenting, as the trucks had no roofing and the temperature was—28° C.

The two padres took a hand with the arrangements and helped to hold back the large numbers of able-bodied men who swarmed round the cars hoping for a lift. Peters felt a hand on his arm and heard a voice say:

'Padre!'

He turned and saw a hollow-cheeked individual with a stubbly face who introduced himself.

'Harras—Lieutenant Harras of the Divisional staff. Have you forgotten me?'

Peters would not have recognized him. A hand wrapped in dirty rags was stretched out towards him and a timid look met his eyes.

'I'm wounded,' he said. 'Can't I—can't I go with them?'

'What, with these?' said Peters scrutinizing him from head to foot—'No, you are still able to walk. But come along with me. Perhaps the Doctor will be able to do something for you.'

'No thanks,' said Harras, sounding hunted and afraid, and his hand disappeared behind his back. Then he muttered something and melted into the crowd.

The drivers were impatient to be off. The doors were slammed, the motors roared and the heavy tyres ground their way through the snow. That was the alarm-signal for those that were left behind. From all sides the slightly wounded and the stragglers rushed to storm the cars, jumping on to the radiators and mudguards and the doors of the drivers' cabins and tried to hoist themselves up the sides of the cars. But the orderlies in the trucks, groping through cargoes of wounded, cursed and hit them on the head and rapped their hands till they let go and dropped into the road like apples off a tree.

There were still hundreds lying in the stable. They could hear the shouting and the noise of the departing tracks; and now no one would come and fetch them away.

The surgeon was working in his loose-box by the dim, flickering light of a lantern. He too felt the tension that drew tight its invisible threads throughout the great room, and buried himself in his bloody work.

Then from the dark corners a hoarse, groaning sound was heard. Suddenly the room was filled with moaning and crying which seemed to come from the depths of human existence.

The dark corners over which the stillness of death had seemed to be brooding, had come to life. The patients were stretching and moving, weary hands were feeling and grasping and, like a thick and glutinous river of lava, a stream of human bodies flowed out into the room. Men without arms or legs, men with head and belly wounds, who had long been comatose or delirious—they all had suddenly become alive and were writhing along the ground, crawling over one another and sliding like a sea-monster with a thousand arms towards the exit.

The surgeon stared at the spectacle with his mouth open, and then shook himself as though to make the incredible picture disappear. The assistants too forgot the man lying on the table with a bullet through his throat and gazed at the stream of groaning men propelling themselves along the central gangway. It seemed to them like a sign from the other world—a vision of the Last Judgment.

But after a while the human wave lost its impetus and the moaning ceased and died down to a thin, helpless whine, followed by a deathly silence like that which had preceded the outburst, leaving the gangway blocked by motionless bodies.

The Doctor wiped his brow. Then he turned with renewed zeal to the body which lay under his knife. Why was he still working? What was the good of cutting and sewing up, of sealing off arteries and cleaning out abscesses? He didn't know and didn't ask. Work had become an end in itself, an escape from reality.

A part of the hospital staff had already driven off and the SMO was preparing to leave. When Peters came by he beckoned to him.

'Padre,' he said, 'walking cases must go on foot to Gumrak. Arrangements for their reception are being made there. I put you in charge of the column.'

Peters looked questioningly at the Doctor:

'And what about all the others?' he asked pointing with his chin at the men who strewed the floor—some hundreds still. This place would soon be in the thick of battle. 'Who is going to stay with them?'

The Doctor's eyes were dark and brooding. Then a quiet voice near by said: 'I am.'

It was the young Catholic priest from the Rhineland. Tears came into the Padre's eyes; for a long time past differences in faith had ceased to exist. During these dreadful days the two men of God had shared their duties. It was hard to say which had been given the better part.

The officer, who had already loaded his stores, said: 'Just count how many men there are lying here and I will leave you supplies for them.' He took out a lead pencil and a well-thumbed note-book and began to calculate. 'Cold food for three days,' he said. 'After that you'll have to . . .' He looked up and met the eyes of the other men. He put the note-book away, with an embarrassed air, cleared his throat and went out.

The medical staff had gone. The surgeon drove off in the last Volkswagen to another place where blood and pus and wounds would be awaiting him. Padre Peters organized his column of walking cases. From all sides men limped and crept up like field-mice driven from their nests by a thunderstorm. Some were supporting themselves on sticks or home-made crutches, some leaned against one another, some walked on their knees and others crawled on all fours. There was someone to lead and give orders and there were canvas bags full of bread and tinned food, guarded by orderlies with rifles ready to shoot. From the other side of the gorge a stream of men flowed to join them—fugitives and stragglers, apparently in good health. Peters drove nobody away. The word 'healthy' had lost its meaning. Over there could be heard the hammering of machine-guns and the hissing discharge of a Stalin Organ followed by crashing explosions in the gorge.

The column slowly set itself in motion like a great caterpillar and by the side of the road men lay and stretched out their arms and begged for help or cursed. Padre Peters marched at the head, the flap of his fur cap falling low on his bearded face. He had turned up the collar of his greatcoat and his knapsack hung on his back. He had left his fur coat with the wounded men in the hospital. Near him two men were struggling forwards. One had a bandage round his head and the other wore a shapeless bundle of rags fastened with string to his foot. Between them they were dragging a third man, hanging with his arms round their shoulders. His head wagged to and fro, like the wooden head of a jointed doll, and his eyes, glassy and disturbed, looked out of black hollows. His feet dragged along the surface of the snow, leaving a wavering track. 'Come on, Schorsch,' panted the two men, themselves scarcely able to move forward. 'Now we're going to the rear, to the hospital. Come along, we'll soon be there.'

Slowly the column wound its way onwards and it was not for

several hours that the Padre dared to look back. Behind him, where the battle was growling and the white carpet of the snowy plain lost itself in grey, lay the hospital from which they had started. He saw a reddish glow and brown gusts of smoke and covered his eyes with his hand.

In the twilight they reached a ravine blocked by snow-drifts. A few trucks had stuck there, up to their axles in snow. They belonged to the convoy of Büssings which had started that morning and there was an uncanny silence round them. No drivers and no orderlies were to be seen and the men in the lorries did not move, for they were dead. The living men climbed up the sides, fell in over the dead bodies and tore off their blankets and greatcoats and, groping among the corpses took away their food.

The column marched on through the night and the following day. Between waking and sleeping Padre Peters shuffled on legs that moved automatically. His feet were flayed lumps of flesh, but he felt no pain. Only a small company that followed him now. Few were left of those who had started from the hospital, but strangers had joined him on the road.

Low houses appeared, a water-tower and railway lines.

It was Gumrak, their goal.

Darkness overhung the place, torn by the yellow flare of parachute lights and the white flashes of exploding bombs. There was a deserted street between low mud cottages and then a brick building that showed no lights. It had been a railway station but was now the hospital. A sentry in a fur coat barred the way. 'Go back!' he croaked. 'Go back, I say. There's no room inside.' He pushed the feeble and exhausted wayfarers back into the night. His orders were to protect the overcrowded people within.

The wanderers sank down on the steps in front of the house and their moans died away in the cold of the advancing night. In the morning they would be cleared away.

They had reached their destination.

'Captain Döhring.'

'Here.'

'Lieutenant Jankuhn.'

236

'Here.'

'Lieutenant Krause.'

'Here.'

'Lieutenant Semprich.'

'Here.'

Amid the clearing of throats and the shuffling of feet the answers to the roll-call sounded hoarse, or sulky, or sometimes overloud, as if in protest against some grievance. Captain Engelhard, who had been shot through the lungs, found the cloud of tobacco smoke and the smell of wet clothes hard to bear. After calling each name he paused for a second to breathe and tried to get a good look at the individual officer, but the small room was so crowded that it was impossible to do this satisfactorily. Here and there he recognized a staff-officer and nodded to him. The other faces were all strange and unknown, uncooperative and obviously waiting for trouble. They belonged to the heads of all the large and small units, baggage, repair-shops, supply services and stores, who inhabited Bunkertown. It had been a job to assemble them all in Unold's new bunker and they had come reluctantly. Why did the staff want them? Why need they interrupt their work?

'All present, sir,' reported Engelhard to the next table. Unold, who had been writing, busily pushed the brandy bottle under the table and rose to his feet. There was a moment of silence. The two red patches on his cheekbones contrasted strikingly with the pallor of his face. There was a gloomy look in his lack-lustre eyes.

'Gentlemen,' he said, 'an Army Order has come through declaring the village of Dubininski a fortified position. Arrangements for defence on a circular perimeter must immediately be put in operation. The Commandant of the fortress will be Colonel Braun, the OC of the Mortar Regiment. All units situated in the Dubininski area are, as from 10.00 hours today, to place themselves under the orders of this Officer. Colonel Braun is not yet here. As his Second-in-Command I speak for him and order all units to consider themselves in a state of emergency. The allotment of sectors will shortly be announced. Battle Headquarters is here. Every unit must have a representative here. Any questions?'

Deep silence. Then everyone started talking and muttering,

more noisily than before. Right in the front a square-shouldered Captain, who had pulled his lambskin cap down over his forehead, started gesticulating.

'But,' he said, 'it can't be done. We have to bake the bread. For weeks we've been working day and night ...'

'And what about our three siege-guns?' put in an officer from the repair-shop. 'The Corps want them ready for the line in ten days. I can't spare a man.'

'Quite right!' said a voice from a safe position in the rear. 'It's nonsense!'

'Absolutely out of the question!'

It became evident that in consequence of other more pressing duties no one would be available for the defence of Dubininski.

Unold felt under the table for the bottle. His hand shook so that the glass ran over. He drained it at one gulp and wiped his mouth and forehead with his handkerchief. Then he glared at the company like a lion-tamer at his rebellious beasts.

'I don't think we understand one another,' he said in quiet, cutting tones. 'We shall not be needing bread or siege-guns any more. In a few hours the Russians will be here. The place will be defended to the last man. General Hube of the Tank Corps has selected a sniper's nest for himself on the line, which he doesn't propose to leave alive. I hope that you now see what I mean. There is no retreat now for anyone and no tomorrow or the day after. There's only here and now. In a word, it's all over.'

An uncanny silence followed his words.

For a moment Unold savoured the effect of his words.

'With regard to the staff,' he continued, 'the other ranks will be formed into a group of riflemen under Captain Gedig. All available officers will constitute a special fighting group, under Captain Engelhard, and go into the line as infantry. Lieutenant Breuer will be adjutant to Colonel Braun. Major Kalweit will command what is left of the Tank Regiment ...'

There was a noise at the door. A man was forcing his way to the front. It was Captain Endrigkeit.

'What's the matter? Don't disturb the meeting,' shouted Unold at him. The Captain saluted and snorted a few times. Then he said:

'I beg to report, Colonel,' he said carefully, 'that the prisoner has gone.' 'What?' said Unold. He had long ago forgotten the case of Lakosch in the stress of the latest emergency. Then he remembered and said impatiently, 'All right, Endrigkeit. I have something here for you . . .' 'No,' interrupted the Captain. 'It's not all right. He's gone.'

'What?' said Unold. 'Do you mean to say that . . .'

Endrigkeit shrugged his shoulders and said: 'When we went to the bunker to fetch him at dawn, the bolt was drawn and there was no one inside.'

Unold pressed his hands on the table and leaned so far forward that the Captain involuntarily recoiled.

'You let him escape, did you?' he whispered. 'You must be mad. I shall arrest you and bring you before a military court. I'll send you to the front with a punishment squad, you incompetent ass.'

Suddenly he realized how meaningless were his threats.

'You'll pay for this, Endrigkeit,' he said through thin sweat-beaded lips. 'We'll talk about this later.'

Colonel Braun was a choleric gentleman with a fat red face. Since morning he had kept his adjutant busy. Breuer had had to go round searching for trenching tools, to argue with irritable heads of units in strange bunkers, to indicate imaginary positions to fighting groups and to endeavour to pick up stragglers in the street and assemble them into a unit. In the evening the Colonel gave him half an hour to attend to his own affairs.

Breuer found the bunker empty and unfamiliar. The three men belonging to Intelligence had already gone off with Captain Gedig. The stove was still alight and the remains of some coffee steamed in a saucepan. Geibel had probably left it for him.

Breuer sat on the bench, took off his cap and pushed back the hair from his forehead. He was very tired. He had faced death a hundred times with the peaceful certainty of a soldier prepared to sacrifice himself. But the idea that the break-through which all had wished to attempt, would never be attempted, that was a bitter thought.

He took up a packet of letters in his hands, letters from Irmgard, his wife. He would not be ready to meet his fate, till they were all burnt to ashes.

He had to write. There would be a messenger today to take the last letters to the airfield. But what was he to write? In Germany they knew nothing and a jealous censor would see to it that they never learnt the truth.

He laid his writing-pad on his knee and wrote:

'My Irmgard,

These lines will go by the last post—do not expect further news of me. I cannot write what is happening here, but I want you to know that we shall not see each other for a long time and, perhaps, never more in this world. I am grateful for all your love and for the years of happiness I had at your side. Now you must go on your way alone. May fate be kind to you and give you strength to bring up our children so that they honour the Commandments of God above those of men. It is not easy for me to write this. I am leaving you in sorrow and with no peace in my soul. Once I believed that I was living, and could die, for a good cause. Pray for us, if you can.

Your Franz.'

Breuer addressed his letter carefully, stuck all his airmail stamps to the envelope and gummed it down.

Once more he looked round. Then he put out the lamp, slung his sub-machine-gun round his neck and climbed up the steps into the night.

Chapter Eleven

WHAT HAVE THEY DONE TO US?

❦

BREUER HAD PASSED a restless night full of fierce, almost unbearable tension which had made him forget the bitter cold. The Russians had not come. It was learned later that the divisions driving down from the north and the south, together with the remnants of the forces from the west which had fallen back on the Rossoshka Valley, had been able to hold up the enemy for a short time. Instead of the Russians, morning had come, and with it an order from Unold instructing members of the Divisional staff to assemble before marching off.

Breuer, with a pain in his back, had clambered out of his hole in the snow and limped into the staff bunker to be greeted with a sardonic smile by Colonel Braun. Outside stood the two command cars, a truck, the vehicle carrying the field-kitchen and some other motors, with their engines running.

Battle headquarters were being transferred to Stalingradski. They had driven off with the Corps Staff and the General who, the day before, had been looking for a suitable rifle-pit to die in.

At every turn of the weary wheels a fragment of self-respect or of faith had broken. The man who climbed down from the cars at the end of the drive hardly dared to look at his neighbour. Breuer knew that he had been a fool to believe that Unold had had any ambition to die a hero's death at Dubininski. But what did he hope to gain by changing the rallying-point and moving from one spot to another? They could not go any farther as the Volga blocked the way. Was this the final break-up, the panic-stricken 'sauve qui peut' inadequately camouflaged under a veneer of military formality?

Breuer had summoned up enough strength to face the final ordeal at Dubininski: now his strength had evaporated. He felt he ought to have stayed in Dubininski. Unold would not have prevented him. He had left Endrigkeit and the military policemen there. But while he was still there, the thought of staying behind had not occurred to Breuer. As a matter of fact when he had first grasped Unold's order, he had felt like a would-be suicide rescued at the last moment. An animal desire to go on living had possessed him and left no room in his mind for any thought beyond a longing to survive. Perhaps there was some way out. Perhaps there was still a chance of liberation.

Meanwhile he was choked with self-disgust.

Woom—— Woom—— Woom——

Another stick of bombs fell in the main ravine. The Russian airmen often dropped their bombs there, sparing the valley at the side, which seemed to contain nothing of importance. A few mortar shells from the far side of the Volga fell here but if the bunkers didn't get a direct hit, they were fairly safe.

Corporal Herbert cursed as he picked up the splinters of glass blown into the bunker by the explosion. He had only just mended a window-pane and had for hours been working to stop the cracks in the front wall of the bunker with paper and pieces of cloth. The new quarters were somewhat draughty and fine snow dust blew through the cracks in the door as far as the middle of the room. The fact that the glassless window afforded a full-sized view of the sun was only a minor consolation.

Geibel was sitting at the table cutting out strips of paper. For days hunger had been nagging at him, but now he hardly noticed it. He felt bitterly about the loss of his friend Lakosch and Herbert's irritable impatience had done nothing to console him. He wondered where Lakosch was now.

'D'you suppose the Russians have any arrangements for prisoners-of-war?' he said quietly to Herbert, squinting over at Breuer's bed. Breuer looked as if he were fast asleep. 'Perhaps they only kill the officers.' 'Oh, shut up! You're crazy,' said Herbert angrily. 'No,' went on Geibel undeterred. 'We're working men, aren't we? If the communists are on the side of the working man . . .' Herbert gave a nasty laugh. 'Don't make me laugh,' he said. 'With that grocer's shop of yours you're a bloated capitalist.'

'Do you think so?' said Geibel, putting down the knife. He had a look of horror in his eyes. 'I do wish that fellow would say something!' He pointed with his thumb over his shoulder at the back wall of the bunker, where a middle-aged man was slitting a light-blue French Zouave jacket. His round head with close-cropped hair was bent and his coarse-looking hands were folded between his knees. He was looking, without interest, at the splash of sunlight on the damp floor.

'If only he'd say something: but he hasn't said a word.'

'Have you seen the Colonel's food?' asked Breuer.

They both started. The Captain was awake. Had he heard their conversation?

'Yes, sir,' stuttered Geibel. 'They made a bit of a fuss to begin with but I fixed things up.'

Timofei Ivanovitch Gontsharov was an engineer officer and a Lieutenant-Colonel in the Red Army. In September 1942 Unold himself had selected him from a POW camp at Taganrog as leader of a newly-formed troop of Cossack auxiliaries.

In November, the day before the ring was closed, he had finally reached them. He had been unable to take over the Cossack troop, who had remained outside the ring at Mariupol. So he had spent the long, depressing weeks sitting around in the staff office, quiet and friendly, a burden to nobody. He had learnt a few phrases of German and had allowed himself to be shown off by Captain Siebel as a curiosity. There were plenty of volunteers, among the Russian POWs who would carry ammunition or clean the officer's boots for a plate of soup, but a Russian Lieutenant-Colonel, who wanted to fight on the side of the Germans was something out of the ordinary.

On the previous day they had suddenly found him standing before the door of the Intelligence bunker accompanied by a staff NCO. Captain Siebel had sent a message with his compliments saying that he supposed that prisoners-of-war were the concern of Intelligence which led to the transfer of POW Gontsharov to

Breuer's section. Just like them to do this, thought Breuer, when their own milk and honey was running short.

The Cossack auxiliaries had been started without consulting Intelligence and Breuer, who was furious, wanted to send the Russian back. However Fröhlich, who had recently been enduring misfortune with equanimity and was busy on some mysterious ploy of his own, had managed to arrange for the Russian to remain. He had long conversations with him which no one understood and when asked what they were all about he answered uncooperatively. But when Fröhlich was absent, which happened often enough, the Russian sat on a bench at the back of the bunker staring into space. He understood very little German, but saw what was happening and must have had a clear understanding of the general situation and of his own position.

In the region round Stalingrad trees were a valuable and much admired rarity. They did not grow on the steppe and in the hollows eaten out by melted snow-water a few clumps of miserable brush-wood were the most you could hope to find. And so the soldiers had named the long deep valley running from the north of the city westwards, which contained groups of sickly-looking alders, the valley of trees.

Colonel von Hermann had sent his car on to the car-park and was walking slowly down the narrow side-path. For the last ten days he had been in command of the Infantry Division on the Volga front. The transfer, for which he had worked and which he had eventually achieved, had been a flight from irksome inactivity to the centre of things, where incessant work and pressing respon-sibilities would leave him no time to himself.

His hopes had been only partly fulfilled. Wiese, the young Lieutenant with the patient, hollow-cheeked face, was a constant source of sad memories. He had acted on impulse in bringing Wiese with him. Now he realized that it had been a mistake. As to his new post being at the centre of things, his division, which belonged to the old establishment of the VIth Army and had had heavy losses in the autumn battles, was sitting comfortably in well-constructed positions on the steep bank of the Volga. The front was stagnant and, apart from occasional small operations by patrols, there was almost nothing doing. Winter clothing was available, the losses had, to some extent, been made good, and reserves of food which had been hidden in defiance of the army orders had been brought out to supplement the rations. Soon after his arrival the Colonel had visited the most advanced posts and had noticed a feeling of security and confidence.

'We can stick it here for two winters more if we have to, Colonel. Ivan won't get through here.' Except for the increasing numbers of units that had been withdrawn it would have been hard not to believe it. Von Hermann told himself that his troops would soon find out what was happening and then, perhaps, he would find forgetfulness in the final battle.

On the path which wound down the steep slope stood an officer, his fur collar turned up over his ears, motionless and grey as the trees. As the Colonel approached, he turned round. 'Ah, von Hermann, glad to see you.' The Colonel's face darkened as he saw the crumpled face with the eyes of a frightened mouse. Major-General Calmus had been his predecessor as Commander of the division. When the news of the encircling of the German armies was made known, he had had a nervous breakdown. Since then his professional activities had been limited to sitting in his bunker and calculating how long the supplies of munitions, food and liquid fuel would hold out. Finally the Army Command had relieved him of his post on grounds of sickness.

'I've been looking into the question of our wood supply', said the General in a whining, nagging voice. 'Up to the New Year ...' 'Don't worry, General,' interrupted the Colonel. 'We shan't need it. In a short time we'll find things hot enough here.'

He went on his way without listening to the frightened babblings of the General—a poor wreck of a man. In one of his fits of sadism the Army Commander had ordered him to stay with the troops. Now he wandered about like a ghost, sat down among the soldiers in their quarters and bored them with his moanings.

Farther down the slope the line of bunkers began. They were not dug-outs or improvised shanties but real dwellings, comfortable and lovingly laid out as if for permanent occupation.

In the OC's bunker the Second-in-Command, a thick-set broad-shouldered officer with a flattened boxer's face was leaning over a map and making heavy strokes with a charcoal pencil. In 1941 he had been one of the few survivors of a time-bomb outrage, which had blown up the soldier's club at Kiev. A broad scar on his forehead and a flickering look in his eyes were reminder of this experience.

'They're doing us down again, Colonel,' he said as his chief came in. 'First they take away one battalion after another and now that we can't spare any more they increase the length of our sector—The latest is that we're to take over from our neighbours on the right another 400 yards as far as . . .'

'Listen to me, Danne,' interrupted the Colonel. 'In the west our front has been smashed. Whether and where we shall find a line to stand on is something I don't know. Perhaps even Pitomnik is untenable now. We have been ordered to defend our rear with our own forces.'

The Second-in-Command's face paled, except for the scar on his forehead which glowed red. He sprang up and threw down his pencil. 'What!' he shouted, 'He has betrayed and sold us—the miserable scoundrel! Good God, I . . .'

Hermann's face had turned to stone.

'Pull yourself together, man,' he said coldly. 'After all you're a soldier, aren't you? Let me look at that map.'

The staff of the VIth Army had not expected a major attack by the Soviet forces so early in the year. Nevertheless when the Russians delivered their blow, they were not unprepared. Within the ring, positions had been provided in the rear with shorter lines of defence, which would make up for anticipated losses in men and material. On the map drawn up by the General Staff the names of flowers given to these lines were quite impressive. On the actual terrain the beaten and disintegrated troops saw nothing of these positions—'reception lines' they called them. They clung to hollows and ruins of houses, Russian dug-outs and rifle-pits and old half-destroyed flak positions, without knowing what was happening to right and left of them, defending their lives against superior forces when they still had the strength to resist. And it was in fact a miracle that during the first days of the attack the enemy who had brought up forces from the north, south and west including swarms of tanks and aircraft and who made use of massed artillery at the points of attack did not succeed in smashing up the Cauldron completely and that a German front of some sort continued to exist. This miracle was due on the one side to the courage of despair and the crazy faith of the defenders, and on the other to the unwillingness of the attackers to risk their lives in order to take a single machine-gun or attack a handful of half-frozen riflemen just to gain time, when they knew that the over-ripe fruit would fall into their hands in a day or two. And possibly too the great bluff was still working. The legend of invincibility, which Hitler had given to the army he had created out of nothing in four short years, and with which he had deceived the whole world. Perhaps too the Russian Moujik envisaged 'Frietz', who had after all penetrated to Moscow and Stalingrad, as an uncannily formidable opponent even in his present emaciated, ragged and miserable state.

The routine work of the Army Command during these days was almost always the same. The mornings were comparatively peaceful. Towards noon the telephone began to buzz and the telephone and wireless messages reporting alarming incidents piled up on the tables—— In one place the enemy were attacking without pause, in another a battalion had been dispersed, here a big breach had been made in the line and there the enemy tanks were through. One message reported that a staff had been surprised and were fighting the enemy at close-quarters. And what was worse was that no more news came from many units. These conditions gave rise to an epidemic of frenzied activity. Tanks which were lying wrecked somewhere in the snow, were allotted to particular crews which had already been dispersed and were straggling over the country. Forces which only existed on paper were directed to points which had long been occupied by the Russians. Trucks which lay burnt out by the roadside were being sent with ammunition which had long since been shot away to batteries, whose guns had, in the meantime, been put out of action or were in the hands of the enemy. In the evening the situation was checked up—on paper. Then followed a few short hours of rest till the next day when new batches of bad news found their way through the tortuous service channels to Army HQ and spread fresh anxiety and alarm.

Colonel Unold and Captain Engelhard had been harnessed to one of these teams. Soon after arriving at Stalingradski Unold had presented himself at Army Staff HQ and had reported that he had a complete divisional staff, at present unemployed. 'Unemployed,' said the Chief of Staff with a chilly smile. 'That can be remedied.' Since then the two men had been sitting in the Intelligence section busy with maps, reports and orders, while among their orphaned personnel malicious rumours were circulating about their sudden disappearance. However, one day orders from Colonel Unold had reached Captain Siebel and Lieutenant Breuer telling them to report in light marching order at Army Staff HQ.

The Intelligence Office was a large room with a low ceiling supported on props. Papers were heaped on desks and map-tables and a soldier was pasting cellophane over the narrow window-slits. Frequent bombing had made it clear that repairs were a waste of time. The other occupant of the room was an elderly officer in a field-grey greatcoat with a fur lining and the shoulder-badges of a Lieutenant-Colonel. From under his peaked cap, a narrow, lined face with a grey moustache looked out. His gaze rested for a moment on the newcomers and then turned to the wall. By his feet was a new, leather trunk. 'Is Colonel Unold here?' asked Siebel. 'He's with the Chief, sir,' answered the soldier from the window. 'He's sure to be back soon.' 'Let's hope so,' said the old Colonel grumpily, without moving his eyes from the wall. 'Been hanging about here for nearly half an hour. An odd way of doing business, I must say. Things weren't like that in the old Prussian Army.' 'There have been a lot of changes since then,' remarked Siebel, winking at Breuer. The old gentleman swallowed the bait and turning to Siebel said in an interested voice: 'Do you know what happened to me at the Pitomnik airport today? I never saw such a catastrophic muddle. Can't understand how such a thing is possible.'

Two hours ago he had returned from a course and was now in search of his unit. Breuer listened to him attentively. That face, that voice . . . he knew the man but couldn't remember from where.

A side door opened and Unold swept in with a rolled map under his arm.

'Aha, there you are, Siebel. I've got something new for you to do.' He unrolled the map on the table. 'Excuse me,' said the stranger, 'I've already been waiting here for half an hour. I came to ask for information as to where my columns are. I've just flown in . . .'

'Oh, just flown in, have you? Very nice,' interrupted Unold impatiently. 'Well, we need officers as badly as we need bread. Place yourself under the orders of the Captain here. Don't worry about rank, he is an experienced staff-officer. You'd better come and look over here. Here is the railway-line.'

The Lieutenant-Colonel was speechless for a moment. He fidgeted nervously with his pince-nez—'Excuse me,' he then said, 'there must be a misunderstanding. I am an artillery officer, I command a supply column. In the autumn my columns were at Karpovka and there . . .'

'Yes, yes,' broke in Unold angrily. 'You don't have to tell me. I'm not an idiot! Your columns must have been shot to pieces long ago. And your men are somewhere in the line; don't worry about them any more. You are now working, under Captain Siebel, on a matter of the highest importance . . . let me . . .'

The old gentleman began to tremble and stamp around like a naughty schoolboy—— 'Unheard of!' he cried. 'We are directly under the army. You can't give me orders. I shall . . .' Unold stood up. 'Do you know where you are? We have martial law here, sir— *Martial Law*. And we don't treat it lightly.' The older man opened his mouth a few times like a fish on dry land, but no sound came out. Staring helplessly at Unold, he started wiping his spectacles with his handkerchief, as though they were responsible for his not understanding what it was all about.

Unold turned away and rolled out the map once more.

'Look, Siebel,' he said, 'this is how things stand. The by-pass to the west between Gumrak and Voroponovo has been settled on as the inner line of defence—in case of emergency. A regular line has got to be built up here with bunkers, snipers' nests, rifle-pits, anti-tank positions and so on. That's your job. You must barricade all the railway crossings and pick up everyone coming from the west. Everyone, including drivers of vehicles. The only exceptions are members of the staff and wounded men. Vehicles must be taken to one side and abandoned. We shan't need them any more. It's essential that the work should be done with the utmost speed. Is that clear?'

Siebel's face grew hard.

'Who's to man the road-blocks?'

'The Field-Police and the 51st Corps is under your orders.'

'Entrenching tools?'

Unold's eyelids began to twitch and he drummed with his fingers on the map.

'Good God, man, don't make difficulties about trifles. You'll have to manage those things for yourself.'

'For myself . . . !' cried Siebel, pulling his fur cap from his head and throwing it on the table. Then, leaning on his good arm, he went on: 'Colonel, I've seen all this before. You draw your finger across the map, and that's the new line of defence. The poor sod who gets the order collects the blame if things go wrong. You've got him by the short hairs. But not me, Colonel, not me. Give me three battalions of pioneers and I'll build you a super line in three days. But if you say "you must manage for yourself" I say "can't be done".'

Unold's yellow face grew paler. 'Siebel,' he whispered, 'Are you crazy?'

There was a loud whizzing sound and simultaneously with the following crash an invisible hand tore the cellophane from the window. A cloud of dust and snow filled the room. The blast drove the three officers against the wall. When the dust had subsided Unold pressed the map into Siebel's hand and said: 'Now, off you go, gentlemen,' and pushed the three of them out of the bunker.

The Talovo depression, which ran in a gentle curve more or less following the loop-line and slowly tapering until it reached the Volga, looked peaceful enough in the noon-day sun. Its slopes were covered with bushes, overtopped at intervals by a few low trees, between which the wooden façades of bunkers looked like week-end cottages. At the bottom horses were pasturing and in places washing was hanging out to dry. A steaming field-kitchen was diffusing a delicious smell of pea-soup through the valley. Not far away a slaughter-house party were at work. The joints and carcasses of freshly slaughtered beasts looked rosy and appetizing as they hung on the walls of the sheds.

Breuer took this idyllic scene for a mirage. Siebel, who wanted to drive over the projected line of defence, had taken Breuer with him as far as the head of the valley. Breuer was to prepare billets for the troops. Now he was on his way to the battle HQ of the Corps, which had been holding a portion of the Volga front since the autumn.

Soon he was sitting on a black leather chair facing two Ordnance officers. They had received him courteously, but slightly distantly.

'We've had instructions,' they said. 'We know that Captain Siebel has been ordered to prepare a line of defence over there.'

'Over there', in fact, meant some three kilometres to the rear.

Breuer was painfully conscious of the contrast between the well-cared for hands and faces of these people, their highly-polished riding-boots, the fresh-looking medal ribbons on their elegant tunics and his own ragged and louse-ridden shabbiness. The spotless bunker, with framed oil paintings on the walls, an Astrakhan rug on the boarded floor and yellow, polished writing-tables was furnished as comfortably as a room at home. After apologizing for his own appearance, he began to talk of the last days and weeks.

The two officers listened with polite interest, saying: 'Yes, we heard something about it. Terrible show, isn't it?' as though they were discussing an earthquake in Peru.

'It's an astounding development,' said a youngish cavalry Captain with a soft freckled face. Here on the Volga everything has been absolutely quiet for weeks. The Russians won't get through here.'

This sounded very self-satisfied to Breuer, though it was said in all innocence. Good heavens, he thought, these people still don't understand!

'You're sitting in well-constructed positions,' he said hotly, 'but what good will that do you? I beg you to try and grasp the situation. In a few days, perhaps a few hours, the battle-front will be a few hundred yards to your rear.'

The officers nodded anxiously. Apart from anything else, they were worried about the poor fellow in front of them. His nerve seemed to have gone. They heard what he had got to say, but they did not grasp its implications.

Towards the west the Talovo ravine opened out into a flat depression looking like a village square. It seemed to be skirted with low, wooden cottages which in fact were the wooden frontages of bunkers with their doors and windows, which had been built into the steep sides of the depression. Smoke was curling up over a few bunkers, but the place gave the impression of haunted loneliness. On one of the doors was a notice saying 'Ranger's Hut'. The officer accompanying Breuer opened the door with a key—'Come in please,' he said. Breuer found himself in a large room, with panelled walls. On one side was a great stove made of mud bricks with the joints painted white, which could also be used as a cooking range. In front of it there were benches built into the ground and cottage chairs which, with an oak table, formed a comfortable living corner. The big window was provided with black-out shutters and flowered curtains in red and white. At the end of the room were two three-storeyed sets of berths.

Breuer looked at the Ordnance officer.

'Pretty, isn't it?' said the latter, somewhat embarrassed, and clearly worried as to whether the standard of comfort would meet the requirements of the Army staff. 'The Field Police of one of our infantry divisions have installed themselves here for the winter. They've gone out to do some cordoning jobs. It'll be some time before they're back.'

They would never come back.

He opened a side-door and the two men found themselves in a bar. It was a perfectly good bar with stools, counter, and red walls covered with spirited paintings of dancing couples and half-naked girls as well as lines from popular songs. The shelves behind the counter were, of course, empty. Against the wall stood a heavy German stove.

The Ordnance officer shook his head and smiled, saying: 'Very ritzy!' He went on: 'I hope you'll be all right here. Everything is at your disposal. You get your telephone connections through the Corps exchange, and you ask for Extension 5. Now I must leave you.'

Breuer carried an armful of firewood into the bunker and lit the stove. He pulled off his felt boots, hung his socks up to dry and stretched his legs towards the fire. He closed his eyes and thought of nothing, like a shipwrecked mariner feeling the planks of the life-boat under his feet——

After he had rested he went out to find the supplies bunker.

'Aha, the Siebel mob,' said a Commissariat officer in friendly greeting. 'I see that there are five of you, so I'll give you five day's rations all together, that'll save you the trouble of coming here every day.'

He laid out a few loaves on the table, a couple of tins of meat and a tin of coffee. Then he weighed out a great lump of butter—real butter—and finally produced a sausage, as thick as a small tree and as long as a man's fore-arm.

'From our own butcher,' he said. 'Horseflesh, of course, but good quality, believe me. Sign for it here?'

A bottle suddenly appeared on the table.

'Martell,' he said, 'for officers' messes—five marks the bottle. I can spare you one. . . .'

It was getting dark and the winter night was drawing on, quiet and peaceful. Breuer sat before the stove eating bread and butter, while on the top the hot water for coffee was boiling. He gave a start; the wooden ring with glass bulbs on the ceiling had burst into blinding light. Breuer stared at the brightness till his eyes smarted. Electric light, Dubininski, 100 grams of bread . . . Where was he? He walked on tiptoe to the switch by the door and turned it on and off, giggling happily to himself. Then he stopped and put his hand to his eyes.

It was long after nightfall when Siebel and the Lieutenant-Colonel came in, powdered with snow and half-frozen. They found Breuer standing by the fire roasting slices of sausage. Breuer looked at the Captain's tortured face.

'What was it like there?'

Siebel pulled off his cap and slung it sideways through the air. 'To hell with it!' he said. For the first time he became conscious of the unfamiliar surroundings and said: 'What the devil's happened here?'

Breuer grinned and said: 'Father Christmas has been here.' Then he told him what had happened during the day. Siebel shook his head as he listened.

'Well, let's have some supper,' he said. 'After that, who cares?'

The Lieutenant-Colonel seemed less surprised at everything than the other two men. He had already unpacked his trunk and taken out a pair of slippers. Now he examined the beds and complained of the hard mattress. Breuer gazed reflectively at his wrinkled face and his moustache and the parting in the middle of his grey hair. It seemed strange and yet somehow familiar to him. Where had he met this man before?

They ate and drank and learnt how to laugh again. Afterwards they fell into their beds and their sleep was deep and dreamless.

Not far from the tents, bunkers and sheds of the airfield lay the village of Pitomnik. A dozen snowed-up cottages and a multitude of white, ice-bound vehicles standing stiff and dead. Everything living in this polar settlement had been forced by the cold and the incessant bombing to creep under the earth, which was riddled with holes like a giant molehill.

Lieutenant Harras was sitting in one of the holes, squatting on the bare earth with his knees drawn up and his back against a greasy wall. Wedged in between the bodies of strangers, he was dozing with half-open eyes. Hunger, exhaustion and the events of the last days had left their mark on him; his face was covered with stubble and hardly distinguishable from the cracked surface of the brownish-grey wall. His wounded hand lay on his knee, throbbing and ticking like a clock.

The bunker was full of men cowering round the walls. In the middle sat a Supply Officer at a table with a candle on it. In front of him was a pile of tins and loaves of bread and near him an aluminium bowl of butter. He was doing sums and making entries and only occasionally and unwillingly looking past the candle's narrow circle of light into the darkness. Then the door-flap opened to admit persons seeking protection and with them a blast from the icy outside weather. Harras gave a dirty side-long glance at the table. When he had come from the airfield, he had asked the Supply Officer for rations. 'What unit? How many men?' asked the other. 'I'm alone—displaced.' 'Sorry, I can't give you anything. Rations can only be issued to units.' Several times during the course of the afternoon this answer had been given to hungry individuals, who did not always take it lying down. But there was a pistol on the table—and the safety-catch was off.

Hunger and rage were maddening Harras. If he had had the strength he would have slugged the bastard in the mouth—the stupid, obstinate, bureaucrat! He couldn't remember when he had last eaten—— Two tins of corned beef had been pinched from him by some lousy fellow, before he had had time to read the labels. What a life! thought Harras bitterly. They wouldn't have dared to steal from an officer in the old days.

He closed his eyes and his features contracted under the nagging pain which ran from his wounded hand to his elbow. Harras had somehow to believe that the bullet from his pistol which had passed through the palm of his left hand had been discharged accidentally. He had seriously believed that such an injury would entitle him to be flown home. Now there were hundreds lying in bunkers and tents waiting for transport—men without arms, without legs, with bellies shot through or fractured skulls. It would have been better for him to stay with the Russians. It couldn't have been much worse on their side. But who could have guessed that this was coming?

Harras felt someone tugging his sleeve. He looked round sleepily.

'Lieutenant,' said a thin voice coming from a man with a face like a shrew-mouse and a pair of lively eyes like buttons. 'You haven't anything to eat, have you?'

Harras closed his eyes again. An idiotic question didn't deserve an answer.

'Can you tell me where the staff are quartered?' asked the shrew-mouse undeterred. Harras grunted something that sounded like 'idiot'. He had no desire for conversation.

'I think they'd find something to eat for a man who could tell them that he had been on the other side, with the Russians.'

Harras pricked up his ears but some of the other men seemed to be paying attention.

'Were you with the Russkis? Come on, man, tell us about it.'

The shrew-mouse, flattered by this unexpected interest, said:

'I'll tell you. They caught us at Dubininski or whatever that hole was called, me and two other chaps. They started by delousing us all over, even our boots, we thought they might do us in. But then a man in a leather coat came in and things began to hum. The Russians are sharp, that's what they are. They gave us back all the things they'd taken from us and fed us as well. Then the man in the leather coat asked us if we wanted to go back to our side. Neumann was afraid they'd shoot us in the back, but the other bloke and I said 'yes' at once and they let us go . . .'

'Just like that, without conditions?'

'Yes, and the man in the leather coat said we could tell them how we had been treated, and that the soldiers should make an end of the war and that Hitler was to blame for everything.'

Harras listened, embarrassed. 'Tell me,' he asked, 'did you meet any Germans over there? I mean German civilians.'

'German civilians?' repeated the man, looking at Harras without understanding. 'The bloke in the leather coat could speak German, but not very well. There was another fellow in our soldier's kit, who spoke German properly. A red-headed man with freckles.'

'In German uniform? I bet he was a Commissar in disguise.'

'Yes, or a Jew. They all know German, the devils. Red-haired, you said, with freckles. I know a fellow like that. He used to peddle mousetraps in '32 in our village in Finkenwerder.'

'Yes' went on the shrew-mouse, who had become somewhat subdued on seeing that his experiences seemed to have such varied interpretations, 'and the man who looked like a soldier said that nobody was going to get shot and we ought to ask the German Sergeant-Major who had been there once, as he knew exactly. A man with a name like a dog. Do you know anyone like that, Lieutenant?'

Harras had gone to sleep again.

Some hours later the silence was torn asunder by a few sharp detonations, following swiftly on one another. Machine-gun fire broke out and the sound of cries was heard in the bunker. Harras's subconscious registered 'Air Raid' and his weary head sank down once more.

Then someone shouted through the flap of the bunker 'Out! The Russkis are here.'

The Supply Officer was the first to spring to his feet. Harras continued to sit leaning against the wall. His exhausted body struggled against the impulse to wake up. That's grand, he thought, half-asleep. At least there's room in here. But the bitter cold brought him to his senses. The bunker was almost empty. The candle was still flickering on the table, and he jumped up and saw someone creeping about the floor and scratching up butter from the ground and pushing it into his mouth. Harras stepped over him and found another man crouching in a corner by the door. Harras took him by the shoulder and shook him, saying: 'Hey, get up. This is it —the Russians are here.' The man stared at him in silence and did not move. When Harras had forced his way through the narrow entrance, he was carried away by a raging whirlpool of humanity which swept him into the tumult of the flash-lit night. The earth was spewing up men from holes in the ground; the air was full of shooting and wild cries: the howling of motor-horns, the rattle of skid-chains and the sound of heavy wheels pounding through the snow. Harras felt himself being pressed against the sides of swaying vehicles, with clusters of men hanging on to them; he stumbled over bodies and saw by the light of the flames on blazing house-tops the contorted faces of officers shouting orders and the pistol barrels of gesticulating Field-Police. Coloured fire-balls were lobbing up into the sky and on one side was a parachute-flare. Reports and crashes came from all directions. Tracer bullets flew just over the heads of the crowd.

Harras took in all this, wide awake by now. The piercing cold which pricked his face had fully aroused him. Unable to help himself, he floated in the middle of the stream like a piece of wood, neither knowing nor asking where he was going.

Suddenly the pressure lightened, and he heard the words 'To

Stalingrad,' which caught the mood of the crowd as a spark catches dry tinder. So the stream of men poured eastwards out into the darkness of the steppe.

Somewhere in midstream an open personnel car was swimming. In the back seat was sitting a single officer in a fur coat, Colonel Steigmann. He sat very stiffly with his head leaning back. A Colonel without a regiment: a head without a body.

Harras shuffled along the broad track levelled out by a tractor. A little while back he had fallen, but had managed to pull himself up. Death was waiting for him everywhere: in the knee-deep snow at the side of the road and on the highway from wheels and skid-chains. Meanwhile the frost was creeping up his limbs and driving all the warmth he had out of his body. It had reached his chest and at every breath he took he felt as though needles were piercing his lungs. The men marched onwards silent and shadow-like, uttering no sound as they fought to get near the cars, and no cry as they collapsed. Only the cars seemed to be alive, as they snorted and groaned and howled their warnings into the darkness.

A truck full of boxes was standing by the roadside and near it a fur-clad figure holding a loaf of bread in his outstretched hand. 'I'll swop bread for gas!' he croaked, 'who'll give me a drop of gas for this bread?' The stream pushed past him and no one seemed to hear him. But then someone struck him and grabbed the bread . . . With a cry of rage the soldier sprang forward. They grappled with one another and one of them fell to the ground with a gurgling cry, which was soon silenced as a truck passed over him . . . In a moment the crowd were swarming over the boxes in the car.

Harras felt as if he were on stilts as he moved forwards; he had no sensation in his limbs. On the right-hand side of the road an artillery column had halted, three light 4-inch field howitzers with their tractor in front. Almost a complete battery in battle order—something that hadn't been seen for months. Near the leading gun the battery officer was standing. He had laid an arm on the barrel of the gun—not a very safe thing to do, for on a night like this a man's flesh could freeze to the metal. He stood there staring into the darkness. He ought to have blown up his guns when he came to the end of his ammunition, but he hadn't had the heart to carry out the order and had retired on his own initiative with the howitzers. They had 'borrowed' gasolene from staff cars and had been able to push on as far as this, but now they could get no farther. 'Remove the breech-blocks. Prepare to proceed on foot,' ordered the officer in a voice he didn't recognize.

A truck had left the road and got temporarily stuck in a drift. Immediately some of the walkers tried to climb into it. The men inside fended them off angrily. Harras staggered alongside the vehicle. By this time he could neither see nor hear. His brain had become a lump of ice, incapable of shaping a thought.

He collapsed against the wooden side of the vehicle and his knees gave way. He looked up once more at the star-sprinkled night sky and saw a face looking down at him and the arm of the man to whom the face belonged raised to strike him.

'Lieutenant, is it you?' A hand clutched at his coat collar.

'Give us a hand, chaps. It's one of our officers.' Hands seized him and drew him up. Tumbling over sacks and boxes, he came to rest in a soft corner. A fur coat and some blankets were thrown to him.

'How did you get here, Lieutenant?' The truck belonged to the baggage train and the men in it to the battalion staff—Lehmann, Warrant Officer Werner and Josupat, who had recognized him in the darkness in spite of his changed appearance. A hand held a bottle to his mouth. He drank and felt the fiery liquid coursing through his limbs. His face relaxed into a helpless smile, but he could not speak. . . .

Among the vehicles carried along with the stream of fleeing men in the Talovo depression was an open car, a Wanderer with a four-wheel drive. The road having come to a stop, the driver leant back to ask Colonel Steigmann for fresh instructions, but the Colonel did not move. He looked strangely stiff as he sat there in his corner and the driver felt uneasy and got out. When he took hold of the Colonel's sleeve, his body fell against him. He was already cold. The blood on his temple was congealed. It had not been a back-fire. . . .

And all this chaos and confusion, despair and death, had been caused by a trifling incident. A Russian advance party with two or three tanks had pushed forward into Pitomnik and after firing a few bursts had withdrawn.

The old Lieutenant-Colonel had lunched well in the friendly bunker at the extremity of the Talovo Valley and had settled down to a cup of coffee in the living-room. The two other men had gone out early leaving him to guard the house. Things outside looked very uncomfortable. The window-glass was coated with ice a quarter of an inch thick and he could see the stove eating up the logs, without giving out much warmth. He did not understand what Captain Siebel's party were supposed to be doing. On the previous day they had driven along the lonely railway embankment and had inspected the Field-Police detachments, which stood idle and half-frozen at the road-blocks. Even the Captain didn't seem to know what to do next. It was impossible to know what the Army Command were aiming at, and he couldn't grasp the idea of a whole army being surrounded. Nothing like that had happened in the First World War. Things had, indeed, changed since the days of the old Prussian Army. In any case he was heartily sick of the whole business. He would look about him for a day or two and then set out in search of his columns. After all one didn't leave ammunition columns lying about like umbrellas.

With a curse the old man flung a book on the table and stood up. He couldn't understand all the noise outside. He threw open the door and the icy wind prevented him from breathing and made him cough. The square had filled up with men and motor-cars. Before the entrance stood a car with the hood down and something looking like a polar-bear in front of it.

A voice called 'Hi, you!' The Colonel was shaken by another fit of coughing. The polar-bear turned round and stared at him for a moment, before sinking down once more over the running engine.

The Colonel shut the door with difficulty and put the last blocks of wood on the fire. Then he pulled down the black-out curtains and turned up the electric light. He turned back to his book . . .

Suddenly the door flew open and an icy draught blew into the room. The Colonel put down his book.

'What's all this?' he said, as he took off his pince-nez. In a moment he found himself looking speechlessly at five or six men, evidently soldiers, but in what a state!

The old officer rose slowly to his feet. 'What is the meaning of this?' he said, half aloud, trying to control his voice. 'Where have you come from?'

The soldiers stopped where they were, looking stupidly at the brightly-lit scene. They carried no arms, and their bodies were covered with blankets and old sacks. Their heads and limbs were enveloped in rags and the patches of bare flesh showing between them were swollen and blue. The Colonel couldn't think what was happening and cried out in a tone of disgust——

'Are you mad?'

The leading man took his cap off his head and twisted it in his hands. Out of the left side of his face, which was swollen, stared an overlarge eye, while the other side which was grey and hollow twitched incessantly, giving him a cunning, clownish aspect.

'Excuse me, sir,' he said in a hoarse, rusty voice. 'We thought ... we wanted ...'

'And so you just crashed in here?' said the Colonel, by now shaking with rage. 'This is a staff billet, do you understand? A staff billet!'

'We've come from Pitomnik. The Russians are in there. We've been running all day.'

'That's all very well,' said the Colonel. He had suddenly become quite calm. After all, these were poor fellows, and it was a waste of time to address them in military language. They had probably been through some frightful experience. . . . 'Very well,' he continued, 'but, you see, this is a staff billet and we have important work to do. You must understand that.' And then he was ashamed of himself for being so soft and resumed the attitude of a superior officer: strict and inexorable. 'That's all,' he said sharply. 'About turn, quick march!'

It was a mystery to the soldiers. Their frozen brains could only understand one thing—unless they could now find a warm place to rest in, they were finished. Here was a bunker, brightly lit and warm, almost empty and seemingly prepared for them by a good fairy. That they could understand. But the Colonel was mistaken in his judgment of them. They still were soldiers. In their confused brains there was still something which reacted to epaulets and a commanding voice . . . They moved slowly back and squeezed themselves through the narrow door into the night. . . .

The Colonel turned the key in the lock, to prevent this happening again, and took up his book again. But the incident continued to worry him. He couldn't believe such a thing possible. Even in the débâcle of 1918 which had been bad enough, he had seen nothing like that. Suddenly he recounted that they had said the Russians were in Pitomnik, where he had landed the day before. Absurd!

Hours later Breuer came back alone. Siebel had dropped him at the entrance to the valley, and had gone on alone to the Army Staff HQ. Breuer found the bunker very cold and untidy. The Lieutenant-Colonel, wearing his fur coat and cap with his trunk packed on the floor in front of him, received Breuer crossly.

'Back at last, are you?' he said. 'A nice state of affairs. I was on the point of going away.'

'You can do whatever you like,' said Breuer. 'Our work here is finished.'

He fell exhausted to the bench in the corner. His eyes were still full of images of the panic-stricken stampede. What was going to happen, when he reported to the Army Staff that their plan was wrecked and their mission impracticable? Siebel would have to pay . . .

The old officer said angrily: 'In the first war things were different. In 1918 I took my machine-gun company intact and in perfect order back over the Rhine. But of course this famous Army Command is to blame, this handful of ignorant men who let a Lance-Corporal lead them by the nose.'

Breuer stared at him in the half-light then scales seemed to fall from his eyes and a storm of rage overwhelmed him. He sprang at the old man, seized him by his coat collar and shook him till he fell on his knees.

'Who is to blame? You say the Army Command. I'll tell you who is to blame. You are to blame! You with your "Stahlhelm", your Sedan anniversaries and your damned songs, poisoning the minds of children—you are guilty and you alone, Herr Doktor Strackwitz.'

The Lieutenant-Colonel's eyes started out of his head. He broke loose with a swift movement, grabbed his trunk and tumbled out of the bunker.

The Talovo Valley was no longer peaceful. The way back, which ran at right angles to the roads leading into Stalingrad, had very little traffic on it and they progressed at a good speed. Breuer had tucked himself into a corner seat and tried to sleep in spite of the cold. He did not succeed. His nerves were still jumping. The flood of fugitives from Pitomnik had marked the beginning of the collapse, the first warning of the chaos to come. They had been helpless in the face of this tragic rout and the mission entrusted to them by the Army Staff seemed a mockery. Prepared for the worst, Siebel had driven back to report to Unold that his orders could not be carried out. Breuer had expected to see him down-graded or put under arrest. But when he came back, rather late, he was a Major! The Commander, who, in view of the special situation, had been granted the right to make promotions up to the rank of Major General and award decorations up to the Knight's Cross, had personally announced this special promotion in recognition of 'outstanding services in the defence of the Fortress'. Siebel, who had had no opportunity of making a detailed report about his mission, found himself relieved of it. The further construction of defence line 'Sunflower' would be taken over by the 3rd Motorized Infantry Division. Siebel had driven away before anyone from the motorized division had appeared.

When they got to the railway crossing at Gumrak they found they could go no farther. The road was choked with people. Parachute lights were swinging over the village and a house was burning on the right. Siebel got out of the car and led the way for the driver to take it over the snow through a collection of vehicles and crowds of cursing soldiers till finally, after a violent exchange of discourtesies with an officer, he managed to get it safely over the railway embankment.

When he was back in the car and wrapped up in his rugs he said to Breuer:

'Tonight is my wedding-night.'

Breuer looked at him mystified . . .

'Wedding-night? What do you mean?'

'Long-distance marriage, by proxy. Done by the Army Radio via the High Command. Paulus himself recommended it—he understands about that sort of thing. In two hours I got a message of confirmation from my fiancée.'

When they arrived at the Staff HQ at Stalingradski they found to their astonishment that Unold and Engelhard had rejoined them.

Their bunker was nothing like the splendid quarters Unold had had built for himself recently at Dubininski. That they were still sitting in this small and dirty dug-out late at night was due to Engelhard's exaggerated sense of what was correct. He could not admit that such a surprising double event—marriage and promotion—in the career of an officer in this staff, should be passed over in silence.

Unold had been mystified by the Commander's unexpected announcement and when, shortly after Siebel had been relieved of his mission by the army, Engelhard suggested to him that they should get up a small improvised celebration, he had not answered. Engelhard had taken his silence for consent and had invited Siebel and Breuer to come round for a drink. He had managed to get hold of four aluminium mugs and produced a bottle of Benedictine from his own store. Siebel took a couple of bottles of cognac from his pockets and set them on the table, saying: 'This is really my party.'

He placed one of the bottles between his knees, pulled out the cork with his good hand and poured the brandy into the mugs.

'Cheers,' he said. 'To my wedding-night!' Captain Engelhard smiled. He had managed to get hold of two epaulets and was looking forward to fixing them to Siebel's shoulders.

'To your promotion, Major,' he said and raised his mug.

Siebel put his drink down, untasted. He looked the other up and down.

'Yes,' he said, 'to that too—— Damnation,' and drank it down at a draught. 'Now she's sitting at home crying. . . .' And he slammed his mug on the table.

Engelhard made a wry face.

'Take it easy, please,' he said, turning his head to the dark corner of the bunker. 'The Colonel is resting. It's been a hard day.'

For the first time the two guests saw that there was a man lying under a blanket on the camp-bed. It was Unold. He was lying flat on his back, his eyes were closed and his mouth open. On a stool near the bed stood a framed photograph—and by it, ready to hand, a pistol. Siebel gazed for a few moments silently into the corner. Then he turned, 'A hard day, yes,' he said quietly. 'I'm surprised that you noticed it. After all you saw nothing and know nothing of what happened . . . You didn't see the German army rolling in the filth. You've been just sitting here, sketching out defence lines on paper. But it's finished, man. Finished and done with . . .'

Engelhard did not raise his glass. Why couldn't they shut up? He had looked forward to spending the evening talking about other things, but he saw that this was going to be impossible.

'Do you really think so, Major?' he said darkly.

'Well, I don't believe the staff are under any illusions as to our power to defend ourselves, so we've only one thing to do! Sell our lives as dearly as we can and to die as decently as we are able. When there's no other way out, there's always a pistol.'

'Decently!' snorted Siebel bitterly. 'Starving, frozen—dying like beasts in the snow—— What a night, Engelhard! You should have been there to see—— Decent? There's no decency here, in life or in death. He has lied and betrayed us—cheated us of our soldier's honour and of the chance of a decent soldier's death. The man has ruined more than an army—it can't be mended.'

'Major, I beg you!' said Engelhard, honestly shocked. 'We're all in, but even so we should behave with self control. . . . The super-human, historic personality of the Führer is not subject to our criticism. He is above good or evil.'

He threw a swift glance at the camp-bed, but no sign came to confirm his sentiments. The Colonel seemed to be far away.

Major Siebel was dangerously drunk.

'You don't have to explain to me what decent behaviour is,' he said with a calm lucidity which went strangely with his disordered expression. 'I didn't win my Knight's Cross at an office table. It cost me my arm which is rotting somewhere in a mud hole on the

Volchov. I'm ready to lose the other or a leg or both, but not my head, sir, no thanks. I need that still and I mean to get out of here.'

Engelhard wanted to answer, but was checked by a gesture.

'You all think the same as I do, only you haven't the guts to say so. If there was a chance of getting an air-lift out of here, you'd be off like a shot.'

'Major!'

'Of course you would! Good behaviour means having the courage to tell the truth. I don't mean to die like a dog here, and I'm not going to blow my brains out. I want to go back home again, Engelhard, if it takes me five years or ten or fifteen to get there—partly for her sake of course, so that this day shan't be without meaning, but first and foremost to pay off the score that I owe to this herd of swine.'

Siebel was shouting now and Engelhard's only worry was that Unold might wake up. He seemed to be sleeping deeply for he did not move.

'Cheers!' said Major Siebel. His face was crumpling and tears were running from his eyes. He put down his mug and stroked his brow with the back of his hand. Then, leaning on the table with outstretched hand he pushed himself to his feet and stood there with his legs apart and his head bowed, like a wounded bull.

'I've had enough,' he said. 'Come along, Breuer. There's no sense in getting drunk. We've got to keep awake, damn it. Well, Engelhard, no offence meant and many thanks to you for helping me to celebrate my wedding-day.'

Soon afterwards Pitomnik was lost for good and in the west and south the front was withdrawn to the railway line which surrounded the town of Stalingrad in a wide circle. Only the northern front of the salient, frequently attacked and desperately contested, still held firm. In consequence the Russian plan to split the Cauldron into four segments and smash them in turn failed for the time being. A respite was granted to the condemned armies, who continued to hope for the promised relief.

This hope no longer contained any element of enthusiasm; it was dumb and bitter and cherished by exhausted spirits who simply could not endure the naked truth. But it lent the men the strength to resist to the end. Fuel and ammunition had almost run out. The stream of air borne supplies had practically dried up. The alternative air field at Gumrak was under fire by day and night, and landing on the crater-pitted and ill-marked runway under a hail of hostile bombs and shells without any fighter cover, was a life-or-death adventure. Improvised sledges, made out of gasolene cans, were used by the exhausted pioneers to drag the scanty supplies to the men in the line, who crouched behind anti-tank or machine-guns in pill-boxes made of snow and ice and often enough had no weapons but their rifle-butts and side-arms. At a point on the railway embankment south of Gumrak four men with an anti-tank gun shot up twelve Russian tanks with their last twelve rounds before they themselves fell beside their gun.

Farther to the north a group of twenty men under the command of a Major, who had been holding the Russians off for a whole day, fought their way out and rejoined their unit. On all sides miracles of daring and resource occurred in the midst of the slaughter. They had to hold out. The Führer had promised help. He would not, *could* not sacrifice a whole army. The relief must be near. Twenty machine-guns of a completely new type had recently been flown in —wonderful weapons capable of firing 2,000 shots a minute. The only trouble was that they didn't have the 2,000 shots. . . . However, it showed they weren't forgotten. They had to stick it out.

Only the senior staff officers had given up hope. They knew the truth and only worried about one thing. *How* was it going to end? In mid-December the instructions were that no officer should allow himself to be taken alive. He had to shoot himself. Since then things had changed, and now the official view was that officers should share the fate of the troops, whatever that might mean. Even the Chief of the Army Staff had lost his faith, though his great blue eyes had lost none of their brilliance. He sent his chief orderly officer to Hitler begging for help within forty-eight hours. The orderly officer never came back and help never came either. There was none to come.

One day Lieutenant-Colonel Unold ordered his staff to meet him in Captain Gedig's bunker into which he had recently moved. Breuer, who went across with Fröhlich, was astonished to find so many people there. There were a number of faces he had not seen for weeks. They were all crowded into the small bunker, looking helplessly and with trepidation at the Colonel, who received them lying on a camp-bed. Unold had not bothered about his divisional staff for a long time. It must be something unusual that had made him suddenly think of them. The walls of the room were draped with blankets, which swallowed every sound and robbed voices of their resonance. Unold was unwell, as Engelhard had explained in a whisper. The suspense and uncertainty of the last few days had worn him out completely.

Engelhard bent down and reported that all were present, upon which Unold sat up and, supporting himself with his left hand, looked round the company with wavering eyes. When he came to Lieutenant von Horn's arrogant face he stopped and said: 'My God, Horn, can't you take off your eye-glass?' The Lieutenant clicked his heels together and bowed slightly from the hips before replying with a kind of impertinent politeness—'Certainly, sir.'

'Gentlemen,' said Unold in a voice that had neither colour nor resonance, 'for some time our division has had no *de facto* existence. Now I have to inform you that from today it has ceased to exist *de jure*. The few remaining men belonging to the Artillery Regiment and the Signals, as well as the remnants of the Tank Regiment are now under the command of Colonel Lunitz. They will be known as the Fighting Group Lunitz and will be at the disposal of the army. What arrangements are being made for the officers and other personnel of the divisional staff, I do not know. . . . Our division has carried its colours with honour as far as Stalingrad. As we hand them back today, we do so with a consciousness of their proud and glorious past.'

Unold's voice quavered and his face trembled. The others, who had never seen him look like this before, were deeply shocked.

Meanwhile Captain Gedig had placed two bottles of French brandy on the table, survivals from Unold's carefully hoarded mess allowance.

'We have no glasses,' said Unold, 'so let's pass the bottle round like they do in the Navy.'

They walked along the edge of the ravine back to the Intelligence Section. As they strode into the teeth of the wind Fröhlich said to Breuer: 'I've got something I'd like to say to you, and now's the time to say it.'

'Hm,' growled Breuer discouragingly. He had lost interest in Fröhlich's fantasies.

'Now that the division no longer exists,' went on Fröhlich, 'I've worked out a plan for getting away.'

Breuer stopped dead and began to laugh.

'You, Fröhlich! I thought the Führer was coming to fetch us away! Too bad if he finds you've already gone.'

'The Führer *is* coming,' replied Fröhlich with a wave of his hand. 'He keeps his word. But . . . perhaps he'll be too late. One has to take precautions . . .'

Breuer gave a sigh.

'Do you still believe in the columns of tanks on the road that follows the River Don?' he said, like a schoolmaster talking to a child. 'How far away do you think our main front-line is now? At least 200 kilometres. And do you propose to get there on foot? This is mid-winter and it would take weeks to cover the distance . . . Even if we could collect enough food, and managed to get past the Russians, we shouldn't get more than a dozen miles. The first night out would be our last.'

Fröhlich shook his head. 'I know all that, I'm not an ass. Of course we must drive.'

Breuer shrugged as they went into their bunker. Horn had developed a similar plan. An armoured car, loaded with provisions with ten men inside with M.G.s and sub-machine-guns, and at the last moment a surprise dash through the Russian lines . . . It would have been highly dramatic and heroic, but it would still have been suicide. Breuer took off his coat and went to the stove. Herbert and Geibel were not back, only the Russian was sitting in his accustomed place and cutting kindling wood for the fire.

Fröhlich sat down at the table and folded his bony hands. 'Won't you listen to me for ten minutes?' he said. 'I really believe that with a bit of luck we can get over there in twenty-four hours, or at the most two days. I've worked everything out very carefully.'

'Very well, fire away then.'

Breuer had taken in his second pair of trousers which he had left hanging in the frosty air in front of the door and was looking to see how the lice stood a temperature of minus 28 degrees. Then he said to Fröhlich: 'I don't suppose you'll want to drive the Command car, but perhaps you think Major Kalweit will put his last tank at your disposal.'

Fröhlich who usually flared up very easily, paid no attention to the sarcasm. He thoughtfully unfolded his plan.

Breuer listened without any particular interest. He had already found half a dozen lice, which had come to life in the warmth of the bunker. Suddenly he put down the trousers he had been examining. What was Fröhlich saying? To lie doggo in a bunker while the Russians came in, and then to get themselves driven off disguised as a POWs truck with Gontsharov as guard?

'Well,' said Breuer, looking at the other man. 'That sounds interesting.'

It was indeed a bright idea and one that hadn't occurred to anyone in the Cauldron. That was why Fröhlich had been so lively since the arrival of the Russian, and why he had spent hours whispering to him.

Breuer asked what Gontsharov had to say. Would he agree?

'Of course he will,' laughed Fröhlich. 'If he doesn't he'll be much worse off than we are.'

Breuer looked at the Russian with real interest for the first time. A wave of hope flooded over him.

'And after that?'

The rest of the programme had been carefully thought out. It seemed feasible as long as there was a Russian officer available, who knew the ropes. The escapers were to beg a lift on an empty truck and take it with them to the west 'for the conveyance of important prisoners to the GHQ of the Russian Army.' As soon as a favourable opportunity presented itself they would—and this was unavoidable—have to liquidate the driver and his mate. The 'POWs' would then transform themselves into a party of convalescent Russian soldiers on the way from the hospital to their units at the front and travelling in an empty vehicle.

'We've already got Russian kit,' said Fröhlich. 'We'll have to take it in a parcel. Herbert and Geibel can wear the clothes of the driver and his pal. I believe that in one day we can get near the front and after that we only need a little luck.'

Breuer was prowling up and down the bunker like a caged lion.

'I really believe it might work!'

He took out his purse, the flap of which was decorated with a captured komsomol badge, a red-star from a Russian military cap and three 'Kubiki', the diamond-shaped collar-badges of Russian staff-officers.

'This might come in handy,' he said as he picked up the red symbols and held them out for Gontsharov to look at. Gontsharov grinned and produced something similar from his own pocket. 'Fröhlich, if this really comes off . . .!' But suddenly Breuer groaned. 'What about the gas, man? We haven't enough.'

Fröhlich smiled wearily.

'Every Russian truck has to keep a full tank in reserve—it's part of the regulations. That would take us more than 300 kilometres.'

Breuer's excitement rose with every word. At last, it seemed, they would be able to do something instead of waiting passively for the end. He spread out the map of the Don Bend and, after looking at it said: 'We mustn't go to the west. We'd never get over the bridges. We must go south first and then in the direction of Rostov. That's safer. I've got a Russian automatic rifle I can let Gontsharov have . . . but listen . . . Major Siebel . . . we must take him with us. After all it was he who made us a present of the Russian—didn't he?'

Fröhlich was doubtful at first, but eventually agreed.

'Keep it under your hat,' he said. 'Besides us, no one on the staff must have an inkling of our plan.'

Breuer nodded and fell to thinking.

'We must know the number of some Russian division in the Rostov region,' he murmured. 'Haven't we got their order of battle.'

Suddenly he looked up, his face pale as he stammered——

'No, it's all nonsense—can't be done . . . we've got no papers and we must have them to get through the controls.'

Fröhlich explained in a tone of superiority: 'We shall have the papers of the two Russians, shan't we? And Gontsharov will write us out our marching orders. He knows what those things ought to look like. We can fake the stamp with a copying-pencil and damp blotting-paper. It's very easy to do and a big, bold stamp is just what Ivan likes.'

Herbert and Geibel, who came back soon afterwards, found their stable companions in a state of great activity. When they heard the plan they smiled confidently. Only Geibel turned pale, when he learned how it was proposed to deal with the two Russians. Herbert, with his deft hands, at once set to work to copy the Soviet emblem from a coin and Gonsharov did the signature. Between them they produced a fine, impressive office-stamp.

Later they asked Major Siebel to come over. When they told him, he was beside himself with excitement. 'Fröhlich!' he cried, 'if the fellow gets us home, I'll give him a permanent job on my place, where he'll be able to live happily to the end of his bloody life. You might translate that for him.'

The Russian gazed at Siebel with his small, impenetrable eyes and said, 'good' in an indifferent voice.

Chapter Twelve

GUILTY

◠◠◠

PEACE HAD RETURNED to the divisional staff. The men were sitting in their bunkers, dozing or sleeping. The most uncanny thing was that the inexhaustible stream of rumours had suddenly dried up. There was, however, something in the wind—'something decisive.'

In the morning Geibel came back with coffee from the kitchens. His slack face was mottled with colour, this time not caused by the cold. His eyes looked more helpless than ever.

'It's . . . it's starting,' he said.

'What's starting?'

'The whole staff is going into the line with Captain Fackelmann . . . Everybody, even the kitchen staff. Only an orderly is to remain behind with Colonel Unold's driver and Corporal Schmalfuss.'

Breuer glanced at the interpreter who was gnawing his lower lip with his horse-like teeth.

'And the officers?' he asked.

Geibel shrugged his shoulders. 'Nothing was said about them.'

'Just a moment,' said Breuer, grabbing his cap and running across to the Colonel's bunker.

Behind the door he heard excited voices. He knocked on the door and opened it without waiting for a 'Come-in'. There he saw four men—Unold, Major Kalweit, Colonel Müller and Major Siebel. They were standing round the table with their heads bent over a map. As Breuer came in they all stopped talking and stared at him as if they were forgers caught in the act. Then Unold shouted at him:

'What's the matter now? For God's sake, man! Don't come barging in here like that!'

Breuer withdrew cautiously and, as he was waiting irresolutely outside, the door suddenly flew open. The old Army Medical Colonel walked by, without a glance. Major Kalweit followed, also in a great hurry; and last of all Siebel appeared. He was bareheaded and visibly upset as he hurried by, however, after a few steps he stopped and came back.

'Yes, Breuer,' he looked at the toes of Breuer's boots and the furrows on his forehead looked like a storm on a lake. 'We're flying out.'

Breuer looked at him without a word.

Siebel went on, still looking at the ground. 'Kalweit has been sent for as tank-specialist and General Hube has been summoned to organize the supplies from outside the ring . . . they're taking me out too, because of this contraption of mine, I suppose.'

He made a movement with the shoulder from which his useless arm was hanging. His eyes met Breuer's but he quickly looked away.

'Give my love to the old country,' Breuer said tonelessly, 'and good-bye for now.'

He raised his hand and then let it drop. It was impossible to shake hands with the Major.

He looked around him distractedly. Could he go to Unold after this? No, with dragging feet he walked down into the valley, feeling very much alone. Then he made up his mind to call on Captain Gedig the Adjutant.

'Ah, Breuer, it's you.'

The Captain hardly seemed to be listening. 'Of course you're staying with us . . . that is, I really don't know, perhaps . . . the Colonel hasn't yet . . . you'd better wait for a decision.'

There was no longer a common destiny. The ship was sinking and the order of the day was 'every man for himself'.

He went back to his bunker.

'Put your things together,' he said to Fröhlich, 'and tell Gontsharov to get ready. We're going into the line with this group. I think our moment has come.'

The officers commanding divisional units had assembled in Colonel von Hermann's bunker.

The first to appear, accompanied by his Adjutant, was Colonel Welle, who commanded the single remaining infantry regiment. A thickset, elderly gentleman, whose bloodshot eyes glared through the dim lenses of a pair of army spectacles. He seldom came to the divisional HQ and spent all his time in his own bunker, which was lined with railway sleepers and situated below one of the streets in the western suburb. Here he had been sitting for four months by the flickering light of a wretched kerosene lamp, entering the losses of his regiment in a much-thumbed note-book. He had become a troglodyte. The ruined city with its piles of debris and rubble, its smells of gas and smouldering wood had taken possession of his spirit. Open country, fresh air and a valley with real trees no longer fitted into his conception of the world.

A little later Lieutenant-Colonel Zedwitz, who had been in command of the regiment on the right flank since October, came in. He was haggard and bony and on top of his long wrinkled neck was perched a strikingly small head with patches of fluff growing above his collar, so that he looked like a vulture. When he had been attached to the Corps Staff he had had a row with his chief, which was why he had been sent to command fighting troops. He hoped soon to be recalled to the General Staff and endeavoured to achieve this by doing well at the front. In the regiment it was said that he was after a Knight's Cross, which did not increase his popularity.

The others trooped in one after another. A grey-haired Colonel of Artillery, who suffered from rheumatism, and the much younger chiefs of independent departments as well as the members of the divisional staff. The reason for the meeting was unknown and the air of the small crowded room was full of speculation.

Colonel von Hermann, who sat writing at his work table, greeted the officers as they arrived with a curt nod which contrasted strangely with his usual courteous welcome. When Danne announced that all were present, he rose to his feet. For a few moments he looked at his audience in silence. His expression was grave and reserved.

'Gentlemen,' he began quietly. 'I have asked you to come here in order to tell you about a plan which is being considered by the army, and to get your views on it. The operation in question is called "The Multi-directional Break-out."'

A surprised murmur ran through the crowded bunker. The Colonel took a sheet of paper from his table and looked at it, then he continued: 'The plan provides that every division on the north, east and south fronts with all their fighting troops, reinforced by survivors from air forces retreating from the western front, should be formed into independent fighting groups, each 200 strong, and, without artillery preparation, should advance to storm the enemy positions with the object of fighting their way through until they can effect a junction with the German front.'

The Colonel gazed quietly into the helpless faces of his officers. Then he started again; quiet and apparently quite uninterested in what he was saying:

'According to verbal explanations communicated by Corps HQ the division should break through on a front equal to the line they occupy, cross the Volga and proceed to a point some four kilometres to the east. There they should join up with other detachments from the Corps. Then they should swing in a body towards the south, and after crossing the Volga once more south of Beketovka should join up with the other units of the army.'

While he was speaking a current of uneasiness flowed through the room. Colonel Welle cleared his throat noisily several times, then said: 'And how is all that going to be done? I don't understand. What about supplies? A plan like that needs preparation! To cross the Volga and throw the Russians out of their positions on the steep banks now, after we've been trying unsuccessfully to do this very thing for the last five months . . . Madness, that's what it is.'

Colonel von Hermann's face remained perfectly impassive.

'What is your opinion, Colonel Zedwitz?'

'It's a crazy idea, when one comes to think of it.' His adam's apple leapt up and down in the open neck of his battle-dress. 'It's much too late now. If there's a chance for some of the army to fight their way out, I think . . .'

The uneasiness was gnawing. The Colonel raised his hand and the murmuring died down.

'This chance no longer exists,' he said. 'Individuals might be able to get through here and there, but there would be no hope for the army or for any appreciable portion of it. We must not misunderstand one another. This plan has nothing to do with a tactical break-out by our forces. It has been proposed in order to implement the Führer's order about fighting to the last man and the last cartridge.'

Someone from the back said: 'Is it meant to be a mass-suicide, or is there some military objective to be gained?'

'The military objective,' answered the Colonel, undisturbed, 'is to do the enemy as much damage as possible and to create confusion behind his lines.'

Everybody started talking, but a clear voice was heard asking: 'What's going to happen to the wounded?'

It was Captain Martens, of the reconnaissance section.

'Yes, of course—— What about the wounded? What'll happen to them?'

The Colonel called for quiet once more and, as he spoke, his voice sounded like an over-stretched wire. The paper in his hand shook.

'The plan,' he explained, 'says nothing about the badly wounded. It is proposed to constitute a covering line along the railway embankment from Voroponovo to Gumrak for the walking cases, to protect the rear of the division who will be engaged in the break-out. These men must not be told what the real situation is. They would be told that they are being put into the line to facilitate impending relief operations.'

There was a moment of silence and then the storm broke loose.

'What a filthy idea! Who thought up that dirty bit of double-crossing?'

Colonel von Hermann did not know and he had not dared to ask the Corps. It was whispered that the Chief of Staff of the Army or one of the Corps Commanders had invented it.

This time the Colonel did not call the meeting to order. The reactions of the officers gave him the answer he wanted. His face relaxed and his voice sounded less strained, as he asked each officer in turn to give him an opinion. There was only one opinion. Even Zedwitz thought the plan was 'questionable'.

Colonel von Hermann breathed a sigh of relief. 'Thank you,' he said. 'I hadn't expected any other answer.'

Shortly afterwards he reported to the Corps Commander by telephone that the leaders of units of his division considered the plan of the Multi-directional Break-out 'unworthy of serious discussion'.

'Ah yes,' said the General indifferently, 'that plan. Thanks. I don't think we shall hear more of it. No one seemed to be really keen on it . . . By the way, my dear Hermann, before I forget, your promotion to Major-General has come through. I've just heard from Army HQ and it's a pleasure to be the first to congratulate you.'

'My respectful thanks, General,' replied von Hermann. When the connection was cut off, he still held the receiver in his hand.

The world had shrunk to the size of a white platter overhung by a low grey lid of sky. By the entrance to the Stalingrad ravine, where the army vehicles had been laid up, stood the soldiers belonging to the divisional staff ready to march off to some point in the line. Altogether about fifty men—the clerks from Intelligence, divisional staff, and paymaster's offices, the registration and courts-martial clerks, men from the 'Weapons and Tools Department', map-drawers, messengers, stretcher-bearers, orderlies, drivers and cooks.

They had formed up in line and were standing there with their rifles slung on their backs or clasped between their legs, their kit-bags at their feet. Three weeks before most of the available winter clothing had been served out to the 'fortress' battalions and most of the men on this parade had clothed themselves in their whole stock of undergarments and woollen wear, so that their battle-dresses and light greatcoats looked like bursting their buttons from the pressure. Luckily for them, the weather was not so cold as it had been.

What was going to happen next?

The men stood and waited for their officers, none of whom had yet shown up with the exception of Captain Fackelmann, who was trotting up and down the line like an excited hen. There had been talk of 'defence of the airfield'. That sounded harmless, but why didn't the officers come? Unrest and bitterness brooded over the ranks like a cloud.

'Unold! Where's Unold? The Colonel should be here.'

The little Captain got more and more nervous. He waved his arms helplessly.

'Be quiet, please, chaps,' he said. 'Listen to me. The Colonel is . . . detained on duty. He has a new appointment. He sends you his best wishes——'

An angry cry greeted these words.

'You can't fool us. He's flown away.'

The Captain was relieved to see Breuer coming with Fröhlich and the Russian. When Breuer explained in a quiet voice that they wanted to go into the line with the men, although they had had no positive orders to do so, he thanked him warmly. He didn't understand why none of the active officers was in charge of this obscure operation and why everything had been left to him, a temporary Captain and a dug-out and one of the latest to join the staff. Meantime the men had calmed down somewhat. They were staring at the Russian who, in his grey fur cap, his brown greatcoat, his blanket rolled over his shoulder, a pistol at his belt and an automatic rifle in his hand, cut a remarkable figure. He looked as though he thought his own participation in the scene was the most natural thing in the world. The men said nothing and seemed slightly ashamed of doubting him.

It was almost dark when three trucks rolled up to drive Fackelmann's group to its destination. The vehicles were strange and so were the drivers, and the latter gave uncivil and evasive answers to the questions put to them.

The drive seemed endless. When at last they halted, it was pitch dark outside and the order came to dismount.

The trucks emptied themselves to the accompaniment of jostling and suppressed curses. There was a hum of voices, and here and there single cries. Slender beams of light from torches slipped through the darkness. A faint light issued from the entrance to a bunker, as big as the gate of an Egyptian tomb.

Someone called for Captain Fackelmann.

'Here I am, in front here. I'm coming at once.'

The mouth of the bunker blazed up and swallowed him. The atmosphere was exciting and full of uncertainty. Gumrak Airfield, Northern Front and Gontchara Gulley were names being whispered among the men, but they did not mean much.

When Fackelmann returned the men started to move off along an uneven, undefined footpath. The darkness was cold and dank. There was a gentle clink of rifles and cook-pots and here and there a suppressed curse could be heard, when a marcher made a false step.

Fackelmann, who was panting along the path just in front of Breuer, suddenly fell back a pace or two and clutched Breuer's arm.

'Unold was in there,' he whispered. 'He's working out the defence of the airfield with Colonel Fuchs. Don't tell the men. He ought to have shown himself, don't you think? At least said good-bye to the chaps. I mean to say . . .'

He fell silent when he received no answer.

The path curved to the right over smooth, snowy hillocks and through unexpected hollows. Each man clung to the belt of the man in front, so as not to lose contact. They breathed noisily and cursed under their breath. On the left, behind them, yellow flares were drawing stripes across the sky and making the path visible from time to time. Grumbling noises like a distant thunderstorm followed them as they marched. On the right a coloured beacon-light showed the position of the airfield.

'Ha . . . alt!'

The marchers seemed to have reached their destination. Lights blazed out and the night air resounded with confused shouts and whistles.

Breuer had lost the Russian and Fröhlich in the darkness. Nor did he know where Geibel and Herbert had got to. He pushed his way forward, stumbling over a length of wire and narrowly missed a steep ice slope which ran down into a bunker. Gentle gramophone music was welling from the earth.

Someone turned a torch on to his face. 'Is that you, Breuer?' said the voice of Captain Fackelmann. 'I've just heard that there isn't room for all of us here. What had we better do? This is Captain Lange who commands this sector.'

'How do you do,' said a rusty voice. 'Fackelmann is right. My quarters are chock-a-block. They won't take more than twenty men. If you go forward into the valley, about 300 yards from here, you're sure to find empty bunkers. They all cleared off yesterday.'

'Three hundred yards farther on?' said Fackelmann in a husky voice.

'Don't you worry,' said Lange. 'This is a sort of safety line for all emergencies. You'll find the whole of the 44th Infantry Division on ahead.'

'Is that so?' said Fackelmann without conviction. 'In that case I'll leave the Rosner and Gotthard groups here. That makes nineteen men, including you, Breuer. We'll make other arrangements in the morning.'

'I've still got room for an officer in my bunker,' said Captain Lange.

Breuer did not like this at all, but he couldn't very well refuse. Meanwhile the members of the various groups had found one another and the men were distributed to the various posts. Breuer found an opportunity to explain things to his men, who had to go forward. He himself reluctantly stayed behind.

The bunker was bright and warm and the Captain sat comfortably in a basket chair. He had a low forehead and bushy eyebrows which joined across his nose. A Sergeant-Major in Flak uni orm got up from another cane chair and saluted, turning his fishlike eyes on Breuer but without interest. He seemed to be tolerably drunk.

'This is Wilhelm,' explained the Captain.

Breuer took off his greatcoat and laid down the things he was carrying and Wilhelm tried to help him.

In a recess at the side there were two double camp-beds rigged one above the other. On one of them a man lay, making a moaning sound like a wounded animal. From down below Breuer could see nothing except two huge feet in felt boots which stuck beyond the edge of the bunk—one of the soles had a large hole in it, which had been stuffed with newspaper.

'Your bunk is up here, Lieutenant,' said the Captain, hanging his greatcoat on the protruding feet. 'Don't worry about that fellow, he's too far gone to notice anything.'

On a table covered with a bright-green cloth stood a half-empty bottle and by it a blue portable gramophone. The Captain felt behind a curtain and put a third glass on the table, which he filled up.

'Cheers!' he said, and they clinked glasses. The Captain emptied his glass at a single draught and wiped his lips with the back of his hand. 'Put on a record, Wilhelm,' he cried.

The Sergeant-Major turned over the record and put the needle on the disc. It scratched terribly and poured out a flood of tinny dance music to which an effeminate man's voice crooned:

> Now Dolly has it good,
> She sits in Hollywood,
> Beside Clark Gable
> At one table.

It had been a popular song years ago. The record was worn out and there was a crack in it. Breuer wondered how it had got there.

'Now let's feed our faces,' said the Captain. He fished out a loaf bread from behind the curtain, together with a box containing butter and a smoked sausage from which he hacked a piece as broad as his hand. 'You must be hungry,' he said.

Breuer reached for the food. He was too cold and hungry to ask questions. After eating three slices, he said at last: 'And where did this manna drop from?'

'From on high of course, what did you think?' laughed the Captain, stretching himself in his chair. 'Things like that fall from heaven, hereabouts. Yesterday we picked up thirty-five of these truncheons.' He swung the sausage in his hand like a rubber cosh. 'The only thing is, you have to watch out that the box they're packed in doesn't fall on your head.'

'Aren't parachute supplies supposed to be handed in for distribution?' asked Breuer, who remembered a very strict order on this subject.

'Handed in?' growled the Captain, sticking his fists in the

pockets of his riding-breeches. 'Handed in? When they've been starving us to death for weeks?'

Breuer ate and drank and a feeling of warmth and well-being flowed through his limbs. For the first time that evening he had the curiosity to look at his companion closely. The Captain was wearing a sea-green shirt and his light-grey breeches were faced with leather at the knees and tucked into a pair of soft, brightly polished riding-boots.

'Cheers!' said the Captain. 'Next time we meet we shall be older.'

Breuer held his glass to the light. The white Bordeaux gleamed golden. It seemed ages since he had drunk out of a proper wine-glass.

'Did this fall from heaven too?' he asked.

'No,' laughed the Captain. 'We have other sources of supply. If you want riding-boots, a dress tunic or ladies' underclothes, or maybe a coffee-set, you can have them all.' As he spoke he pushed a cigar box across to Breuer. 'Just look at the bands,' he said. 'Genuine imports from Sumatra—fit for a millionaire!'

He leaned back in his chair, stretched out his legs and blew smoke rings at the ceiling, while the gramophone went on crooning:

> In love with Harold Lloyd
> In love with Conrad Veidt

In the corner the wounded man continued to groan monotonously.

'That was a bit of a party, Wilhelm, the day before yesterday, wasn't it?' said the Captain, winking at the Sergeant-Major who sat stupid and sleepy beside him. 'You should have been there to see how these Pay Corps fellows ran, when they heard the front line was coming here. They were gone in a flash and left everything behind, boxes and suitcases full of things they'd been hoarding—luxuries of all kinds, fantastic food and as for the drink—we were all paralytic.'

Even the Sergeant-Major's fishlike face assumed a glassy grin. He wound up the gramophone which was running down in a series of gurgles.

'Unfortunately all the stuff is lying out there in the open, ready for anyone to liberate,' went on the Captain cheerfully. 'In the day-time of course Ivan keeps plastering it with shells. He's already smashed up two of the trucks. I told the young fellows to wait till it was dark, but their fingers were itching to get at the stuff, especi-ally the drink. Four of them were done in by a shell. Otto, the chap behind there, he caught a packet as he was trying to pull out a case of vino. He got a splinter in the crutch.'

Suddenly Breuer felt very tired. He was no longer used to drink-ing wine and the bunker was overheated. He excused himself and crawled into his bunk. Above him the used-up air hung thick and heavy. He soon fell into an uneasy sleep, pierced by confused noises. He vaguely heard crashes, bumps and rumbles far away and then the drumming of a 'sewing-machine' which rattled around for a while and then crackled off into the distance. Meanwhile the gramophone went on quacking—

> Now Dolly has it good
> She lives in Hollywood
> Across the briny sea
> No such damn luck for me.

Lieutenant Wiese's position as orderly officer to General von Her-mann was much resented by the other staff-officers. Wiese, how-ever, remained quite unaware of their attitude. Since the tragedy of Dubininski he had been incapable of thinking clearly. He felt that he had nothing more to fear and nothing more to hope for—no mission in life and no goal. He had come to the end.

General von Hermann, a hard task-master to himself and to those who worked for him, gave Wiese very little to do. When he saw him, and that was seldom, he met him with an embarrassed friendliness. He wondered why he had brought him along, but did not take himself to task for having done so. Wiese repaid his Chief's forbearance, which annoyed the others, by a weary, hope-less gratitude such as a dying man might feel for his doctor.

One day when he was standing before his Chief's table he noticed that the General looked at him long and reflectively.

At last he said: 'Lieutenant Wiese, I have received an order from

Corps HQ. The division has to appoint a courier for the army to go to Army Group Headquarters.'

Wiese's face remained without expression.

'You are that courier.'

'Yes, sir,' murmured Wiese. Suddenly the blood rushed to his face and he stammered: 'Me? How can I go, Colonel—I mean General. It isn't possible. I can't do it.'

The General gazed at him sternly. Nothing in his face revealed what he was thinking. In fact, he was thinking of a day in November, when the photo was still standing on his table, and he remembered saying to this boy: 'Don't take it too much to heart. We don't only need soldiers in this world.' There he had been sympathetic but during the last few weeks he had been thinking about the profession which he had embraced. He had come to realize that every professional attitude of mind, including that of the soldier, was necessarily one-sided. The youngster who stood in front of him with flushed cheeks and twitching face was certainly no soldier. But the others, for the most part, weren't born to be soldiers either. They were labourers, honest craftsmen, small employees, peasants, technicians—all pressed into a single mould by a cruel destiny. Suddenly it seemed important to General von Hermann that someone who had looked into the abyss, as Wiese had, should take his knowledge over there and keep it, so that there would be an answer to the questions that would be asked one day. The General now knew that the impulse that had come to him, as he held that awkward message from Corps HQ, had been a good one. He realized that there was a meaning in the inspiration that had led him to pick out this man and save his life, so that he might bear witness for the dead.

'You are to be the courier,' repeated the General with an emphasis which allowed of no contradiction. 'You must report to Captain Sander, who will see about your papers and the car. Tomorrow morning at 9.00 hours you must be at the Army Staff HQ, Intelligence section.'

When he saw that Wiese's resistance had weakened he adopted a friendlier tone.

'I've chosen you for service reasons, and on personal grounds.'

He picked up something from the table and said: 'Take this packet and give it to my wife. The address is on it. Tell her that . . . that I've tried to behave like a soldier and a Christian. And tell her about that other thing—I can't tell her in a letter.' The General had striven to speak in a practical, businesslike tone, but without success. As he spoke the expression on Wiese's face had suddenly changed. The life flowed back into it.

'But I don't know,' he stammered helplessly. 'You've never told me, sir . . . I mean about Ferdi . . . and how he died.'

'How do you mean?' said von Hermann in painful embarrassment. 'You don't know? But I thought that you yourself . . . Weren't you there when it happened?'

Wiese grew as white as chalk and the blackness of night came into his eyes—— So that was what he had done! He felt his knees giving way under him.

The General walked up to him, full of pity. The sternness had gone from his face. He put his hand protectively on Wiese's shoulder.

'Tell her about it, my boy,' he said, 'as far as you can—may God help you.'

Wiese's head was spinning. A tide of love and respect for this man flooded through him. He would have liked to tell the General, but he did nothing of the sort. He said: 'At your orders, General.'

Wiese completed the arrangements for his flight in feverish haste. He did not notice the spiteful looks nor hear the unkind remarks made behind his back. 'The young man's in a devil of a hurry, all of a sudden.' 'Yes, of course, just what you'd expect.' 'Doesn't seem to feel embarrassed about it.' And when anyone sarcastically wished him '*bon voyage*', he looked as though he did not understand.

Wiese saw no prospect of freedom before him, only a task to perform. He felt himself weighed down by a superhuman burden and believed that he could only shake it off by committing a monstrous deed. He was to take messages to the Army Group. He would find his way to the Führer's HQ somehow or other. He would pretend to be carrying some special, private message to be delivered personally to Hitler. And then he would shoot. He had had to shoot six bullets at his friend but he still had two cartridges in the magazine . . .

As he drove to the airport he kept urging the driver to go faster. Every minute seemed to him precious and irreplaceable.

It may have been because of his feverish haste that Wiese never reached the airport. As they drove out of the village of Gumrak they came under fire from a group of Russian bombers. The car was riddled with shrapnel, overturned at the side of the road, and completely destroyed by fire.

Breuer was rocked in his bed by enemy gunfire and awakened out of a weary sleep. He pushed back the heavy sheepskin coat which covered him and sat up cautiously so as not to knock his head against the ceiling. The grey light of dawn was filtering in at the window. His neighbour's groans had ceased. The man in the next bunk was motionless. His nose looked sharp and white and his mouth hung open. He looked as if he had framed a word which would never be spoken.

Captain Lange was down below, already dressed and prepared for action; he was having an argument with the sentry.

'How long did you say this had been going on?'

The man snorted noisily through his dripping nose. A dirty puddle had formed round his snow-sprinkled felt boots.

'Oh, quite a time, Herr Hauptmann,' he said, wiping the moisture off his face with the back of his hand—'Must be about three hours already.'

'Damnation!' said the Captain.

About fifty yards behind the bunkers there was a road leading to the west. Men were moving along it in small groups at a considerable distance from each other. Here and there was a vehicle or a gun and then again men in thick clusters or extended lines. Some of them were drawing sledges with baggage on them or wounded men or machine-guns. They were marching eastward.

The Captain and Breuer went up and challenged them.

'Who are you and where do you come from?'

No one looked up. They trotted along the track with their faces muffled and their rifles dangling on their backs. They didn't even look up when a mortar-shell roared over their heads and the two officers threw themselves down in the snow by the roadside.

At last a group arrived which had preserved some semblance of order. There was an officer with them who stopped for a moment and said:

'We're the cyclist-squadron from the 44th Division.'

'Where are you going?'

The officer shrugged his shoulders and said: 'Oh, anywhere.' He looked along the road. A truck full of wounded men rushed noisily by.

'And what's over there?' asked Lange, pointing with his chin towards the west. 'Over there? That's the end. We're the last.'

The officer waved his hand and then stumped after his men.

Lange turned pale and looked at Breuer. 'Damnation!' he said once more.

The abandoned bunkers in the gulley could comfortably house a company at full strength, so that the twenty men whom Breuer brought up with him were easily accommodated. A number of bunks, tables and stools were still available and there was even a kitchen bunker with two built-in boilers, pots and pans and plenty of firewood. The previous occupants seemed to have cleared out in a tremendous hurry. In spite of everything Fackelmann's men had little sleep that night; their anxious OC kept them busy digging trenches. He was visibly relieved when Breuer appeared.

'I want you to look at the position,' he said, 'and to tell me if the two machine-guns are in the right place. Fröhlich gave me some help; as you know I haven't a clue.' The sweat was streaming down his yellow, waxen face from under his fur cap.

'How does the line run?' asked Breuer.

The Captain gave him a dejected look—'I thought you would know that. Is it so important?'

'Have we at least got support on either side of us?'

'The gulley doesn't run any farther to the west. There's nothing there. But on the left we have Captain Lange with his people, haven't we? We've just finished patching up the telephone line to them. And farther to the right—well, I don't know. The Pioneers are supposed to be somewhere about.'

Breuer hadn't the heart to tell this helpless creature that the front did not exist any more and that very soon the situation here would be desperate. He suddenly began to feel desperate. These men had been personally known to him for a long time. They needed a leader able to cope with this fiendish situation—someone to give them strength and courage to meet the final crisis. Fackelmann couldn't do that and Breuer, an old infantry officer who could, was he going to steal away and leave them, without a thought for any-one but himself. Before, it had all seemed so simple, but now it wasn't simple at all. Admittedly he was there of his own volition, unattached, without orders and responsible to nobody, and ad-mittedly there was no military logic in putting these men into the line. They could neither change nor save anything, and the opera-tion was the last convulsive death-twitch of the apparatus of com-mand. But he got no comfort from such thoughts. His duty as a human being was clear: he must help in whatever way he could.

He inspected the positions with Fröhlich. Good work had been done overnight. Snipers' nests had been dug at intervals of about twenty paces on the upper face of the gulley, and most of the men were resting in bunkers.

On the right wing, far up the gulley, Corporal Herbert and Gontsharov were looking after a machine-gun behind a bank of snow. Geibel was sleeping in the bunker which Fröhlich had re-served for Breuer's group. The Russian was laughing all over his wrinkled face. He shook Breuer firmly by the hand.

'Goot,' he said, 'all goot—I bring you to home.' He slapped Herbert on the back. 'And you too,' he said to Fröhlich, boxing at him playfully. 'I bring you all to home.' He gave a booming laugh, which brought some astonished faces to the loopholes in the snipers' nests.

Breuer had to laugh too. What an extraordinary fellow the Russian was! With a man like that they couldn't fail to get through. There was no longer any doubt about it. Their plan of escape was the only thing that made sense any more.

Then Fröhlich took him by the arm and winked at him.

'Look over there, Lieutenant,' he said. 'Do you see anything?' He pointed towards the other side of the gulley, where there was a small embrasure with a few bushes almost covered in snow. Down below there was a hollow which looked as though it had been scratched out by a dog.

'Our hiding place,' whispered Fröhlich. 'There's a bunker behind. We've plastered the entrance with snow and the wind has blown the surface quite flat. Great, isn't it? All our things are inside already, including the drink. When the time comes . . .'

Breuer took a deep breath and beamed at the others.

'That's fine,' he said. 'You couldn't have done better. No one is going to shift us from here. Two more days, at most.'

The Gonchara gulley, between thirty and fifty yards across, winds slowly towards the east. To judge by the map it is several kilometres long and reaches almost to the railway leading to Gumrak. Its steep slopes are topped by odd-looking walls of snow and here and there the naked clay is visible along them. Sprawling bushes cover parts of the valley. The footpath which Breuer followed lost itself gradually in individual tracks behind the bushes. The untrodden snow became deeper and progress was difficult. The faint sound of distant motors was carried down-wind.

This was no front—just a desolate patch of no man's land.

After walking for some twenty minutes Breuer came upon fresh tracks. The valley broadened out at the other side of a bend. On the south side the doors and windows of bunkers were visible. There were a few vehicles painted white, roughly camouflaged behind bushes and walls of snow. A soldier came whistling towards Breuer with a few planks under his arm and a hatchet in his hand. When he reached him, he stopped whistling and eyed him suspiciously. Then he walked on without saluting.

Breuer found a Major in one of the bunkers—a small man, looking somehow deformed. His prominent eyes looked over a hooked nose at the unexpected visitor.

'Oh! So you're our new neighbours,' he said in a high but hoarse voice. 'High time you reported, isn't it?' And then he complained that no lateral communications had been established.

After an exchange of ideas it was agreed to prolong the line of defence as far as the middle of the intervening stretch of road. When that had been settled the Major became easier to talk to.

'The day before yesterday there was a Lieutenant-Colonel here,' he said, 'General Staff and so forth. He said that this was the front line and that I was in command of the sector, and we must hold out to the last man. I told him that we'd been fighting the war here for the last four weeks without the benefit of orders from the top brass, and we'd go on doing so. I had no intention of leaving my hole—— But as for my being in command of the front line . . . He cleared off pretty quickly, after that.'

Breuer looked round the roomy bunker which was warm and comfortable. There were flower-patterned curtains on the windows and geraniums growing in flower pots. He asked if there were any troops to the right of there.

'Yes, there's a bridge-building column just behind the next bend. Poor devils! I'm sorry for them.'

The OC Bridgebuilders was a white-haired gentleman, formerly a professor in a technical college. He had a thick scarf round his neck and a cruel cough. He looked at Bruer through rimless glasses. 'This is a ghastly business,' he complained. 'We're a specialized unit, trained to execute the most difficult jobs. We had three most valuable mobile workshops, worth millions of marks, and we've had to blow them all up. Our cars, our machinery—all destroyed. Then there are my men, welders, riveters, carpenters, technical draughtsmen, qualified mathematicians—hand-picked material, every one of them a man of talent . . . they've posted half of them away, God knows where to, and now they're freezing and starving. And the few they have left me . . . just go out and look at them.'

He had another coughing-fit and Breuer picked up his glasses which had fallen into the snow.

'My Adjutant used to be my assistant in Vienna. I have trained him up from boyhood, as you might say. A splendid man with most unusual gifts. He couldn't stand it any longer and put a bullet through his head. He died in my arms. Oh, that devil! that devil!'

The old professor frequently repeated this imprecation as he voiced his complaints. Breuer wondered who he was talking about.

'And now look at us! We're supposed to hold up the Russians with the handful of wretched men. I don't understand the first thing about it. I'm no soldier. That devil! That devil!'

There was nothing and nobody farther to the right. The bridge-builders were all alone and hadn't seen a soul for weeks except some pioneers, next door to them. No one had bothered about them till this Colonel came two days ago. . . .

Breuer climbed up the side of the gulley while the old gentleman, coughing and occasionally cleaning his glasses, panted along beside him.

Before them lay a white, empty plain stretching to the dark grey horizon.

On the right through his field-glasses Breuer could see columns of trucks pushing slowly from north to south. The road must be there, near the railway line from Kotlubani to Gumrak. Were those German vehicles or Russian? He could not make out.

Darkness came down early and to the north he saw the glimmer of tiny flames, a wreath of watch-fires. The wind carried along snatches of song and laughter. It was the Russians, already celebrating their victory. They had nothing more to fear. Occasionally the tac-tac of a machine-gun stuttered over the plain like a burst of ghostly laughter. But to the rear, in the direction of the air-field which they were supposed to be defending, all was dark and still.

The Army High Command had moved from its battle headquarters at Gumrak to a bunker village on the southern edge of the town. where a divisional staff had been obliged to make room for them, It was no longer safe to remain in Gumrak.

The Commander-in-Chief summoned a conference of all the senior commanding officers. Of the five generals who had been left with the encircled forces, two had been flown out of the Cauldron. According to the official version General Hube had been instructed to re-establish the crippled air-supply services, and the General commanding the IVth Corps had sustained a head wound when a beam fell on him during an air raid. Two Generals had been appointed to fill the gaps left by the two Corps Commanders. One of these was the old General with the skipper's beard, whose division had not been saved by the sacrifice of the 200 wounded men.

All the five Generals appeared personally at the conference. The emergency called for a full attendance. The airfield of Gumrak was under gunfire and could no longer be used. The enemy had broken through north of the railway and was now threatening to split the Cauldron into two. The General in command of the northern group was uncertain whether he would be able to find his way back to his corps.

In reply to a despairing appeal for help from the Cauldron, Hitler had sent Field-Marshal Milch to the Don as a special envoy with extraordinary powers. His mission was to step up the supplies to the VIth Army. From his HQ in a special train he had been 'organizing' the dispatch of supplies. But in fact there had been no change. One day forty tons came in, then fifty-two tons and on one occasion 170 . . . In place of material, many consoling messages arrived—bombers, fighters and large transport planes would soon be coming. . . .

'They've let us down,' said the Chief of Staff. 'Hube isn't up to the job. We need someone out there with some punch.' He did not say of whom he was thinking.

There was a discussion about the small airfield at Stalingradski, which had now to be used, and about the possibility of making runways in Stalingrad itself in case Stalingradski were lost, for it was doubtful if it could be held.

The General in command of the southern region reported a new offer of surrender terms from the Russians. 'They came with baskets full of sausages and ham and schnapps, apparently hoping that we'd take the bait. . . .'

The Chief of Staff was furious and the tiger-headed General backed him:

'Of course we sent them back post-haste,' said the bearded General in a soothing voice—— 'Not much point in it any longer, but as long as the no-surrender order remains in force . . .'

'For my part I've given orders to fire on Russian negotiators, and on any of our people who show signs of giving in,' snarled Tiger-Head, drumming with his fingers on the top of the table. 'They won't get me alive!' His green eyes had shrunk to mere slits from which shone a feverish light. He was dangerously ill with stomach trouble and knew he had not long to live.

'Capitulation is out of the question,' said the Chief of Staff.

'We shall fight to the last cartridge. The severest measures must be taken to fight defeatism. You must remember that the shortening of our line has more than balanced our losses. In a way we're getting stronger every day. The town of Stalingrad provides an ideal defensive position. The Russians held out in it for months. We can do the same, but of course the supply situation must be put in order.'

'All this is nonsense, absolute nonsense!' said General von Seydlitz springing to his feet. The muscles of his face stood out in ridges. 'It's a question of days to our final collapse—any *child* could see that.'

'True,' said Hube's successor, ducking his head quickly when he saw the Chief of Staff looking at him.

'But what's happening now?' continued Seydlitz. 'We've got tens of thousands of wounded and sick, whom nobody's looking after. Every day men are dying—not in battle but of cold and hunger. The few survivors are at the end of their tether. We're finished, simply finished. Can't you see that? Without air support and heavy ammunition we can't go on fighting, not against an enemy who's short of nothing. Fighting against T34 tanks and rocket batteries with pistols, rifles and machine-guns is the stone age against the twentieth century.'

'But we have our orders,' said Paulus quietly. 'What do you want us to do?' He found scenes of this kind very painful, though he did not show it.

'Put an end to it all!' cried General Seydlitz. 'Ignore the orders issued by people who are too cowardly to show themselves over here. Capitulate on your own initiative and save the few wounded men who are still alive. After all we're reponsible to the German people and not just to a . . . a . . .'

'You're going too far,' roared Tiger-Head, banging his fist on the table.

General von Seydlitz, bewildered, kept silence for a moment. Then he said:

'Everything has gone too far. Stalingrad is like Beresina on a bigger scale, and if we go on like this Germany'll be like Stalingrad on a bigger scale still. You'll remember what I'm saying then.'

He sank into his chair, the flush faded from his cheeks and he looked very old.

The Chief of Staff played with his pencil and said in tones of false bonhomie: 'Go ahead then. Give yourself up to the Russians.'

'How can I do that?' said von Seydlitz. 'The order to capitulate must apply to the whole army.'

The Chief of Staff continued to smile. He knew the General would never disobey an order, not so long, anyhow, as *he* was holding the reins.

'Thank you, gentlemen,' said General Paulus with an effort. 'I can't act against orders. When orders are disobeyed, everything is at an end. But I think you all agree that I should make further representations to the Führer. I shall describe the situation once more in unequivocal terms and demand freedom of action. That is the most I can do.'

The Generals took their leave. Even General Seydlitz said no more. It was useless. When they had all gone, the Chief of Staff handed the General the draft of an Order of the Day to the troops, adding in casual tones: 'It looks as if Hube was unable to fix things with the people back there. I think I might be able to. . . .'

Paulus looked at the paper and his expression hardened.

'You?' he said. 'You stay here.'

The Chief of Staff raised his eyebrows. He found it hard to conceal his surprise at this unaccustomed resistance.

'General,' he said in emphatic tones, as if he wished to strangle all doubts in regard to the purity of his motives, 'our survival depends on a satisfactory solution of the problem of supplies. Only someone completely familiar with the situation and able to impose his personality . . .'

'You are staying here,' said Paulus once more.

The Chief of Staff said no more. He picked up the order which the Commander had signed without looking at it and went out. This order had been awaiting signature for several days. It was dated 20th January and ran:

'We shall go on hoping for early relief. Reinforcements are already on their way.'

.   .   .   .   .

295

Another day dawned gloomily over the Gonchara Gulley.

Herbert was squatting by a machine-gun and sweeping the horizon with a pair of field-glasses which Breuer had left him. Geibel was sitting on an ammunition box rubbing his arms. He was freezing, inside and out. During the previous night, like all the others, he had slept very badly. They had kept on repeating to themselves the details of their plan of escape. Their hiding place was not twenty yards away. Each of them knew what to do as soon as the attack started.

As soon as it started. . . .

In the meantime Geibel had learnt a lot of things. Since the Russian break-through in the forest region south of Peskovatka, he knew that tanks could not be stopped with bayonets: even a machine-gun made no impression on these devilish creatures. He was now trying to imagine what form the attack would take——

'Do you think they'll start with a barrage . . .?'

Herbert didn't answer. He continued to look through his glasses.

'Perhaps they'll begin with the tanks, what do you think? That would be the best for us, wouldn't it? Then everyone would scram?'

When the Russians had suddenly crashed through between the blockhouses at Peskovatka, the infantry had also cleared out and had left Major Kalweit to clean up. He had shot down two Russian tanks and Lieutenant Dierk, with his four-barrelled flak gun, a third. If only the two were here now. But the Major had flown home and Dierk had gone off with one of the fortress-battalions. And Lakosch? Nowadays he often thought of Lakosch and tried to imagine what he would have said to this or that. He had never missed him so much as now.

A little later Breuer came up to have a look. During the night he had remembered that in two days it would be the 24th and that got on his nerves. However, he showed no sign of nervousness.

'Everything in order, men?'

'Everything's OK, Lieutenant.'

Geibel looked at his chief with beaming eyes and chattering teeth. He suddenly felt great confidence in him. They were going to take him with them and wouldn't leave him to die here. He was infinitely grateful to them. He felt that he had to go home. Elfriede was looking after the business and the child all alone. She was a wonderful kid, worth two of her husband, but she couldn't hold the fort alone for ever. Geibel was convinced that for him the war would be over, once he got across the line.

'What's that over there?'

Herbert handed the field-glasses to Breuer, who wiped the lenses and adjusted the focus. Then he made out what had caught Herbert's attention. Vehicles were driving along: long columns of trucks, several of them abreast it seemed, all pushing eastwards.

'Good heavens,' murmured Breuer, allowing himself for a moment to think that these were German troops. Could they be reinforcements?

'That's Ivan,' said Herbert with a bitter laugh, 'out for a drive.'

Endless lines of Russian vehicles in open marching order without any camouflage rolled by. And nothing happened; no armoured car attacked, no tank showed itself and not a shot was fired.

About noon, when they were getting their meal ready, loud cries were heard on the west side of the gulley and wild bursts of fire. The men left their cooking-pots behind, seized their rifles and stormed out. Breuer was with them and even Fackelmann came trotting along. 'My God,' he groaned, 'my God.'

The men on the top of the slope shouted and beckoned. 'Come here,' they cried, 'the Russians are coming!'

Breuer climbed up the steep face. When he reached the top he could see what was happening. A Russian patrol on snow-shoes had tumbled into a corner between their own line and the rearmost position of the anti-aircraft detachment, who must have seen the four or five white figures, though they were not very easy to make out against the snow. But the Germans here, who were jumping around like clowns, obstructed the line of fire.

'Get back,' shouted Breuer. 'Lie down!'

The men took no notice. They made a confused uproar among themselves till suddenly one of them charged forward followed by another. Soon all of them were rushing to the front shouting 'hurrah'—and waving their rifles. The Russians hesitated, taken aback by the noise, and then turned about and glided away with

long strides towards the west. But the clerks and drivers, the orderlies and cooks, floundered madly through the snow, stumbling
over the skirts of their coats, falling down and getting to their feet
again. As they advanced they fired their rifles, and shouted to give
themselves courage.

The accumulated tension of the last days and the despairing
mood of these amateur soldiers found an outlet in this ridiculous
attack. Fackelmann led them, hobbling through the snow on his
short legs, brandishing his pistol in the air and firing it at random.

From somewhere came the hoarse, wicked stutter of a machine-
gun. Suddenly, around the attackers burst the angry, unannounced
detonations of mortar-shells.

Breuer sprang to his feet.

'Are you crazy?' he roared. 'Halt! Stop! Lie down!'

With long strides he ran after the attackers. Then something
snatched his feet away from under him and flung him flat on the
ground. The last thing he felt was a stab of pain, as sharp as a
needle, which pierced his left eye.

General Paulus sent a signal to the Führer's Headquarters. He described the supplies situation, the lack of quarters for officers and
men, the impossibility of holding the present line, and the absence
of facilities for treating the 16,000 wounded, the message ended:
'Request freedom of action in respect of continuance of struggle as
long as it can be carried on and capitulation when further fighting
impossible.' The answer was received next morning:

'Capitulation out of the question. The army must hold its
positions to the last man and the last cartridge, making by its heroic
resistance an unforgettable contribution to the building up of a
new front and the saving of the western world. Signed Hitler.'

The weather continued comparatively mild and Fackelmann's
group had suffered only a few casualties from frostbite. The foolish
adventure with the Russian patrol had caused their first serious
losses. Hinzel of the registry was shot through the head and killed
instantly. Driver Kloss had had his hip torn open by a splinter from
a mortar shell and the five other wounded men were more or less

badly damaged—Captain Fackelmann had tried to telephone to the rear for medical aid, but couldn't get through.

Breuer lay in the bunker next to the kitchen, where they had put the badly wounded men. The medical orderly had put an emergency bandage on the bleeding and lacerated eye-socket, but the blood kept soaking through. For the moment there was nothing more to be done. The night after the engagement he was still unconscious. Geibel sat up with him, listening anxiously to his irregular breathing and started when the patient threw himself about or uttered unintelligible words.

Fackelmann was anxious. Since the shooting yesterday the Russians had kept up a nuisance fire on the area. That was the result of their folly. He had failed as a leader and he knew he would fail again. The line which he was supposed to be defending was somewhere in front, but he didn't know where and had no communications with it. He tried to get help from the Interpreter Officer, but Fröhlich was of little use. The yellow flashes of the bombardment which tore the black of the night filled him with fear and he crumpled up every time there was an explosion. There was a constant droning of motors all round. It was getting louder now, and it never let up, and there was still no communication with the rear. Ought he to send out a man to look for the fault? He supposed that was the normal thing to do. . . .

When Geibel returned from his guard duty—dead-tired and half-frozen, he met Breuer coming out of the bunker. He looked terrible. His sunken, stubby face with its blood-stained bandage was hardly recognizable. His greatcoat, flecked with rusty spots, hung on his body like a sack. With one hand he was clinging to the frame of the door and in the other he held his kit-bag. His single eye, red-veined and flickering with the light of fever, glared at Geibel.

'I'm . . . I'm going out now.'

His voice, too, was strangely altered. Geibel looked around for help, and he saw Herbert and Fröhlich, who had been called by the medical orderly, running up.

'You can't do that, sir. You must lie down at once.'

'I'm going now,' repeated Breuer like an obstinate child.

'Where do you want to go, for heaven's sake?'

'Anywhere—away from here.'

Fröhlich took Breuer by the arm and shook him. 'And what about our break-out. Our escape?'

'Break-out? You'll have to go alone.'

Yes, they would have to go alone, if at all. It was clear to all three of them that they couldn't take Breuer. But they couldn't just leave him behind.

'Nonsense!' said Fröhlich. 'You've got to come with us, that's obvious. We can't leave you behind here—it's a ridiculous idea——' he laughed. 'It's out of the question!'

Breuer swayed, his head wagging to and fro. But suddenly he pulled himself up and stood stiffly to attention.

'Fröhlich,' he said. 'You've got to take these men across—understand? It's an order. You mustn't bother about me any more. You've got no time for that. If you take me, the whole show will be ruined, as you know very well!'

The three men made no answer. They watched Lieutenant Breuer staggering through the snowy valley and knew they would never see him again.

The mortar-bombardment to which the Gonchara Gulley was subjected throughout the night grew more intense in the morning. A Russian patrol made a reconnaissance in the direction of the pioneers on the left, but otherwise there were no troop movements.

Captain Fackelmann was waiting to be connected with the rear, but it was more than an hour before the telephone engineers turned up. They reported that they had gone back as far as the rear position and found the line in order—but nobody there.

'How do you mean, no one there?' The Captain couldn't believe his ears. 'What does that mean?'

'The bunkers are all empty. There's not a soul to be seen. There's a lot of gear and kit left behind and the telephone apparatus. We rang up the airfield, but there was no answer from there either.'

No one there? No one behind them? They had been forgotten or written off as a lost handful of men . . . The Captain stood in helpless silence.

About half an hour later voices shouted through the gulley: 'tanks, tanks.'

'Look out, they're coming! Look out!'

Fackelmann walked through the running, shouting men to the machine-gun position. He remained quite calm. When he got there, he saw the enemy tanks—about twenty of them. The Russians were doing them proud. They could afford to. They were still a long way off, but they were clearly not in a hurry. Perhaps they were really afraid of something. An advance guard of three preceded the convoy and it was easy to make them out. They crawled forward like dirty grey cockroaches over a white handkerchief.

The Captain put his hands over his eyes and held his breath. There was no German line in front of him—nothing but the enemy in overwhelming force. And behind him there was nothing, no one in command, no one to give orders. He was alone in the presence of God and his conscience, with the lives of some fifty Germans in his hands.

And then something extraordinary happened. Captain Fackelmann, a temporary officer, a little business man from a little German town, found the strength to come to a decision at which two dozen Generals and a Commander-in-Chief had balked—the only decision a responsible man could take.

He looked round to find Fröhlich in order to arrange the details; but Fröhlich was nowhere to be seen. He had run to the bunker to find Herbert. They must clear out at once as the open side of the bunker was exposed to enemy fire. They were feverishly putting their last remaining possessions together. They had given the agreed signal and the two others would soon join them. The decisive moment was at hand.

Then the door opened. In the doorway stood Captain Fackelmann. The two men looked at him in alarm. As they stared up at him, he seemed bigger, much bigger than usual. He put his head forward in order to be able to see better in the half light and opened his mouth to say something.

At that moment a crash tore the silence. A fearful blast whirled the two men against the wall. Earth and beams came clattering down and soon nothing was to be seen through the fog of thick, hot dust.

After a while Fröhlich pulled himself up. He groaned as he felt his limbs. He could see nothing, for his eyes were full of dust from the choking cloud which still filled the room. There was a smell of sulphur and scorched flesh.

Fröhlich listened intently but heard nothing. His ears felt as if they had been stuffed with wax.

'Herbert,' he cried. 'Are you there?'

In the distance he heard a high, piping voice.

'Yes . . . ha—have you anything to smoke?'

Without thinking Fröhlich pulled a cigarette out of the pocket of his tunic, tore it in two and held out half of it in the direction of the voice. He felt a hand come in contact with his own. A match blazed and the men smoked in silence. Gradually the dust settled and the dreary daylight grew visible through the empty doorway. At their feet covered in earth and debris lay a body—or rather what had been a body, but was now only a heap of dirt and rags. A shell from a tank gun had struck the Captain full in the back, torn him in two and buried itself in the back wall of the bunker.

Suddenly Fröhlich started to his feet.

'Come out,' he cried. 'Come over to our hide-out. I'll go and fetch the others.' He found Geibel at once. He was standing with his back against the door of the neighbouring bunker, shaking like a leaf.

But where was Gontsharov?

Fröhlich searched for him everywhere and ran, calling his name, through the bunkers, and taking no precautions. Not a sign of him. The Russian was not there. He had disappeared and left no trace.

Then it began to dawn on Fröhlich that the fellow had betrayed them. He had left the sinking ship and gone back to his own people. What else could they have expected? And they had built all their hopes on the Russian.

In the madness of despair he grabbed the holster of his pistol, but then, looking around the chaotic scene, from which the Russian tanks had long since disappeared, he saw a handful of distraught men crowding round him like shipwrecked mariners. When he saw their eyes, he put the pistol back in its holster.

After a moment's hesitation he stretched out his arm and shouted at the top of his voice.

'Listen, everyone, I'm in command now. Fackelmann Group assemble—ready to march away.'

A few minutes later the remnants of Fackelmann's front-line fighters marched off in tolerable order to the south, unmolested by the enemy.

Chapter Thirteen

HORROR AT GUMRAK

❦

SOME FIFTEEN KILOMETRES from the western edge of the city of
Stalingrad, at a point where the north road coming from Kotlubany
leads into the great circular roads around the city, and streets from
all points of the compass converge, there are rows of dreary wooden
cottages, a few railway buildings and a water tower. From the beginning of the battle this place was recognized as a focal point and
was the scene of violent fighting. And even now, though hardly
more than a heap of rubble, its proximity to the airfield and Army
HQ, with its concentration of roads and network of communications, made it a constant target. Troops marching in column
avoided the place and vehicles obliged to come that way raced
through it singly like hunted animals, dodging the craters dotted
over the highway.

It was in this place that the Field Hospital of the VIth Army had
for some time past maintained a final assembly point for the sick
and wounded men of twenty-two divisions—a final goal and haven
of hope for tens of thousands of miserable human wrecks. They
dreamed of this place, of warmth and comfort, of nurses in white
uniforms and of the road to freedom as they lay groaning in
delirium or shivering with cold on the trucks which brought them
from the front.

In fact Gumrak was nothing but a transit camp for the immense
burial ground that stretched farther and farther into the steppe.

Padre Peters now lived here. It was a place of fear, which from
the outset had seemed to him an earthly purgatory. Of the people
who had come there with him, hardly one was left alive. But there
were plenty of others, new ones all the time . . . shortly after his
arrival the resident Chaplain was killed by a stray bomb. Peters had

304

quietly taken his place. He had found quarters in a dark dug-out, hardly the height of a man. At dawn every morning he started on his rounds through huts, which were gradually being transformed into miserable rubbish heaps or stinking craters. He climbed down holes and hollows into which men had crawled like dying animals, hastened along the shattered sleepers to the goods-wagons.

There they lay—badly-wounded cases or men who could not walk any farther—thirty or forty in a single wagon, wrapped in rags and bedded down on dirty straw or simply on the floorboards, keeping themselves warm by huddling together or by means of bonfires which they lit between the lines. There was no one there to attend to them, if there had been, it would not have helped them much, for the Army Staff had cancelled the sixty-gramme bread ration for the wounded on the ground that those who cannot fight, shall not eat. The walking cases dragged themselves to a near-by pump to wait for the horse-drawn carts. Before the unsuspecting driver understood what was happening they would throw themselves with pocket-knives, pieces of metal or just their bare hands on to the trembling horse and cut it to pieces, carrying away with them shreds of steaming flesh. Those who could walk a little better used to hobble along to the overcrowded hospital tent to beg a plate of soup.

Padre Peters scavenged for his wounded in the rubble heaps of ruined houses, and brought them rags and singed garments taken from the dead. He crouched with them on the bare boards of the goods-wagons, when the bombs were falling and red-hot splinters came singing through the walls, and he helped them to put out fires as they occurred.

Peters closed the eyes of the dead or held dying hands or prayed or gave the last sacraments with tea and a crust of bread. But words of consolation came with difficulty to his lips.

Once Padre Peters celebrated a baptism. In one of the huts there lay a soldier, the son of working people from Altona, a lad of twenty-three with an injury to his spine, who begged to be christened. He also begged the Padre not to tell his father in Germany, who would be annoyed.

Peters lit a candle and baptized him with due ceremony, and the others in the room who looked on, were touched or embarrassed or just curious. Two days later the Padre found him lying quiet and peaceful in his corner, with his hands folded on his breast: he was dead. The stub of his baptismal candle was burning at the head of his bunk.

But all the while the Chaplain's mood became gloomier. During the long, lonely, bomb-riddled nights he looked for strength in prayer and no longer found it. Hours of wild despair alternated with periods of lethargy and inertia. The deep sleep of exhaustion seldom brought him relief and his only food was coffee and tea. He no longer bothered about solid food and soon he was only a shadow of his former self. His chin was covered with grey stubble and in his hollow ashen face his eyes burnt feverishly. He paid less and less attention to what he was doing and his actions were meaningless and mechanical. In his struggle to exist his intelligence and sense of service became dim. Only occasionally did individual images fix themselves in his consciousness, and they were often the most horrifying.

For instance before the door of one of the high goods-wagons, they had made a stairway of hard frozen corpses.

Or the case of the three Roumanians run over by a truck. No one came to take them away. Every day Peters passed the corpses and every day he noticed that there was some change in the way they looked. The pools of blood were frozen and brown and the bodies became grey and insignificant after a while. Trucks drove over them regardless till at last they were rolled flat.

Then there was the soldier in front of the railway building. He lay there, weeping and begging to be taken in, clasping the sentry's knee. The sentry shook him off saying good-humouredly 'No it can't be done—don't make trouble.' Peters went by without a word. The next day he saw the man again in exactly the same place, lying on his side with his arms outstretched. His mop of ash-blond hair had been trodden into the snow and frozen tears, like pearls of ice, glittered on his face.

But that was only the beginning. Now this high stone railway building had become a landmark for miles around, a ghastly focus of misery and despair. The bombs which had destroyed everything around it had by a strange chance left the building almost untouched. But one day a bomb fell into the cesspool by the wall and, without doing any other damage, blew out all the windows. The glass had to be replaced by bricks or boards with the result that inside the building there was perpetual darkness. The sick and wounded lay in the passages, rooms and corners side by side or on top of one another and starved and died in their own ordure. No one came to take out the corpses. The building exhaled a pestilential smell, which frightened all living things away. Two stout-hearted medical orderlies and a wounded man, who could still walk ventured to the place occasionally, bringing fir-cones to burn and cooking-pots full of snow.

In this house of the dead Peters twice held religious services. By the light of a candle he stepped on and over soft bodies and limbs, heedless of groans or curses, till he reached the passage which connected the two great rooms with one another. Here he sat down with the Holy Scripture on his knee and the candle in his hand and read. He took as his theme the 90th Psalm.

'Lord, thou has been our refuge . . .'

A foul, choking atmosphere surrounded him and he felt the hot breath of the patients as they panted and groaned.

'Thou turnest man to destruction and sayest "Come again, ye children of men".'

Padre Peters used the last of his strength for these services, and as he performed them he felt that his eyes could once again see and recognize, while his hoarse voice vibrated with its old confidence.

'Man is not forsaken, no. He is in God's hand. And our need and suffering, they, too, come from God. He alone knows the meaning of our ordeal. We must humbly bow and suffer.'

'But God performs miracles,' cried an agonized voice from the darkness. 'Why doesn't he perform a miracle for us?'

'God performs miracles for those who have faith,' answered Peters sternly. And he defended his God to them, defended Him forcefully, while the first spears of doubt pricked his weary spirit. Over and over again he would say 'And are you guiltless? Can you say you have not deserved all this? Have you ever thought about God in all your doings?' For him God had become the jealous God of the Old Testament, the God of Battles. In the gloom he would see burning eyes fixed on him and in his heart a voice cried 'Let them not suffer so terribly, O Lord. Let me bear their sufferings. Take me, if Thou needest a sacrifice.'

After these hours of anguish he would return to his bunker dripping with sweat and full of despair. Huddled in a corner he would hunt through the Scriptures for words of consolation. The text swam before his eyes and he knew he could not bear this much longer. The vessel of his soul was drained dry.

Padre Peters might well have ended in misery but for Corporal Brezel.

One morning, during his first few days in Gumrak, when he felt stronger than he did later, Peters had climbed up a rickety ladder to the attics of the railway building. Pushing through a tin-lined, trap-door he found himself in a dark passage, in which stood blistered cans and other rubbish, but also considerable stocks of what Peters first thought were lengths of timber. On a closer view he recognized that they were the frozen legs of horses. Puzzled he went on to a low wooden door, opened it and gave a cry of surprise. He was looking into a small, very tidy room. It contained a camp-bed, a crackling stove, and pictures from illustrated papers on the walls. There was a small window looking eastwards and in front of it a table, at which sat a soldier. At first all that Peters could make out was a flowing mane, but when the soldier took off his horn-rimmed glasses, stood up and greeted the newcomer with a bow, introducing himself as Corporal Brezel.

For months Brezel had been living alone in this secret room. In this airy and dangerous roof-top, undisturbed by the noise of falling bombs or the suffering beneath his feet, he was writing the history of his division, an infantry division which had distinguished itself in Poland and France and then had found its way to Stalingrad via Shitomir, Kiev and Voronesh. The task had been entrusted to him by his Divisional Commander in the victorious days of autumn and he took it very seriously. His table was piled with dossiers, decrees, letters, accounts of individual experiences, photos and other original documents which he exhibited to Peters.

Brezel was a poet by profession and, before the war, had written about the Revolution and the Soul of Germany in verse so striking and intelligible that the National Socialist provincial press had regularly published his contributions.

At the same time Brezel was a thoroughly practical man with a considerable talent for organization, and the history of the division was not his only military responsibility. He was in charge of a troop of Russian prisoners of war, who worked in the village on clearance operations and road repairs. Up to December a section of this troop had been detailed for slaughtering animals, which meant that there were pickings for all, including the Corporal. Hence the frozen horses' legs. Meanwhile Brezel's troop had shrunk to six men, and he could leave them to their own devices.

Peters visited Brezel a couple of times, sipped hot tea with him and nibbled at half a crust of bread.

One day Brezel appeared, with a friendly smile, in the Padre's bunker. In the early morning a bomb had come through his window, penetrated the opposite wall and exploded in the street. Brezel had decided, after this incident, to bring the history of his division, to an abrupt conclusion. He had divided the haunches of horseflesh among his Russians and told them to beat it. Then he moved out himself.

'Graciously God gave a sign, and his servant heeded the warning——'

were the last words of Brezel's colourful report.

Since then he had been acting as sacristan and cleaner to the Chaplain. He kept the bunker clean, discouraged unbidden guests, collected firewood, saw to the lighting and managed to procure supplies from all sorts of mysterious sources. He would arrive with a handful of dry bread, a small bowl of thin soup or a handful of meal from the hospital.

Brezel was always friendly, good-humoured and untouched by the deadening world around him. Neither bombs, grenades nor dying men interfered with his healthy slumbers. But he went on his way with wakeful senses and an animal's keen scent for danger and an unerring instinct which led him to the most secret sources of life. Thus it was that he remained alive and kept the Padre alive. He had taken a shy liking to Peters, whose unlikeness to himself had attracted him and awakened his desire to be of service.

In any case, he soon had reason to worry about the Chaplain, whose behaviour grew more and more strange. He often sat for hours without moving, staring into the distance and apparently not hearing what was said to him. Or else he seemed to be looking round the bunker for some mysterious thing which he could never find, mumbling unintelligibly to himself. Sometimes he would go away suddenly leaving Brezel to wait anxiously for his return.

Once he returned from a walk with two shapeless overshoes of plaited straw which he hid under his bunk. Later Brezel heard him groaning and tossing on his bed and thought he could distinguish the words 'thou shalt not steal . . . thou shalt not steal . . .' In the middle of the night Peters crept out without a cloak or a hat into the cold. It was not to relieve himself, for he remained outside for a long time. Next morning the straw shoes were no longer there. Later Brezel saw them again. The driver of a Russian peasant cart was busily feeding them to his horse.

Then there was the incident of the bread ration. In his restlessness Peters used often to go to the airfield, where the arriving and departing planes gave an illusion of a life that had long since vanished from the dead city. One day, on his way back, he saw two men dragging a strip of canvas. When he came near he saw that it was piled high with loaves of bread. Excitedly he quickened his steps till he caught up with them. They eyed him uneasily but he planted himself in front of them.

'Where are you going?' he asked. The soldiers put down their burden and looked at him. His attitude made them conclude that he was a senior officer and they began to stammer out an explanation: 'It's for . . .' they seemed to have perfectly clear consciences. Very often the planes did not land but dropped supplies by parachute which did not always fall where they were aimed.

'Yes, yes, we know all about that,' said Peters in a hectoring voice—— 'You're going to stuff yourselves alone, aren't you? And what about the others? Let me look!' and he pulled back the canvas and seemed to be making calculations. 'Two hundred and forty . . . 416 times 7 . . . 824' and then he burst out: 'You've got to give up five loaves, d'you understand? Five loaves—that's fair and human.'

'Very good, Major!' they agreed, pleased to have got off so cheaply. The Padre picked up the loaves with trembling hands. He pushed one into the pocket of his overcoat, tearing the cloth as he did so, and crammed the others under his arms. Then he hurried away. The two soldiers looked after him in amazement. There was something abnormal about the affair.

When the Padre returned to the bunker with his booty, Brezel's eyes popped out of his head. Peters gave the impression of being drunk.

'Ha! What do you say now?' he exulted, rubbing his hands together. 'Yes, Papa's come back from town.' Cutting one of the loaves in two, he handed half to Brezel. 'We'll do ourselves proud today and make the rest last for a week.' He pushed the remaining loaves under his bunk beside the machine-gun. 'For a week we can live like the Kings of France!'

He broke off great chunks of bread and pushed them into his mouth, laughing and joking as he chewed them. Brezel was gradually infected by his unnatural hilarity. Peters had not realized what immense trouble his friend took to get anything at all to eat—now they had five whole loaves. Brezel scratched up the remnants of his coffee and they began to feast, while Peters described his adventure in high-flown language. A feeling of envy came over Brezel as he discovered this unknown side of the Padre's character but with the envy was mingled a half-conscious feeling of disillusionment.

They were still eating, when a visitor arrived. It was the medical orderly from the hospital in the ravine, a Franciscan monk from a cloister in Silesia, a slim little man with eyes as clear as a mountain lake. He was usually a welcome guest in the bunker, but today his visit was inopportune and he was received in embarrassed silence. He sat down all unsuspecting. Brezel poured him out a can of coffee and Peters cut off a slice of his bread and gave it to him.

'Many thanks, Padre,' said the monk politely, but he neither drank nor ate. He told them about the great difficulties they had been having in the hospital tent and said that they had no longer enough supplies for the patients' daily cup of soup.

The two men suddenly lost their appetite. Peters looked uneasily round the room. Then he rummaged under his bunk and produced a loaf which he handed to his guest.

'There!' he said in a voice harsh with embarrassment. 'That's for you.'

'Oh!' said the Franciscan in incredulous astonishment. 'Oh, Padre!' He carefully took the loaf in his hand, smelt it and stroked it with his fingertips. 'Can I really take it with me?' His eyes took on a dreamy brilliance as he said, 'What pleasure this will give.'

Padre Peters stared at him as if he were a ghost. His face turned ashen pale and he began to tremble all over. Then he knelt down by his bed again and pulled out the remaining loaves from underneath, one after the other. 'There, take them all,' he said. 'All of them.'

Brezel wanted to jump up but he felt as if he were nailed to his seat. He opened his mouth and tried to speak, but only gaped silently as he waved his hand helplessly in the air.

The monk did not understand what was happening. He looked at Peters and then at the loaves under his arm and then at Peters again. 'O Lord, my God,' he stammered. Four loaves meant six kilos of bread, which could be divided into 120 slices—120 poor men on the verge of starvation would each have fifty grams of bread today. . . .

When he had gone Brezel got up and slipped out like a whipped dog. But Peters sat on his bed with his head in his hands weeping.

Breuer stumbled back through the gulley. Under the broad, blood-crusted field-dressing that covered his forehead, eye and ear a throbbing pain bored into the back of his head. Faintly behind him he could hear the rattle of a machine-gun, a few clear reports, the sound of a challenge and the cry of a wounded man. Breuer's comrades were back there—Fröhlich, Geibel and Herbert. Perhaps they were preparing their getaway—without him. With him, in his present state, they could never have brought it off. He thought of their plans without regret and realized that he had never been confident about them. At some other time of year perhaps, but not in the last days of January. 'Breuer, on 24th January!' Now he remembered that tomorrow was the 24th.

Where should he make for now? He didn't know, but thought that if his legs would carry him so far he would try and get to the staff at Stalingradski, if there still was a staff. Or to a dressing-station, a bunker or a fox-hole into which he could creep—only tomorrow was the 24th.

The gulley grew broader and ran into the plain. On the right lay the line of bunkers, in which they had spent the night two days before. They were as empty as the high road behind them. Not a soul to be seen, no movement, no life.

Breuer tottered on, passing vehicles, snow embankments and roofs of bunkers. Guns pointed their muzzles into the air: there was a wireless car with a mast and a network of wires, fringed with snow, but everything was abandoned and frozen stiff.

Breuer stopped for a while because he found the loneliness paralysing. Suddenly he saw, at the entrance to a bunker, a white figure as motionless as himself, staring fixedly like a marble statue.

'Hey——' shouted Breuer. The sound of his voice, breaking the silence, frightened him. The other man started and vanished as if he had been swallowed up by the earth. Breuer felt his knees weaken and longed to hide himself in the earth as well. Then he was overwhelmed by fear and longed to be with men and to hear a human voice. He hurried on until at last he recognized the faint outline of a water-tower that he took to be Gumrak.

A broad, beaten track led there and Breuer started to follow it. On the right of the road lay the immense air field, the hulks of ruined aircraft half-buried in the snow. On the runway stood a great, grey JU 52, apparently undamaged, but abandoned.

Shells were now flying overhead and he could hear them exploding in front of him, while a nuisance fire was being kept up on the western side of the village. He wondered if he should avoid the danger zone by making a detour through the snow field, but felt that he no longer had the strength. He stayed on the road.

The village took shape as he approached it and the uniform whiteness of the snow became multi-coloured. The white shaded off to grey and brown and was often pitted with black craters. Along the road were heaps of rubble and charred wood from some of which a yellowish smoke was rising. There was a strong smell of burning everywhere but this was mingled with another smell, sweetish and heavy, which Breuer remembered well from the autumn fields of Poland and through which he had marched in France and Russia till the frosts and snows of winter stifled it. It was all around him in spite of 40 degrees of frost—the smell of decaying flesh.

A shrivelled figure was rummaging in a heap of rubble, wearing a dirty blanket round its body and bent like an old woman. While Breuer looked at this strange apparition, he felt the air suddenly becoming heavy and full of danger. His instinct prompted him to take a few hurried steps towards the spot where the figure had just disappeared into the ground and just as the blast from a shell was reaching him he slipped into a deep hollow. Half stunned, he got to his feet and pushed his way, through an opening, to where the darkness was fitfully lit by a flickering fire. A small opening admitted a thin shaft of daylight. Breuer stood there, his head bowed and his back pressed against the entrance while his head touched the flimsy metal roof. On the ash-covered ground he saw human figures lying. And suddenly he was overpowered by that horrible stench which he had already smelt outside. Breuer knew that the figures on the ground were dead men, corpses, rotting here in this meaningless warmth that issued from the crackling stove, before which the man he had seen outside was squatting and tending the fire. The red glow of the flames disclosed a withered face distorted by a lunatic grin.

Breuer struggled for breath. He had to go into the open. Cold and snow and bombs were human. But this stench of burning and putrefaction was inhuman and unbearable. In frantic haste he tugged at the planks, but they would not give way.

Then something made him turn round, he thought that someone had spoken his name. Was this the beginning of madness? He listened trembling but only heard the crackling of the stove and the chattering of his own teeth. But there it was again—a soft and distant sound.

'Breuer.'

It wasn't the man by the stove. The voice came from the corner. Once more he heard it, more urgent now and quite unmistakable.

'Breuer.'

Stepping over motionless bodies as soft as the soggy ground, Breuer made his way to the corner, while fear chilled his spine. Even in the corner there was a huddled heap of corpses. The firelight fell on greenish, glazed faces with turned-up eyeballs and open mouths.

Breuer saw a pair of eyes gazing at him from dark, hollow sockets. On a heap of filthy clothing a transparent hand was moving its fingers. At last came the faint sound of a voice. 'Yes, Breuer,' it said. 'It's me. God is not mocked. . . .'

Breuer sought feverishly in this altered face for the once familiar features.

'You?' he stammered. 'You here? Wiese, my God!' And then his helplessness fell from him, and with it the sense of his own misery. He must fetch a doctor. What was going on here was not to be endured in a world which God had made. But the two burning eyes held him back and rooted him to the spot.

'Stay here,' said the voice. 'There's nothing you can do.' For a moment Wiese closed his eyes in exhaustion and then focused them, with an agonized effort, on his friend.

'I thought I knew better than the others,' he said painfully. 'I saw it coming. And I did nothing to stop it. But God has punished me. He is not mocked. . . .'

'The others,' whispered the voice, 'didn't know, but I knew from the beginning and did nothing to stop it.'

The grey face seemed to be shrinking, and on each side of the nose were runnels of sweat.

'Now it's too late. There's no way back.'

The damp wood smouldered in the stove as the kneeling cripple carefully pushed the pieces into the flames with his mutilated hand.

'That man,' said the voice, 'looks after me. He nursed . . . the others . . . till . . . they died. I don't need anything.'

Breuer knelt beside his friend. His fingers stroked the bloodencrusted folds of his discoloured greatcoat, and touched his cold hands, which felt like lumps of tallow. He could think of nothing to say.

Then Wiese's voice murmured softly: 'Look in the right hand pocket of my tunic.'

Breuer hesitated, but under the compulsion of those eyes he cautiously put his hand under Wiese's coat and felt a soft, sticky mass. Overcoming his disgust he pulled out the remains of a pocket-book, saturated with pus. It was Wiese's collection of poems from which he had often read bits to his mess-mates.

'Take it with you,' said the voice. 'Take it to my mother.'

Breuer felt a lump in his throat. A feeling of anger and helplessness filled him and he almost envied the friend, who was going to die.

'Wiese,' he faltered, 'I don't know if I can. I may not . . .'

The steady eyes went on staring at him.

'You'll get home, Breuer . . . I know it. Go now.'

Breuer slipped the notebook into his pocket and looked round helplessly. The firelight flickered over the dead bodies and gave them a gruesome appearance of life.

'You don't belong here, Breuer. You belong to the living——Go!'

And Breuer went——

He reeled into the open air like a drunken man and staggered over the mounds and the shell-torn road. He longed to see his fellow men, but here, too, the village seemed to have been swept clean.

Suddenly he ran into a man who was painfully pulling himself out of some smoking ruins. Breuer stared him in the face and then gripped his arm.

'Padre!' he cried.

Peters' ravaged face gave a fleeting sign of recognition——

'Ah, Breuer.'

'Padre, Wiese—Lieutenant Wiese is lying in a hole in the ground. He's dying. . . .'

Peters tried to remember. 'Wiese,' he said wearily, 'the little Lieutenant. Yes, many are dying here. There's a doctor over there. Come with me.'

Gumrak was being abandoned and the doctor had come to look after the wounded men in the village, who could do something to help themselves. He realized from Breuer's description that there was nothing to be done for Wiese. 'I'll see,' he growled, and pushed away the hand that was pulling at his sleeve. Then, seeing Breuer's bloody bandage, he felt sorry. 'What's the matter with you?' he said. 'An eye-wound?' He felt the dressing and said: 'We'd better not touch it.' Then he wrote a few words on a card and handed it to Breuer saying—— 'With an eye injury you can fly out without special approval from the army. At present they're flying from Stalingradski, but I don't know how long it'll go on. You'd better hurry up!'

Breuer stood and stared at the card.

Could he really fly out?

Was it as simple as all that?

A wave of emotion swept over him, wiping out everything: Stalingrad, the last months of misery, the pain of his wound and his dying friend. A bright vision rose before him, of home, Irmgard, his children and the house by the lake.

In his hand he held a passport to freedom and life.

At the back of his mind was the omen of the 24th—but hope had taken possession of him. He was going to live.

He hurried off towards the air field at Stalingradski.

Chapter Fourteen

NO WAY BACK

THE AIR FIELD AT Stalingradski was the last in the shrunken ring. The only gateway into the outer world. The other world, gilded by memory, was waiting, ninety flying minutes away.

Within a few hours, this last gateway might be closed for ever.

There was a road running somewhere towards the south. To the left of it was a ravine. By the roadside was a notice saying 'This way to the airfield offices.' The signpost pointed down the steep slope towards a wooden hoarding along a pathway flanked by low bushes. With his wound-pass between his lips, Breuer slid down this icy winding path and pushed his way through a half-open door. He found himself in a room full of smoke and people—a medley of soldiers waiting in surly silence. By the window someone was hammering on a typewriter.

Breuer pushed forward till he got to the barrier. There a black-haired officer was sitting behind a table. As he fumbled among his papers he kept eyeing the faces of the men leaning on the barrier. Breuer held his wound-pass under the nose of the officer, who gave it a casual glance and said: 'It needs the signature of the PMO.'

Breuer's heart missed a beat.

'I don't understand,' he said, 'I was told . . .'

'Then you've been told wrong,' snorted the officer. 'No one gets through here unless his papers have been countersigned by the PMO.'

Breuer held on to the railing, speechless. The men standing round grinned maliciously. This seemed to irritate the air-officer, who took the paper once more.

'An eye-wound,' he growled as he spelt out the doctor's diagnosis. 'Leave the thing here,' he decided. 'It must go over to Doctor

Rinoldi. Perhaps he'll sign it. Doesn't that suit you? You're not the only one. Wait outside in the square.'

Breuer was shocked to see the officer throw the paper carelessly into a heap of others. A few moments ago he wouldn't have parted with it for anything in the world. Now a word had made it worthless until another signature restored its value.

Breuer stepped outside. The day had suddenly grown dark and grey. He was dead tired and starving and the pain of his wound was worse than before. Freedom, had seemed within his grasp, but now it had retreated to an infinite distance.

He crept up the slope on all fours and crossed a road flanked with high bushes. Then he found himself on the edge of the air field, a piece of snowy steppe like a spotty, torn tablecloth. It was dotted with mounds of snow, which might have been graves.

Wrecked machines lay all around, some already buried in snow and others looking strange and dark against the white background. Little coloured flags were standing here and there and men with hand-sleighs waited idly by a truck.

As Breuer drew nearer he saw a clump of people, a solid mass of bodies. He could see their faces distorted by hate and rage, their arms gesticulating wildly and clenched fists and sticks raised in the air. There was a sound of breaking crutches and bodies falling heavily to the ground. Those that fell got up, if they could, and struggled once more into the crowd. Some slithered back groaning or pulled themselves along by means of wooden pegs which they drove into the beaten snow-track, or clung to the legs and skirts of the standing men who kicked them, pushed them and trampled them down. All round lay a ring of wrecked bodies, the twitching or motionless victims of this devil's cauldron.

Breuer gazed at this ghastly scene, but did not understand what he saw. The broad, deserted field, under its coating of snow, the dead wrecks of aircraft and this bitter struggle of unchained passions: it was ghostly and meaningless. He had expected to see tents for the wounded, zealous doctors and orderlies, energetic flight-personnel and a string of machines ready to fly them to the land of freedom.

He looked closely at the man who was standing twenty yards to one side of him with legs apart and a pinched face sunk into his turned-up fur collar. He looked ready to spring and had the wide-awake look of a lion-tamer. In his hand he had a cocked pistol.

'Get into line,' he rasped. 'Three ranks in line I tell you.' His voice sounded like a spoon scraping a rusty bucket, but the mob cowered. Then the tumult grew louder again and single, piercing cries rose above it.

Breuer began to understand what was happening. The people were struggling for priority—everyone wanted to get the first place—a senseless, hopeless, lunatic struggle. There were Germans, Austrians, Luxemburgers, Croats and Roumanians all mixed up together—workers, peasants and townspeople, Protestants and Catholics, rich and poor, fathers and sons . . . They were not soldiers any more, scarcely human beings, even.

The officer in charge kept his eyes fixed on the sky. Soon Breuer could hear the rise and fall of motors growing louder and louder, though the grey canopy of cloud was impenetrable.

'You pack of swine, you bloody morons,' barked the officer, waving his pistol—— 'Form into line, blast you! If you don't obey, I'll tell the pilot not to land. Then no one will get away.' He knew they would listen, because they were entirely in his hands.

It was he alone who decided whether they should live or die.

Suddenly a huge shadow swept over their heads, and a flare went up. Would the pilot chance a landing? Everyone fell silent, looking at the sky.

During these few moments a little group of men had separated themselves from the mob and cries and curses were heard. 'I'm first, I'm a Colonel.' 'Shut your trap, you bastard!' 'Keep your hands off!' Suddenly, something like a queue had separated itself from the mob, which was still staring upwards.

Meanwhile the plane, a Heinkel 111, had circled very low. It thundered over the heads of the crowd and the slipstream from its propellers sucked up the snow from the ground. When it reached the end of the air field it turned and settled down to make a landing. About 100 yards from the waiting crowd the propellers slowed up and stopped and the plane came to a halt. A door was flung open and a flight of landing-steps appeared. A man climbed out, stretched his arms and legs pleasurably and remained standing with his hands in his pockets by the gangway. A truck came rumbling up and casks and boxes were unloaded in feverish haste and stowed in the lorry. One of the men stood near by with his carbine at the ready.

The officer in charge dashed after the group that had separated itself from the crowd and counted off twelve of them. Standing at a safe distance he kept the others covered. 'Not a step farther,' he shouted. 'Anyone who moves gets a bullet in his guts.'

They knew that he meant business and no one dared to cross the invisible line marked by the point of his pistol. Meanwhile, the twelve raced across the field like hunted hares. The Roumanian lost his hat but did not turn to pick it up. Another man limped panting behind the pack and suddenly fell flat on his face in the snow, but he pulled himself up and hobbled onwards, waving his arms wildly. The man by the aircraft, a cigarette between his lips, checked the papers casually and the men disappeared into the dark hull.

Breuer stared absentmindedly at the machine and saw a shabby leather jacket and a yellow brief-case. Somehow they were familiar and revived a distant memory which he could not pin down.

They had begun to swing the propellers of the Heinkel once more. The plane made a detour and lumbered nearly to the other end of the air field.

'A nice prospect, don't you think?' said a voice. Breuer saw a fresh-complexioned, clean-shaven face, smiling at him. He had noticed the man in the office, taking an energetic line with the officials. The latter had called him 'Major' and treated him with extreme politeness.

Meanwhile the Heinkel had begun to gather speed, though it was still not airborne. Its wings almost grazed the crowd and the officer in charge had to spring to one side to avoid being knocked down. Then a man detached himself from the others and with a desperate jump managed to get hold of one of the wings and to pull himself up with hands and legs on to the surface. The control-officer sprang forward with a cry of rage, raised his pistol and fired. The report was drowned by the noise of the motors, but the man reared up, clutched at the air with his hands and pitched heavily into the snow. A few moments later the plane was airborne.

'An idiot!' said the Major to Breuer. 'Let's get out of the wind, it's no use milling around here with all these people. I suppose you're waiting for your ticket.' Breuer nodded without speaking. The Major took up his leather suit-case and strode off with a swagger to sit in the shelter of a wrecked JU. Breuer wished he could lie here and let himself be carried to some quiet wilderness. He had still to fight for his life and he knew that he had no strength left for fighting. Tomorrow was the 24th! The spectre was there once more, huge and paralysing.

'Let's hope the fellow with the tickets turns up,' said the Major. He had taken out his cigarettes and offered one to Breuer. 'You can't trust these chaps. Of course it's not much fun to be sending other fellows away, when you're obliged to stay yourself.'

'Yes,' murmured Breuer. He was looking at a shadow circling over the airfield. It looked as though the pilot was worried about his landing. The Major chattered cheerfully on. 'Cripples and invalids are being flown out, but it's damned stupid. They'll only fill the hospitals at home. They ought to be lifting out healthy infantry-men, tank-soldiers, specialists or staff officers. . . . They talk about ruthlessness, but when it comes to the point . . .'

Breuer didn't answer. The second machine was coming in to land and one of the snow mounds suddenly came to life. A figure rose to its feet, twirled round on its axis and staggered, waving its arms, on to the runway.

Shouts went up from all sides. The tip of a wing struck the man, lifting him off his legs. His body struck the earth like a stone, but the plane had been thrown off course. It struck an obstacle and its under-carriage broke away. The hull scraped noisily along for a while, leaving a dark furrow in the snow, and then, tilting on to its side, lay there motionless.

That was the end of that.

Gumrak was a smouldering, crackling heap of ruins. From the debris of houses came a mixed smell of burning and putrefaction which the fresh breath of newly-fallen snow could not efface, nor the east wind blow away.

The road was sprinkled with dead bodies. But from the holes in the ground and the heaps of rubble and the burnt-out railway carriages other beings crawled out into the unaccustomed light and joined the convoy, supporting themselves on half-burnt pieces of salvaged wood which served them as sticks and crutches.

Slowly, painfully, they made their way towards Stalingrad. After they had gone, the village was silent. The Russian bombers no longer found it a worth-while target and even the periodical artillery bombardment ceased. Only occasionally a single shell broke the silence and crashed against the ruined walls or corrugated roofs.

After that came small, silent groups of armed men, who marched through without halting. Rifle-fire and the hoarse rattle of machine-guns could be heard from the north and west.

Corporal Brezel saw the changes with growing unrest. Since the field-hospital in the gulley had been evacuated, it had been difficult to find anything to eat. He roamed aimlessly through the deserted village, rummaging in the refuse and wondering if he should go or stay and if he dared to go alone. When he had almost made up his mind, fear drove him back to the bunker. Padre Peters lay on his bunk in a fever. He was so weak that he could not creep outside to relieve himself and the stench in the dug-out was unbearable.

One day Brezel shook the sick man and said: 'The Russkis will be here soon. We must go.'

But Peters did not react. He stared into the distance and made incoherent sounds. Brezel gave up trying to help him, collected his few possessions and packed them in his hand-sleigh while the tears traced dirty stripes down his cheeks. After walking for fifty yards or so he flew into a rage turned about and hurried into the bunker.

'Come along, you idiot,' he cried and pulled Peters from his bed. He pulled his overcoat over the Padre's body and forced his fur cap on his head and then drove him out with blows. Peters made no attempt to resist. He swayed a little as he walked and blinked helplessly in the daylight, but he remained on his feet.

Brezel handed him a flask filled with tea. The hot liquid and the keen winter air brought the Padre partly to his senses. He took a few deep breaths, gave Brezel a sidelong glance and then trotted on silently beside him. Eventually they found their way out of the village and crossed the railway line.

By the roadside someone was lying. He had been bedded comfortably in the snow and was lying on his back under a horse blanket. His hands were dirty and brown but below the surface was visible the bluish pallor of death. His face too, dried up like a shrivelled apple, was the face of a dead man, but his sunken eyes followed the men as they passed him.

The Padre did not stop at first, but then a text came back to him from the Gospel of St Luke, *They looked on him and passed by*. He remembered his own inaugural sermon and the life came back to his eyes: They 'looked on him and passed by.' he murmured as he stopped. Brezel was some way ahead before he noticed. He turned and walked up to the Padre, feeling that he might have to drag him along on the sleigh.

'What's up, Padre? Come along now!' But Peters cried: 'It's not true, we were not the last men in Gumrak.'

When Brezel tried to catch hold of him, he pushed him away.

'Away!' he shouted.

'Get thee behind me, Satan!'

Brezel was afraid he was out of his mind. He shook the Padre, then ran back to the sleigh and hurried on. He was afraid and did not dare to look round.

Peters walked back to the man lying by the roadside and knelt down beside him. He took his flask from its case and moistened the dying man's lips, then he pillowed his head on his lap and prayed.

'Thy will be done. Thy will, O Lord, only Thy will, which Thou dost reveal to us so gloriously. We are but vessels to receive Thy will!'

In those few, quiet minutes, Padre Peters found the way back. He closed the dead man's eyes, put him back on his pillow and drew the blanket carefully over his face. Then he stood up and looked round him with new vision.

Brezel had disappeared. From the direction of Gorodishche, he

324

heard the rumble of a heavy bombardment, and from nearer at hand came an occasional crackle of machine-gun fire. Peters breathed heavily. The fever had left him and with it the dreadful helplessness of the past few days; his head was clear once more and he still had a mission to perform.

Padre Peters walked back to Gumrak.

A strange hush lay over the village. Nothing had changed since they had left . . . and yet for him, everything was different. It no longer looked dead and forsaken. The shattered mud huts and heaps of rubble were breathing, the earth breathed and through the walls pierced the eyes of countless men looking to him for help. Everywhere, he thought, are men who can no longer help themselves and to whom no one brings help. 'They looked on him and passed by.' The sacrificed, the forsaken, the lost . . . Peters hesitated: in a short time the Russians would be there, 'O God,' he stammered. 'What shall I do? Help me, O Lord. Show me the way.'

Suddenly the light came to him. He must go to meet the Russians and surrender the place as a hospital with all its sick and wounded. He would ignore the army order forbidding the surrender of wounded men to the enemy. Of what value now were the commands of men?

The Padre dragged himself out of the village. The mist hung thickly over the steppe. Then he saw them—a few, small, hardly visible figures gliding sideways over the snow. Four, five . . . seven men. They spread out as they came nearer. Peters closed his eyes for an instant and then he felt inspired by the courage of the martyrs of old. He pulled out his cross and held it high over his head crying: '*Christos Voskresty*'—' Christ is risen. I am a priest.'

The Russians grew larger as they glided towards him. They approached cautiously with their pistols ready for use until at last they had surrounded the bearded man with the cross. Their childish, undeveloped Ukranian faces were full of astonishment.

'*Christos Voskresty*,' said the Padre once more—it sounded like an entreaty or an almost hopeless prayer.

The leader of the patrol, a square-shouldered fellow, a head taller than the others, broke the spell. He dropped his hand and walked up to Peters. 'Little Father,' he said and laid a heavy hand on Peters' shoulder, shaking him good-humouredly.

'Little Father.'

The Russian laughed heartily, while in the background two of his men secretly made the sign of the cross.

Then Padre Peters fell on his knees and buried his face in his hands.

'There he is!'

The Major jumped to his feet. 'Who?' asked Breuer, waking with a start.

'The fellow with the tickets.' The Major was already hurrying to the spot and Breuer followed as fast as his feet would carry him. The man, who was surrounded by an excited rabble, was the officer from the control hut. Was it an aircraft engine that he heard or the racing of his heart? The officer seemed to have nerves of steel. He was taking his time. He laboriously deciphered the names on the cards and checked the pay-books. It seemed to take hours.

Meanwhile the plane was circling overhead. At last Breuer had a card in his hand. On it was scribbled in pencil: 'Approved—Rinoldi.' The PMO's visa, the official confirmation by the Highest Authority of the decision that Oberleutnant Breuer, Intelligence officer on the staff of a non-existent Panzer Division, was authorized to leave the Stalingrad area.

The grey shadow of the plane was still wheeling over the airfield and to the west a plume of yellow smoke showed the direction of the wind.

Silence gripped the airfield and even the officer in charge stared tensely upward. The drone of the motors was as nerve-racking as the rasping of a circular saw. Then something came loose from the hull, a white hood unfolded itself and hovered slowly downwards. Half a dozen blackish objects trailed after it and struck the ground noisily. The pioneers hurried forward with their handsleighs, but the JU looped round the field and vanished into the distance.

Down below pandemonium broke out.

The control-officer darted back and fired a few pistol-shots into the air. Then he shouted: 'Keep your heads!—more machines are coming! Fifty more JUs are scheduled. There'll be plenty of room for everyone.'

His luck was in, for with the sound of the departing plane mingled a new tone and once more excitement spread through the waiting crowd.

'What did I say?' cried the officer. 'You'll all be able to get away.'

As the new plane methodically lost height its under-carriage was lowered. It was another Heinkel, and the pilot effected a masterly landing. The supervising officer had moved to one side, but now he turned and ran across to the little group, where Breuer was standing. He seized them and pushed them towards the aircraft, counting them as he did so.

'One—two—three.'

'Don't forget me,' cried Breuer. He pulled a fur-clad Roumanian to one side and held out his card saying—'Eye-wound.'

The officer growled, but gave him a push towards the aircraft.

'Seven—eight—nine.'

The Major with the smartly-bandaged arm whispered something to the control-officer and was also pushed towards the plane.

'Eleven—twelve.'

It was over in a few seconds and the control-officer was just able to get back to his post in time to keep the crowd in order at the point of his pistol.

The twelve hurried across the field as though the hounds of Hell were after them. The plane was still being unloaded—boxes and barrels tumbled noisily out. A wooden box burst open and loaves of bread rolled into the snow. The pilot, who also held a pistol in his hand, saw to it that there was no delay.

At last the gangway was free and the first passengers climbed up. Breuer, his nose pressed against a musty-smelling greatcoat, was pushed up the steps. Behind him followed the Major in a tearing hurry.

'Get along, hurry up,' he cried.

What happened then was never clear to Breuer when he thought it over later.

He might have missed his footing on the slippery stairway or perhaps the impatient Major threw him off balance. All he knew was that his strength suddenly gave out, he knocked his head against the metal covering of the fuselage and everything turned black.

The slipstream of the propeller brought him back to consciousness. He heard the engine roaring and a huge rubber-tyred wheel narrowly missed him as it crunched through the snow. He pulled himself to his feet and looked after the plane as it glided away. Then he bent down to pick up his cap, took hold of his bundle and walked to the side. He was still holding his card. He looked at it as if he had never seen it before, and then tore it up deliberately and watched the wind carrying the scraps away. He knew instinctively that no more planes would land in Stalingrad and he remembered that Wiese had said, as he lay dying: 'There is no way back.' His only chance had been thrown away.

Breuer felt that Stalingrad had become something more than a geographical conception, and that no one could escape it, even if he fled to the farthest ends of the earth. Every man who had been here was branded for life.

The day was drawing to a close. To the north, gunfire drew a chain of sparkling flashes, coming slowly nearer. The noise of the crowd was sometimes broken by a dull crash and yellow-grey smoke arose from a black crater. The crowd was quieter now, and an old Roumanian Colonel, spluttering hoarse orders, had succeeded in forming them into three ranks. No one seemed to notice that the control-officer had gone away.

Breuer did not know where he wanted to go. Suddenly, he caught sight of a pair of familiar felt boots with black toecaps, leather bands along the seams and a buckle at the back. He saw that the boots belonged to a man who was being propped up by a companion. The first man had a temporary splint on one arm, a bandaged neck, a chalky-white deeply shadowed face and a pair of sunken eyes.

'Dierk . . . Good God, man . . . what are you doing here?'

The eyes gazed at Breuer and the mouth tried to form words. The man supporting Dierk was a Sergeant-Major from the Flak.

'I'll help you hold him up,' said Breuer.

'But . . .' said the Sergeant-Major hesitating, 'they say there'll be more machines. The Lieutenant can't walk.'

'There won't be any more,' said Breuer. 'Look over there.'

He nodded towards the north where the red glow of the barrage was climbing higher and higher into the sky.

They held Dierk under the armpits and dragged him along. He looked from one to another and faint groans came from his lips. His feet slithered under him.

'Shot in the neck,' said the Sergeant-Major, 'and a few splinters in his arm. The bone was gone. He copped one in the left leg, too.'

On the highway which led from the middle of the town to the road leading to Kotluban, a broad stream of men and vehicles was flowing towards the south. Deadly tired, wounded men, driven once more from their fox-holes; dispersed units which yesterday were holding a sector of the line; small improvised fighting groups assembled for some unimportant duty and vaguely ordered to proceed to some uncertain point on the fringe of the town; staffs on the run from Stalingradski and Gorodishche; stragglers flushed out of their secret hiding-places . . . and again wounded, displaced, miserable spectral figures from the limbo of a broken army.

After wandering aimlessly for hours through the wilderness of snow the former Fackelmann Group, together with a few pioneers and building technicians from the Gulley, had reached this high road in fairly good order. There they had been merged in the great stream of fugitives and had split up into small pockets which soon dissolved.

For a long time Interpreter Fröhlich had been alone, though he was hardly aware of it. His desire for leadership had quickly evaporated. His companions no longer looked to him for support and they had now all deserted him. He trudged along with his lower lip stuck out and his teeth gritted together. For the first time he felt the shock of the failure of his plan. What a swine that fellow Gontsharov was! Still, it might have been worse. The Russian might have killed them on the road or sold them to the first NKVD post for a return ticket to Russia. It was rage that drove Fröhlich on. They would never get him—he would see to that! In the pocket of his overcoat were two spare belts with thirty cartridges each and the sound they made, as they knocked together, was comforting.

Somewhere in front Geibel and Herbert were swimming in the human stream, yet they were alone, for the first time in their lives. Quite alone, no longer protected by the sides of a truck or the walls of a bunker. Now no one gave them orders, or called them to eat, to wake up, to fight or to die. The community had thrust them out and left them driving along through darkness and ruin.

Herbert, a slender and delicate looking man was walking unexpectedly well, Geibel had reached the end of his strength. He shuffled painfully through the brown, trampled snow. Since early morning he had eaten nothing, but neither hunger nor thrist disturbed him. All feeling seemed to be concentrated in his feet, which were raw and covered with blisters.

'Herbert,' he said, 'I—I can't go on any longer.'

'Of course you can! You can go on if you try.'

'Is there much farther to go?' he asked.

'No, not now. Come along, man.'

While they were still in the Gulley, a sort of catchword had run through the ranks. 'Meeting-place at the Gorki-Theatre. Colonel Lunitz will be there. That's where the remains of the division must reassemble.' Herbert consoled his companion by reminding him of the rendezvous.

Geibel suddenly stood still and looked at Herbert with an expression of childish astonishment on his face. Then he slowly drew his hand out of his glove and felt with bare fingers along his padded trousers.

'What's wrong now?' asked Herbert.

Geibel stretched out his hand to his friend, and whispered: 'blood'.

'Blood, blood!' said Herbert, mimicking him. 'What's the fuss about? Just a scratch, you lead-swinger. Come on now, get moving!'

He grasped Geibel by the arm and pushed him forwards, though he felt a cold chill in his heart. Geibel draped his blanket over his shoulders and shuffled on, shuddering with the cold.

A voice behind them screamed: 'Tanks, Tanks!'

The moving stream was checked. Cars crashed their gears and bumped against one another as they tried to get out of the line of fire. On the road the marchers crowded together like sheep, all staring to the left where five tanks in open order were slowly moving along at an acute angle to the main road. Their guns were firing but their shells struck the ground a long way away from the procession of moving men and cars. It looked as though they meant to miss.

'Tanks, Tanks!'

Four cars belonging to a signals unit had halted on the side of the road. They were for use on construction works and were carrying a complete building plant. The signals people lost their nerve, jumped down from the vehicles, threw their rifles away and ran screaming on to the snowfield. Others followed and soon whole groups of men could be seen pushing off through snow that came up to their knees towards the west. It was a stupid, childish, senseless stampede.

Fröhlich noticed that the high road round him was emptying itself. A truck with its motor still running had halted near him. The driver jumped out and, after a few wild leaps, flung himself to the ground. The tanks were now very close. Fröhlich hesitated for a moment and then crawled under the truck. He heard the sound of feet running by and a vehicle from behind ran into the truck and pushed it forward a bit. Then the first of the tanks rattled by, its caterpillar-tracks flinging chunks of yellow snow in the air. Fröhlich edged forward in order to be able to get a better view of the road. He held his sub-machine-gun in his hand. The tank swung round to avoid a truck which was lying on its side. The hatch of the turret was open and in it a man was standing waving his cap and calling in German and laughing. 'Come along, all of you—come to us.'

Fröhlich raised his gun, pulled the trigger and the butt of his weapon hammered against his shoulder. He fired some fifteen rounds, which rattled like hailstones against the cast-steel. The Russian in the turret threw his head back with a gurgling cry and slowly slipped down. Finally only his hand remained visible and the cap it had held fell into the snow.

After a while Fröhlich crept out. There was no one on the road. The tanks had turned round and were driving a great crowd of men over the steppe to the north. Fröhlich walked to the Russian's cap, spat on it and then kicked it off the road.

In the meantime a handful of men had assembled, including the driver of the truck. Hurriedly and still shaking with fear they with started the motor. Fröhlich and a few others climbed on board and the vehicle set off along the road at breakneck speed.

Herbert and Geibel heard the noise of the truck, but did not bother to look round. Geibel was breathing heavily and his limp grew worse and worse. Finally he stopped dead. He was as white as a handkerchief and the sweat was standing out on his forehead. Herbert felt a stab of nausea when he saw the blood seeping through his friend's felt boot.

'You'd better sit down, you old slacker!' he said. He had to leave the boot alone, but was able to pull down Geibel's trousers. The insides were full of blood, the leg was swollen and there was a deep wound above the knee. It was a wonder that Geibel had been able to walk so far. Herbert pulled off his overcoat and tunic and tore strips from his shirt to make a bandage.

'It's nothing,' he stammered, 'Just a little flesh-wound—a deep scratch, that's all.'

Geibel only groaned softly. Luckily Fröhlich recognized them, and gave them both a lift on the truck.

His brush with the tank had given Fröhlich new self-confidence and he tried to communicate it to the others.

'We've got to stick it for another week. That's not long, and then you'll see something to make you sit up!'

Nobody listened. Geibel had his head on Herbert's lap. His eyes were closed and he whimpered gently as the truck jolted along. The others were sitting round a small sack of oats lazily chewing the ears and spitting the husks on to the ground.

General von Hermann watched the end coming. He did not behave like his predecessor, who roamed through the bunkers whining for rescue, nor did he share the attitude of his staff, who still cherished fantastic hopes and plans. He saw everything with untroubled sober clearness. It really was the end. Beyond it there was nothing.

His division, a mere skeleton, was fighting on two fronts. Undisturbed by the swarms of fugitives who filled the hollows and dug-outs, the division went on fighting with the courage of despair and melted away in the process. The General conducted this last fight with the toughness of a man of steel. He had deserters and looters shot and imposed draconian penalties for misuse of stores or ammunition, while marauding stragglers were driven from his area by force of arms. Since he had heard of Wiese's death, he had become a sort of robot, an automaton that functioned perfectly. There were no more discussions or conferences with his officers and there was no personal touch in his relations with them. His sympathy and humanity seemed to have dried up. His officers, accustomed to horrors in these grim days, shuddered beneath his icy glance and even the hot-blooded Colonel Danne shunned his presence.

They had received an order to fight to the last man and the last cartridge. This order was valid. A soldier could not ask questions: he had only to obey.

Such thoughts passed through the mind of General von Hermann during those short, ash-pale winter days, when, as the person responsible for its fulfilment, he carried out the order with inexorable vigour. But when at night he lay sleepless with fatigue on his camp-bed, other thoughts came crowding into his brain, and nothing was clear any longer.

Should an order be obeyed unconditionally, even if it was an affront to conscience? '*God with us*' was still stamped on the buckles of their belts, but it was a lie. Hitler was a criminal, the guilt was universal and nothing could excuse it. Those who were part of the system shared the guilt—and Stalingrad was the first instalment of their punishment.

The General tossed on his bed. Should they revolt against this demented Corporal? He knew that such plans had been secretly considered by some of the Army High Command, but he had always refused to entertain them. That would mean revolt. The very word was repugnant to him. No, it was all too late, too late——

The General passed his hand over his eyes. He suddenly felt that the whole of his past life had been misdirected and that it would be wonderful to be able to leave it all behind and begin again. Foolish dreams! He could not break the rigid mould in which the tradition of generations had imprisoned him. And for whom was he dreaming? His son, Ferdi, for whom a new life would have been worth while, was dead. Burnt alive almost before his father's eyes . . . *Oh Absalom, my son, my son.*

A semi-official message had come from the Army High Command saying: 'It is not dishonourable to attempt a break-out. It is not dishonourable to turn one's weapons against oneself. It is not dishonourable to go into captivity.' That was an order, and a valid one as long as it was not withdrawn. But the nearer the front came to the army battle position the more fluid and unclear its outlines became. Why talk of honour here? It had been trampled underfoot a thousand times. In Stalingrad, Hitler's Wehrmacht had lost the mask that had covered its face and what now appeared behind it was a grinning skull.

General von Hermann got up to face another new day with its claims. He knew that he could not break away or even dream of doing so. He no longer wished to. He was a General defending a position and he must play his part to the end. Others could look for a cheap way out for themselves. For him there was only one way—a way without hope or faith or loyalty or honour, perhaps, but not without dignity.

The night sky, lit by an invisible moon and a multitude of fires, looked like a canopy of copper-coloured cotton-wool. Something like a huge caterpillar crawled, shuffling and panting over the shadowless snow. It seemed to have no beginning and no end. Its thousand-footed body worked itself painfully out of the flickering ring of fire to the north and lost itself in the night mists.

Breuer, the Sergeant-Major and Dierk were a tiny fraction of this caterpillar, Dierk was as heavy as a log of wood. His eyes were closed and he was breathing in short, noisy gasps. They slithered past piled-up cars and dark wreckage; over wavy ice or ankle-deep, crumbly snow, sometimes as part of a mass of humanity and sometimes almost alone.

Every hundred steps they halted and Dierk opened his eyes as if he expected to see a miracle. Every time he saw only the same figures, the same cars moving by in the mist, and the faces of his two companions, glistening with sweat despite the cold. They didn't know if he was fully conscious, but from time to time they rubbed snow on his mouth, which seemed to do him good.

The road was once more blocked with cars: horns hooted, men shouted and torches flashed. Suddenly a small car came hooting along. It skidded over to the right and they were just able to pull Dierk out of the way. The car halted and an officer, standing on the foot-board, shouted orders to the people behind. A tank loomed up and rumbled past, followed by two or three personnel cars.

'Farther to the right, Willy. To the right . . . yes, that's it. Now you can go on.'

Something was glittering in the officer's face. The ray of a torch kindled a small spark on the piece of glass sticking in his eye.

'Herr van Horn!'

The officer bent down. 'Is that you, Breuer? Rendezvous at the theatre, you know, for the last act of the play.' He was moving as he said these words. His little convoy had already disappeared.

'Give us a lift,' called Breuer, but his words were lost in the mist, which was getting thicker and thicker. A mist accompanied by twenty degrees of frost.

Dierk's feet trailed along the ground. His eyes were closed and he hung between them like a corpse. If they let go of him, he would just fall to the ground. The Sergeant-Major wiped his face with the back of his glove and looked at Breuer.

'All up! Finished . . .'

That was the end. Nothing more to do—*Rien ne va plus*.

Breuer stared into the mist. The caterpillar of men and cars crept by, but he and his companions no longer belonged to it. Alone they could probably make it, but not with this half-dead man. If they left him lying here with the others with whom the road was strewn, he would freeze to death without noticing it. If they left him. . . .

'Look over there!'

The Sergeant-Major had been peering to the right so Breuer looked in the same direction, but he saw nothing. Then for a few moments a pale surface, appeared, a nebulous shadow that vanished again. But the path before their feet, that led towards it, was real.

Without a word they picked up Dierk and dragged him to the right. Behind them the road with its noises disappeared. In front of them a pale indefinable something grew into a house—a clumsy-looking wooden box with windows and doors barricaded by tree-trunks.

They scouted round it, like hounds, scenting whether it was alive or dead. The house seemed to be deserted. Then they saw that behind it was a second house giving out warmth and smoke through the mist.

They hammered on the door and shouted. From inside they heard a shuffling noise. A board creaked—and then silence.

'Open the door, damn you!'

They knew that someone was behind the plank walls.

'You'd better open or we'll shoot your bellies full of holes.'

A wooden bolt creaked and the door was slowly opened. A man in uniform was standing there and, over his shoulder, a girl looked at them anxiously.

'These are staff quarters,' growled the man in an outlandish accent. 'You can't come in.'

'This man's badly wounded, we're coming in.'

Holding their pistols in their hands they pushed Dierk forward into the dark hall. The man and the girl made way for them and whispered behind their backs. They stumbled over invisible objects, knocked against boards and posts and found themselves in a brightly lit kitchen. There were soldiers squatting on the floor, busy with their bandages or drinking tea out of the lids of saucepans. Others were clustered round the fire from which came a smell of toasting. An old woman with a grey headcloth was busy but when she saw the new guests, she came tripping forward and said in Russian:

'Officers? Please come this way,' and opened a door and pushed the three inside. 'Sit down,' she said and her small, wrinkled face beamed with friendly welcome.

They found themselves in a warm and homely room. There were two beds in the middle with heaped-up pillows on them and a table with a tablecloth. By the wall stood an ancient plush-covered sofa on which a well-fed NCO, with oily, parted hair was sitting with his arm round a girl's shoulder. The girl stood up, drew down her bright red pullover and smoothed her short skirt. With a sidelong glance from her black eyes she pushed past the strangers and went out. The NCO screwed up his eyes and stared at the pistol which Breuer was still holding in his hand. Then he got up, too, murmured something in a strange language, lounged casually about the room for a little and followed the girl out.

They took off Dierk's greatcoat and felt boots and laid him on one of the beds. He did not move. Then they sat down on the sofa, just as they were, with their caps on their heads and the collars of their snow-powdered overcoats still turned up. They did not speak, but blinked at the electric light globe hanging over the table under an enamel shade. Slowly the dry warmth of the room filtered through their clothes to their bodies. Two hundred yards away the stream of stragglers was moving along the road.

The Babushka came and put a steaming samovar on the table. She nodded to them and babbled a blessing. Then they sprang up and pulled off their wet clothes laughing and slapping each other on the back with cries of 'What the hell!' and 'Well I'll be damned!' and 'Who'd have thought it?' There were slices of bread for them to eat, rusks, tinned meat warmed in the cook-pots, meat-loaf and a packet of little cigars. Dierk was given hot tea, and sighed deeply with satisfaction. What they had gone through during the day already belonged to the past.

The man who had opened the door, a Regimental Colour-Sergeant, had joined the party. He did not speak much, but they learnt from him that they were occupying the office of a Croatian Artillery Regiment which was attached to the 100th Light Infantry Division, whose front was on the Volga, facing east. They had no responsibility for the other points of the compass.

Chapter Fifteen

THE LAST HOURS

THE MORNING SKY hung over the land like a mask of damp sacking. The main road, a dirty yellow strip of crumbled snow ploughed up by countless wheels and footmarks, was almost deserted. In places the wind had blown the snow off leaving blank strips of steel-grey ice.

The three men felt rested and revived. They had breakfasted plentifully with the Croats. The morning air was invigorating after the stuffiness of the house. Even Dierk had recovered some of his strength and was not so helpless as before.

By the road stood a poster saying:

ATTENTION

This street is under observation by the enemy. Persons using it, do so at their own risk.

The District Commandant.

They grinned as they read the notice.

Suddenly some men came running down the street which was unusual; people no longer ran in Stalingrad. They were gesticulating and calling to one another. The stream slowed down and formed into small, helpless groups. Breuer picked up a few scraps of talk. 'Yes, now at this moment . . . two divisions . . . the District Office itself . . .'

'Hey, what's the matter? What's that you're saying?' he asked.

The man was out of breath. His eyes glittered with excitement.

'Two SS Divisions, Captain . . . They've broken through and are fighting on the edge of the town . . . The District Office has sent us out to spread the news.'

Breuer held Dierk's arm in a firmer grip and looked at the Sergeant-Major.

He waited with Dierk in the street, while Breuer pushed slowly through the crowd. He reached a barrier behind which Field-Police, with steel helmets and glistening medals on their chests kept guard, and asked about the rumour he had heard.

'We don't know, sir,' said the soldier indignantly. 'We haven't any information. We didn't start the rumour.'

There was unfortunately no accommodation at present. The authorities were busy reorganizing. In two or three hours perhaps. . . .

Breuer worked his way back. Perhaps they were not lying, but unwilling or unable to recognize the truth. Breuer felt something like admiration for these highly polished soldiers, the embodiment of Prussian spit and polish, who talked of re-organization to the end.

They walked through the riddled city, joining a procession of aimless wanderers, passing ruins, wreckage and human beings as they went. The fog persisted and prevented the artillery from firing and the airmen from dropping bombs. A respite for the wreckage of a broken army which was floating into the ruins of a shattered city.

Exhaustion led the three men to a house, which looked undamaged. A black-haired fellow with a cigarette in his mouth was emptying a bucket beside the door. He eyed them distrustfully and then started shouting loudly in Roumanian.

They felt their way through a dark hall, opened the first door they came to and a stream of warm air flowed out to meet them. Round a table a number of men were grouped with their heads pillowed on their arms, asleep. Others were squatting on the floor or lying along the walls. They were all Roumanians. One of them stood up and cried: 'Full house, all occupied.'

But the house was not full according to the standards of accommodation which prevailed outside Stalingrad. They pushed the man aside without a word and laid Dierk on the boards by the wall. Breuer put his blanket under his head and he immediately went to sleep. They sat beside him, unpacked their provisions and began to eat. All at once a watchful silence fell round them.

They ate their meal hastily and packed the remains of their provisions with care. They could see that the other men were sick with hunger, and did not want to tantalize them.

In the night Breuer felt someone running his fingers over him. He struck out hard and the hand vanished noiselessly. Suddenly he felt it was too dangerous to talk aloud, so he whispered to the Sergeant-Major. 'We must keep watch . . . take it in turns, two hours each. Tomorrow we must get away from here or they'll do us in. They'd cut our throats for a bit of biscuit!'

The building in which the District Commander's Office was housed was a stone colossus, and a target visible from a great distance. Yet in the midst of a forest of ruins, it had remained almost unscathed. It looked as though respect for the City Soviet, which had had its headquarters here, had laid a sort of taboo on the building.

The District Commander of Central Stalingrad had been sitting in his bomb-proof cellars since the autumn. He was an old General, unfit for other duties, with a dozen clerks to look after the papers and a posse of Field-Police. When they first took over there had been important things to be done. Plans for the reopening and exploitation of the great city on the Volga had been prepared. Now the personnel pretended to be busy with their meaningless masses of papers, but their first concern was not to lose their safe quarters. They could no longer do anything useful, and were unable to keep order on the floors above their heads.

The upper floors were a rookery of fugitives and stragglers who had flowed into the ruined city from south, west and north. Swarms of wounded and sick men from the caves in front of the city, exhausted stragglers and gangs of men who went out to commit robberies by night. Among them were Croats and Roumanians, Russian 'Hivis', railwaymen belonging to a party who had been sent to examine the railway station and consider how best it could be used. There was also a German woman—or so they said. . . .

The name 'District Commander's Office' worked like a magnet. It had a flavour of order and security and revived blunted memories of leave and ration-cards. Men squeezed into the already over-crowded rooms and used the squares of parquet flooring to make open fires, so that smoke streamed in clouds down the long corridors. In the tiled lavatories the excrement was two feet high and exhausted sufferers from diarrhoea had to climb over strangely shaped, hard-frozen heaps of ordure. A shell often tore a hole in the wall and the dead remained lying there, frozen stiff, until new visitors dragged them out into the passages and rearranged the room.

The Commander's Office had thrown up the sponge. Since an officious military policeman, who had ventured upstairs alone, had been found with a fractured skull in the courtyard, they contented themselves with posting a guard to control entries and exits to the ground floor and cellars.

Herbert and Geibel were lucky. It was dark when a car put them down near the District Commander's Office. 'What a huge hospital,' Herbert had said. 'They'll look after you properly here.' When he saw the crowd milling round the entrance and the steel-helmeted Field-Police, he searched until he found a boarded-up side door. After a struggle he managed to pull out two half-rotten planks and to squeeze himself and the semi-conscious Geibel through the opening. They spent the night on the dark, ice-cold staircase, close together in a corner. Herbert tried to get some warmth from Geibel's high temperature, but did not succeed in falling asleep. Geibel moaned and tossed about, sometimes muttering unintelligible sentences.

As soon as it was light Herbert went scouting. He hoped to find a doctor or a medical orderly. He found nothing of the kind, but only rooms, large and small, stinking, smoky and crammed with people. He was received with curses and a piece of tile flew past his head. The building reeled and trembled under the impact of shells and the echo of the explosions ran along the corridors.

Suddenly Herbert felt he could go no farther. He pushed his way through a half-open door and leant against the wall. The room was almost dark and a suffocating stench made him hold his breath, but it was warm and quiet. For a moment everything turned black before his eyes.

'What's wrong with you?' asked a voice. 'Nothing,' murmured Herbert. 'I'm only dead-beat.' Instinctively, he raised his hand expecting that something would be thrown at him.

'Nothing?' repeated the voice, 'Nothing at all the matter?' It was incredible that anyone should be wandering around Stalingrad with nothing the matter with him. Herbert tried to see the speaker in the half-light and at last saw a figure sitting up very straight on the ground at the other side of the door. The man's face was crowned with a pointed skin cap with the flaps sewn together at the back. His small hands were lying on a cape which covered his legs. He looked like a curious cross between a Buddha and a garden-dwarf.

'There's nothing wrong with me,' said Herbert, as though he ought to be ashamed of such an unsatisfactory reply. 'But down below I've got a friend who's in a very bad way.'

The dwarf seemed appeased and said graciously: 'Then you can stay here. You can help me make up the fire and we can get that man over there out of the room. He stinks already. I've tried to move him but I can't manage it alone.'

Herbert's eyes gradually accustomed themselves to the feeble light, which filtered through two openings in the boarded windows, and began to notice details. The floor of the room was thickly covered with people. Most of them did not move, but here and there one heard a rattling snore, which sounded very loud in the uncanny silence that filled the room. Under one of the windows someone was standing and cutting narrow strips from his greatcoat with a pair of scissors. From time to time he held the strips to the light to look at them, 'Won't do,' he muttered, and went on cutting.

'He's been here six days,' said the dwarf. 'You can talk to him as much as you please, but he can't hear you. He doesn't drink anything either. In the whole six days, he hasn't had a drink.' His lively eyes followed Herbert's wandering glance with the pride of a fair-ground showman trotting out his best exhibits.

'Look over there,' he said, pointing to the left. The man he indicated had no left arm. With his right hand he clutched the bleeding stump. His body was swaying from side to side with the regularity of a pendulum.

'That's a Lieutenant. The day before yesterday he came in quite alone. He doesn't hear a thing either and only wakes up when you bring him some snow-water. That reminds me—snow. You'll have to fetch it for us—twice a day with all our saucepans. We had another character who had nothing the matter with him, only a bullet through the arm, but yesterday morning he went off. He said he couldn't stand it any longer, the bloody fool! I can't go downstairs.'

He pulled back the cape from his feet. Two black domino-boxes were revealed, their ends cut off. Through the holes stuck the bare skeletons of his ten toes. Herbert looked at them with watery eyes and a lump in his throat.

'At first they used to hurt,' said the dwarf, gazing at his feet affectionately. 'Now they don't hurt any longer. I don't notice them at all. Handy, isn't it?'

He got carefully to his feet, leaning against the wall and walked stiffly over the prostrate bodies as though on stilts. With difficulty they carried the dead man outside. He was already beginning to smell, but out in the corridor the frost would preserve him. Then Herbert fetched Geibel from below. They bedded him down in the place vacated by the corpse. His face was red and swollen and he was unconscious.

Near Geibel lay a man with a strangely beautiful face. He had delicate, blueish-white, transparent skin; his eyes seemed to be gazing at some radiant horizon, and a childish smile played round his mouth as if he were waiting for something delightful to happen. His hands moved carefully over the blanket as if he were picking flowers. But the blanket that covered him looked odd. It seemed to be coated with a thick, horny layer of shiny black rubber.

The dwarf looked at Herbert and seemed to enjoy his puzzled expression. Then he said: 'Lice—nothing but lice. Interesting, isn't it?'

Herbert bent down and saw that the blanket was in fact alive with myriads of lice.

During the night there was a shot. Herbert wiped something wet from his face and crawled whimpering under his blanket.

Next day they saw that the Lieutenant with the stump of an arm had blown his brains out.

'Well, let's have a look at your little trouble.'

The young doctor had a friendly face and gentle hands in spite of the incessant comings and goings in the underground ante-room he used as a clinic.

Breuer was sitting in a threadbare arm-chair, upholstered with tapestry. He looked into the dull light which came through the dirty window, while the doctor carefully undid the bandage. Around him he saw the familiar faces of officers he had known of old . . . Captain Eichert, Lieutenant Bonte, the little black-haired Adjutant, the two Company-Officers of the Old Tank Regiment, the Paymaster Schwiderski from Danzig, whom everyone called Zahte. They watched the Doctor without interest. They were all wounded. Lieutenant Findeisen had been wounded five times, but each bullet had missed a vital spot. His last wound was a perforation of both cheeks as he was working his way alone through the Russian cordon. Now his face was swollen and his speech was like that of an aristocratic music-mistress.

'You must have bled like a stuck pig,' said the Doctor to Breuer. 'Perhaps that's what saved you. That and the frost. It's a miracle that the wound remained clean.'

In the last twenty-four hours there had been a chain of miracles. He remembered the Bessarabian German, who knew Captain Wilhelmi, the German liaison officer, whom Breuer had once met in Businovka. This man knew of the cellar in which his divisional staff were quartered and, in return for three cigarettes, he had guided Breuer over the Tsaritsa Gulley as far as here. When the Roumanian Captain informed him that there was no accommodation and that the General was sharing a room with eight men, Breuer, who by this time was resigned to adversity, suddenly saw Eichert, whom he had long believed to be dead. Eichert had said: 'Breuer? Of course you must come to us. You've often saved me from the quill-drivers. I see you've got Dierk with you, and Hermann. Hurry along and settle in. We can feed three more mouths.' Miracles still happened, only one shouldn't try to force them. Breuer now realized that he was not going to die in Stalingrad. He was going farther, but where and for what he couldn't guess. The walls around him were full of signs, but he could not read them.

'This is going to hurt.' With a jerk the doctor pulled off the rest of the blood-crusted bandages. A fierce pain shot through Breuer's head and visions chased one another like lightning flashes over a screen.

Then he heard the Doctor saying 'the eye itself doesn't seem to be damaged. Keep your right eye shut with your hand and try to open your left one . . . can you see anything?'

Breuer made an effort to raise the scab-covered lid and said: 'Yes, I see something. Just a faint glimmer. I believe it's getting lighter.'

The remnants of a flak battery were housed in a timbered hut in the western portion of the town. They had managed to get a 2-inch gun into position there and occasionally fired a shot down the street to break the monotony. From time to time some unknown officer would appear and speak with emphatic gestures of new lines and positions. They assented to everything he said and grinned cynically when his back was turned. Under the command of their square-built Captain they were waging a private war. They had salvaged two supply bombs and had more than enough to eat— which was, after all, the most important thing.

Interpreter Fröhlich had found a refuge here two days previously. A sub-machine-gun with ammunition was an asset, and moreover he spoke Russian. Such a man might be useful, since no one knew what would happen next. They put up with him and listened good-humouredly to his fantastic views on the situation. Sometimes they handed him a piece of bread or the remains of a tin of corned beef, so that Fröhlich managed to regain some of his strength.

But he did not want to remain there. He had no desire to be picked up by the enemy before the Führer came. Next day he would clear out. He had tucked away some of the provisions given him by the flak people. He had cut the bread into slices and packed it carefully in the legs of his felt boots which he never took off and had hidden two tins of sardines and a sausage in the lining of his greatcoat.

Next morning, when Fröhlich was nearly ready to break away,

the Colour Sergeant-Major came into the room holding on to somebody who looked like a tramp.

'At last,' he said, 'we've caught the swine who's been grabbing our food.'

His prisoner was wearing a torn and faded greatcoat and a crust of dirt covered his face. His chin was covered with stubble an inch long like the bristles of a scrubbing brush. Matted hair hung over his forehead. Round his left hand was bound a dirty rag which gave off a revolting smell. He looked as though he had been wallowing all day in a pit full of liquid manure.

The Captain stood up.

'So you've been pinching our stuff, have you, you filthy brute?' He struck the man in the face with the side of his hand. 'Robbing your comrades, eh?' They searched the man and then pulled off his coat. 'Look here, sir,' said the Sergeant-Major, 'a brown belt and a Mauser. Seems to be an officer. He's cut off his shoulder tabs, but you can see the ends quite clearly.' 'What! An officer? That's too much . . . leave us for a moment, Gerke.'

The Captain came closer. 'Are you an officer?' he asked.

The man didn't answer. He looked like a rat in a trap and his feverish eyes darted from side to side.

'Let me see your pay-book.'

The man fumbled in his breast-pocket and brought out a greasy book. The Captain turned over the pages and then threw it on the table.

'Aren't you ashamed of grabbing other people's food?'

'I don't know,' muttered the man. 'It was hunger . . . I was so confused . . .' He licked up the dark blood trickling from his nose to his mouth.

The Captain pursed his lips and gazed at the man in silence. Then he took out his watch and said: 'You have your pistol. Disappear over there. I give you five minutes. You understand me, don't you?'

The man raised his hand in an unsteady gesture, as though he wished to express something for which he could not find words. Then he turned round and staggered out of the room. Fröhlich sat by the table with chattering teeth. The stolen bread was burning a hole in his boots. The Captain looked morosely at his watch.

After an interval the Colour Sergeant-Major came back. 'Nothing's happened so far, sir,' he said.

'You'd better go and help him,' said the Captain, lighting a cigarette and walking to the window.

Fröhlich picked up the pay-book and looked at the first page on which was entered the word 'Corporal'. Below it framed in a black square was the entry:

'*1. 10. 1940 Sergeant,*' and a line below:

'*23. 12. 1942 Lieutenant.*' Written below in fluent official handwriting was the name *Günther Harras* . . . Fröhlich felt sick and pushed the book away as though it scorched his fingers.

'All over,' said the Colour Sergeant-Major stiffly, when he came back.

'Good,' said the Captain.

A mortar bombarded the house with obstinate regularity. A shell would fall in the street and then one in the courtyard without any warning detonation. Overhead was a ceiling of reinforced concrete and above that four storeys of almost undamaged masonry, on which no measly mortar-shells would make much impression. But collecting firewood for the stove, which they did by turns, had become a dangerous job.

Breuer spent as much of the day as was possible sleeping. Wrapped in his blanket and greatcoat with his kit-bag for a pillow he slept on the bare cement floor, undisturbed by the explosions and by the cries of the men in the 'hospital'. Waking up was like surfacing out of a submarine world of immeasurable limpidity, but strength and peace remained with him.

As soon as he was awake, people came and asked him questions.

'You were on the staff, after all. You must know something. What do you think is going to happen?'

'Me? I don't know anything, but I believe it's all over.'

'What! All over! You don't believe we'll be rescued? You must be mad.'

Lieutenant Schulz, a man with an unbroken line of eyebrows over unquiet eyes, brandished a paper before him saying:

'Here's an order of the day—from Paulus, dated 20th January: "*Let us go on hoping for the relief, which is already on the way.*" He wouldn't write that, unless . . . or do you think that Paulus is betraying us? That the Führer is betraying us?'

Breuer shrugged his shoulders and said: 'At Hill 102 the Russians have reached the Volga. I heard that yesterday, so now there are two Stalingrad Cauldrons for Hitler to relieve.'

He said no more, out of sympathy for the men. As a detachment of the anti-tank brigade they had fought and fled in the Rossoshka Valley, as Fortress-Battalion I on the heights of Kasatchi, as the Eichert Combat Group at Pitomnik and finally on the railway embankment, where this pathetic little band had shot down six tanks. Their dead lay all over the long road to the Volga. They had done more than one had any right to ask of human beings and they had had no time to think things over. Now they had the time. . . .

'Yes,' said the Adjutant. 'The whole thing's a fraud. I've thought that for a long time, too. No one's coming to pull us out of here. But I don't propose to die like a dog here; I won't do it.' He shouted the last words and waved his wounded arm like a club. Dierk looked at him in astonishment. His arm was now tidily bandaged and the bullet in his neck had missed bones and arteries. The Doctor thought he had a good chance of getting through.

Every day Eichert and his assistant went their rounds. The Doctor distributed pills and powders. The pills were made of dry bread, rolled up small, and the powders of flour and salt. Eichert spoke of their coming release. He said what he believed and also many things which he no longer believed. There was, too, a daily distribution of soup—the lid of a saucepan full of hot water mixed with flour or barley.

When they came back from their rounds, they were soaked with sweat. Once they calculated how many men they had visited. It came to well over 500, but that included the dead. . . .

They couldn't deal with the corpses, nor could they do anything about typhoid and dysentery. The time for that had passed.

'What ought we to do?' Eichert asked the others. 'Do *you* see any way out?'

They were silent. Dierk's questioning eyes looked round his comrade's faces. It was hard to abandon all hope. They had known blitz attacks, blitz victories, advances and battles in the Cauldron: they had known defensive actions and retreats: no man can know, beforehand, what it is to be destroyed.

The end came from the west with a 100 flaming cannon-mouths, which tore the thin lines of defence to rags; it drove a mob of running, screaming, falling men before it, smashed the last three German guns and fell like a roaring, bursting wave over the line of dug-outs. To the frantic eyes of the fugitives it looked like a huge, blazing torch.

Then came a crazy order carried by a man on a motor-cycle. 'The division is to face south and hold its positions till the last cartridge has been fired.' That meant three fronts instead of two, but there was no division left—no regiment, not even a battalion. It would have been hard to make up a company.

This is how the end came. . . .

'All over,' said General von Hermann, getting up from his chair. Colonel Danne stood up too, sweeping maps and orders from the table. He walked up to the General and said:

'There's a transport vehicle standing by, General, with two machine-guns, some hand-grenades and sub-machine-guns. Provisions and enough gas for 400 kilometres. Steger wants to go with you and Captain Martens, Colonel Zeidwitz and a Sergeant-Major from the Pioneers.'

The General looked at the wall.

'There's nothing dishonourable about it, sir,' went on the Colonel hurriedly. 'The Army Staff have done it and the Intelligence people are taking a Horch across the Volga.'

The General continued to look at the wall.

'Do what you think right, Danne,' he said, giving an odd twist to his mouth. 'I won't keep you back—neither you nor anyone else now. Everyone must go his own way.'

Under the flickering eyes of the Colonel, he began to do some strange things. First he took out his best tunic with the red tabs and put it on. It was slightly creased, but that couldn't be helped. Then he laid out all his decorations, the bright clasp of the Knight's Order, the Iron Cross First Class with clasp, the Tank medal, the silver wound decoration and the Knight's Cross. Then he stroked down his smooth, carefully-parted hair, looked at himself in the glass to see that he was properly shaved and put on his field-service cap.

'Good-bye, Danne,' he said.

The Colonel did not move. He just stared at the General.

Outside there was a white, chalky-looking sun. The firing had stopped and from the sector immediately to the left, black clouds of smoke were rising. Human flotsam from the other side of the rampart was streaming over, gunners from their demolished firing positions and leaderless groups of survivors from the division next door. The General didn't seem to notice all this. He had flung his old cape without badges of rank over his shoulders and the butt of a carbine showed beneath it. He had not far to go.

A solitary figure stood in the road—a Colonel in white camouflage with a white fur cap. He was struggling vainly to stop the fleeing men. No one paid any attention to him. He was the Commander of the annihilated division from further down the line.

'You're wasting your time,' said Hermann as he went by. 'Come along with me.'

The man he addressed gave him a puzzled look through his glasses. He thought he understood. A General in the front line could work wonders. In front of them lay the ramparts, built centuries ago as a protection against the attacks of Asiatic nomads. Even now they had their part to play. The twentieth century needed them still. Separated by longish gaps, a few soldiers were lying below the top and firing their rifles. There was even a machine-gun letting off a few weak bursts. Six hundred yards away, the snow was dotted with black figures—Russian soldiers—coming in three waves in overwhelming force. They marched as if they were out for a walk. Another machine-gun started barking on the left and the Colonel marked, with grim satisfaction, that the Russian lines were falling into disorder. Then a fountain of snow and dirt splashed him in the face. He drew back his head in alarm and all around he heard the whistle and hum of bullets. It was a damned silly idea to expose oneself to fire up here and it had done no good; none of the men had followed them. Cautiously, keeping his face down in the snow, he pushed himself back a little and looked around for his neighbour.

Half a dozen paces away General von Hermann was standing upright on the rampart. He was shooting with his rifle and his cape had slipped from his shoulders.

'Lie down!' cried the Colonel. 'Lie down!' he cried again, oblivious of the General's superior rank. 'Are you mad?'

Suddenly he realized that General von Hermann was not concerned about the risk of being hit. The two machine-guns kept on hammering. Now the Russians were about 500 yards away working their way forwards on their bellies and their shooting was wild. This unexpected resistance seemed to have enraged them.

General von Hermann stood there and fired. He aimed carefully, fired slowly, reloaded and aimed again.

The Colonel turned away and shut his eyes. He imagined the General throwing up his arms and writhing in pain on the ground, or shot through the eyes and blindly groping. He was expecting something gruesome, something terrible, but nothing happened. The machine-guns to right and left of him went on tack-tacking, as though hastening towards some unknown goal.

After a long time the Colonel looked up. The place where the General had been standing was empty and the General was lying at full length at the foot of the rampart. The Colonel breathed deeply and an immense feeling of relief flooded over him. He cautiously slid down the slope but the General did not move. He lay on his back with his eyes wide open, staring sightlessly into the sky. There was a small hole in the middle of his forehead with one drop of blood oozing from it.

The Colonel knelt down and closed the General's eyes. In his fingers he felt the cold of death, which was beginning to take possession of the body and his eyes clung to the dead man's Knight's Cross.

'A hero,' he murmured as he left him. The Divisional and Corps Commanders and the Generals on the Army Staff called General von

Hermann a hero, too, when the story of his last gesture reached them. 'The hero of Stalingrad.' They said it happily and without envy, heartily glad that one of them, at least, had conducted himself with dignity to the end.

The news penetrated to the outside world. Propaganda seized hold of it with greedy fingers and built it into a myth. 'Generals and Grenadiers shoulder to shoulder in the final battle under the floating banner of the Swastika,' was the story that they told at home.

Clear, cold weather had returned and, with the sun hanging like a pale metallic disc high above the ruins, the flying men had come back. Their planes crawled over the sky as pale and transparent as lice, looking distant and uninterested. The crashing detonations of bursting bombs, amplified by the resonance of the empty walls of ruined dwelling houses and factories, seemed to have no connection with them. But every day, the appearance of the city changed. Houses disappeared overnight, mountains of rubble grew out of nowhere, and clouds of powdery dust from the ruins filled the air. Piece by piece, the city was dying.

One day Sergeant-Major Addicks went out and did not return. They found him in the courtyard, with a splinter in his hip, already half-frozen. They dragged him in and laid him on the ground in their room. 'He'll be lucky if he's still alive tomorrow morning,' said the Doctor. 'Lucky? Why Lucky?' asked Eichert, and the question seemed to hang about the walls.

Much had happened since the previous day. There was no more talk of defence nor of rescue. A new army order had come from the Roumanians saying that no food was to be issued to wounded men incapable of fighting.

The paper was passed from hand to hand and read by all of them. No one said a word. After a while Captain Eichert got up and went out. When he came back, he said: 'I have placed our party under General Bratescu's orders. He is the senior officer available. He has declared this block a field-hospital and ordered Red Cross flags to be flown to distinguish it. Food will be issued to all without distinction. We can't go out and collect wounded men, but anyone who finds his way to us will be taken in and looked after.'

Rumours flew around. The Russians were said to have got through to the Volga in the neighbourhood of the oil refinery. General von Seydlitz had been arrested for allowing Commanders of units freedom of action. 'Tigerhead' was now in command of the central area. His orders were unequivocal.

'The following persons will be shot:

(1) Anyone having relations with the enemy:

(2) Anyone taking possession of parachuted supplies:

(3) Anyone ceasing to resist, unless ordered to do so:

(4) Anyone preparing to break out on his own initiative.'

Luckily there was not enough ammunition left for all these shootings.

The denizens of the cellar had given up louse-hunting, which no longer amused them. They sat on the floor and dozed, waiting for something to happen. Perhaps for a relief or for a decisive army order or for some unknown event which would put an end to this nightmare.

Bombs kept falling outside, sounding like the echoes in a cave full of stalactites. Sometimes a shiver ran through the cracked walls and chunks of plaster fell from the ceiling and split on the concrete floor. A direct hit would provide the answer to every question.

Breuer fingered his bandage and tried to look under it with his wounded eye. He was happy to be able to see a narrow streak of light but what he saw seemed cock-eyed and out of focus with the vision of his good eye. 'The obliquus superior muscle has been cut or grazed,' the Doctor said: 'It will have to be operated on later.' He had said 'later', unable, apparently, to get out of the conventional habits of thought. Perhaps, Breuer thought, it might be a good thing not to see objects from the normal angle.

In the evening some people came in from the hospital to tell the Captain that a supplies canister had been dropped over the building. It had sailed quite low over the courtyard and must be somewhere in the ruins behind.

Bonte and Schwarz went with them and came back after half an hour with the thing. They marched in with cries of triumph. The canister contained wheaten bread, meat-loaf in tins, bottles of mineral water and a dozen large sausages.

They measured out the spoils. Five hundred portions of bread and sausages. There was enough left over for a celebration.

They were in the middle of their feast, when they heard steps in the corridor—threatening, official steps. In the doorway stood a fat fellow in a fur coat with two soldiers in steel-helmets, with carbines in their hands looking over his shoulders.

'Salvage Company 13, Staff Paymaster Wegener,' he announced energetically with a casual salute. Eichert raised his chin, narrowing his eyes to two slits. 'Yes?' he said quietly, 'what do you want?'

The Paymaster surveyed the room, looking pale and wretched. Nowadays even paymasters were hungry.

'You have appropriated a parachute canister,' he said, his voice quivering with official indignation. 'You know what that means. You will now hand over the total contents of the canister. Further action will follow.'

'Certainly not,' growled Findeisen as he cut a piece of *hartwurst* into small slices. He could only bite with his front teeth and he found this kind of sausage a problem.

'I can have you shot—you must have heard of the special army orders,' said the Paymaster, somewhat ill-at-ease. He had expected his entry to make a greater impression. 'Hand over that stuff and I won't report the matter.'

'I suppose you'll eat it,' cried Bonte. The soldiers with the tin-hats were handling their carbines noisily.

Captain Eichert rose slowly to his feet. With his left hand he reached for the sub-machine-gun, which was hanging on the wall. Then he said: 'Now listen to me, you lousy bastard. I'm going to count up to three. If your silly face is still here then, my gun will go off!' He pushed back the safety catch.

'One . . .'

'Captain,' cried the Paymaster hysterically.

'Two . . .'

The men in the background had disappeared, but the Paymaster was still there looking like a ghost.

'Three!' The door shut behind him as well.

'Pigheaded fool!' said Findeisen munching. He had not allowed the incident to interrupt his meal. Eichert had dropped his pistol and sunk back into his chair with his arms hanging slackly.

The Doctor was quite right; Addicks was dead by the morning. During the night he groaned a few times and talked a little in his unintelligible low-German. Now he was lying there with the lines smoothed out of his face and touch of pride about his sunken mouth. Between two bouts of firing they carried him into the courtyard, knowing that the dying city would bury him under snow and rubble.

At about three in the afternoon a stick of bombs fell, bringing down a portion of the house. As they cowered against the walls listening to the thunder above their heads they thought that the end had come. But the reinforced concrete held firm. Only the coffee-pot on the stove was once more filled with dust. In the wing where the wounded were housed, things were worse. Some of the cellars in that part of the building had been demolished, and the patients buried.

That evening they cleared the passage leading into the court-yard. If they hadn't done so, the General would not have found his way to their refuge. Hearing a noise in the ante-room and curt, military answers coming from the Doctor, they judged that some-thing unusual was going on. Then they saw the General standing in the doorway. The wavering light of a lantern was reflected by the gold braid on his collar and the yellow eyes under his bushy eye-brows. Two officers stood behind him, their sub-machine-guns ready to fire.

'What sort of a club is this?' he asked. It was the General responsible for the 'will be shot' orders, but they didn't know the Tiger by sight. Captain Eichert reported, saying who they were.

By this time everyone had stood up, except Lieutenant Dierk who remained seated by the wall.

'There are only wounded men here, General,' said Eichert. 'This cellar is part of the hospital where there are 500 wounded men to whom nobody, except ourselves, pays any attention.'

'Wounded, wounded,' said the General, mimicking him. 'I, too, am wounded, sir! Have you any idea where the front line runs?'

The front consisted of a handful of cripples, bribed by a few pieces of bread, and a Colonel who wanted to become a General before he went into captivity.

'The front is a line dividing right from wrong, General. We and you are not on the same side.' It was Breuer who said these words.

Perhaps, after all, it was not Breuer. . . . Perhaps it was Lieutenant Wiese, who lay frozen beneath a layer of corrugated iron, stones and earth at Gumrak. Or Corporal Lakosch: or Captain Endrigkeit who got a bullet through his head at Dubininski. The living were no longer really alive and the dead were not yet dead. Still chained to bodies preserved by the frost, their shadows haunted the cellars and bunkers and streets of the dying town. In the twilight moments between waking and sleeping one could see them and hear their voices. Dierk, still dumb, whose pale grey eyes seemed to pierce the walls and whose hands were forever feeling after the invisible, could certainly see them. Breuer, too, caught sight of them in dark corners. Even Captain Eichert seemed to see them when the pain of his head wound shot through his brain. The speech of soldiers was not equal to dealing with the uncanny phenomena of the twilight state. But sometimes a word escaped which even the speaker listened to, wandering and afraid.

'. . . between right and wrong, General.'

Seconds passed, during which the only sound was the crackling of the lamps and the trickling of plaster dust from the cracked walls. The General pushed his head forward and gazed at Breuer like a biologist examining an unusual specimen. He had mounted a gun in front of his bunker with the intention of discharging it himself if anyone refused to obey orders. Suddenly his face lost its puckers as if some enlightenment had come to him. Mad, no doubt, he thought, completely crazy. Not by any means the first lunatic he had encountered in Stalingrad. He looked once more at the faces of the officers, who did not flinch. Mad, of course. How could they be anything else? He knew he had cancer of the stomach. He had three months to live or perhaps four, but in Stalingrad death would have none of him. Mortar shells, bombs from planes and rifle bullets all missed him. In his bunker, in front of which he had mounted the gun, were six boxes ready packed, two thermos flasks, an unbreakable plastic dinner service and a piece of catskin to rub on his sciatica. He had three months or four . . .

'All right,' muttered the General, and the ghost of a smile played round the corners of his mouth. 'This place is a hospital. Come along.' He fastened his coat and walked out with short steps. His escort clattered after him. Those who remained behind looked for a while at the closed door before they sat down again.

The man by the window had cut his overcoat to pieces. By him was a pile of fragments of cloth. Now he was engaged in cutting up his blanket. 'It doesn't fit,' he muttered.

Geibel was a little better. His temperature was down and with Herbert's help he was even able to hobble to the latrines, but the pains in his leg were still severe. Herbert fetched a double ration of soup from the field-kitchen in the courtyard every day at noon. This he shared with Geibel and the dwarf. He had given the cook a gold piece to do him this favour—a twenty-mark piece bearing the head of William II—a christening gift, which from his childhood he had always worn on a chain round his neck.

An ambulance unit was now billeted in the cellars. The Senior Medical Officer ordered the dead bodies to be removed. His men laid them out in piles under the roof of the coach house. They were frozen stiff, and sounded like wooden blocks being thrown about. Soon there was room for no more. The Paymasters sat in the cellars and kept their books. They sorted the thick bundle of Reichsbank notes, and Treasury notes, which they had to burn, and wrote down every single number on their lists. No one kept a list of the dead.

'We'd better put the hopeless cases outside in the corridors,' said the Senior Medical Officer. His assistant looked at him, puzzled. 'Out in the corridors,' he repeated, adding quietly: 'Freezing is an easy death.'

They carried out the hopeless cases.

For the 'promising' cases, there was some hope. The surgeon

was working in a room on the first floor. He worked day and night and hardly ever took off his bloodstained rubber apron. He operated mostly without anaesthetics. Narcotics were in short supply and had to be reserved for serious amputations. The screams of the patients could be heard right up to the top of the building.

It became harder and harder to find clean snow. The snow was befouled with urine and excrement, but this did not deter some of the men from using it for drinking water. One day Herbert spent a long time hunting for clean snow: he came back to find that Geibel had disappeared.

'They've taken him away,' said the dwarf, in a tearful voice. 'I don't know where; they didn't say.'

Herbert wandered down all the corridors where the hopeless cases were lying and searched all the rooms, but he did not find Geibel.

The noise of fighting increased. The courtyard and the street were under fire from mortars as well as from artillery, although the Russians were obviously trying to spare the building itself. Rifle and machine-gun fire was also increasing in force.

Meanwhile Geibel was lying on the operating table. The surgeon had decided to take off his leg and had approved the use of an anaesthetic. But he didn't need it, for a bomb crashed through the wall and reduced the table, the windows and the walls to a heap of debris. When they pulled Geibel out, he was no longer a case with a future, though he was still alive.

The explosion had caused indirect, as well as direct damage to the 'promising' cases, for the surgeon had had both his hands blown off.

In the courtyard two guns had been mounted and were firing over the street into the ruins through which the Russians were advancing. The Senior Medical Officer begged them to respect the Red Cross and to change the position of the guns, but in vain. After a while well-aimed mortar fire silenced the guns.

Herbert went on searching the corridors and rooms. Twice he passed Geibel without recognizing him.

Soon the Russian infantry came across the street in a broad line. Firing had ceased. The doctors, wearing head-dress and belts, stood in the main entrance and prepared to surrender the building as a hospital.

'Walking cases out into the street,' said the Russian Major.

'Doctors too?'

'Yes, doctors and orderlies. All who can walk.'

Men streamed out of the entrances, out of the heaps of debris, and out of the cellars. Others, who could still walk, put on bandages for show and filtered in among the seriously wounded. They trusted the flag with the Red Cross which flapped wearily over the entrance. The line of men in the street grew longer and longer. Russian sentries counted the numbers but they made mistakes and shouted and cursed when they had to start again.

Herbert ran along the lines in search of Geibel calling 'Walter, Walter!' He had never called him by his Christian name before. A Russian gave him a push with the butt of his rifle and drove him into line.

They were a hundred yards from the building when Herbert looked round. He raised his fist to his mouth and bit into his glove to prevent himself from screaming. The great, grey building was in flames.

Among the unnumbered men who perished in the fire was Corporal Walter Geibel, twenty-six years old, formerly a shop-keeper in Chemnitz.

Next morning brought no light. The cellar window was filled up with debris. It was hopeless to think of clearing up the mess under the continual fire of the mortars. They had to depend on the tiny flames of the lamps and the flicker of the fire in the stove. Occasionally Breuer and his companions took a few steps into the court-yard where the light of the frosty day was almost more than their eyes could bear. At other times they sat in gloomy silence, each busy with his own thoughts.

Towards midday they had visitors. When they saw their thick sheepskin coats and the blankets round their shoulders, they mis-took them for Russians.

Later they recognized Captain Gedig, the Adjutant of the divi-sion. He had with him Lieutenant Stenzel, a thin-faced young man, who knew Lieutenant Bonte from the Military School and from service in Yugoslavia and greeted him warmly.

'Pack up and come with us. We're clearing out.'

'What's that? Sit down first and tell us.'

The third visitor, a gangling boy, remained in the background unobserved until Breuer went up to him.

'Fröhlich, by God!'

He took the interpreter by the shoulders shook him and drew him into the light.

'Is it really you, Fröhlich? Yes, of course it is.'

The interpreter stared at him without recognition. He craned his neck forward and listened.

'There,' he said, raising his forefinger. 'Up there . . . aircraft . . . German ones . . . they're coming tomorrow.'

His adam's apple jumped up and down in the opening of his tunic.

'Fröhlich!' exclaimed Breuer once more. He looked helplessly at the other two, who shrugged their shoulders. After a bit Gedig said: 'It's quite true about the aircraft. There were six bombers flying very high, but you could see the black crosses quite clearly. It's a long time since they came over by day.'

'How's your father these days?' said Bonte to his friend. General Stenzel commanded a division in the south of the town. A shadow crossed the face of the young man. 'I don't know,' he said. 'The day before yesterday he said good-bye to me. He's probably dead by now, shot or poisoned. I don't know which. They have all killed themselves there—the Intelligence Officer, the Doctor, the two Regimental Commanders . . .'

Silence fell.

'Now you want to get out?' asked Eichert in a hoarse, excited voice.

'Yes, Captain, eastwards over the Volga and then south through the Kalmuck steppes. There's a chance—it's the only one.'

Bonte beat rhythmically on the table with his splint and Fröhlich squatted on the ground next to Dierk. 'Tomorrow,' he whispered. 'Parachute troops—two divisions—huge transport planes—tomorrow.'

'Do you want to go with them, Gedig?' asked Breuer. 'What about the others? Unold, Engelhard . . .'

'Unold . . . haven't heard about him?' Gedig's voice grew lively. 'Unold got away on the last plane—with a few papers from the Army staff under his arm and a courier's pass he had made out for himself. The Chief of Staff nearly went off his rocker when they found out. The day before they had promoted Unold to full Colonel. So the Chief reported him to the army group in Germany and Unold was shot when he arrived.'

Breuer leant his head on his hand and saw the air field in his mind's eye. A milling mob, a leather coat, a brief-case, a grey face . . .

'And Engelhard?' he asked.

'Major Engelhard had a crying fit when the news came. We took his pistol away from him and I don't know what he's doing now . . . or whether he's alive.'

'Unold was a cold, bloodless brute,' said Eichert. 'I never liked him or his cheesy, pale face . . . but this . . .'

'Six days too early,' said Gedig. 'Today it might count as a heroic action. Lots of people would be glad enough to take the risk today, but now it can't be done. The plan to create an air strip in the town has gone west. The only thing's left are consolation prizes to pin to heroic chests.'

'And now you want to get away?' asked Eichert with a quaver in his voice.

'Tonight,' said young Stenzel. 'There are four of us. We could take four more.'

In the end it was agreed that Bonte and Gedig should go. The others decided to remain. The Russians, after all, were human beings.

Later that day the army wireless sent a radio message to Hitler's Headquarters:

'To the Führer

The Sixth Army greet their Führer on the 10th anniversary of his accession to power. The swastika still flies over Stalingrad.

May our struggle inspire our contemporaries and coming generations of soldiers never to capitulate, however desperate the situation. Then will Germany be victorious. Hail, my Führer.

Paulus
Commander-in-Chief.'

Chapter Sixteen

THE GODS ARE OVERTHROWN

❦

'THIS IS DEUTSCHLANDSENDER. In a few minutes you will hear a broadcast of the rally to celebrate the tenth anniversary of the National Socialist régime, which is being held at the Sport Palace in Berlin. Reichsmarschall Göring will be making a special broadcast to German forces everywhere.'

The men in the cellar clustered round the radio. Hunger and misery were forgotten and distance banished. They felt at home again, they felt that they still belonged. They heard the Hohenfriedberger March and then 'Old Comrades' . . . Then the voice of the announcer was heard again, but this time against the background of a crowded hall.

'We are standing in the gallery of the Sport Palace. The seats round us are occupied by the chiefs of the Party, the State and the Forces. Below us four blocks of seats are filled with officer cadets of the three branches of the Forces and the Waffen SS. Their young, fresh faces reflect the importance of the moment.'

More and more people crowded into the cellar. They stood leaning against the walls or squatting or lying on the ground—men from the hospital, wounded men from the neighbouring cellars and Roumanians from General Bratescu's staff. Now they were all awake and tense. The atmosphere of the distant hall in Berlin had communicated itself to them and held them under its spell. They were waiting—waiting for something they couldn't precisely define, something extraordinary. They remembered Hitler's words: 'You can depend on me with rocklike confidence.' At this moment they forgot that they had ever doubted his words.

Confused shouts of command rang out and the sharp clicking of hundreds of heels. The voice of the announcer died away to a whisper——

'The Reichsmarschall is entering the hall . . . He is striding down the central gangway followed by his staff. Behind him . . .'

then came a number of unintelligible sounds, words of command and so on.

'The Commanders salute and he raises his baton.'

Göring, the Reichsmarschall. He had promised to send supplies to Stalingrad—in transport planes by moonlight. They had forgotten this for the moment. They were ready to forget everything, if only they could hear the one thing for which they waited:

'Comrades.'

The clear and surprisingly young voice with its mixture of toughness and joviality sounded near and resonant. Göring was speaking. People had made countless jokes about him and his human weaknesses and it was known that he enjoyed a joke against himself. They trusted him more than the others, the cold fanatics about whom no one dared to joke. The men in the cellar stirred expectantly.

'Comrades, you are standing here today as representatives of the whole German Wehrmacht. I mean my words to be a call addressed today to all comrades belonging to the forces, wherever they may be fulfilling their duties at this moment—a call to remember the day when the destiny of the German Empire was changed from its foundations.'

They listened and waited. For the moment nothing could be heard in the cellar except their heavy breathing and this ringing voice, which sounded so near. But next came one of the set speeches they had listened to so often. Suddenly they grew anxious and began to say to themselves: perhaps he's going to say nothing about us, nothing about Stalingrad? For weeks the army announcements had contained no word of them. Perhaps they'd all been written off as dead and forgotten.

At last Göring began to speak about the war against the Soviet Union——

'And now, Comrades, whether Field Marshals or recruits, I beg you just to consider the position of our Führer, when his political genius became aware of the deadly danger that threatened us.'

The listeners were too hungry and exhausted to consider the Führer's position very fully. They hoped he'd make it short.

'Our Führer was then faced by the gravest decision of his life. His perspicacity, his far-sightedness and his political and strategical genius enabled our Leader to realize that this would be the most difficult of all his campaigns.'

A noise in the hospital distracted their attention. One of the two orderlies broke noisily into the room.

'Captain,' he said. 'There's an officer here who says we must remove the Red Cross flag.' Behind the man appeared the angry red face of a Major with the Knight's Cross hanging round his neck.

'It's an insult, dammit, to show that flag,' he shouted.

'Hold your tongue,' said Eichert. 'Sit down and listen. Göring is speaking.'

The Major looked round as though he expected to see the Reichsmarschall in person in a corner of this cellar. But he took off his cap and sat down near the radio.

'Then destiny found a means of testing the quality of our troops who had been hurrying unchecked from one victory to another. It was not the foe but the elements that halted the advance of our victorious troops for the first time. . . .'

The Paymaster grinned sourly. He had been in the retreat from Moscow, when the thermometer showed 30 degrees below zero. Three brand new Siberian divisions had chased his lot back almost as far as Smolensk. Three-quarters of their effectives and almost the whole of their material had been left on the high road . . .

'Then the second winter in the East . . . bitter enough to cast its icy spell on everything—rivers, lakes and marshes. The soft ground where one formerly could hold the line with a few companies was suddenly turned to ice and the whole country became traversable by the enemy forces——'

'Everyone knows that,' grumbled Findeisen to himself. The second winter had never been properly planned and should never have been undertaken! Why was he stirring up the old dirt? The men at Stalingrad did not want apologies.

'At this moment we are witnessing the enemy's last gigantic effort to restore the situation. . . . Weary old men, boys of sixteen years, are being pushed into the fighting line. The human element is undernourished and half frozen and their tanks are the worse for wear.'

A few men started laughing. They had not laughed for a long time and their laughter did not sound cheerful. 'Who's he talking to?' asked Eichert, looking round the room.

'But I am convinced that this is their very last effort—the last reserve they can squeeze out of their people. The Russians have a ruthlessness which is more than ruthless. It is pure barbarism. The Bolsheviks have no respect whatever for human life. They regard their people merely as means to an end. Their leadership is brutal in the extreme. But in spite of all we have beaten them up to now and we'll beat them again.'

'Beat them,' roared a voice from behind. 'Beat them! Yes today! To arms! Man your positions!'

It was Fröhlich. He had got up from his place and was waving a sub-machine-gun over his head. They had a job to overpower him and push him down into his corner. In the confusion one of the wires of the radio got broken and the transmission was interrupted. When Findeisen had repaired the damage amid the impatient growls and curses of the audience and quiet had been restored, they at last heard that word for which they had all been waiting—Stalingrad.

'This will remain as the greatest struggle of heroes in our history. The achievements of our grenadiers, pioneers, gunners, flak-gunners and all the others from the General to the humblest private are unique. With unbroken courage, though exhausted and worn out, they are defending every building, every stone against over-whelming enemy forces. . . .'

The silence in Eichert's cellar had become so oppressive that no one seemed to breathe. What did he mean by history? They were waiting for a decisive word, an order of the day. But it seemed as if the man over there in the distance was not speaking *to* them but *of* them; as one might speak of the dead. And what he was saying about them was not true. Their faces grew hard and watchful.

'Soldiers, most of you will have heard of a similar example taken from the history of our great and powerful continent of Europe. . . . Two and a half thousand years ago there stood in a narrow pass in Greece Leonidas with three hundred Spartans. Then, as now, the onrush of the eastern hordes broke itself against the resistance of nordic man; the defenders fought and fought till the last man was killed. And in this pass a sentence is inscribed.'

'They're putting us into our coffins,' said Eichert. 'They're burying us alive.'

'. . . will become a proverb in the history of our times: "When you come to Germany, tell them you have seen in Stalingrad . . ."'

'Our graves!' screamed Fröhlich in his corner. 'Our graves!'

'. . . the law, the law which commands us to die for the safety of our people, for Germany. The warriors of Stalingrad must die. The law has commanded it, the law of Honour and our Leader in the war. This law . . .'

'The law of incompetence and obstinacy,' hissed Findeisen, his eyes full of tears of impotent rage.

'In the last analysis, though this may seem a hard saying, it is all one to the soldier whether he dies in battle in Stalingrad or Rzev or the African desert. If he offers up his life . . .'

'No!'

Eichert leapt to his feet and pulled the radio from the table so that it fell crashing to the ground. Then he took the hatchet they used for chopping firewood and brought it crashing down on the set. The glass was splintered and the voice died away, drowned by the cries of the listeners, who fell over one another as they retreated from their positions round the table.

Then there was silence once more. The men felt stiff and paralysed. The horror was over, but the voice of the speaker went on echoing through the room. They had been written off, pronounced dead, buried alive. Over their tomb their leaders were carving a monument to perpetuate a myth which would one day draw new victims to the altar of sacrifice. And there was nothing they could do about it.

They knew that no word, no further order would come to them, either from their Führer or from the Commander-in-Chief of this unhappy army. Nor from anyone else whose rank or position entitled him to give orders. They looked at Captain Eichert, who was still standing over the smashed radio and gazing at the hatchet in his hand.

Near the cross-roads west of Stalingrad's Red Square stood the ruins of a business house—ruins with strong walls. Only the roof and the upper storeys had been demolished. Down below the ceilings had taken the weight of the falling debris and still lay firm between the stone walls. This building was at once a 'front' and a battle-headquarters. In the extensive cellars, among hundreds of wounded men, Colonel Lunitz was camping with his fighters. On the ground floor and the first storey the windows were barricaded with sandbags and bricks. That was the front line, for the Russians had already occupied the Gorki Theatre directly opposite.

The Colonel's quarters consisted of a small cellar with room for three plank beds against the walls and in the middle of a narrow wooden table. Round it sat three men: Colonel Lunitz, Doctor Vondel and Supply-Sergeant Negendank. The Colonel was leaning against the damp wall with his arms folded across his chest. He looked at the flame that was consuming the last of their gasolene. They wouldn't need any more since the single tank they had brought into the town with them had been knocked out. It lay a hundred yards away at the next street corner with Lieutenant von Horn inside. A bullet had struck him in the eye, straight through his monocle. What was the use of petrol now except to provide light and warmth?

Outside someone was blundering over the legs of the wounded men in the corridor. The door was opened and a soldier powdered with snow came in with his rifle in his hand. He saluted and said: 'Colonel, there's someone outside.'

'What d'you mean? Someone?' There was more than 'someone'; there were three Russian tanks.

The man wiped the drip from his nose with the back of his hand.

'Over there at the theatre—there's a man who keeps shouting across to us. Won't you come and see for yourself, sir?'

The Colonel got up grumbling and pulled the hood of his white camouflage jacket over his head. The other men went with him. They climbed to the first floor and took up their positions at an opening where a window had been. Across the square, was the theatre, a huge building with a pretentious pillared façade and a broad stairway. There seemed to be no movement in the building and the tanks below showed no sign of life.

'He'll come back, Colonel,' said the soldier. 'He's already been twice.'

They stood for a few minutes in the cold and then a door opened in the theatre and a man came out. He put a megaphone to his lips and called out:

'Colonel Lunitz, Colonel Lunitz—by order of the Soviet Command, the building is to be evacuated by 1600 hours—I repeat 1600 hours. If this order is not carried out, the building will be destroyed. I repeat . . .'

Colonel Lunitz screwed up his eyes. They knew his name, and the man who shouted wore a German officer's uniform. And he spoke German without an accent. Nothing surprised the Colonel any longer.

'What madness!' he growled as they went down to their cellar. 'It's quite impossible, with all the wounded.' Moreover the south front of Red Square had to be held at all costs until early next morning. These were his orders and the house he occupied was the key to the whole position.

'What do they want? They're not usually in such a hurry,' said Doctor Vondel. 'Tomorrow everything will be over anyway.'

They fell to considering the ultimatum, and at last the Supply-Sergeant said:

'How would it be if someone went across, Colonel?'

'Go across? To the Russians? Absolute lunacy.'

'Well, you know, they're quite intelligent. Perhaps someone could talk to them and come to some arrangement.'

'Why not?' said the Colonel, after a while. 'What have we got to lose? Very well, I'll go myself. If they don't let me come back . . .' He shrugged his shoulders meaning that then that idiot Vondel would have to make out as best he could. Everything had become rather meaningless.

They tied a comparatively white vest to a pole by the sleeves and the Colonel waved his flag of truce as he walked by the tanks and across the square. The others watched him from the first floor. He climbed slowly up the steps and knocked at the door. Two Russians received him, one of them a woman. They did not blindfold him and allowed him to keep his pistol, but the muzzle of the sub-machine-gun which he felt pressing into his back was unpleasant. They led him through cellars, over courtyards and across various streets. Wood fires were burning everywhere with Russian soldiers squatting in front of them, warming their hands or holding saucepans over the flames. They were talking and laughing and someone was playing a harmonica. The woman walked by the Colonel. She wore the uniform of the Red Army with a Lieutenant's badges of rank. She was young and had a cigarette stuck between her bright red lips. The looks that she cast at the Colonel were not friendly.

At last they reached an isolated block-house. Here a Russian Major greeted the Colonel. He had a fat greasy face, smelt of spirits and was obviously in a good temper.

'Ah, Colonel Lunitz, good, good! I very good German speak. Have learnt at school at Ivanovo. Do you think I very good German speak?'

Colonel Lunitz confirmed this politely. These are the victors, he thought. They looked more like impoverished *petits bourgeois*.

The Colonel, slightly embarrassed, explained that the time allowed was too short for an evacuation and asked whether, in view of the numbers of the wounded, the Russians could extend it.

'Then immediately hand over house with all men and everything,' proposed the Major.

Colonel Lunitz regretted that he couldn't accept this. He had orders from the army, which tied his hands until the following morning. Couldn't they wait until the next day? If they did he would refrain from counter-attacks. Got to bluff, he thought, my only chance.

The Major pushed his cap over his forehead and scratched the back of his head. 'I not know,' he said. 'Speak with the General.'

He fiddled with the knobs of a radio transmitter standing on a chair by the wall. At last he got the connection. After a longish palaver, he beckoned to the Colonel and handed him the receiver ceremoniously. Colonel Lunitz introduced himself in military fashion. Then a voice said in German: 'What do you want? Speak slowly.'

Once more the Colonel explained his requirements. It was a tedious business, interrupted by failures to hear and misunderstandings. Moreover it sounded as if each sentence had first to be translated into Russian.

Suddenly there was a crack and the connection was interrupted. The Major cursed and started turning the different knobs without success and finally picked up the instrument and shook it angrily. Nothing happened. He looked at the Colonel helplessly.

'I have an idea,' Lunitz said: 'Tonight we'll abstain from military action and tomorrow morning at four o'clock I'll give myself up with all my people.'

He had to repeat this twice before the Major understood. He thought for a while, then a smile crept over his face.

'Good,' he said. 'Tonight rest, sleep, no shooting . . . tomorrow you with all men finish, prisoner of war. Good! But if not, then I shoot, understand? No pardon then!' He made a mischievously threatening gesture with his forefinger.

The Colonel did not smile.

'You needn't worry,' he said stiffly. 'I keep my word.'

They shook hands on it. Very politely, now, they conducted the Colonel back to his battle headquarters. The Colonel was monosyllabic and reserved. He had come to the end. The war, his military career—everything had ended for him. He had never dreamed of such a shaming, unsoldierly finale. He was bitterly ashamed of such a squalid end.

But then he began to feel a certain satisfaction at having fixed things up so cleverly. The Army Staff would be safe that night and the Army Order was being carried out. No one could have done better. Now he would go round and tell the men what had been arranged.

As far as it was in his power, not one more of them was going to lose his life for Hitler's sake.

During the night none of them slept. They knew it was the last night before the last day, but they didn't know what would come after. Nevertheless, since everything had been decided, they felt relieved.

There they sat brooding, while their bandages dried by the stove. Even Dierk had joined them at the table for the first time since he had come. Only Fröhlich was snoring in his corner.

Findeisen, who was standing by the door, as it still hurt him to sit down, suddenly let down his trousers and began to snip at them with a pair of nail-scissors.

'What's the matter with you?' asked Schwarz surprised.

'Do you think I'm going to leave my wedding ring to be grabbed by these bastards. I'm going to sew it in here under the flap of my breeches. Nobody'll find it there.' Findeisen replied.

After a while Schwarz fetched his box and rummaged about in it irresolutely. 'What's one to do with all this mess?' he growled.

'Put on everything you can,' advised Findeisen, 'and throw the rest away. That was my old man's advice. He was in Siberia in the first war.'

After a while they all started looking through their clothes. Schwarz's bottomless box provided Breuer with a light grey, very lousy, pullover and Dierk with a lambskin waistcoat with long sleeves. Breuer helped him carefully to put it on and during the process saw a fleeting smile pass over Dierk's face. He breathed a sigh of relief. He had never seen Dierk smile—not even before he was wounded.

The Paymaster had not talked much during the preparations. At one point he disappeared and when he came back he had his arms full of tins.

'There you are!' he said curtly and tumbled the stuff out on the table—kilo tins of liver sausage.

'Good God,' exclaimed Findeisen. 'Why wait till now to produce the goods. The fellow allows us to go hungry for weeks and then asks us to stuff ourselves with liver sausage.'

'How could I guess that you'd be celebrating so soon?' he answered. 'One's got to take precautions.'

'Then take the precaution of putting the rest of your hoard on the table, you miser,' said Schwarz cutting open one of the tins with his knife. 'If you don't, Ivan will grab it for himself tomorrow.' With a heavy heart the Paymaster produced three boxes of cigars and a bundle of banknotes. 'You can light your cigars with them,' he said, 'but please don't try to spend them. I have to establish that I destroyed the whole issue.'

'Who will you report to?'

'That doesn't matter. Everything must be done in due and proper order.'

Eichert remained silent and apparently uninterested, alone with his thoughts.

'I'm not going to shoot myself,' he said quietly. 'Men should not meddle with destiny . . . But how will it all turn out? I'm a soldier and always have been one——'

Breuer sat down by the Captain.

'We all of us drag round a load of ballast, the heritage of centuries. . . . We'll have a lot to throw away.'

Eichert raised his heavy eyelids and gazed at him. 'But can one?' he asked dispiritedly.

'We're Germans,' said Breuer. 'We have always been Germans —brought up on poems and songs and prayers and orders as though nothing else existed on earth. From these harmless things a monstrosity has come into being to which we are all bound by a common guilt. Perhaps we shall have to find the strength to throw this away, too.'

'What will remain then?' murmured Eichert. 'You will remain ... and I ... and Dierk and General Bratescu ... and Ivan Kropotkin and Lyuba Karlova and a woman called Irmgard Breuer—many people, countless people—each one of them by God's will a little world which will at least be taken seriously! Only the individual remains.'

Eichert made a disparaging gesture 'The individual,' he said, 'the savage beast that preys on his fellows ...'

'No I mean one's fellow-man as a vocation.'

It was past midnight when the sentries pushed a Russian into the room.

'We caught this man by the theatre, sir. He's stopped one.'

The Russian held his bleeding left hand in the air. In his right he was carelessly dangling his rifle which no one had taken from him.

Eichert beckoned to the Doctor and said: 'Bandage him up and let him go.'

The Doctor examined the hand, which the Russian held out to him unconcernedly as he looked curiously round the room. He was tall and broad and his face was clean-shaven and well-nourished. A tuft of fair hair projected from under his fur cap. A Siberian, perhaps.

The Doctor, having bandaged the wound tidily, clapped the Russian on the shoulder and said: 'Buzz off.'

The Russian's face gradually expanded in a broad grin.

They looked at him in silence as he marched out comfortable and happy.

Suddenly they realized that not only a battle but a war had been lost in Stalingrad ...

In Colonel Lunitz's cellar they were eating the last of their provisions. Rusks, two tins of liver-sausage and cheese in tubes. There were also cigarettes and a bottle of Hennessy. These things had been kept for a special occasion, for the day of rescue or the day of capitulation. This was the end. But life would go on, an unknown, unimaginable life. There was no point in thinking about it on this, their last night of freedom. Better to think of the past and to let the mind wander back to distant days in the homeland. They would see one another again, perhaps sometime. . . .

Suddenly, a man stood in the room, though no one had seen him coming in. It was one of their officers in a steel-helmet with hand-grenades in his belt, a sub-machine-gun slung over his chest and the insignia of the Field-Police. He stood near the door with his hand raised to the salute.

'Colonel Lunitz, please come with me to the Chief of Staff.'

The three men were silent. The Colonel wrinkled up his forehead and a shadow fell over his face. He looked at the officer who was still standing to attention.

'All right, I'll come in a minute.'

The officer did not budge.

'Is there anything else?'

'Sorry, Colonel, my orders are to accompany you.'

The weather-beaten face of the Colonel became olive-green. He slowly rose to his feet and buckled his belt.

'Well, good-bye gentlemen,' he said quickly. 'Good luck. If anything unforeseen should happen, you know what to do.'

Outside the distant stars were glittering as he branched off to the right. His men were crouching under the remains of walls—a man every ten to twenty yards and a few machine-guns, some of which still had one belt of ammunition. It was the last bulwark, a rickety one that would give way at the first push.

The Colonel whispered the pass-word and turned on his torch for a moment.

'It's me . . . Colonel Lunitz . . . Tonight you can rest and tomorrow the trouble will be over. I give you my word. I can't tell you more than that.'

He distributed cigarettes, shook hands with the men, and gave them friendly pats on the shoulder. They were the last of his men. They had trusted him. Now he had to lead them into an uncertain, but doubtless brutally hard, captivity. Would they understand? Would they grasp the fact that there was no longer anything here for an honest man to die for?

The Colonel was alone. He lit a cigarette under the shelter of a wall. What now? The Field-Police officer's visit was almost like an arrest. They must surely have got wind of his negotiations with the Russians. What that might lead to was clear. 'Anyone who negotiates with the enemy will be shot.' The Colonel felt for the holster of his pistol. Perhaps they would expect him to put a bullet through his head and save them the dirty work, but he wasn't going to do that. They could do the business themselves, if they had the courage, but not before he had unburdened himself in straightforward, unadorned words. He had a lot to get off his chest.

'Lunitz!' The Chief rose and gave him his hand. He was alone. 'You're late, Colonel Lunitz.'

'I was inspecting the security line on the south side, General.'

'Is that so? Well, sit down.'

The Colonel sat down stiffly on the edge of a chair. He was tense and vigilant.

The Chief filled two liqueur glasses. 'All in order?' he asked. His face gave nothing away.

'Yes, General, I can guarantee the safety of the Army Staff tonight.'

'Hm, yes . . . Your health, Lunitz.' The General looked at him with wide eyes and a faint smile.

'You know, Lunitz, you are our last defence.'

The Chief lit a cigarette and pushed the box over to the Colonel, who did not take one. He knew the Chief and was on his guard.

Then it came—the harmless, casual sentence:

'I hear you've been talking to the Russians . . .' There was a clink as a glass fell to the ground.

'Yes,' he said in an uncontrolled voice, 'yes, I have.'

Then he recovered and reported in crisp clear language. He concealed nothing, not even the fact that in the morning he was to order a cease-fire. Only the drops of sweat on his forehead betrayed his tension.

The Chief did not interrupt him. He sat in silence, watching the smoke of his cigarette, then he sprang to his feet and walked up and down.

'Crazy!' he cried. 'Simply crazy!'

He stopped in front of the Colonel and said: 'You seem to be negotiating here and there with all and sundry . . . no one comes to us, the Army Staff.'

Colonel Lunitz thought he had misunderstood.

'What d'you mean, General?' he stammered.

'Well, dammit,' spluttered the General, 'we're the people they should negotiate with.'

'If that's all,' Lunitz managed to say at last. 'If you want to get in touch with the Russians . . . that is . . . I mean if that's all. . . .' He straightened up with an energetic gesture. 'I think I can promise you, General, that tomorrow morning at whatever hour you wish a Russian delegate will be at your cellar door.'

The General looked at him intently from blue eyes, which had lost none of their brilliance, and said:

'Very good, Lunitz, do that.' Then he came up to the Colonel and looked reflectively at the medal ribbons on his tunic. 'I want you to get me right, Lunitz,' he said. 'We've carried out the Führer's order, haven't we? But we must spare the world the spectacle of a German Army Staff being chased across the battlefield by the enemy.'

The Colonel's bearing was stiff and firm, and his face was like a wooden mask.

'I repeat, General,' he said curtly, 'in order to avoid misunderstandings: I myself shall order my men to cease fire at 0400 hours and shall then surrender. At 0730 hours a Russian delegate with full powers to negotiate will be here.'

'Yes, yes,' said the General impatiently. 'Quite so. And now, good night.'

The Colonel walked back to his headquarters through darkness, which reeked of burning gas and death. His head was spinning.

It had been so simple, and it had come so suddenly.

The Army Staff was capitulating. Not on behalf of the VIth Army—that was forbidden. But 'to spare the world the shameful spectacle . . .' The little men were dead and their leaders were running away.

Suddenly Lunitz was shaken by an irresistible fit of laughter. It was a terrible laugh, ringing grotesquely over the empty square and echoing against the ruined walls.

During the night they prepared for their journey into the unknown. Now they were waiting. It was 31st January 1943.

Since dawn Breuer had been standing with Fröhlich at the entrance leading into Theatre Square. He had shaken the interpreter out of his leaden sleep and had dragged him to the place where they now stood. Fröhlich said nothing and his eyes, full of fever, ranged up and down the western side of the square. Breuer's stomach was rumbling and the sausage he had eaten made him belch. The Red Cross flag floated over their heads and it was bitterly cold. A bullet whistled over them from time to time, and there was an occasional distant explosion. The broad, white square was empty and lifeless with a few mutilated trees reaching upwards with their leafless branches.

Then they saw something that Breuer was never to forget.

From the south side of the square two small points began to move towards them. As they got nearer they were seen to be two Russian soldiers. With their short legs made shapeless by their clumsy boots, which caught in the skirts of their overcoats, they staggered and stumbled through the snow.

'Come!' they cried. 'Come!'

Breuer gripped the interpreter's arm and felt Fröhlich trembling all over.

The two Russians were now close at hand. They gesticulated wildly turning now towards the Kommandantur, now towards the south, calling out to the Germans 'Come . . . come all!' They did not look at all like victors.

The rifle-fire had become livelier and in the north-west corner a machine-gun began to rattle.

Breuer felt the blood pulsing in his neck. 'An officer,' he called to the Russians. 'We want an officer with full powers, do you understand?' He pulled Fröhlich round and said: 'Open your mouth, dammit, you can speak Russian—tell them we want an officer.'

The interpreter looked wildly round. He appeared to have just woken up. With a jerk he tore himself loose.

'No,' he cried. 'No.'

Then he started running across the square to the west, shouting all the time 'No, no, no.'

Breuer called after him, but he knew that no shout would stop him.

Fröhlich kept on running—falling and getting up again. His cape billowed out behind him.

He was still shouting when a second machine-gun began to bark. Fröhlich leapt high in the air, clutching at his stomach; then he fell and rolled over twice. The echo of his cries was still resounding through the square while he lay there motionless, a small dark patch on the broad white surface.

In the dark basement room of the ruined building on Red Square General Paulus was sleeping on his bed. He had stayed up very late, wandering uneasily up and down the cellar which was to be the scene of his last battle. Heavy gun and mortar-fire was directed on the building above him. He had taken refuge in a curtained corner, where his radio stood—it was his spiritual home. There he had listened to a wonderful performance of 'Don Giovanni'. The melodies were still haunting his sleep and his face, freed from its ugly twitch, looked strangely handsome.

The curtain moved. It was the Chief of Staff coming in softly. He walked up to the bed and gazed at the sleeper for a while with an inscrutable expression on his face.

Then he gently touched the Commander-in-Chief's shoulder.

Paulus started and before he was properly awake the famous twitch reappeared on his face. He opened his eyes.

'Yes, what is it?'

'May I be allowed, sir, to congratulate you respectfully on the high honour that has been conferred on you,' said the Chief of Staff smiling.

'What do you mean? What's happened?'

'We've just received a message from the Führer, informing us of your promotion to Field-Marshal: effective today.'

'Ah,' said Paulus and listened. It was remarkably quiet and the shooting had stopped.

'Yes . . . and what else?' he asked hesitantly.

'What else? Ah, yes. The Russians are at the door.'

'Oh,' said the Field-Marshal, rubbing his forehead. The General gazed at him with a serious expression.

'Do you wish to negotiate yourself, sir,' he asked meaningly.

With a deprecating gesture Paulus said:

'Oh no, no. You can do that better alone.' The Chief bowed silently. Of course he could do it better alone. He had, as a matter of fact, done everything else alone. Everything that had happened in the Cauldron and was still happening was his doing. Just in case the agreement made with Colonel Lunitz didn't work out, he had sent off the interpreter of the 51st Corps, a special service officer and a former ensign in the Tsarist Army. He would certainly get on well enough with the Russians to accompany the delegation as intermediary. Now they were waiting in his room—a Panzer Lieutenant, whom the interpreter had produced, a Colonel brought by Lunitz and Major-General Laskin, the Chief of Staff of the 64th Army, representing the Russian Commander-in-Chief. That was all *his* work. The newly created Field-Marshal had had nothing to do with it.

He had done something else as well. He had sent out a last radio signal, before smashing the transmitter. It read: 'Russians at the door. We are destroying.' It was a clever, diplomatic message as it left unclear *what* was being destroyed. Was it the secret papers and the radio stations, the helpless cripples in their burrows, General and private, shoulder to shoulder, or the Army Staff with the Field-Marshal at its head? Hitler could interpret it as he pleased.

'Has the Field-Marshal any special instructions?' he asked politely.

'No—or rather yes. Try and arrange for us to keep our cars and perhaps a truck . . .'

The negotiations with the Russian officers did not last long. General Laskin demanded the surrender of all the German troops in the Cauldron on the same conditions as those previously offered. The Chief of Staff refused on the ground that he was no longer in a

380

position to transmit orders. He could only capitulate on behalf of the Army Staff and the security units grouped round Red Square. He did not behave like a beaten leader commending the remnants of his forces to the indulgence of the conqueror. He behaved like a king distributing tokens of his goodwill. In many places the killing and dying went on, especially in the isolated northern part of the town.

The square in front of Army Staff Headquarters presented a curious spectacle. German soldiers in steel helmets, rifles in hand, stood fraternizing with Russian soldiers in front of the stinking, smouldering background of the dead city. They jabbered unintelligibly to each other and laughed, showed each other photographs and exchanged cigarettes. They looked like extras in a war film taking a lunch break. Behind them men were piling trunks and boxes into a truck, which the Russians had generously left to the staff for this purpose. All around lay the bodies of men killed during the recent fighting. They were covered with snow and dirt and could hardly be recognized as men.

In Eichert's cellar they had kept awake and waited and the end came upon them as they were sleeping the sleep of exhaustion.

When, disturbed by the noise outside, they walked weary and confused into the corridor they found the Russians already there. General Bratescu was discussing the surrender with an officer. When he saw Eichert he beckoned to him.

The Russian said to Eichert: 'Let them all line up in fours.' He was a tall, quiet, cool-looking man. On his collar he wore a rectangular badge in red enamel showing that he was a Lieutenant-Colonel.

Eichert said: 'We have a lot of wounded who can't be moved.'

'Very well. Let all the walking cases line up. Those that cannot walk remain here.'

'And the Doctor, too, and the medical orderlies?'

'You have Doctor here? Good—doctors can stay.'

Then they came swarming out of all the holes and hiding places in the ruined house—bearded, grimy cave-dwellers whose eyes were unused to daylight. They felt their way along the walls; some were on crutches and others leant on sticks. At such a moment who was going to admit that he couldn't walk? They came up and looked at the Russians. They saw the end, the irrevocable end, which no word, no order and no message from the Führer could avert. For weeks they had known what was coming, but they had gone on hoping until the last, dreadful moment. . . .

Then a strange change came over these men's faces. All the appearance of life which they had still preserved in the midst of the killing and dying seemed to fade away, and their faces turned to masks of stone.

Suddenly a cry rang out, a well-known cry, repeated so often that no one really thought about its meaning. Others took it up and soon a hundred voices were echoing through the gloomy cellars: 'Heil Hitler!'

With irony and hatred the shout was taken up. It rose and fell and finally faded to a whisper, back in the cellars where the dying men lay.

'We're not soldiers any longer,' said Eichert bitterly. 'Now we must learn to be men again.'

THE BALANCE SHEET

FOR TWO DAYS more the northern end of the Cauldron was subjected to the massed fire of Russian guns and a ceaseless rain of bombs from countless aircraft. General Strecker, who commanded the XIth Corps, sat in his dug-out and stared morosely at his folded hands. Divisional and regimental commanders begged him to give up the struggle and surrender to the enemy. The grey-haired East Prussian shook his head and said: 'No—I could never look the German people in the face again.'

His communications with the Army Staff had long since been cut but the broadcasts from Berlin told him of the collapse of the central sector. He imagined that Paulus and his staff had died in the holocaust.

The Commanders of units saw the last of their men running away *en masse*. The Cauldron was dissolving in chaos and flight. When on 2nd February at 1000 hours the General signed the order to surrender, he had no troops left.

On the 76th day after the beginning of the Soviet encirclement offensive, the battle of Stalingrad came to an end. The curtain fell on the greatest military disaster in German history.

Thirteen infantry, three motorized and three tank divisions of the German Army, one flak-division belonging to the air-force and two Roumanian divisions had been liquidated—a total of twenty-two divisions, the combined establishment of two armies.

According to official reports by the Soviet authorities, 142,000 German and Roumanian dead were counted on the battlefields.

Of the thirty-four Generals in the Cauldron, seven had been flown out—five of them in good health and unwounded, and two wounded, one slightly and the other seriously. One General was killed in battle, one committed suicide and one disappeared.

Ninety-one thousand spiritually and physically broken men went into captivity, including about two thousand five hundred officers and twenty-four Generals, headed by a Field-Marshal and two full Generals.

More than half of these died in the concentration camps of Beketovka, Krassnoarmeisk and Frolov during the epidemic of typhus in the spring of 1943. Tens of thousands died during the long trek to the prison camps of Central Asia or in the forest camps and quarries.

When the war ended, less than five thousand of them were still alive.

In the spring of 1943 the Commander-in-Chief of the disbanded Army Group B, General Freiherr von Weichs, and his Chief of Staff were paying a farewell visit to the Führer's Headquarters. At that moment the first letters from the Stalingrad prisoners of war had reached Germany via Turkey. During luncheon, at which only a few people were present, these two officers expressed the hope that this mail might be distributed without delay, so that the relatives might be relieved of the burden of uncertainty that had been weighing on them for months.

Hitler put down his knife and fork and looked up. His expression dumbfounded those sitting round the table.

Then he said: 'The duty of the men of Stalingrad is to be dead.'